Hanging in the Balance

Hanging in the Balance

Catherine Gagnon

For Anne-Marie McDonald

PROLOGUE
ONCE UPON AN OLYMPIANS' HISTORY

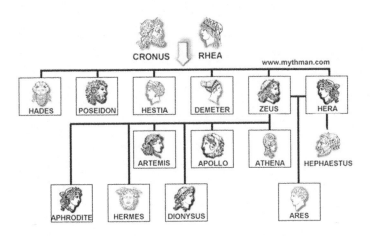

In Olympia, there are twelve Olympian ruling gods and goddesses who lived high above the clouds of Atlantis on the one and only majestic Mount Olympus, a Mount erecting from the far corner of the Atlantean city. The guardians of the universe once interfered in the affairs of humans but had soon grown tired of their vices, deciding it to be safer, more enjoyable, and far less dramatic to remain in the beauty of Atlantis. Although choosing to withdraw from human society, they resorted to staying away, partying heartily but continued to plot lurid intrigues like famine, natural disasters and war.

Amongst the children of Cronus, king of the Titans and the god of time, particularly time when viewed as a destructive force, and Rhea, mother of the gods, and goddess of female fertility, motherhood, representing the eternal flow of time and generations. Foremost was Zeus, king of the Olympians, who ruled the Heavens. His brother Hades presided over the Underworld, and the other brother, Poseidon, had dominion over the Seas. Hera, queen of the gods, goddess of marriage, women, the sky and the stars of heaven. She was also a sister and wife to Zeus, along with Demeter, goddess of agriculture, grain and bread who sustained mankind with the earth's rich bounty. And lastly, Hestia, virgin goddess of the family hearth.

The offsprings of Zeus made up the bulk of the Olympians. They consisted of the goddess of Wisdom, Athena; Apollo, god of Prophecy and Healing, and his twin sister Artemis, goddess of the Hunt; Hermes, the clever and mischievous messenger god; and eventually his last one, Dionysus, the ever-popular god of Wine.

With his wife Hera, Zeus fathered Ares, the greatly despised god of War; and Hephaestus, industrious god of the Forge.

Aphrodite, goddess of love, beauty, pleasure, and procreation, was daughter of Uranus, primordial god of the sky, and Dione, Titan goddess of the oracle of Dodona.

Although Hades and Poseidon both possessed splendid palaces in their respective domains, they often visited Mount Olympus when summoned by Zeus.

When Dionysus was permitted to enter and dwell at Olympus, Hestia, goddess of the Home and Hearth, gave up her place for him to reside on earth, because it was believed that thirteen was an unlucky number and all were afraid it would bring bad omens. Demeter, goddess of the Harvest, also abandoned Olympus in utter disgust when she discovered Hades had kidnapped her daughter, Persephone, and Zeus chose to do nothing about it.

Thetis, goddess of the sea and the leader of the fifty Nereids. Like many sea gods, she possessed the power to change her shape at will. Because of a prophecy which said she was destined to bear a son greater than his father Zeus, just as Zeus had dethroned his father to lead the succeeding pantheon. In order to prevent said prophecy Zeus ensured a mortal father for her eventual offsprings. Zeus and his brother Poseidon made arrangements for her to marry a human man, Peleus, which she blatantly refused. With the help of other sea gods, they found Thetis while she was sleeping, bound her tightly to keep her from escaping by changing forms.

She did shift into many shapes, becoming flame, water, a raging lioness, and a serpent but to no avail as Peleus held fast. Subdued, she then consented to marry him in a ceremony attended by all the gods of Atlantis. She bore a son named Achilles. In her desperate attempts to protect her son during the Trojan War, Thetis called in almost all her favors from the gods. After Achilles' death, Thetis began plotting her revenge for her sentence in the earth realm and marrying a mortal human. She called in the last of her favors to attempt the impossible: making sure the prophecy of her offspring by Zeus would come to be.

INTRODUCTION

The cruise boat glided along the water at its slowest speed. Families gathered around the boat's port side to admire the extraordinary wildlife surrounding them. They had seen a few sea otters already and now the Captain's voice echoed through the ship's sound system to announce their new discovery: Orca's. A full herd or two of the beautiful fearless mammals were circling the boat. Everyone watched in wonder as they popped in and out of the water.

"The killer whale, also referred to as the orca whale or orca, belongs to the oceanic dolphin family. Killer whales are found in all oceans, from the frigid Arctic and Antarctic regions to tropical seas. Killer whales as a species, have a diverse diet, although individual populations often specialize their types of prey. Some feed exclusively on fish, while others hunt marine mammals. The Killer whales, or Orcas, are Apex predators meaning they have no natural predators of their own and are at the top of their food chain. Orcas are highly social; some populations are composed of matrilineal family groups called pods, which are the most stable of any animal species. They have highly sophisticated hunting techniques and vocal behaviors, which are often specific to a particular group and passed through generations. They are sometimes called the wolves of the sea, because they hunt in groups like wolf packs." The Captain explained like he did hundreds of times before, but new to those now standing on his boat pointing in amazement at the sight. Running around were two young boys holding a doll with its owner frantically trying to catch up to them. The eight-year-old dark-haired Serena tried desperately to catch up to her mean older twelve-year-old twin brothers, who always found a way to be cruel to her in any way possible. She had been chasing them around the boat, trying to make her way through the crowd and not lose sight of her dolly. Reaching the bow of the boat, the boys stopped waiting for their sister to catch up to them.

"Give me back my doll!" She yelled out in desperation.

"You can have your precious doll," One of them said.

"As long as you can come and get it!" The other finished sadistically as he held the doll between the bars and hung it over the water. Watching from his cabin, the Captain noticed the boys torturing the little girl. He hated little brats, but especially the parents who obviously never gave the time of day to take care of their problem! Usually, he would not even meddle. He was not paid to babysit! But the desperation in that little girl worried him. He picked up his microphone to say something but it was too late. The little girl, trying to reach for her doll, tripped on what he assumed were shoelaces and she launched forward right in between the bars and fell overboard. He slammed the lever down to take the boat to a complete stop.

"Bloody hell!" He cursed. The crowd started to panic when they realized what happened from the screams of the little girl and the boys screaming too loud for anyone to understand what they were saying.

"Man overboard!" The Captain yelled through the ship's speakers. Seeing a couple running to bow, what he assumed were the parents finally giving a rat's ass about their child. The mother screamed in complete panic as her husband held her from jumping into the water herself. Serena struggled to stay afloat as the weight of her clothes pulled her underwater.

She splashed around in panic and shock as the water chilled her right to the bone. She began sinking, unable to stay above water. Opening her eyes under water, she came face to face with an Orca staring directly into her eyes. The Orca used its nose to lift her up to the surface, allowing her to gasp for air.

5

On the boat, the chaotic crowd fell silent at the scene unfolding in front of them. A group of the Orcas had created a circle around Serena, who was leaning against the mammal helping her stay afloat. Time stood still for a few moments.

"Have you ever seen anything like this?" One of the workers asked the Captain as they watched in disbelief.

"Never seen or heard anything remotely resembling this behavior from these bastards!" He answered, chewing on his toothpick.

"What do you think they are doing?" The worker asked, deeply intrigued. Dolphins maybe.... but Killer Whales?

"I don't know but let's not wait to find out." The Captain said, ticked off that his staff was not doing anything. The Captain yanked the Life ring out of his hands, threw it overboard then spit out his toothpick.

"Grab on!" He yelled out as loud as he could for the child to hear him. Falling a few feet away from her, the Orca helped Serena swim towards the life ring. The rest of the pod stayed put, not moving from their previous formation. She grabbed onto the life ring and locked eyes with the mammal again. It was almost like she was somewhat frozen and entranced. Serena's mother shouted her name, snapping her out of it. Following the instructions of the adults shouting from the boat, she slipped it over her head and hung on tightly. They began pulling her up slowly until she was safely in reach and they could pull her back onto the deck. Someone gave the Captain a bunch of blankets. He snatched one and wrapped it tightly around the little girl but realized she wasn't even shivering. He touched her skin, no signs of anything close to hypothermia. How was that even possible? She should at least be cold as hell.

"Serena!" The girl's mother called out as she pulled her towards her to hug her with tears of relief running down her cheeks. The Captain stood back up and looked overboard. Gone. Not even one left. He looked at the family, wondering what in god's name had occurred?!

But he shook it off and decided it was best to simply forget about it. Even though he knew he would never forget the little girl floating amidst a pod of Killer Whales staring straight into the eyes of the beast like they somehow had a deep connection. One of life's mysteries he supposed.

*****

The doors opened and there she stood, Iris, female messenger of the gods. She wore a dark blue bewitching dress to reflect the deep colors of the sea that suited her perfectly shaped and slender body complemented by golden winged sandals on her feet. Her divine blond ringlets placed perfectly on her head. She stopped a few feet short of the throne and bowed her head respectively as she leaned her caduceus on the marble floor beneath her feet. Poseidon always admired her beauty, making her messages slightly more bearable if she happened to bear bad news. On his right, sat his wife Amphitrite, beautiful beyond description herself, with long and wavy hair, black as midnight, and brilliant brown eyes. Her hair was held back by a thin net of bright pearls and silk. She wore a white silk dress and stood proudly next to her husband. She smiled kindly at the messenger as she looked in her direction, always the friendly welcoming one. On his left, sat his son and heir Triton. His tall six-foot ten height and strong muscular upper body was almost identical to his father, although he wore his mother's brilliant brown eyes, wavy, but brown hair, and her charming, welcoming smile.

"Welcome dear Iris." Amphitrite said kindly.

"Greetings." Iris answered simply with a nod. She waved her right hand above her caduceus that produced a large round bubble of water. Suddenly, a scene unfolded from inside it where a pod of orcas swam majestically around something or someone. After a few moments of waiting, they saw the image of a child. She was dressed in human clothing with dark brown wavy hair flowing in the water. She was swimming amid the mammals surrounding her. Their pod mother swam to the child, and seeing through her eyes, they watched as the pendant she wore around her neck slipped out from under her clothing. The pendant was a carefully braided dark brown leather cord with a wire wrapped moonstone hanging in the center. The wire wrapping around the moonstone depicted a symbol that was unmistakable. Everyone in sight

7

watched in disbelief.

"Thetis....can it be?" Amphitrite managed to mutter.

"It certainly seems like the necklace came from no other than the sea goddess herself." Poseidon answered in deep thought. He stood to take a closer look at the child and the necklace followed by Amphitrite and Triton.

"An amulet." Triton concluded upon further examination. To a human eye, the moonstone would look like a simple and plain necklace. But to a god's eye, once looked upon, one could see the stone, filled with a cloud like mist in its center. It was enchanted, imbued by incredible power.

"It certainly would explain how she has managed to stay hidden for so long, and how she could hide a daughter as well." Poseidon answered scratching his white beard.

"The only reason she would have to hide the child with an amulet..." Amphitrite trailed off looking at the child.

"The child is an immortal." Poseidon finished his wife's sentence. Both looked at Triton. There had been a prophecy that Thetis's child would become greater than Zeus and in order to ensure a mortal father for her eventual offspring, Poseidon and his brother Zeus had made arrangements for her to marry a human named Peleus, but she bluntly refused. They had advised Peleus to find Thetis when she was asleep and bind her tightly to keep her from escaping by changing forms. Thetis was a shape shifter amongst other things, and shifted into flame, water, a raging lioness, and a serpent, fighting for her life. Subdued, she then consented to marry him. Thetis had long disappeared and never was seen or heard from for an exceptionally long time. No one had known what had become of her. Even now, this unclear message left many questions unanswered. First and foremost, who could be the father? One thing was for certain, this would change things. The image of the child vanished, and the bubble of water dispersed itself.

"Thank you, Iris." Amphitrite dismissed the messenger. They waited until she had gone, and the heavy doors closed behind her.

"Triton, we must find the child." Poseidon stated in deep thought. It was unknown what this meant exactly. Their interpretation of the prophecy was that she would bear a son however giving this new information, their interpretation could be very wrong.

"This might prove difficult considering she is protected." Amphitrite said as she sat down. They were not dealing with a simple task. Thetis was certainly not the strongest foe, but she was obviously cunning. She had managed to stay hidden this long and would not come crawling back on her own anytime soon.

"The amulet will only hold until the child becomes of age. She is a sea goddess. The amulet suggests she may not know it yet, but the full moon will draw her to the sea and the moment she steps into the water will give us her location." Triton answered his mother. With the command of the seas, it would not be difficult at all.

"And every other interested party for that matter." Poseidon stated deeply concerned. Poseidon knew too well what this could mean. They had sensed an imminent shift in the balance and they were beginning to understand why. With the help of his son Triton, they had been able to keep things under control. But the number of Scylla's followers continued to grow, and the rift between mermaids and mermen grew stronger. Scylla was a beautiful naiad, a type of water nymph 'female spirit' who mostly resides over fountains, wells, springs, streams, brooks, and other bodies of freshwater claimed by Poseidon, but out of angered jealousy, Amphitrite had turned her into a sea monster by poisoning the water of the spring where Scylla would bathe. Ever since then, Scylla had begun a quest for vengeance against Amphitrite and her family, affecting not only their immortal world, but creating havoc for humans as well.

CHAPTER 1
SERENA

She slid her key in the lock, box in one hand, and nervously opened the door, pushing it with her foot. She took a deep breath, smiled, and walked in. She had worked hard to get here. Her family moved around a lot, never staying more than a few years in the same city. She had always dreamed of coming back to Hawaii as this place always felt like home to her. Her mother, for some reason, had always refused to explain why she was terrified beyond belief of water, and would never allow them near any form of open water, fresh or salt, lake, or ocean. They had always lived amidst the busy city life. Her, on the other hand, preferred the quiet outskirts. Even more, the smell of the ocean and the sound of the waves crashing. Of course, her mother had quite a conniption when she told her she was moving to Hawaii. She had begged, cried...everything under the sun, but Serena had made up her mind and there was nothing her mother could say to change it. She was twenty-nine years old, almost thirty, and an adult. She had gone to school and worked as a nurse for the last few years but had been miserable and completely unhappy with her mother's life choices for her. She had always wanted to be a marine biologist, but her mother would have nothing to do with it. It had taken her twenty-eight years to finally have a backbone and do something to change her path in life. She knew most people struggled with it, but she had taken matters into her own hands when she finally realized no one else was in charge of her happiness but herself. Pleasing her mother was already a difficult task to begin with, and even then, it was always a struggle. Her mother could deal with her own unhappiness, she had her own life to deal with. She had been an overprotective mother all her life. Serena always had the feeling like they were running from something… and she had enough. She did a total one eighty with her life and career then decided to move to Hawaii. Her life was not imperfect. She had the job and the parents, although she was not too successful with relationships. It seemed she just could not quite settle until she met Brian. They had been together for almost six years when things completely fell apart. She had caught him right in the act of cheating on her one night when she had not been feeling well and switched her shift around so she could go home early. It seemed like that had been where the tides had turned. She could have let it destroy her completely or pretended to move on and continue her life feeling completely unsatisfied…but she did not want to. It took almost a whole year to get everything prepared and ready. Having applied for work transfers and internships, she wanted to make sure she had everything set to start her new life. She was starting school in a few days, and since she already had a lot of biology majors with her nursing degree, she only had to go back to take the courses she was lacking for her dream job. A nearby marine park had agreed to take her on as an apprentice and had kindly given her a few hours a week as side credits. In the meantime, she found a job at a cute little café by the beach literally a few blocks away from her apartment. With both jobs, and her savings, she would be able to start things on the right foot. Was she scared? Hell yeah! This was all new to her. But there was an unmistakable smile on her face as she entered the threshold of her new home. She set her box on the table, looked around then walked to her back-patio doors. The beach is right in her backyard! What else could she have asked for? She pulled the door open to let the ocean breeze in. For the first time in her life, she felt completely at peace.

The delivery service had already come by with the rest of her things. After pouring herself a glass of wine, she tackled her boxes as she knew it would take a while to get everything in its place. She peeked at her watch and realized she only had thirty minutes left before the start of her first shift at the café. She did not want to be late for that! So, she grabbed her backpack and pulled out the white t-shirt with 'Chez Lily' written on it and decided to wear it with her favorite jean skirt. She hurried to change, then slipped her heavy brown wavy hair into a ponytail, grabbed her purse and on her way she went!

The owners of the cafe were an older retired couple. Their daughter and son managed the day to day run of the place and seemed quite nice when she met them. They of course did not understand why someone with her education and experience would want to work for minimum wage at a lowly cafe instead of making a nurse's salary. But to Serena, it was not about the money. It was about a fresh new start, in a place where she was at peace with herself. She had serving experience from working in a pub in her College days so that part was easy...still, she could not help but feel a few jitters as she approached the little quaint café. She found herself taking a deep breath before entering. The place always seemed to have a steady flow of traffic. She had not taken more than three steps into the café when a waitress apron was thrown at her.

"Thank God you're here!" Ellie, the owner's daughter exclaimed in desperation. "Tracey called in sick and I couldn't reach anyone else." She explained as she grabbed a dirty plate from a customer's table with a friendly smile. Serena hurried to slip the apron on. It was not that the place was packed or hectic at all, but it sure sounded like Ellie was a bit overwhelmed! Serena still had a few minutes before her shift officially started, but she moved quickly to match Ellie's pace and started bussing tables.

"Excuse me, can I get today's Lily's Special?" Someone asked as she passed by.

"Sure, no problem. Coming right up." She smiled kindly even though she had no clue what he was talking about. She walked towards the front counter and noticed the chalkboard on the back wall. It was beautifully decorated in colorful chalk art that highlighted the Daily Specials.

"Memorize that board!" Ellie shouted as she started to pass through the swinging doors, pushing her way through the right door, she looked back and motioned for Serena to follow.

"Right door in, left door out." She put her tray of dirty dishes on a dolly sitting in the hallway, then leaned back against the wall with a heavy sigh. She looked exhausted and overwhelmed.

"Thank Goodness you're here!" She repeated. Ellie was a cute petite long blond-haired woman in her late twenties with sparkling blue eyes.

She was heavier set but owned her roundness with her cuteness.

"You don't know how long I've begged for them to hire some help." Ellie trailed off as she gave Serena a once over. Ellie thought Serena had a radiant glow about her. She was an incredibly beautiful woman with a slender build, amazingly beautiful brown wavy hair, and those green eyes! There was something captivating about her. It was more than just beauty. When she smiled, it was serene. And her name was Serena? Go figure! She understood why her father had hired her. He could not have said no! She wiped her hands on her apron to shake herself out of this trance.

"I'm Ellie by the way." She introduced herself with a giggle over the fact that in her moment of panic, she felt she had been rude and forgotten her manners.

"Nice to meet you Ellie." Serena greeted back. Ellie couldn't explain it, but as she firmly shook her hand, she felt a sense of relief and was able to completely relax and feel utterly comfortable to the point she barely remembered why she was in a panic to begin with.

The rest of the day had gone surprisingly well. If Serena was unsure or uncomfortable, she did not show it. She greeted everyone with a kind smile and served everyone in a timely fashion. Hiring someone new was always a gamble, but the customers seemed to love her and judging by the tips Ellie was sure Serena was going to be an asset. Ellie walked to the front of the cafe and turned over the sign to 'closed'.

Serena was glad when the day was over as she hung her apron behind the counter. She could not wait to go home and finally dip her toes in the ocean. She was used to being on her feet and working long hours, but she had to adjust to a new routine and getting back into the groove would take some time.

"Thanks for your help today." Ellie said gratefully.

"My pleasure." Serena said as she smiled. She loved feeling useful and could feel that Ellie really appreciated it.

"We will see you tomorrow then?" Ellie asked tentatively to Serena's surprise. Why wouldn't she be? she thought.

"Bright and early." Serena reassured and noticed Ellie looked somewhat relieved. Ellie unlocked the door and opened it to let Serena out.

"Enjoy your evening then." Ellie said with a warm smile.

"Oh, I will, the beach is calling me!" Serena said with excitement as she walked out the door. Ellie chuckled as she watched her leave then waved goodbye. She knew Serena was not from here, but by the way she spoke about the beach, it almost sounded like she was a kid going to a candy store. It reminded her that perhaps she took her beach lifestyle for granted. If she were suddenly unable to enjoy the smell of the ocean, she would definitely miss it! She knew going anywhere remotely away from this was totally out of the question. Maybe she appreciated it more than she thought.

*****

It did not take Serena long for her shoes to come off as she threw her keys on the counter. She wanted some fresh air, so she cracked the sliding door open to let the warm ocean breeze in before she dropped onto her sofa like a stone!

She could not believe how tired she was after working a mere eight-hour shift! Granted, she had not stopped for a break all day, but it was not like she had never worked a long shift in the hospital before. Must be the jet lag. Her body never seemed to adjust to the time change very well. She closed her eyes and took a deep long breath of the sweet ocean air. It truly was divine! Nothing in the world could compare to the fresh salty smell and the sound of the waves. She wanted to get up and dip her feet in the water, but her body was like a dead weight preventing her from moving. Her eyes closed for a second, then she heard something. *"Meow"* Was she dreaming, or did she just hear a cat? *"Meow"* Hmmm... it could not be her imagination. She sat up and looked around. *"Meow"*. There it was again. So much for relaxing! She thought as she finally mustered enough energy to get up on her feet. It seemed to come from outside. She walked to her patio door and spotted a little creature right there at the door. Curious, she opened the door. The cat wasted no time and walked right in. Serena peeked outside to see if anyone was out there looking for a lost pet but alas no one. The cat suddenly rubbed against her leg and started purring like she was home.

"Hey there," She said as she picked up the new furry friend. As she started to pet the cat gently, she noticed the collar. Peeking at it, she noticed the strange green stitching on the back of the collar with no names, but the little medallion seemed so strangely familiar. She could swear it looked like a mini version of a necklace her mother always wore. How strange! She leaned on the stool by her breakfast bar and watched this little cat who seemed extremely friendly and comfortable here. Serena picked her up and put her down on the counter and stared at her intently. The cat meowed before sweetly licking her on the nose and scurrying off the counter to disappear around the corner towards her bedroom. Why was this cat so familiar in her new abode? Could it have belonged to the previous owners of her condo? Could there be another explanation? She would have to find out. She followed the cat into her bedroom to find her lying comfortably on her bed. The cat sure did not waste any time making herself at home! What was she going to do now? She decided that maybe it would follow her outside if she went for a stroll. So, she left the patio door slightly open, at least open enough for the cat to fit through and continued her walk. Peeking periodically behind and around her, she didn't seem to see the cat anywhere. When she got home an hour or so later, the cat was waiting for her by the door, inside her condo.

Chapter 2
Triton

The waves crashed and rumbled like a washing machine. The heavy winds he created caused chaotic rainfall with thunder and lighting crackling in the background. Below, the current flowed with such strength the sea creatures had no choice but to go along for the ride. But that was the point wasn't it? Controlling the movement of the water and creating havoc amongst them was part of the game.

As the heavy spear flung a few inches from his face, he swiftly moved his body in a twisting motion to dodge it while mumbling a command. A lightning strike followed, crashing down from above and hitting the water right where he commanded. You could barely hear the Sirens' screams of agony as the electricity shot through their wretched scaly bodies. Triton had no idea where they all came from, but he was certain Scylla and Charybdis had something to do with this. Scylla, once a lover of his father, was relentless in her quest for revenge against Poseidon for turning her into the tentacle monster that she was. As for Charybdis, Triton was not sure where the tides had turned. Daughter of Poseidon herself, she had always supported her father's relationship with Zeus, until Zeus had turned her into the bladder monster she is now. Triton mused that maybe Scylla and Charybdis' bitterness and fury towards him was due to the lack of protection from their Father, Poseidon. It still did not make much sense to him because everyone knew Zeus was untouchable and Poseidon was unable to protect them from Zeus. No one was. There had been whispers that the numbers of mermaids were growing, and that others such as Brizo (goddess of sailors), Ceto (goddess of the dangers of the ocean and sea monsters), Doris (goddess of the sea's bounty, wife of Nereus) and Leucothea (another sea goddess who aided sailors in distress) with many other sea nymphs joined together.

At first, Poseidon and his people had only laughed at the futility of women gathering against men. But no matter how his father chose to ignore the situation, the problem was growing and creating havoc across the Worlds. More and more were joining their cause, even Cymopoleia (another daughter of his father, one of his favorites, goddess of giant storm waves) had recently been known to have joined them. They had lost many mermen in this fight, and Triton knew now that it was more than just a senseless feud. It was war. A war that was taking a toll not only on Poseidon's legacy, but in all oceans and bodies of water across all the Worlds. The balance was shifting, and they all knew what happened when there was a shift.

Needless to say, it was not good. The balance had been stable for over two thousand human years. It has been so long that some blindly chose to ignore the change. It was only since the news came of Thetis' offspring that his father had begun to understand the risk of said offspring falling into his adversary's hands. It would simply be catastrophic.

The water trembled as a series of loud screeches erupted ahead. The Sea Nymphs were the front line of attack, lined up like a shield of defence. They disperse a screech so unbearable to the ear, creating the perfect distraction for the powerful mermaids to make their move. Triton swirled around and retaliated with his trident sending lightning charges immediately disabling half of the nymphs and injuring most of the mermaids.

And there it was, another sea monster coming for Triton. Conjured by the goddesses themselves, these were more difficult to fight off. Glancing towards his two allies Thaumas and Phorcys, they realized they had to work together. Picking up his conch, he blew loudly, not only to make the storms grow fiercer, but also to call up more men to fight. Triton could not tell how long it would take for reinforcements to arrive, but he hoped they would not take too long. Triton grunted in frustration as yet another spear flew by and nicked his left arm. He had warned his father that the growing numbers were starting to become more than a mere nuisance. This was getting out of hand. His frustration grew with each blow of his trident. With each spear he blocked and each whirlpool he sent with a heavy shockwave towards the enemy line. He looked sharply behind him while he punched through a siren charging in front of him. He then threw his elbow at another one attempting to sneak into his blind spot on his left. This battle was going to hurt both sides although he had no doubt his side would win. Although his chances were much greater once the reinforcements arrived. A loud thunder rumbled around him and he knew they were close. He closed his eyes tightly and took a deep breath to listen. The encroaching rumble was the battle call of the reinforcements as they drew closer. The rumble quickly turned into an unbearable high-pitched scream repelling the sirens and creatures charging at them. The mermaids and those wretched sirens were unrelenting as they charged on bravely fighting against the sonic attack coming from Triton.

"Let's finish this!" He instructed the others frustrated beyond measure. Although Triton stood by his father without question, he disliked meddling in these types of quarrels, especially if it took him away from his quest in the earth realm. It was a tedious task, as Thetis had done an excellent job staying hidden for so long. He had to admit he was beginning to enjoy the quiet lifestyle maybe a little too much and his father was growing impatient. Each day that passed made him stay away from "his people ", as his father liked to put it. His father was concerned that he preferred to live amongst the humans than with his own people. Triton had to admit he had found the perfect haven in the Hawaiian Islands and its people. He found "his people" were too dramatic and self-centered for his taste, and it was exhausting. It seemed they had forgotten the sole reason for their existence was to be the guardians of the fragile balance of the universe, which meant guarding the so-called "humans" they disdained so much. But this bloody feud was growing into a full-blown war, and the worst part is no one really knew how or why it even grew to this proportion. What was really brewing in their reasoning? Who's behind these wretched sirens and mermaids? There must be something immense hiding in the shadows supporting them or these battles are completely pointless as we outnumber and overpower them. There is only suffering in store for these wretched sirens and ghoulish monsters they were unleashing in these battles and perhaps, if this continued to grow, the humans. Unless this had to do with Thetis and her offspring somehow. It had to be, for no one, absolutely no one, could go against Zeus and his allies. As a final push, Triton's mermen joined together and created a gigantic whirlpool, with their song creating a crippling rumble loud enough to completely disable and disorient anyone that wasn't mer giving them the distraction they needed to advance and completely overtake them. The wretched sirens, knowing they were defeated, scattered as they attempted to withdraw in a futile escape. But there could be no escaping. Zeus and Poseidon would not allow this tirade to continue and wanted to eliminate anyone taking part in it. Triton pummeled through with his sword and trident, slicing the monsters protecting the wretched sirens into pieces. From the corner of his eye, he saw a dozen of them to his right and a smaller group to his left. Turning a blind eye, he decided to let the bigger group go. Then slashed his way through the smaller group in disgust. Not at the creatures, but he hated the senseless killings. He wasn't like his father, killing only made matters worse in his opinion. Triton had not pushed their foe into battle, they had done so on their own accord and would have to suffer the dire consequences. As the remaining mermen slashed the remaining few, Triton lowered his sword and trident watching the grim scenery unfold. Blood stained the waters, with arms, heads, tentacles, and tails floating like a scene in a horrible nightmare. Sirens were normally a peaceful kind. Their numbers have dwindled in the past few decades and this war would not help their population. He could not understand how they could be so wretched to involve themselves in such a senseless feud.

His heart was heavy as he closed his eyes to draw in the thick death fueled water through his gills then exhaled slowly through his mouth. The exhalation created a different type of whirlpool; an end of a battle whirlpool that would slowly gather all the dead and discard them by dragging them deep into the depths of the ocean, never to be found again. An offering to the ruler of its kingdom: Poseidon.

CHAPTER 3
THETIS

Quietly, she pushed the door of Serena's bedroom open so as to not wake her. Looking around, she noticed Serena had not wasted any time making herself at home. She had acquired a nice little make-up dresser, sitting along the wall opposite her bed, which still laid directly on the floor. She stopped to look at the family portrait she had placed carefully surrounded by a vase of fresh flowers and with her favorite Orca figure she had kept since she was a child, since that day on the cruise boat. Little Serena begged her for hours to get her one. She had given in, figuring after what she had been through it was the least, she could do. Of all her childhood memorabilia, this was the only one she could not part with. She kneeled next to Serena's bed and saw that she still had the necklace around her neck. At least she kept her promise to keep it on, not that she could remove it anyway, but Serena didn't know that. She is a loyal daughter. Being so far from home, she wasn't sure Serena would keep her promise. Serena, of course, did not understand the importance and the reasoning behind it but believed her mother when she said it was an old tradition and superstition. She hovered her hand over the necklace, as the stone trapped inside the metal wire glowed lightly. She frowned in frustration. She had been warned that the amulet might not be strong enough to hold past the first full moon of her coming of age which was only four weeks away. After the incident at sea, she noticed the amulet was weakening as it flickered on occasion. It was unnoticeable to the human eye of course, just as the spell hidden within it intended but she noticed.

After the incident, Thetis had traveled back to a place she had not been since before the birth of her daughter, Atlantis. He had looked at the amulet and recharged it but warned her there would not be any telling what the powers of the full moon might do, especially to the one who is coming of age. There was a time, amongst their kind, that would determine the coming of age of their young. Where the powers of the full moon would define their destiny. Serena's destiny remains undefined as long as she is hidden. She had been hiding from her realm and her kind for an exceptionally long time with limited access to any way to obtain such information. To search for it would be too dangerous and the risk of her being found was too great. One thing had been clear, Serena's destiny was connected to the prophecy. This prophecy foretold that she would bear a son more powerful than Zeus himself. A prophecy many tried to silence by forcing her to marry a mere mortal from earth. This son was revealed as a figure of cosmic capacity, quite capable of unsettling the divine order. Fearing this prophecy which nearly caused her death had given her no other choice but to vanish. She smiled at the thought of the lengths she had gone through to make this happen. Zeus himself had been fooled and had no idea she had borne a child from him. Of course, she was extremely disappointed to find out she was carrying a daughter, until she had reason to believe that her daughter was the key. This human world has been the best place to keep her hidden. Their belief in our gods' existence had dwindled down to nothing, making it that much easier to hide amongst them. A race, a world that for so long had treated them as gods now completely ignored the roots of their existence. Indeed, most of this world had completely lost the knowledge of them and so, the rest of the 'gods' (as the human's called them) continued to reign over all the other worlds, serving their purpose quietly. They were still the guardians of life, the universe, in their own domain, overseen by the father of all, Zeus. Humans were left to believe they were in charge of their own fate. It had only taken a few centuries to notice the shift. Something changed in this world that is creating havoc. Ares was always busy with his talk of war. Humans were easy prey when it came to hatefulness and greed. This fact will never change. It would only shift from age to age. But the change she talked about was much bigger than anything she had seen in this world before. The climate changes in this world made her believe that something was brewing. As it grew, so did her belief that Serena was connected to it all. She had used everything in her power to keep Serena hidden for so long, afraid of what would become of her if she were to be found. One crazy act of fate had thrown her daughter into the one thing that could potentially awaken the beast, the open water. She would be foolish to think that nothing had come of this act of fate. The blood that ran through Serena's veins was straight from Zeus himself, and the power that would run through that blood was too strong to contain. She was certain that someone had noticed. Orca's had been well known in the seas to have been given the intelligence to carry out tasks and orders from Poseidon. They were rulers in this world, and in a twist of fate, she had fallen right amid them! She did not want to take Serena anywhere near them. It was James, her human husband in her current age, that convinced her to take the kids. She followed along to make sure nothing would happen. Foolishly, she had let her guard down ONE TIME, and the incident happened. She knew all too well that no matter how hard one would attempt to change fate; it had a path of its own. It has been said that there would be a child that would surpass the power of Zeus and trying to prevent this fate would be futile. Having been assured she would bear a child from an Olympian God, she fooled Zeus into bedding her. Because the prophecy foretold, she would bear a son, she was convinced it would be so. But fate had other plans. The prophecy said *a child* would be born that would change everything. The interpretation of this child being a boy may have been misread by the Gods. It was their fault. She sighed heavily and as quietly as possible not to wake Serena while she carefully removed her own necklace. She then pressed her amulet against Serenas then closed her eyes and whispered a few words to recharge the amulet's protection. But this time, the stone struggled. Something was fighting her...

CHAPTER 4
SERENA

Serena awoke suddenly with an intense feeling that she was not alone followed by a feeling of extreme heat on her chest where her necklace sat. She placed a hand on it and felt a strange warmth coming from it. Her heart was racing as she looked around the room, only to find the cat staring intently at her from the floor. When she made eye contact, the cat jumped up on her bed and gently rubbed up against her. She had to admit, there was something comforting about its presence. Once she managed to calm herself down a bit, she threw the covers off and went to the bathroom. She splashed her face with cold water and looked into the mirror. She thought she had been having a bad dream until she noticed a small burn mark on her chest in the shape of her amulet! She noticed the glimmer of the moon reflecting in the mirror. It was a full moon. Turning to look out the window, she noticed how round and full it was shining up there above the ocean. She was not sure she would be able to fall back to sleep, but she knew she would have to try.

Her alarm clock rang in what felt like moments after she fell back asleep. She wanted to throw that clock across the room but felt the cat purring comfortably at her feet which somehow calmed her. If she wanted to have a nice cup of coffee before heading to work, she needed to get up now.

Walking into the Café, she noticed Ellie was nowhere to be found. She saw a young man speaking to customers. He had an amazing genuine smile. He stood about six feet tall with short honey blond hair that he spiked slightly at the front. He wore a white t-shirt showing off his muscular arms with one hand tucked into his khaki shorts. She couldn't take her eyes off of him as she put her apron on. Tying it behind her, she turned to grab her notepad and pen to slip it in one of her front pockets.

"You must be Serena." He said, obviously surprising her. She couldn't believe how sparkling and clear his eyes were. Clear blue, like the ocean. He had heard nothing but good things from Ellie who couldn't seem to shut up about how 'pretty' she looked and how nice she was.

Now he knew what an understatement 'pretty' had been.

"Uh...yes." She answered, shaking herself out of her thoughts. "Yes I am."

"Liam." He introduced himself with a nod as he leaned over the counter. "Ellie's brother." He explained as he noticed the puzzled look on her face. She could see the resemblance now. The blond hair, the blue eyes, and the kind smile.

"Nice to meet you." She said, feeling a bit uncomfortable for some strange reason. She quickly turned to look at the daily specials. Same as the day before, except for the soup. She took some notes down and decided to get straight to work.

"So, what's a girl like you doing all the way out here?" He asked bluntly full of curiosity. His folks had mentioned a few things about her like she seemed to be highly intelligent and couldn't understand why she would up and leave her life behind to start a new one so far away from home. The question seemed to make her a bit uncomfortable, she frowned slightly and tensed her shoulders.

"Sometimes life just takes us on a different path. Mine simply required a major overhaul." Serena answered.

"All the way out here? That takes a lot of guts." Liam said admirably. He had always been close to his family, and he simply didn't see himself ever leaving the island. He would miss it all too much. He couldn't imagine what could possibly make someone leave everything they knew and everyone they loved. But then again, he didn't know her circumstances. Not everyone was so lucky. He grew up in a good home with loving parents. Serena smiled at him without sadness, fear, or regret, she seemed peaceful.

"Excuse-me?" A customer said waving them down for service. Saved by the bell! Serena thought as she hurried to the table to avoid further interrogation. Not that she needed to defend her decision making but she couldn't help the uneasiness she felt in the pit of her stomach.

*****

Serena had just finished a jog on the sandy beaches of Waimanalo beach. She had always chosen running as a way to escape, vent or clear her mind. Coming to Hawaii and doing it with sand under her feet had just made it that much better. For some reason, she always blared the Evanescence albums on her ipod, finding it gave her the motivation and rhythm she was looking for. It was by far the heaviest type of music she listened to, preferring mostly pop style music on a normal basis. But there was something about that particular artist that just seemed to fit with her exercise and her need to release. As she arrived at her back patio door, she grabbed her legs for a nice runner's stretch then she looked at the time. She was sweaty and sticky, good thing she lived right by the beach. She peaked at the waters of the calm enough ocean in front of her and decided it was much more inviting than a cold shower. She stripped down to the red bikini under her workout shorts and tank top then ran to the water with the biggest grin of the north pacific. She dove in as she reached deep enough waters, letting it cool every inch of her body. It amazed her how much it could not only wash off the sweat, but the anxiety roaming through her mind much more effectively than running ever had. Maybe she needed to switch up her release methods. She pushed herself off the ocean floor and burst to the surface fighting the urge to cry out in ecstasy. She did let out a yelp, but only of surprise as she came face to face with a stranger. The girl appeared to be about eighteen or nineteen years old. She was about Serena's height and had long, thick bright red hair clinging to her perfect slender curves. She had red lashes and cute freckles across the high cheekbones of her heart shaped features. Her deep brown eyes reminded her of someone, but she just couldn't seem to place them.

"Hello new neighbor." She said with a voice that suited the features of the stranger in front of her. It was sweet and kind.

"Hi! I'm sorry...you just surprised me." Serena said with a hand on her chest trying to appease her pounding heart.

"It's alright." The girl replied sweetly. "I did come out of nowhere."

"And we are neighbors?" Serena asked curiously, certain she had never seen this girl before.

"Yes, of sorts. I live with my father a few doors down. " She explained kindly with sparkling eyes.

"I'm Serena." Serena introduced herself as she stretched out her hand. The girl looked at her hand and Serena swore she seemed hesitant at the gesture.

"I'm… Arianna." Arianna said as she finally took the hand. Serena thought she had hesitated a little too long, this girl was definitely on the strange side.

"Nice to meet you." Serena said with a friendly smile. She hadn't had the time to make any friends outside of work since she had arrived and it felt great to meet new people. "Are you from Hawaii then?" Serena then asked curiously. The way Arianna had hesitated on the handshake made her think maybe she was native to Hawaii and was used to a more traditional greeting.

"No, I just followed my father here. Seemed like it was worth the adventure." Arianna replied with an excitement that seemed surreal.

"And you?" Arianna asked curiously.

"No...I just moved here not that long ago. But, I too was looking for a little 'adventure'." Serena said with a friendly wink.

"Sure seems like a great place to start does it not?" Arianna asked, her gaze taking in the paradise around them. Serena thought there was something off about the way she spoke, definitely not the speech of someone her age. But, she could sense the girl was eager for friendship.

"Sure does." Serena answered as she dipped her hair back in the water to smooth it out of her face, then made her way towards her home. Arianna followed closely behind her confirming her suspicion of her need for a friend.

"Is that where you live?" Arianna asked, pointing at her abode as they stepped closer to her back steps.

"Sure is." Serena answered proudly as she twisted her hair to let out the water, then fluffed it in a futile attempt at drying it somewhat before she went back into her house.

"Would you like to come in for a drink?" Serena asked as she could see Arianna didn't seem to want to leave.

"That would be lovely." Arianna said with a grin. Lovely? As strange as her choice of word was, she seemed harmless and kind of lonely. Serena slid the back patio door open and made her way around her kitchen island to grab some glasses in her cupboard. She took out some ice cubes from the freezer and popped them in the glasses then grabbed a pitcher of lemonade she had made the day before. All this while Arianna watched her intently and her eyes scanned her surroundings. Serena's cat meowed as she made her way to Arianna slowly and Serena watched as Arianna jumped back with a look of sheer fear in her eyes.

"Don't worry, the cat is quite friendly." Serena said as she poured the lemonade and then placed it back in the fridge. Arianna studied the cat with wide eyes as if she had never come face to face with one or even seen one. She walked back around and handed Arianna a glass and she watched as the girl sipped it slowly then smiled as if pleased. Serena picked up her cat gently petting it on the head.

"I haven't named her yet, as the medallion seems to indicate she belongs to someone." Serena said as she kissed her gently on the head, the cat returning the sweet gesture by licking her nose. Arianna smiled and tentatively reached out a hand to pet the cat as if she was about to touch a venomous snake. Then, her eyes caught a glimpse of the medallion dangling from the collar and she recoiled taking a step back. Arianna gulped the lemonade down quickly and set the glass on the counter.

"I best be going." Arianna said, seeming to be in a hurry all of a sudden.

"Well, it was nice to meet you Arianna." Serena said with a smile as she rubbed her cat's head again.

"It was a great pleasure for me as well, thank you." Arianna said genuinely.

"Will I see you again?" Arianna asked, her eyes sparkling with anticipation.

"You know where I live." Serena answered with a smile. Arianna nodded then turned to leave but walked right into the door. Serena bit her lower lip trying not to laugh, but a chuckle still managed to escape. She opened the door for Arianna and watched her leave curiously as she slid the door shut then waved at her. "What a strange girl." Serena said with a frown to her cat who simply meowed in agreement.

CHAPTER 5
SERENA

Serena grabbed a mug out of her cupboard, poured herself some hot water and slipped in a lemon herbal tea bag. She dipped it a few times then let it sink to the bottom of her cup before walking to her patio door. She pulled it open and drew in a few deep breaths of the fresh saltwater air as she leaned against the doorframe. She took a sip of her tea and stared at the waves beyond the beach and could not help but crack a smile. There had always been something about this place that brought her peace, it was her happy place. She could not explain the stillness she felt in the depth of her soul, but it was something deeply comforting and profound, like it reached every part of her being and filled her with inexplicable peace. It was as if the air directly affected her nervous system in a way nothing else could. Sometimes she wondered if this is what it felt like to be high on drugs? It is not like she could really test that theory, or at least, she had no inkling to do so. She looked at the clock on the wall as an alarm sounded from her phone sitting on her kitchen table. She felt a twinge of nervousness settle in the pit of her stomach as she thought of the day ahead. She put her mug in the sink after rinsing it, grabbed her backpack sitting on the kitchen chair and slipped her phone into the side pocket. As she stepped out of her home and locked the door behind her, she exhaled a breath she did not realize she was holding. She walked along glad she had checked out the marina earlier in the week so she would know how to get there. The last thing she wanted was to be late on her first day as an intern. She reached the gates then stopped and smiled as she read the archway "Sea Life Park Hawaii". This is the entrance of the park where she was to begin her new journey learning about sea life. It was too early in the morning for the park to be open to visitors, but she remembered an email instructing her to use the employee entrance to find the office. She spotted the employee entrance then once through she quickly found a building to her left past the ticket booths that seemed like the office she was looking for.

"Aloha!" An employee greeted her kindly as they passed by her.

"Aloha!" Serena responded shyly.

"Can I help you find someone?" She asked, obviously noticing the uncertainty written all over Serena's face.

"I'm looking for Tristan. In the office?" She asked tentatively. The employee smiled at the mention of the name.

"Up ahead to your left near the conservation center." She replied pointing her gaze and right hand down the path ahead.

"Mahalo." Serena replied gratefully with a polite nod. The employee smiled and then was on her way. Serena grabbed her backpack handles and continued. She peaked at her watch and felt relieved she still had a good twenty minutes or so before her shift. This park was so exciting to her as she spotted the shark gallery to her right. She had not had the time to explore everything yet, in fact, she had only seen pictures and a map on the internet. But she knew she would have plenty of time to get to that later. She stopped as she saw a little "office" sign above a small building hiding behind the conservation center. As she walked in, she noticed it seemed like a garage bay more than an office. Buckets, nets, wetsuits, hoses and more types of equipment were stacked neatly labeled all around. She heard some noise coming from further back and she cleared her throat.

"Hello?" She asked, trying to get someone's attention as no one seemed to be there.

"Back here." A deep, rough voice shouted back. She noticed surf boards, clamps, metal tables laying about and some clothing racks towards the back where the voice had come from. She moved towards the sound, as it seemed like someone was moving things around back there. As she made her way around the racks, she saw him. He was bent over looking at a gauge attached to a tank. When he stood, her eyes widened in total shock. He stood about six feet four inches tall with big broad shoulders. His white tank top showed off his dark tanned skin and muscular build outlined with tribal tattoos covering what looked like his entire left shoulder down his upper left arm. He had shoulder length dark brown wavy hair. She tripped clumsily on a piece of black hose of some sort on the floor but managed to catch herself from falling, but not without alerting him of her presence. He looked behind his left shoulder at the sound and saw her as he turned. His expression softened somewhat highlighting his broad face with a neatly trimmed full beard and dark brown eyes that seemed to look right through her. He smiled gently, raising a scarred eyebrow as he noticed her discomfort and maybe what looked like shyness. This was not his first experience with interns, but as he looked at her, his fears of perhaps another flighty, thrill seeking, high on life tourist vanished. She stood just a little shorter than he did, her frame seemed to come close to what he had expected from the soft confident voice he had heard over the phone interview they had done. She wore blue jean shorts with a braided black leather belt and a tucked in white t-shirt that brought out her beautiful oval shaped ocean green eyes. Her brown wavy hair had been neatly braided into two braids, one on each side of her head. It wasn't often he could admit he was going to enjoy this internship. She had seemed smart and grounded from their phone conversations, and she wore the look completely.

"Welcome Serena, I'm Tristan." He said after clearing his throat and realizing he was probably taking a bit too long to answer. His pause had made her somewhat uncomfortable, feeling like she was under some intense scrutiny. But he sounded sincere. He pulled out his hand.

"Thank you." She replied. As he took her right hand in for a handshake, there was a strange spark that startled her. It felt like an electric shock from his hand to hers that ran right through her. Did it come from her hand and go to his? Or from him to her? She was perplexed by this, not that he wasn't an attractive man, that he certainly was, but she had most definitely never in her lifetime felt this reaction from anyone before. His expression remained unreadable, although she thought she could detect slight surprise behind his dark eyes. Their hands remained locked together for what seemed like an eternity, but in reality, it was simply a few moments longer than a usual handshake. Perhaps we both needed to process what had just happened. She quickly noticed his upper left arm was covered by a neatly wrapped bandage seeming to cover a significant gash. Although she quit her nursing job, her years of experience told her that the state of his wound dictated it had not been thoroughly checked by a healthcare provider. He finally pulled away, turning from her gaze to grab some papers on the table behind them.

"I have some papers for you to sign." Tristan said calmly, hiding how totally baffled he felt by the interaction. How was this possible? He glanced at his right hand where he could still feel the sting of the spark from the handshake. He grabbed the papers and turned back to face her, his eyes drifting again noticing the strange necklace adorning her beautifully shaped neck. It was a leather braided cord with a simple knot tying a beautiful wire wrapped moonstone.

"I suppose I have to sign my life away and release you from any newbie clumsiness that I'm sure I'm about to unleash upon you." Serena said sarcastically, curling the left corner of her mouth into a smile, perhaps trying to ease the strange tension that lingered as she grabbed the papers. It didn't help the matter that he held his grip on the papers a little too long, making her tug somewhat on them. Tristan seemed to come back to the moment, realizing he wasn't responding quickly enough and he needed to snap out of it. He just couldn't shake this strange feeling. He finally returned the friendly smile, making her sigh silently in relief. This was definitely on the top of Serena's most bizarre introductions. Hoping it would not remain this way between them, otherwise, it was going to be a very long year!

"You have nothing to worry about, this is not my first rodeo." Tristan

33

finally replied calmly trying to put her at ease. Hundreds of interns had come his way, but he had a feeling that none of them would ever come close to this one. He smiled reminding himself that fate could not have done a better job. Of all the strangers coming from different corners of the planet, it brought this one right to his doorstep.

Serena's job at the café had been so perfect, she had been able to fit right in like she totally belonged there and had been part of the team forever. Ellie and Liam had welcomed her with open arms, and with maybe a little desperation, but made her feel right at home, nevertheless. She had picked up on the duties with ease and had managed fairly well for someone who hadn't worked in a restaurant in quite some time. Not that she did not feel welcomed with Tristan, it was just a strange feeling all together. He seemed friendly and from his touch, truly kind. But the calluses on his hands and the bandaged arm made her think of him as a marine or army sergeant more than a marine park manager. She peaked at the stack of papers, feeling like it would take her a few hours to go through the pile.

"Just sign the first paper on the top of the pile for now, you can read the rest of the paperwork at home." Tristan instructed, seeing a slight look of desperation on her face, as most people did. He chuckled as he saw a look of total relief cross her face. Serena's eyes scanned the first page, noticing it was mostly about scuba diving, she felt butterflies of excitement rumbling in belly. This internship included many hours of sea scuba diving, exploring, tagging, discovering, and she could not wait to get started. With a sparkle in her eyes, she bit her lower lip out of habit as she read on excitingly.

"I've already completed the lessons on the online platform." She said searching her pockets for a pen.

"Wow, then we can get started as soon as tomorrow." Tristan said, impressed with her initiative. He reached for a pen on the table and handed it to her.

"Thank you. That is awesome! I can't wait!" Serena exclaimed as she grabbed the pen eagerly to sign the document. She felt like a little girl! She had watched all the videos, done all the training, but she had never actually been under water that long!

Tristan swore he could see her dancing in excitement. He watched her intently. He was happy to see she was dressed appropriately for the job. He had seen quite a few interns come through the marina either underdressed or overdressed trying to impress him. Serena looked completely at ease and in her element dressed in simple jean shorts and a white t-shirt. She was quite tall, as he usually towered over most people and liked that she was only head shorter than he was.

"You should get someone to look at that." Serena said simply with that cheeky smile as she noticed the distant look on his face and his hand laying on the bandaged arm. He cleared his throat, realizing he had completely zoned out for a moment and hoped she did not notice him studying her.

"Maybe I will." Tristan said, grabbing the signed paper she was trying to hand him for far too long. He walked to a small desk that seemed entirely out of place along the bay wall and placed it neatly in the first drawer. Serena knew his type all too well. Her inner nurse was cringing, but she didn't want to overstep. Tough army guy who had better things to do then get themselves checked out.

"Ready to go?" Tristan asked motioning to the fully loaded golf cart waiting in the garage bay entrance. The cart was full of buckets of fish, shovels, gloves, hoses, and a long metal stick with a funny looking clamp she assumed was some sort of feeding tool.

"Yes sir." Serena answered, following Tristan to the golf cart. She swung herself up on the seat and grabbed the handle just as the cart jerked forward.

Tristan noticed a smile cross Serena's face as she braced herself for the ride. Others had often used dramatic screams, or screeches in some pathetic attempt to get his attention. Little did they know they were never going to get it. Most of the recruits coming through were never memorable. Although some came with the best intentions but realized quickly that the internship program was way more then they had bargained for.

"Here we go." Tristan said smiling back. As the cart moved along,

Serena was taken aback by the sheer size of the marina. She had studied maps and pictures, but they did not do this place justice. They drove up a small, paved road until it opened up into the pool section where a sea lion sculpture was displayed nicely in the center of three pools. As they got closer, she noticed the sea lions swimming in the pool. They quickly recognized the sound of the golf cart and made their way to the mouth of the pool to greet them. Tristan stopped the cart in time for six sea lions to leap out of the water in unison. One of them gazed from her to Tristan and back again with a series of loud funny barks.

"Now now, be patient Suzie." Tristan answered as he jumped out making his way to the back of golf cart. Serena couldn't help but feel they were staring at her. The one Tristan had called Suzie stood up and clapped her fins repeatedly. They were so cute with the white freckles and big black eyes. She instinctively grabbed a bucket out of the back of the cart. Tristan was pleasantly surprised at her motivation and attentiveness; most people would simply go right to the animals leaving him having to yell out for assistance. Serena followed close behind as Tristan unlocked the gate, her eyes never leaving the mammals. Tristan pulled the door open and motioned for her to go in.

"Thank you." Serena said as she leaned her body to hold the door while Tristan gathered supplies and followed her in. The barks grew louder as they watched impatiently for Tristan to hurry towards them with their breakfast. Four of the six sea lions including Suzie continued to eagerly bark for their breakfast as two remained back in the pool floating lazily on the water clearly not as hungry.

"You can leave the supplies here." Tristan motioned to a little shed by the gates. Serena placed the bucket down along the wall and followed behind as Tristan walked towards the animals. He plunged his hand in the bucket, pulling out a handful of sardines and threw it at Suzie who caught it gracefully and clapped her fins in gratitude. Serena watched, eyes gleaming in fascination. She has dreamed of this moment for as long as she could remember. The call of the ocean and discovering the life within it has finally come true. She felt most connected to sea mammals especially, dolphins, whales, and sea lions. She couldn't explain why but the idea of swimming freely with them, playing with them as they surrounded her filled her with comfort. Out of the corner of her eye, she caught a glimpse of the two sea lions laying alone, quietly in their corner. The smallest one's eyes caught hers and she could swear the sea lion was staring right through her. Serena noticed scarring around the left eye and puss building in the corners of both. Her smile faded as she realized there was a deep sadness there. Tristan followed her gaze and saw the color draining from her face.

"That's Nibblet and Brawler," He started to explain as he continued to feed. "They are two females who were rescued separately a few months apart and quickly bonded during their recovery. Nibblet there," He motioned to the smallest one with the scarring on her face. "She's the runt and Brawler is the troublemaker. They were released separately but could not cope and went back to the shelter in Cali. They weren't doing very well so I agreed to take them in. Unfortunately, it's not going so well here either." He explained solemnly.

Serena could not take her focus off of Nibblet. She felt connected somehow.

"Can I try?" She asked, following her instincts.

"Sure, there are gloves ov-" She threw her hand in the bucket of sardines before Tristan could finish. The cold water sent a refreshing jolt up her arm and without hesitation she threw the handful of sardines at Suzie while keeping her eyes on Nibblet and Brawler. Did they just move closer? Serena thought. The four hungry seals surrounded Serena while barking and clapping their fins as they eagerly ate their breakfast. Caught up in the excitement, Serena failed to notice she was being herded towards the water. Tristan noticed the behaviour but was too fascinated to stop as he was curious to see how Serena would handle the situation. He watched intently wondering if they really were trying to get her in the water or if they were just excited. He had never seen them act this way towards any other intern.

"Serena, watch out!" Tristan called out as he tried to reach for her, but it was too late. Serena tumbled backwards, bucket still in hand, slipping on the wet surface and landing straight in the cold pool. The sea lions jumped in after her. The shock of the water temperature sent a rush through her body, she was trying to hang on to the bucket, but it seemed to drag her down faster. Fearing the salt water, she kept her eyes shut but she needed to see where she was going. She opened her left eye slowly, then her right...no burning! How was that possible? Now was not the time to ponder life's mysteries! She scolded herself. She sank a lot further than she anticipated and struggled to swim towards the surface. The sea lions started swimming around her in a rapid frenzy, making her dizzy and disoriented. She was running out of air and could not see the surface anymore. Suddenly she felt an intense burning sensation behind her ears. She never felt anything like this before. In a moment of sheer panic, she dropped the bucket and made a frantic break for the surface. She gasped for air as her head broke through the water, and it took her a few moments to realize she was hearing Tristan's voice yelling from the platform.

"Are you ok?" She finally heard him repeat for the third time. Was he smiling? And if he was, how was her drowning on her first day amusing to him? Her blood started to boil at the thought. She did not know him very well but had not pegged him for someone who enjoyed watching someone go through a near death experience. It took her a moment to put herself together. She felt her ears again and the burning sensation was gone. Was she imagining it? What was that? She was just about to swim towards the platform when she was met with two black eyes staring right through her. This must be Nibblet, she mused.

"Are you ok?" Serena heard a voice call out as she was approaching the platform. She shook her head as the voice was not the familiar voice of Tristan. She looked up at Tristan who now held out a hand to assist her. Was it him? It has to be him, she questioned. As she looked around, there was no one else in sight so it had to be Tristan. She reached for his hand, tempted for a second to pull him in with her in retribution for the smirk on his face. Tristan pulled his hand away instinctively as if reading her mind. "Don't even think about it." Tristan warned as he reached out again.

How did he do that? Was she that predictable? Serena reached for it again, annoyed and wanting to just get out of the water. As Tristan pulled her out, he noticed the amulet around her neck flickered.

"Please stay." The same voice called out again, but this time strangely fading out and sounding somewhat muffled as she was pulled out of the water.

"What did you say?" Serena asked Tristan in confusion. Surprised, he looked at her, his smirk now disappearing from his face.

"I...didn't say anything." Tristan said dubiously as he looked back at Nibblet. Confused, Serena followed his gaze. Nibblet simply turned around and swam away.

"I... dropped the bucket." Serena said apologetically following his gaze in the pool.

"Don't worry, I'll get it later." Tristan retorted, turning away from her as he picked up his bucket and walked towards the gates.

"Wait, you're just going to walk away like nothing happened?" Serena asked in shock and somewhat upset at his carelessness over the strange situation. How could he just walk away like that? Tristan took a moment to collect his thoughts before he turned around. The slight tremble in her voice and the shock she was feeling was an obvious sign she didn't understand what was happening. He took a deep breath, knowing he would have to choose his words very carefully.

"Sea lions can be quite playful, as you may have now noticed." Tristan answered simply as he turned to face her. Looking at Serena, he realized the appropriate clothing she was wearing was not so 'appropriate' anymore. Tristan couldn't help but notice her perfectly shaped breasts with hard nipples peeking right through her freshly wet, white T-shirt. Even if he attempted not to look, he was not blind to something so obviously perfectly shaped. Dripping wet from head to toe, Serena looked quite stunningly cute and it was difficult not to smile.

"Sea lions are 'quite' playful." Serena repeated sarcastically while crossing her arms over her wet chest, suddenly realizing by his gaze she was wearing a now WET white t-shirt. If it wasn't for the smirk, she could have taken him a little more seriously. She was normally a quiet calm person, but it took every ounce of her being to remain contained. Tristan simply acted like this was an everyday occurrence and was enjoying himself a little too much for her liking.

"So, the sea lions..." Serena began dubiously. "Do they always make a habit of christening every new intern that pops in by throwing them in the pool?" She asked rhetorically with great annoyance. "Wait," She said, glaring at him. "Did you train them to do that?" The truth is, she did not know this man at all. He could have totally set this entire thing up.

"You give me way too much credit." Tristan said with a chuckle as he turned around and opened the gate. The truth was, he could have, but the sea lions came up with this all on their own. Sea lions were like the dogs of the ocean. Playful, and for the most part friendly. They always had two things on their mind: eat and play. Tristan sounded honest enough, but it was simply too hard to believe in what just happened. Serena was completely speechless and remained that way for most of the day. Her clothes eventually dried, and she continued to be pleasant, but remained quiet.

Tristan wondered if he should send her home a little early as he could feel something had shaken her to the core. Something she had to be confronted with. Something detrimentally important that could not continue to be avoided for much longer. But, pushing her too quickly would not do anyone any good.

CHAPTER 6
TRISTAN

As Tristan maneuvered the cart back down the path towards his office, Serena remained distant and deep in thought but still tried to pay attention to Tristan's chatter as he drove. Her work as a nurse had taught her to always be focused no matter what was happening in her life, or around her. She paid attention to every detail Tristan laid out for her; how much food to give, and to be careful with animals like the sting rays, who were, for the most part, gentle creatures if not disturbed in the wrong way. She took this internship seriously and wanted to be a professional. Perhaps this connection she felt with Tristan had given her a false sense of security. Maybe her pride was a little hurt from the sea lion incident, even if he had somehow orchestrated the whole thing in some strange initiation for newbies. Her ego would eventually heal, she told herself. It was quite humiliating if she was completely honest with herself. She might as well have stripped off her clothing and pranced around naked in front of him. Note to self: never wear a white t-shirt without a swimsuit AGAIN near water. Lesson learned.

They pulled into the hangar where they first met in Tristan's office. The door slowly began to lower as she jumped off the cart. There was a woman waiting for them there. She was mid-sized, with dark black hair braided down her back, big brown eyes with long, beautiful lashes and a

41

smooth Hawaiian complexion. She wore a light cotton jumpsuit in vivid Hawaiian colors over a simple white tank top. She had a white and yellow plumeria flower tucked behind her ear which were adorned with long feather earrings. She was simply a stunningly beautiful woman.

"Aloha, you must be Kelena." The woman greeted kindly as she walked towards her. She placed a traditional white plumeria lei around her neck and leaned over for the traditional Hawaiian greeting leaning her forehead against hers.

"Kelena is your Hawaiian name." The woman explained as she noticed the slight look of confusion on Serena's face.

"Aloha." Serena said while closing her eyes returning the kind welcome as their foreheads touched for some time. Serena had witnessed a little bit of the friendly Hawaiian culture since her arrival and was already in love with it all. This was a Hawaiian warmth at its best. The hands embracing her were filled with warmth and kindness like she had never experienced before. The woman pulled back slowly, catching a glimpse of the necklace around Serena's neck.

"What a beautiful necklace!" She said as she touched it slightly, noticing the strange sparkle the stone emulated. Serena appeared oblivious.

"I am Ailani Iwalani Naluai." Ailani introduced herself. Serena noticed a wedding band and wondered if perhaps she was married to Tristan.

"Oh, my mother gave this to me." Serena answered as she tucked the necklace back under her t-shirt. She knew the necklace was quite plain and not worth much, except that it was the only special present her mother ever gave her. Being a cold person, her mother was never one for gifting, saying it was a terrible tradition meant to spoil the souls of humans.

"I am Tristan's partner and long-time *friend*." Ailani explained emphasizing the "friend" word as she noticed Serena glance at her hand then at Tristan. Serena felt a little heat rise to her cheeks as she realized she was caught.

"Lovely to meet you, you have a beautiful name." Serena replied. *Beautiful name with a beautiful face* she wanted to say, but she was certain this woman had heard it many times before. She was not going to be *that* intern.

"We had an eventful day today, so you can go home." Tristan said to Serena with a little too much emphasis on 'eventful' to peak Ailani's curiosity as he busied himself coiling a hose around his arm.

"Eventful?" Ailani asked with an honest frown on her face. Obviously, she seemed completely unaware of anything remotely connected to what happened.

"Sea lions somehow thought I would enjoy bathing with them." Serena answered nonchalantly as she grabbed her backpack that was hung up on the hangar wall. Ailani chuckled with disbelief as this was certainly something she had not heard of before.

"How can that be?" Ailani asked Tristan. "Since most of our sea lions are rescues, they are always a bit shy with newcomers."

"Not today." Tristan answered with a coy smile as he glanced at Serena whose cheeks seemed to burn redder by the second.

"I guess they really like me then." Serena shrugged as she pulled the strap of her backpack on.

"See you tomorrow?" Serena asked Tristan.

"Of course! First day out in the water," He replied as he opened a trunk and threw the coiled hose in. He walked to her and put his hand on Serena's shoulder.

"Try to get some rest, you'll need it." He added. The touch of his big hand was warm and sent another strange sensation through her. It was not as harsh and obvious as when they had shaken hands earlier in the day, but it was a slight tingle that could not be missed. She wondered again if he had sensed this or was she the only one having this strange sensation?

"I will." Serena answered tiredly as she pulled away awkwardly and walked away.

"See you tomorrow Kelena." Ailani waved and watched her leave curiously. She waited until Serena was completely out of sight before turning back to Tristan. When he saw Ailani was starring, he cleared his throat and went to the small desk to grab some papers.

"Who is this woman?" Ailani asked inquisitively, her eyes drilling

Tristan intensely and even though he was avoiding her gaze, he could feel it on him.

"It's a long story." He muttered under his breath trying to avoid the subject. Ailani walked to Tristan and took the clipboard he was fiddling with out of his hands. She put her hands on each side of his face, forcing him to look her right in her eyes. She stood about a foot and a half shorter than he was, but she knew how to stand her ground.

"You know you cannot lie to me Pu'ole." Ailani whispered softly, calling him by the name she had always called him. She named him after the Triton trumpet shell. These shells are used in Hawaiian culture as blowing shells in important ceremonies and commonly named after the Greek god Triton who was believed to have used this shell. It was the tone of voice he could not resist, and even though she held no true power over him, they had known each other too long and he could not withstand it.

"Na-maka-o-Kaha-i." Tristan complied with an answer. It was the simplest way to explain it, in such few short words. Namaka was what the Hawaiian's called the goddess of water and the sea. He did not mean it literally and Ailani knew that, but what exactly did that mean? She backed away, a confused look of disbelief crossing her face, which was to be expected.

"You sensed it when you touched the amulet." Tristan stated, watching her intently. She turned away, leaning against the wall, silent for a few long moments.

"It simply cannot be." Ailani muttered questioning the powers that be. "How is this possible? That she just shows up into our midst out of nowhere?" She thought out loud, baffled. They have often had discussions that many believed Namaka's spirit would come back someday. She would be the one to bring great change to this world. The rising waters, floods, tsunamis, and many other natural disasters growing across the world was proof the world was in chaos. It was becoming clear that something or someone was needed to restore the world's balance. The world was always brought back into balance when it was thrown into the midst of chaos. It was the way of the universe.

"I can honestly say I have no idea." Tristan said as he picked up the clipboard again and looked down at the form signed by Serena. He had lived long enough not to be too shocked at what fate could reveal. And even Zeus could not stop what was coming.

CHAPTER 7
SERENA

Serena walked through the door and slammed it behind her with her left foot. She dropped her backpack in the entrance, walked to her kitchen, and dropped her keys on the kitchen counter. She jumped on her barstool and leaned her elbows against the counter of her kitchen island. She closed her eyes and rubbed her temples, trying to ease the growing headache that had been looming since the incident with the sea lions. These headaches have plagued her since the day she had fallen overboard amongst the pod of orcas. It was strange how she remembered that day. Some details are completely gone from Serena's memory, except for the part where time seemed to stand still, and she came face to face with her; the leader of the orca pod. The orca's eyes were completely mesmerizing, and she could have sworn she had heard the orca say something. It wasn't a spoken word like humans uttered through their vocal cords and mouth, but somewhat like a whisper echoing through her mind. Those words will be forever imprinted into Serena's soul; *Don't be afraid Namaka*. That is when the headaches started. Since then, they are triggered by memories of that day, bad dreams or when she is near bodies of water. It pounded in her head like shockwaves and not much could ease the pain in its wake. Most of the time, she could bear it, pushing the memories or thoughts to the back of her mind like a door to a room. As long as the door was shut, she was fine. But situations like facing Nibblet in the pool threw the door wide open and the flood of pain that followed made it extremely difficult to bear. She had to use every bit of concentration she could muster to withstand the strange painful waves. It usually left her seeming distant and quiet, but it was the only thing she could do to remain functional. In fact, it had dampened many, if not all of her possible relationships whether friendship or in her love life. No one could really understand what she went through and how could she even attempt to explain what she was experiencing? Her mother was the only one who knew part of her pain. She had often spoken to her mother about the headaches, but she simply replied that she must have an intense allergic reaction to the water. Her mother would warn her to do everything in her power to stay away from it if she wanted to live a normal life, and that if she dared to speak to anyone about it they would probably put her in the nuthouse. And so, she had, for the most part, listened to her, as the headaches did disappear. As long as she stayed away from bodies of water, she could manage it, but the truth was, she couldn't. It was a feeling she just could not put into words. The pull of the ocean she felt and the calling to come to Hawaii and be surrounded by the source of this excruciating pain was irresistible. It was well worth it for the great sense of peace and belonging that overwhelmed her. Serena knew in her soul this was truly her home, that was enough to live through this wretched pain.

CHAPTER 8
TRITON

Tristan watched the sunset fall on the horizon of Kailua beach. He stood, standing on the edge of the ocean with the waves caressing his feet as he dug his toes into the soft white sand. Tristan took a deep cleansing breath as he allowed the sound of the crashing waves to ease his mind. This part of the beach during their winter season was generally quiet from tourists or locals, separated by boulders from the main Kailua beach. Coming to watch the sunset was the part of his daily routine he enjoyed the most. Watching the waves crash on the beach and the colors of the sky burst in beauty as if buckets of pink, gray, white, and red paint had been randomly thrown at the sky. It had taken him an exceptionally long time to adjust to living in this realm. He had always chosen to live by his father and mother's side for as long as he could remember, but things had changed when they had discovered Thetis' offspring was in this realm. Against his own wishes, he had been sent away from the paradise of the Atlantean realm to this one. No one had regarded the earth realm with much interest in what seemed like thousands of years, finding humans rather boring and predictable. Atlanteans were never meant to reside in this earth realm for too long. It was known that too many Atlanteans living here would disrupt the universal balance between all realms. But there laid the problem. It was too easy for some lower Atlanteans known as demi-gods to realize the power they held over the humans in this earth realm. It was irresistible. Earth was one of the only realms where the demi-gods could access their god-like powers. Unlike higher class Atlanteans known as Olympians, they had power over all realms. It became very tempting for demi-gods to find their way to earth and meddle to gain a foothold of power. And that was what the true purpose of the Olympians; to protect this fragile balance and the inhabitants of the realms.

* * * * *

Triton closed his eyes as he took a deep cleansing breath of fresh salty air. Living in Atlantis had many benefits, mostly for the fresh mountain air that was incomparable to anything he could find on earth, but the salty ocean air was slowly growing on him and so were the humans. Well, they were much easier to deal with then, he had originally thought. He tried not to meddle too much by staying out of the way but coming to Hawaii was a change for the better. The people here held customs, beliefs and ways of life that reminded him of his home and of his people, minus some of the complicated politics of Atlantis. Triton had decided to stay in Hawaii. It was a central point, close to most of the portals and it is surrounded by water and sea life. He could come and go as he needed to continue his search. He had now realized that they could live a fulfilling life in this realm if so chosen IF they did not meddle. He met some demi-gods who had made this choice and in whom he had a strong bond with. One in particular he would find difficult to walk away from. Except things have taken an interesting turn indeed. He opened his eyes again, hearing the distant sound of the conch shell calling him home. To the human ear, the sound would adapt to the human environment. On a rainy day, it would be masked by thunder. On a clear day, it would be a gust of wind or a flock of birds flying overhead. Taking in another breath, he glanced around quickly to make sure the coast was clear. When it was, he stripped down naked, threw his clothes in a bush behind him then ran into the ocean and swam home. It took merely a few hours before Triton leaped out of the pool portal and onto the rock platform guarded by two Atlantean guards, wearing platinum chest plates encrusted in gold with

Plato's Atlantis symbols holding heavy spears. The pool portals were not usually guarded, but since the discovery of Thetis' foul play, it was decided by Zeus that the portals should be monitored closely. As Triton walked towards them, one guard handed Triton a blue and green satin sleeveless knee length robe with symbols and markings of the Poseidon kingdom.

"Thank you." Triton said with a nod, grateful to this change as he would normally have to hunt for coverings before he wandered about Atlantis completely naked. Obviously, they had sensed his arrival and had prepared accordingly. The guards nodded respectfully, hitting their left shoulder with a right-hand fist in the Atlantean greeting to higher class. Walking out of the skillfully built cavern, he climbed up the stairs into the streets of Atlantis. Unlike what most humans believed; Atlantis is the central realm that controls the diverse universe. It is connected to all the other realms through intricate gateways built by the Olympians long ago. Each species was given their own realm, as the Olympians realized they could not co-exist. Having power in the earth realm caused it to be more chaotic and it was therefore forbidden for races such as the cyclopes or satyrs to live in the earth realm. Even mermaids and mermen had been forbidden, their powers also too great for that realm. Triton made his way through the busy streets where merchants of all realms gathered to do business to the city's southwest quarter, passing citizens from different realms; cyclopes, satyrs, all going about their usual business, some bowing their heads respectfully as their eyes met. He finally reached the ocean side of the city. He took off the robe and plunged into the water to make his way to Poseidon's kingdom which sat in the depth of the ocean beneath Atlantis.

As Triton approached the tall white and yellow gold-plated gates of the palace, they opened as if they knew he was coming. The gates had been built to sense the presence of Atlanteans but guard against intruders. There, at the top of the stairs stood his mother dressed in her official white silk toga with the golden belt held together by a buckle encrusted with Poseidon's symbol. This traditional clothing made it easier to maneuver in their underwater world and it was also standard dress for official gatherings. Her hair neatly braided into a crown upon her head. Triton fell to one knee, taking his mother's right hand and slightly kissing it with deep love and respect.

"Mother." Triton said as he placed the back of her hand on his forehead. With her left hand, she ran her fingers through her son's curly dark hair.

"Triton, my son, we have so much to discuss." She said as she raised him up with her right hand. Their foreheads touched in a family greeting, resembling the one the Hawaiians used. It was then that she noticed the bandage on his left arm. A perplexed, somewhat worried look crossed her face.

"A simple little scuff, nothing the healing pools of Atlantis cannot fix." He replied to ease her worry. Truth was, he normally would come straight to Atlantis after a battle to plunge himself in her healing pools but his mission to find Thetis' offspring had meant he had not been able to return as often as he'd like. Juggling between that and the growing tension in some realms, he found it refreshing every time he came back home and took in his first breath of Atlantean air.

"It is as I feared, isn't it? War is knocking at our doors and your father is too blind to see it." Amphitrite said with worry, her fingers lightly stroking her son's bandage. Triton nodded solemnly.

Like Triton, her beloved son, she had sensed the seriousness of the growing situation, especially since they had heard of Thetis' duplicity. This offspring of hers could make things much worse for Atlantis, maybe even threaten its existence. They swam together down the marble halls of the Poseidon palace, walls covered in artistic glass mosaics depicting the vast history of their kingdom. The halls were filled with thick obsidian columns decorated with all types of sea creatures celebrating a time where all creatures lived in unity. Both swam silently, longing for that simplicity to return.

"Any advances on your search?" Amphitrite asked hopefully as she took her son's arm in hers. Triton stopped for a mere second, his face expressionless making it difficult to see what was on his mind. Triton was always very reserved and excellent at keeping his game face. His emotions and expression controlled, making it extremely difficult for his enemies to foresee his actions. But, she was his mother, and a slight spark in the corner of his eyes might be overlooked by anyone else, but not her.

"Perhaps I have made some headway." Triton answered almost in a whisper, unwilling to give too much information especially in the hollow halls of the palace where information could reach the ears of their opposers.

"Oh?" Amphitrite asked inquisitively with curiosity as she guided him down a hallway to their left. They swam up a set of stairs into the open-aired cavern of the sacred Atlantean healing pool. Triton emerged from the water, transforming back into his human form. Pulling on his satin robe, even if wet, would procure at least some decency in the presence of his mother.

"Perhaps we can discuss it further after you have enjoyed some Atlantean commodities." Amphitrite smirked with intent. Walking behind her son she tugged at his robe to get a closer look at the amassing tattoos on the left side of his chiseled body. She traced the outline of the tattoos with her fingers, curious as to why her son would adopt such gross human behavior. Tattoos in Atlantis were used for branding cattle. She hadn't spent much time in the earth realm enough to recognize the markings, but they seemed to be of a tribal nature. She wondered if perhaps her son was spending too much time with humans.

"What exactly did you have in mind mother?" Triton replied while untying his robe.

"What kind of mother would I be if I couldn't help my son unwind when he comes home." Amphitrite answered earnestly. Triton walked into the pool as his mother departed, plunging back into the water behind him.

This pool was built within the rock of the Atlantean ground and fed through the realm's sacred mountains above. They were hot and full of regenerative properties, filled with ambrosia, the sweet nectar of the gods. Triton closed his eyes and allowed the intense pleasure of the healing properties to take over. He felt a tingle in his arm as the nectar slowly knitted the open wound in his arm back together. He sighed heavily, enjoying this sensation of being massaged by multiple warm hands at once. Like the sound of the conch shell, it was something humans would never in their lifetime understand. There was no denying he had missed being home, in the comforts it provided. He suddenly felt a presence joining him. He opened his eyes to see a divine woman dropping her thin red satin robe at her feet revealing her perfectly shaped body bearing only gold arm bands in the shape of Poseidon, the tail wrapping itself around her arms. The armbands are obviously a gift from Poseidon himself to give her free roaming of the kingdom. Her dark brown hair placed in hundreds of small braids upon her head, held together by a brass head circlet. Her chest covered in tribal tattoos adorning her neck. Her blue eyes, cold and seductive on a mission to please the sea god. Autonoe, a sea nymph, one of Triton's most favored mistresses from his past, most certainly sent by his mother. Except that was in his past. In the days where he resided and lived within the kingdom, before he lived amongst humans within the earth realm, he would have welcomed this gift. Things are not that simple anymore. The prophecy coming to life with meeting Serena has now bonded their fates. The thought of her made his hand tingle with the spark of their first meeting.

"It is good to see you again, master." The sea nymph said seductively into his ear and nibbled his earlobe, sending a shiver down his thick muscular neckline. Her fingers lightly caressed his chest and continued tickling down his abs to his cock. Wanting to push her aside but he fell to her seductive ways. Triton took the nymph by the waist and placed her on his lap filling her with his thickening member. The Nymph moaned in deep pleasure as she felt the hardness of her master swelling inside her, pumping in rhythmic slow motions. She gripped the tangling curls of his hair and pulled it passionately. His eyes still closed, focusing on the moment, the hot water, the beautiful sea nymph doing all she could do to pleasure him. As a sea nymph, Autonoe could sense the desires of her masters and fulfill their deepest fantasies. Whether it was to change her appearance, her voice or any physical traits she felt they wanted. She found Triton's mouth and kissed it fervently, wrapping her legs around his thick athletic waist pulling him in deeper. She pressed her breasts tight against his chest which brought him closer to climax. She gave him everything he wanted. He opened his eyes only to find the face of the woman he was trying to forget. In a frustrated groan, he stopped and almost shoved the nymph violently off him. Angry and insulted by the gesture, the nymph stormed away as quickly as she could.

Triton sank his head under water, letting the sweet nectar of the gods fill his lungs, hoping it would clear his muddled thoughts. He hurried to the mouth of the pool, climbed out grabbing his robe on his way out of the cavern. Knowing the healing pool had worked, he ripped the bandage off his left arm and set it aflame. He dove into the salt water, allowing every inch of the ocean salt to run its course to transform him into his merman form. The salt water, especially from Atlantis, usually did miracles to calm and clear his head but not today. Triton made his way to his quarters, stopping to place his hand on a trident diagram on the marble wall in front of him. The wall moved displaying a thick marble door slowly opening to his private quarters. He was pleasantly reminded of the sheer size of his chambers as he has not been here in quite some time. His enormous bed is carved into the coral wall, encrusted with rubies and diamonds. He swam ahead, opening two double doors to a balcony overlooking the entire kingdom. Past the royal gardens, a medley of village homes and Temples built out of coral and limestone, covered with colorful anemones formed a circulator pattern like Plato's pattern of Atlantis.

Triton changed back into his human form, preferring to keep the merman form for swimming as he is able to breathe with his gills behind his human ears. In truth, he had gotten accustomed to his legs by spending more time on land then he had in centuries. He barely flinched when his mother's hand rested gently on his left shoulder, his gaze never leaving the view of the kingdom.

"What is the matter my son?" Amphitrite inquired trying not to voice the concerns she felt.

She had been making her way to Triton's quarters when she passed an incredibly angry Autonoe. Knowing not enough time had passed since she had sent the sea nymph to be with her son, she could only guess the nymph had not accomplished what she asked her to do,

"What happened, sea nymph?" Amphitrite demanded.

"How dare he treat me this way! Too much human air in his lungs!" Autonoe had shouted angrily. She swam away changing back into her usual nymph form as the tattoos faded with her long hair flowing freely behind her as the braids unraveled.

Amphitrite grabbed Triton's hands to pull him away from his brooding gaze. She looked down at his hands, tracing them with her fingers starting with the right, then with the left. As she traced his left hand, she felt the traces of a magic bond. She focused her motherly senses into Triton's hand, and it began to glow. Her eyes widened in surprise as she followed the glow as it crept up the love line of his massive hand which ran from the fourth finger up to his arm. This line is the vein that runs from the hand straight to the heart, the vein of a Love Lock.

Amphitrite glowered at Triton."How, who?" Amphitrite exclaimed in complete shock. This was something not often seen amongst Atlanteans but could only mean one thing: an unbreakable bond set by destiny tethering two Atlanteans together. It would explain why he would never be able to enjoy a pleasurable encounter with another woman unless it was with whom he was bound to.

"I found her." Triton answered distantly offering little to no information.

"Thetis' offspring?" Amphitrite asked.

"Yes." He answered, still avoiding his mother's gaze.

"And she is still alive?" Amphitrite asked sharply.

"Mother, this wouldn't let me!" He shouted in frustration, shoving his glowing left hand in his mother's face.

Her eyes widened as the realization of his words sunk in. She took his hand and traced the blue shimmering line of the bond again. The mark would prevent him from harming the offspring himself, and then came the implication of what this truly meant. Not only was there a war brewing and many were looking to kill this offspring, but now her own son was bound to her and if it was known, his life would also be at great risk. Triton could not walk away. They were tethered together and would be pulled to each other in a way that was totally out of their control.

"Cursed Atlas father of all Atlanteans!" She cursed angrily as she dropped his hand. A few moments of silence passed as they reflected on the gravity of it all. Zeus and the Olympians had done everything in their power to keep the prophecy from happening in fear of the repercussion of it. Poseidon had always been Zeus' right hand. Triton was always a dedicated son, standing by his father's side until now.

"I was hoping you would enlighten me as to how in the gods names this happened?" Triton asked, his tone slightly angry and accusatory. Bonding had been created by Aphrodite, goddess of love. It was a sacred ceremony that occurred between two gods and only if approved by Zeus himself. Not only was it a symbol of a union, but it was also meant as protection, a carefully crafted political move. It came with great risk if the wrong two bonds were created. It could be catastrophic in the balance of things, and Zeus had rendered it a sacrilege to be done without his blessing. It was a ceremony that occurred on rare occasions of late, as it yielded some undesirable results in the past.

Amphitrite raised her eyebrow and glared at her son sternly making him look away. "Do you honestly believe I would be foolish enough to risk your life? And for what?"

Her condescending tone was not convincing. Triton knew she was hiding something. For the good of the cause, I believe you would do anything. Triton thought. He did not doubt his mother's love for him, but he also suspected he did not know where her loyalty lied. His mother had never supported Zeus's quest to cheat the fates by banishing Thetis to the earth realm, and making Poseidon go along with it all. Thetis was the Queen of the fifty Nereids. Amphitrite was the eldest of the fifty Nereids. Thetis had been her queen long before she married Poseidon.

"Since you spend so much time in the earth realm, perhaps you should question your Hawaiian friends." Amphitrite answered passive aggressively, clearly insulted by her son's accusation.

"What about Laka and Lono?" Triton retorted sarcastically wondering

56

where his mother was going with this. Amphitrite was well aware that her son had spent a lot of time with Laka, the Hawaiian goddess of love, daughter of Aphrodite herself. Laka was sent to the realm to protect it with her husband Lono, the god of peace, son of Apollo.

"You honestly believe a daughter of Aphrodite and a son of Apollo have nothing to do with this?" Amphitrite asked coldly.

"They are my friends, mother." Triton answered, avoiding her gaze, yet he couldn't help but feel a sense of uncertainty towards the two Hawaiians he called friends.

"Oh Triton," Amphitrite scuffed. "You and I both know that Atlantean blood runs through their veins and as much as they would like to pretend they are better than the rest of us, they are not." She wanted to be understanding of her son's new attachment to the human realm, but she also wanted him to face reality. Perhaps it was a little bit of jealousy on her part, after all Triton had never been so distant in thousands of years. Until those two ensnared him.

"You are pushing this too far mother." Triton said, turning away from her irritated.

Amphitrite sighed heavily, closing her eyes tightly to regain control of herself. It was difficult when it came to her son's well being. Mother knows best does she not? "I'm sorry my son," She apologized after following him inside. "This," She said as she took his left hand and gently traced the bond again. "Is difficult to bear." She said through her teeth, more than certain Aphrodite was too afraid to go against Zeus' will. This had to be something those self-absorbed Hawaiians would do. She was certain of it.

"And how do you suppose I feel about this?" Triton asked, yanking his hand away, his mood still foul from his failed encounter with Autonoe. As if he was supposed to accept this fate without a care? Laka and Lono were very aware of the prophecy. Laka was just as surprised as he had been about it all, as far as he could tell. They could see firsthand what damage was being done to their realm. They had been placed there to protect it directly, and they had been eager, maybe too eager to help him on his quest to find Serena. What better way for the god of peace and the goddess of love to stick it to Zeus than to bring this prophecy to fruition by binding him to Serena the second they met? His gaze narrowed in deep consideration of the implications of this plot. They were friends, at least Laka was, and he couldn't help but feel the rise of fury in his belly at the thought of being betrayed. This unwanted bond must have been carefully planned. This is much bigger than Triton anticipated. All he knew, as he stared into his hand, was that he was bound intricately with the daughter of Zeus and Thetis, who was completely unaware of their existence.

"Perhaps something can be done?" Amphitrite asked with a glimpse of hope in her voice. "Visit your friends, they may be able to help you." She said even though in the pit of her stomach, she knew if the fates were involved, there was nothing that could be done.

"I doubt it." Triton answered as he opened an armor chest, digging out his extra-long leather bracers and slipped one on, to cover most of his forearms and hopefully hide the bond. He knew there had to be some truth to his mother's speculations.

He paused and looked at his glowing hand before putting on the bracer. He suddenly felt waves of emotion that did not belong to him run through his body. He closed his hand tightly and dug his nails into his palm to relieve the sense of urgency.

"She is in great danger, mother." Triton said gravely, breaking the silence as he slipped his other bracer on. "And worst of all, she has no idea what power she holds." He closed his eyes again to focus. He saw her face, her smile, the expression of complete loss and confusion as the amulet she wore weakened in the pool's saltwater breaking down the barrier of protection. It was certainly clear she was completely oblivious. The sea lions had done him a favor by throwing her in the pool. It was all the confirmation he needed. If she had known, there would not have been the shock and surprise he had seen displayed on her face when their hands touched, and their bond was created. Triton couldn't understand why Thetis had kept this from Serena. If she wanted her child to fulfil the prophecy, keeping her hidden and oblivious to it all would only put her in danger. He touched his head, feeling the intensity of the headaches

Serena was experiencing and wondered why a mother would do that to her daughter.

"How is it possible?" Amphitrite mused, finding it difficult to understand why the most powerful Atlantean to ever exist had no idea of her power.

"It's the amulet! I don't know who created it but as long as it remains around her neck, it withholds her powers." Triton said, knowing of only a handful of gods who could create such powerful protection, signaling shifting loyalties are imminent.

"Triton, you must get that amulet away from her as quickly as possible." Amphitrite said with great urgency.

"We can never fully understand the prophecy, but you know what you must do. You have to protect her, get her away from that amulet." She said as she placed a hand lovingly on the side of her son's beautiful face to comfort him knowing this would tear him apart.

"You must leave now before she steps into the sea and her identity is revealed and her safety is compromised. She cannot fall into the wrong hands." Amphitrite warned fiercely, gripping his arm with tears in her eyes at the thought of the implications of the dangers to her son.

Triton heeded his mother's advice. He understood the importance of Serena's existence and the threat she posed to their way of life, but he hated feeling like a pawn. He had been treated like a footman his entire life, doing his parent's bidding when he wasn't certain whose agenda he was serving. All he knew at this moment was that he had to protect Serena.

The truth was, he didn't know Serena. What he did know was that she was an Atlantean. He feared her mind couldn't handle the power hidden within her once it was unleashed when the amulet was removed. He still couldn't understand what Thetis' plan had been. If she genuinely wanted to protect Serena, teaching her the ways of Atlanteans and Olympians would have been the only logical solution. Unless she couldn't be sure if her child was really the child of the prophecy.

"If I am not present at this council meeting that I was summoned for, father will send an army to find me." Triton answered remembering why he was there to begin with.

"But can you risk the Olympians finding out about the bond?" Amphitrite added alarmingly. This was quite the dilemma indeed. But Triton had to risk Serena's safety and keep them blind for as long as he could. Sending an army to the earth realm would only attract more danger. He needed time, but he wasn't sure how much of it he had before someone else discovered her. Both decisions put Serena's life at great risk, but he felt it was safer if he attended the council meeting.

CHAPTER 9
TRITON

Triton stood at the entrance of the throne room and marveled at the magnificence of its creation. The hundred foot high cathedral ceilings with giant glass panels were inlaid with brilliant colored glass pieces carefully placed to imitate the pattern of each constellation of the stars. It was supported by thick walls of sparkling white marble with lines of golden intricate patterns representing the complicated, twisted, and intertwined lines of fate. The stone floors had been carefully engraved with the circled symbol of Atlantis. Two thrones sat at the end of the council hall: Zeus' throne on the left and his queen Hera on the right. All the male Olympian's thrones were on the left facing the right and the female Olympians' thrones were all on the right facing the left. Standing in the middle, was a black marble hearth with each of the god's faces embossed around it. It was filled with Greek fire, the sacred fire of the gods. A simple wooden stool sat next to it for its keeper, Hestia, goddess of the hearth to watch over it.

Zeus' throne was the biggest, in fact, it was so large that seven steps had been built leading to it, each one colored with a different color of the rainbow. It was made in black marble with gold lightning bolts etched all over. A large blue covering was laid above it, symbolizing the sky. On the right arm of the throne sat a slick bald eagle calmly resting on it quietly awaiting his master's orders. Many feared this eagle, as it was Zeus' all-seeing eye. A purple ram's fleece covered the seat of his throne, which he shook to create rain over the realms. Zeus, King of the Gods and the god of the sky, weather, law and order, destiny and fate, and kingship, was about the height of most Olympians. He stood tall and although his body was smaller than his brother Poseidon sitting next to him, he was by no means a small man. He wore a golden chest plate, tracing his chiseled muscles. His shoulders are adorned by golden spaulders shaped like eagle wings. Draping behind him was a white cape embellished by golden lightning bolts embroidered along its edges. His glistening bald head intensified his neatly trimmed salt and pepper beard and stern clear blue eyes that demanded respect. He was strong and imposing, shaping the weather according to his temper. He possessed the perfect knowledge and although he could be quite unpredictable, often showed mercy and prudence. In his right hand, he held his beloved lightning bolt, a gift from the cyclopes for freeing them from enslavement.

To Zeus' right, was the throne of his brother Poseidon, god of the sea, earthquakes, floods, drought, and horses which was made of grey-green-white-streaked marble. It was carefully decorated with coral, gold, and shiny white pearls. The arms took the shapes of fearsome sea beasts and he sat on sleek seal skin. Poseidon was nearly seven feet tall and wearing nothing on his thick, strong muscular upper body. His long dark brown hair hung down to the middle of his back with two twisted braids tied with golden clasps snaking each side of his neck and ocean blue eyes sporting his splenetic temper. He was after all the worst tempered, moody, greedy, and known to be quite vengeful when insulted. On his arms, he wore bracers reaching up to his triceps and decorated with bronze fish scales for added protection. He held firmly in his left hand his sacred trident made of celestial bronze forged by the three elder cyclopes during the first Titanomachy.

Next to Poseidon, was the throne of Ares, god of war and battle lust. His throne was made of strong dark brass shaped into realistic looking human skulls meant to represent the humans he killed during the Trojan wars, a display of his prowess. He sat on a cushion made of human skin. It was the least pleasing to look at. He had short, light brown hair, his face bore a light brown stubble and cold icy blue eyes. His left ear was adorned by a large hanging brass cross earring and around his neck was a leather cord with a large brass arrowhead which was used to kill Ekhidnades, the giant son of Echidna, and a great enemy of the gods. He wore a hooded black leather tunic decorated with white gold flames etched along the high collar line. His waist was decorated with a matching large girdle holding his broad sword. His wrist bands of white gold were adorned with bright rubies. Ares was volatile at best, often known to hold no social morals as he was the embodiment of brutal warfare and slaughter. Zeus referred to him on many occasions as the most hateful of the gods.

Apollo's extremely polished golden throne sat next to the god of war, covered with intricate magical inscriptions. Hung above it, was a sun disk with twenty-one rays shaped like arrows as he was the god of the sun and light, oracles, music, song and poetry, archery, healing, plague and disease, and like his sister the protection of the young. He was also the most powerful god of prophecies, foretelling of Thetis and her offspring. Apollo was the most diversified of the gods. Some said he was indecisive when it came to which type of god he wanted to be. He was slightly shorter than the other gods, but nonetheless graced with nicely sculpted muscles, evidence of strength and power. He had short spiked golden blond hair with charming blue eyes and short stubble covering his perfect features. His bright white smile could charm almost any conquest he sought after, and there were many. He wore a fitted full celestial bronze chest plate with a blue cape draped at his back attached to his chest plate with bronze buckles etched with gold and matching gauntlet wristbands. Hanging on his throne was a matching bronze and golden bow and quiver. Apollo was loved by all gods and humans, women, and men, more often than not, he loved them back as well. Unfortunately, his most famous love affairs are the ones that didn't end well. He was the embodiment of the Greek god ideal; he is harmony, reason and moderation personified, a perfect blend of physical superiority and moral virtue.

Next was the throne of Hephaestus, god of fire, smiths, craftsmen, metalworking, stonemasonry, and sculpture. His throne was made out of every kind of precious metal that could be found. The seat was able to swivel, and the arms adjustable. It even moved along with Hephaestus' will. It was a display of his brilliant creative talent. He was as tall as Poseidon, but he was larger, showing every overly bulging muscle across his entire body. He had thick wavy shoulder length black hair adorned by a golden nightshade circlet with the pandora's symbol resting on his forehead. His piercing blue eyes on his broad face were only overshadowed by his dark full beard. He too wore no shirt but chose a ceremonial white over red war leather battle skirt tied by a huge red leather girdle with a golden lion's head. His legs covered by golden grieves with Medusa's head engraved, almost hiding the golden robotic left leg he built himself. The leg he had lost from his fall from Olympus. He was ingenious with his creations and had never been very social as he preferred the quiet solitude of the forges his volcanoes provided him.

Finally, the last one on the right was the stone throne of Hermes, a winged herald and messenger of the gods. He is also a divine trickster and the god of roads, flocks, commerce, and thieves. His throne was simple enough, except for the arms that had been cut to resemble ram heads and its back was engraved with the symbol of the drill Firestarter he invented. For centuries Hermes had preferred the look of a more mature bearded man but had decided it was time for a change. He was now youthful looking and athletically built, with short strawberry blond hair and playful turquoise eyes. He was bare chested, wearing a white knee length skirt with golden trim and a gold belt hosting a beautiful engraving of his double caduceus serpent. In his left hand, he held a wand called a caduceus, given as a gift from Apollo. A golden staff wrapped by two entwined serpents symbolizing peace and restoration and surmounted by wings. Its power varied between bringing peace, putting others to sleep, and being used for travel. He was the only god able to travel between realms, especially between the living and the dead. He loved to help carry the souls to the underworld so much that Hades made him the leader of the souls. He was a darling of a god, always cheerful, good humored, cunning and because he was the messenger god, he was the fastest of the Olympians.

On the left-hand side of Zeus sat the ivory throne of his wife Hera, queen of the gods, and the goddess of marriage, women, the sky, and the stars of heaven. There were three crystal steps leading to her throne and the back was decorated with several golden cuckoos and willow leaves. Above her throne hung a full moon and she sat on a cow skin which she could also use to bring rain upon the realms if Zeus was otherwise engaged. She was a tall, beautiful slim woman with dark brown eyes, long dark brown hair carefully pinned on her head by golden circlets and pearls, with strands of hair hanging down on her shoulders. She wore an elegant floor length white silk dress sewn and embroidered with golden thread. Although she was very physically attractive, her vengeful, vindictive, and high-temper personality drowned out her beauty. She had no concept of justice when angry or jealous, and she could not forgive women with whom Zeus had sexual relations, even if they were innocent of wrongdoings. She despised all of Zeus' illegitimate children and she was known to turn her anger towards mortals. For example, she started the Trojan war simply because Paris, the Trojan prince, chose Aphrodite as the most beautiful woman. Enraged and jealous over the prophecy of an offspring by Thetis, with whom Zeus had fallen madly in love with, she convinced Zeus of Thetis' involvement in the possible destruction of Atlantis, Olympian's and perhaps the entire universe. She is responsible for sealing the sea nymph's fate of banishment to the human realm.

Facing Poseidon and next to the Queen was Demeter, goddess of agriculture, grain and bread who sustained mankind with the earth's rich bounty. Her throne was made with bright green malachite decorated with golden barley, miniature golden pigs and poppies made of rubies glowing blood red against the barley. Demeter was proper and elegant like the queen, except she was broader and fuller, with long straight blond hair, sparkling blue eyes and plump red lips. She wore a white empire waist toga with off the shoulder sleeves, her neck adorned by a beautiful thick golden necklace. Her temper was not as foul as the queen, but she was like most Olympians: quick to anger and display her wrath.

Next was Athena's goddess of wisdom and good counsel, war, the defense of others and heroic endeavors. Her throne was made of gold and ivory, engraved with olive tree branches and a violet crown embedded with bright blue lapis lazuli jewels. The arms finished with carvings of the heads of a smiling Gorgon. A little brown and white Minervian owl was perched obediently on her left shoulder. She had beautiful long thick curly dark brown hair that flowed freely down her back, neatly pinned beneath a celestial steel and golden headdress in the shape of delicate feathers. She wore a matching short breastplate over a white silk, floor length one shoulder dress. Snake shaped thin armbands wrapped around her chiseled upper arms with bronze bracers. Her majestic presence balances the beauty of her curves and her raw physical power. At her feet, resting against her throne was her bronze shield encrusted with Medusa's head. Her grey eyes bore the wisdom she was known for. In fact, Athena was responsible for inspiring all great inventions done by women and was the favorite child of Zeus. She was the moral and military superior to Ares derived in part from the fact that she was the intellectual and civilized side of war and the virtues of justice and skill, whereas Ares was sheer brutality and blood lust.

Next sat the glistening silver throne of Lady Artemis, goddess of the hunt, the moon, wilderness, childbirth, and protector of the girl child until their coming of age. The back of the throne was as polished as a mirror and above it hung a silver crescent moon with twenty-one rays of light made of arrows, as a twin symbol to match with her beloved twin brothers. She was short and athletically built. She wore a gold circlet emblazoned with a crescent moon woven into a blond tightly braided sun kissed hair cascading around the front of her body. Sparkling blue eyes held maturity and wisdom, being the first-born twin had made her a precocious divine older sister. Her crescent moon shaped bow hung by the side of her throne with its quiver. A large white and grey husky sat obediently at her side. She was a goddess of wild nature who loved to dance, usually accompanied by nymphs, in mountains, forests, and marshes. She embodies the ideals of a hunter and a sportsman. Aside from killing games, she also especially protected the young. Her wrath knew no bounds when someone posed a threat to those she protects.

Next to Artemis sat Lady Aphrodite, goddess of love, beauty, and fertility, known for her great feminine beauty and constant smile. Her beauty beguiled mortals and deities alike as she was known as the most alluring of the pantheon. Her throne was as elegant as she was. It was golden and encrusted with sparkling emeralds and aquamarines. The seat was made of swan's down and at her feet was a golden mat with bees, sparrows, and golden apples woven onto it. She was tall, slender, and delicate with shimmering blond wavy hair that hung loosely upon her shoulders. Her head adorned by a thick golden headband where aquamarines sparkled against the honey color of her hair. She was dressed in a simple stunning pink and gold over white satin sleeveless dress. Golden armbands encircling her upper arm and a delicate golden necklace with an aquamarine pendant adorned her long, graceful neck. Around her waist, a golden girdle known to have the power to inspire love and desire for those who wore it. Hera often borrowed it to inspire love from Zeus. Aphrodite held the powers of fertility, pleasure, and eternal youth. The gods were renowned for their patience and she was no exception. Aphrodite could also be short tempered and vengeful, and she would curse women by making them smell so badly, their men would refuse to have sex with them. She took love very seriously and punished those who did not respect it. Men were cursed to never be desired by women. She often started wars and quarrels amongst the Olympians simply because of her beauty and Zeus put an end to it by marrying her to Hephaestus.

In the last throne sat Dionysus, god of wine, vegetation, pleasure, festivity, madness, and wild frenzy. His throne, previously owned by Hestia, was made of gold-plated fir wood. It was decorated with grape clusters carved into amethyst, snakes carved in serpentine, and various horned animals carved in onyx, sard, jade, and carnelian. He was a nice young handsome man with curly long dark brown hair, short stubble, and shiny grey eyes. He wore a simple wine-colored toga with a golden circlet shaped into a grape vine around his head. In his left hand he held a golden staff of giant fennel covered with ivy vines and leaves and topped with a pinecone. He was the last to arrive, and his unusual birth and upbringing marked him as an outsider. He was the only Olympian with a mortal mother. He was often called "the liberator" because his wine, music, and ecstatic dance freed his followers from self-consciousness and the restraints of society. He was a happy god during harvest but languished along with the rest of the earth realm in winter. He was a mostly kind and generous deity but could be cruel when necessary.

Triton clenched his jaw with a twinge of nervousness in his gut as he stepped forward, reaching the stairs to Zeus' throne. He kneeled with reverence in front of the king of the gods. He had always been loyal to his father's causes and alliances, blindly following his orders until this very moment. As a sick twist of fate would have it, he would have to stand there, look straight into the face of the man he revered the most and attempt to keep her safe. It killed him to be in a position to possibly betray his own flesh and blood. The sacred bond he now had with Serena would keep him from intentionally doing anything that could potentially harm her. His only saving grace was that he was surrounded by other Olympians. Amongst them, is the one who had plotted with Thetis and aided her into bedding Zeus and bearing his child. This god also gave her a powerful amulet to protect the child until the right time arrived for her coming of age. But looking around the throne room, he had no idea who could be capable of unsettling the divine order. Whoever had this planned had a sick sense of humor. Trying to outrun a prophecy usually meant it would somehow come back to haunt you. Triton had not directly had a hand in the Olympian's attempt to defy the fates when they banished Thetis to the earth realm. Triton knew that defying the fates had dire consequences, but he followed his father's orders which made him feel like an accomplice. A great lesson in blindly following without question. It seemed like the fates were trying to teach the Olympians a valuable lesson; not to fuck with them.

"Rise Triton, son of Poseidon," Zeus commanded, his voice resonating throughout the grand throne room. "You were given the task of finding Thetis' offspring and have been roaming the earth for quite some time. What news do you bring us?"

Triton rose to his feet obediently.

"Have you found the goddess?" Artemis asked, rephrasing the question.

"I have not found the goddess." Triton answered carefully, choosing his words. What he found was a girl knowing nothing about her true nature. Until that amulet was destroyed, she was simply a human. "But I am close." He added as he knew his initial answer was not satisfactory.

"What do you mean you are close?" Zeus questioned, seemingly annoyed but remained calm and composed, willing to give Poseidon's son the benefit of the doubt. He was a god after all who had never wavered in his loyalty to the Olympians, therefore they had no reason not to trust him.

"I traced the captain of the vessel who saw Thetis and the child falling in the water. It's only a matter of time before we find her." Triton explained carefully. It had not been simple. Triton realized that Thetis was hiding for a very long time and wouldn't give up her location easily, leaving merely breadcrumbs to follow. He had traced the captain and gotten his hands on the manifest of the ship, which had all the addresses of the passengers. He was about to go pay them a visit when he got a call from Serena, whose address just 'happened' to match the last known address of a passenger named 'Cordelia Nereida'. He didn't think it was a mere coincidence that Cordelia was the Celtic goddess of the sea and Nereida was another ancient Greek name for Nereids. He figured it was well worth accepting Serena's internship in the hopes of gaining more information. He wasn't sure that Serena was connected to Thetis until the day they met, and their hands touched. It took more than twenty years of research to get him to this point but what is twenty years to an immortal?

"Triton, we trust that you know what must be done upon finding the offspring?" Ares reminded Triton, emphasizing what 'must' be done. Areas studied Triton carefully. Was that a nervous twitch he noticed in Triton's jaw?

It wasn't surprising that the god of war would suggest killing the offspring. Ares was the god of bloodlust after all. If anyone fueled the present war, Ares had to have a hand in it somehow.

"Let us not be rash," Lady Athena, goddess of wisdom intervened. "Perhaps it would be better if the son of Poseidon brought the offspring here in front of the council." She explained rationally. It made sense she would want to defend another Atlantean.

"I second that proposal." Lord Apollo agreed.

"Preposterous!" Ares disagreed, slamming an angry fist on his throne, making a crack appear on the arm of his throne.

"I agree with Ares, we do not know what the intentions of the offspring will be." Demeter agreed with Ares calmly.

"That is exactly why she must be brought to us, so we can determine if she is a threat or not. She is, first and foremost, your daughter Zeus." Aphrodite said while batting her pretty lashes at the king of the gods in an attempt to protect an innocent.

"If she is surrounded by all of us, what threat could she really pose?" Poseidon said his brows furrowed. After all, Poseidon, Hades and Zeus had overthrown Kronos. How hard could it be to deal with a daughter of Thetis and Zeus? He doubted she was the child mentioned in the prophecy. He was certain that the prophecy spoke of a *son*. Ultimately, the most powerful Olympians to exist were all males.

"Yes, perhaps this is the BIG trick Thetis was planning all along. This offspring could be another Trojan horse sent to destroy us all." Dionysus said mockingly as he took a sip of wine.

"Thetis is not cunning enough to come up with such a scheme." Hermes replied with a chuckle.

"Why would she keep her offspring hidden from us if she intended to have her brought here? No, she kept her hidden for her safety, afraid of what *some* of us might do." Apollo argued. Throwing an accusatory glare at Hera, who was known to be bitter towards Zeus' *other* children.

"Yet she managed to sneak into Mount Olympus, sleep with Zeus and get herself pregnant!" Ares said with complete disgust. Hera tisked.

"Historically, Thetis has done nothing but protect your children and your throne," Hephaestus said defensively to Zeus, infuriated that his beloved foster mother was being called a traitor. "Or have you forgotten what she has done for many of us in times of need?" Hephaestus snarled at Hera to remind her of the kindness Thetis has shown to both him and Dionysus when they were incredibly young.

"That is by no means proof the *bastard* offspring will not be a danger to us all!" Hera exclaimed outraged. She of course would be jealous and greatly offended by the reminder of her husband's infidelity.

"I agree with Hephaestus on this matter. She has proven a fearsome mother who will do anything to protect her beloved children. I doubt she would do anything to risk her daughter's life." Artemis said. She always revered Thetis for protecting other's young and especially her own children. The lengths she had gone to protect Achilles by going to the underworld to bargain for his life was incredible. She felt it was merely impossible for Thetis to put her daughter at risk.

"But she has *never* forgiven you for banishing her to the earth realm and forcing her to marry a mortal." Hera said defensively staring at   Zeus vehemently.

"Enough." Zeus shouted; his voice thundered around the throne room making everything shake in its wake. "We will take a vote as we always do. All those in favor of bringing the offspring in front of the council?" Zeus demanded. Athena, Artemis, Apollo, Hestia, Hermes, Hephaestus, and Dionysus lifted their hands without hesitation. Poseidon stroked his beard, deep in thought over the situation but finally raised his hands.

"Then," Zeus said with a sigh, obviously distraught by the murderous look on his wife's face.

"It has been decided." Zeus stated. "Son of Poseidon," He said, speaking to Triton. "You must find the offspring and bring her to face the council." Zeus ordered although he was unsure how he felt about the ramifications of their decision. He struggled between wanting to see his daughter born of the love of his life Thetis and being afraid of prophesied offspring. But, he knew if she had been raised by Thetis herself, she would not want any harm to come to him. Or at least, that is what he hoped. Thetis was as beautiful as she was kind. A mother who would do *anything* to protect the young.

"Of course, as you command." Triton bowed in reverence while hiding his left arm behind him. He had worn large leather bracers in an attempt to hide the bond marks which glowed in response to thoughts of Serena. Every strong thought or emotion he felt was only answered by a flash of intense panic and fear from Serena's confused mind. These new sensations would take time to control. They were as new to him as they would be to her. He could feel she could sense *something*, and his concern grew for her state of mind. He wasn't sure if the amulet was strong enough to push away all the effects of the tether of the bond. Therefore, until he was certain, he needed to learn to control his emotions to protect Serena. Triton was certain he escaped the suspecting eyes of the Olympians as they did not question him any further. He had his orders but following through might take longer than the gods expected.

Chapter 10
Serena

Serena sat at her kitchen island with her hands wrapped around a cup of tea as she stared outside watching the storm clouds roll away. It was still a gloomy morning, and raindrops were echoing off the roof in a steady beat. It was strange it was raining. She checked the forecast last night and it was supposed to be sunny and clear, perfect for diving however she woke up to this. She knew the weather could change quickly in Hawaii but still. She got up slowly, dropped the tea bag in the garbage and rinsed out her cup before resting it to dry on the counter. She felt a tingle in her hand that reminded her of the spark she felt when she first met Tristan. It had been another restless night for Serena. She was exhausted from the previous day's events at the Marina, and tried reading a book to put herself to sleep. But the headache was too painful for her to concentrate. She then got up, took some ibuprofen, had a nice hot bath, and even drank some warm milk which she shared with her new friend. The grateful cat snuggled up beside her and they both fell asleep to her rhythmic purring. And then the strange dreams began.

Instead of it normally taking place underwater, she found herself immersed in what seemed like an ancient civilization. She stood in the middle of a grand room, looking around curiously. It was filled with colorful history. Cathedral ceilings, tall walls made of marble and polished stone, and engraved with gold. The walls were covered with some markings, but it was too fuzzy to make out the details. The ceilings were mosaics creatively designed in a way that reminded her of a clear starry night sky. She was surrounded by twelve thrones made in different shapes and with different materials, all carved with different engravings, but she couldn't make out the symbols. The ceramic floors below her feet were inlaid with beautiful circle patterns. A pattern she recognized from the history channel, something about Atlantis. She heard an alarming sound and tried to turn her body, but she felt like she moved in slow motion as if she was submerged in water. She caught a glimpse of herself through one of the throne's shiny mirror surfaces and realized she was in a green satin roman toga. As she came to a stop, she saw a blurry figure. Serena focused intently until the figure took the familiar shape of the chiseled muscular body of Tristan. His face was full of concern and he was trying to tell her something. His mouth was moving frantically but there was no sound. Frowning heavily, Serena tried to get her eyes to focus on what Tristan was saying. Even though she couldn't understand what he was trying to tell her, she could sense it's meaning carried great urgency. Her mind filled with feelings of trepidation, uncertainty, great concern and fear. Fear of what? She suddenly realized it wasn't her emotions she was feeling, they were Tristan's. His hand motionned at something behind her.

She turned around in time to see an arrow coming straight at her face.

Serena awoke suddenly, screaming with sweat pouring from her forehead. Her cat quickly curled up in her lap to comfort her. She looked at the time, it was barely six o' clock, but she decided to get up anyway. Thunder rumbled in the distance and she wondered if that had woken her. She rolled out of bed, pulled on a pair of black jogging shorts, slipped on a bikini top and decided to go out for a run before starting her shift at the marina for nine o'clock. With the heavy percussion of her favorite rock band playing in her ears, Serena jogged rhythmically down the beach trying to clear all the confusion she was feeling. She ran for what seemed like hours, unable to stop herself, afraid to feel the strange sensations again. It felt like there was another voice competing with hers in her mind. The voice was male, familiar and deep sounding. It felt so real she could sense his heartbeat. This was impossible. She had to be going crazy. When she finally stopped running, she leaned forward with her hands resting on her knees and caught her breath. She turned off her music and waited, but she heard nothing. Her mind went blank. Maybe what she was feeling was just remnants of the panic from her dream? It had to be.

"Why do you always run this early in the morning?" Arianna's voice asked, baffled as she appeared out of nowhere again. Serena jumped, not really hearing the question, only a mumble and a strange shadow.

"What?" Serena asked Arianna to repeat as she pulled an earbud out of her ear.

"Running, why would you run if there is no one chasing you?" Arianna rephrased, an honest frown of disbelief on her face.

"Oh, I'm not running from anyone...just clearing my head." Serena lied.

"I see. Swimming is much more pleasant, and efficient." Arianna stated looking out at the water, Serena following her gaze.

"You're probably right, but I like the exercise." Serena smiled, still trying to catch her breath.

"Swimming can be a wonderful exercise if you swim far enough, especially through the underwater currents." Arianna replied.

"I...don't like sharks much." Serena said as she stretched a leg, a shiver ran down her spine even though she was covered in hot sweat. She wasn't sure exactly what Arianna was talking about but she did her best at keeping up the friendly conversation.

"The sharks do not particularly like humans and only usually attack if confused or provoked." Arianna said with a sheepish smile as she noticed Serena's look of fear.

"Says the girl who's afraid of a cat? Would rather not test that theory." Serena teased. Arianna's cheeks flared red as she smiled. Serena looked at her watch for the time. "I...need to get ready for my shift at the Marina, can we pick this up later? Meet me around six o' clock at Chez Lily and we can chit chat?" Serena asked not to be rude but she didn't like to be late, especially not today. Arianna's face lit up as she mentioned Marina.

"Sea Life Park?" Arianna asked curiously.

"Yes, I have an internship there." Serena answered with pride.

"That is where my father works I believe." Arianna said as if trying to recall.

"He does? What's his name? Maybe I can say hi?" Serena asked.

"I...better let you go, I also have somewhere I need to be." Arianna said uncomfortably. "I will see if perhaps I can meet you at this Chez Lily." She said as she turned to leave and waved. Serena watched her leave, it was as if she wasn't sure where she was going, looking around before making the decision to turn down the alley next to her house. What was it with this girl?

She ran back home and slipped inside through her patio doors. Sweaty from her senseless run, Serena grabbed a nice cold glass of water and gulped it down as the fingers of her left hand drummed to the beat of the last song she listened to. She looked at her watch, just enough time to change. She ran up the stairs, grabbed a fresh bikini, a pair of blue shorts and a blue tank top. *No chance of showing my breasts to anyone today.* She thought, her cheeks burning red at the thought of the look on his face. He was a man after all and even the half a second his eyes had lingered there was a half a second too long not to notice what he was staring at. At least with a bikini under her teal shirt, she would be covered this time. She was starting to understand why everyone wore bikini tops in Hawaii now. They were surrounded by water, the chances of getting wet were extremely high besides the fact that the inhabitants were always beach ready. So, her new resolution was to do the same from now on. Peeking at her watch again, she had to go so she quickly twisted her hair into a bun, plopping it high on her head and secured it with an elastic. She grabbed her backpack and ran out.

She was excited to get her first day of scuba diving lessons under her belt, yet she couldn't help but wonder how well she would do with this lingering headache. Perhaps it was best that today's lesson was in the pool as the pressure on her head would be a lot less than in the open water. This would give her time to try and get it under control before the next lesson. These were the moments when she wondered if she made the right choice by coming to Hawaii. Her family sure thought she was completely crazy. But she pushed her doubts aside, with keys in hand she locked her door and made her way to the Marina.

Serena stood there looking at the marina door, not hesitating, but simply hoping today wouldn't hold any splashing surprises like the day before. She truly didn't mind that the playful seals pushed her in the water, it was in fact, quite cute on their part. It was the headaches following these types of events she dreaded, and she feared Tristan would mistake that dread for something else. But she couldn't help but feel irritated, no, angry with herself for caring more than she wanted to admit about a man she had just met. She had sworn off the male populace and had decided she would live life in Hawaii to the fullest without letting a man ruin her newfound happiness. She looked at the sky, now completely devoid of clouds, the sun shining brightly above as if the rain was just a bad dream. She slipped her sunglasses up on her head and sighed. She couldn't. No, she wouldn't let Tristan ruin that! Feeling resolved and even though she wasn't quite sure where it came from, defiantly charged through the door of the Marina. Realizing she was speed walking, she slowed down her pace knowing full well she had plenty of time. She had this inexplicable feeling like she was pressed for time somehow, which was completely ridiculous since she was early. Knowing better this time around, she followed the path circling the building to enter through the bay doors, which were already open. She glanced around but couldn't spot anyone. She walked in, making her way to the small double locker standing beside Tristan's small workspace. Opening a locker, she quickly realized it was probably his as it had a backpack stuffed with wrinkled shirts, shorts, and some flip flops. She bit her lower lip instinctively as the musky salty aroma hit her nose. By the smell of it, it seemed he spent most of his time at the marina. She closed the locker door as quietly as she could to avoid being caught snooping. She opened the other locker and was glad to find it empty. Throwing her backpack in, she wondered why she couldn't shake this feeling of anxiety. She took her watch off, peeked at the time and she was still early. She couldn't understand why she had this fluttering feeling in the pit of her stomach. It was as if she was about to miss or be late to something dreadfully important. She shook her head as she closed her locker. She looked up suddenly as she heard the golf cart approaching, somehow knowing it was Tristan. She turned just in time to watch Tristan leap out of the golf cart effortlessly. He wore a shorty, zipped up only to his navel, with the top half hanging off his hips showing his bare muscular chest. With his wet hair tied up in a manbun, he looked like he had just stepped out of the water. Although he was extremely hard to read, Serena could somehow feel his distant frustrated mood. Tristan yanked a hose off a nearby table and threw it in the back of the golf cart, confirming her suspicion of his mood. She cleared her throat to alert him of her presence.

Tristan spun around, forcing a smile at the corner of his mouth. His mood lightened when he saw her brown wavy hair messily placed on top of her head. The teal shirt brightened the features of her face and the bikini top tied around her neck made it clear she had adopted a smarter, more Hawaiian way of dressing herself. He wondered how she managed to pull off looking radiant, yet completely exhausted with dark lines under her eyes.

"Aloha,". Tristan said simply with a nod as he turned to the rack of wetsuits along the wall outside his office. Tristan peered around the rack to get a closer look at Serena to size her for her suit. He took one he thought might fit off the hanger and threw it at her.

"I think that should fit." Tristan said with a smile, feeling a little more at ease now. She caught it, pressed it against her and was certain he was bang on. *Not bad for a guy.* She thought to herself.

"I've had practice." Tristan responded, his eyes darting to hers as he realized the mistake he had just made. He turned away quickly to grab another piece of equipment in an attempt to hide his unease, not seeing the look of bafflement on her face. But he didn't need to, he felt it.

Just how did he do that? Serena wondered. Was it written all over her face? She knew she was clearly not as good at hiding what she was thinking like he was but she never thought she was *this* obvious.

Tristan tightened his jaw in frustration at how quickly he had responded without thinking. Had he not decided, not that long ago he would keep his feelings guarded to make things easier for her? Again, frustration.

Serena pulled off her shirt, glad to have dressed appropriately for the occasion. At this point, he had seen more of her then she was willing to admit. Tristan busied himself by picking up some supplies in a futile attempt to distract himself from her. Normally, he wouldn't even flinch no matter how attractive he found the woman, but this was completely different. As he had assumed, she was perfectly shaped and watching her taking her clothes off sent a heatwave of pleasure through his entire body. He took a long silent breath as he struggled against the bond's magical pull, stiffening him in places that are more challenging to hide. *Cursed Atlas father of all Atlanteans!* He muttered to himself as he turned away again before Serena could detect anything.

"What?" She asked in a muffle voice as she struggled to put the wetsuit on. She froze, feeling a strange heat in her gut, sending goosebumps all over her body and a shiver up her spine.

Tristan sighed quietly, trying to calm himself but became frustrated as he was failing miserably. The power of her amulet was clearly fading, as he sensed her reacting to his emotions. Would he ever get used to someone invading his private thoughts and emotions? Who in their right might would want and enjoy this cruelty? That is precisely what this was, cruelty. Sure, like every Atlantean he enjoyed indulging in the frugalities of sex and other pleasures, but this non-consensual bond is torture. He was bombarded with desire for Serena and he couldn't act on it until she comes of age and the amulet releases her.

"Oh nothing." Tristan mumbled in response trying to conceal the glow creeping up his arm. He grabbed his clipboard to start the paperwork on the diving logs for Serena but he couldn't take his eyes off her.

Serena, still fumbling with her wetsuit, wondered how she was supposed to zip up this thing. Looking behind her, she finally saw the pull rig for the zipper she desperately needed. She reached for it knowing full well her lack of flexibility wouldn't allow her to complete this mission. It was embarrassing to say the least. *Like that's going to happen!* She dropped her arms in defeat, placing them on her hips as she saw Tristan just standing there shuffling supplies, pretending not to notice but she knew he was looking.

"Are you gonna help me or are you going to continue to stand there and enjoy my torment?" Serena snapped in frustration, knitting her eyebrows at his obvious amusement.

But *that* look of amusement was for the fact that Serena was completely oblivious that she was *his* tormentor. Was this his ultimate punishment for playing his part in defying the fates? As much as he tried to remain calm, he couldn't help but smile at how cute she looked frustrated. It was the same look she had on her face when she fell in the seal lion pool. That defiant, exasperated look on her face he simply could not resist.

Serena saw, or maybe felt the change in Tristan's earlier state of mind when she saw him smile at her. She tried to hold her defiant stance, but it was difficult to resist the urge to burst out laughing.

"Didn't your mother teach you how to say please?" Tristan crossed his arms raising his scarred eyebrow.

Damn you and your coolness! Serena cursed silently wondering how he managed to always look so cool and composed. Her mother was definitely not the one to teach her manners. She had her father to thank for that. She always thought her mother acted like a spoiled entitled queen. Her dad sure treated her as such, giving her everything her heart desired. He was a gentle and kind soul and Serena had often wondered why he was with her mother. A pang of regret hit her at the thought of the promise she made to her dad to keep in touch.

"*Please.*" Serena begged with her best puppy dog eyes while batting her eyelashes exaggeratedly.

"There, wasn't so hard now was it?" Tristan asked as he put the clipboard down and made his way behind her. He moved a small loose strand of hair out of the way, not wanting to get it caught in the zipper. The smell of coconut and vanilla coming from her hair and the slight scent of sweat was intoxicating and made him pause for a moment. Serena could feel his hot breath on the back of her neck sending another wave of goosebumps across her body. She closed her eyes trying to slow down her breathing and calm her rapid heartbeat. It pounded so loud she was afraid he could hear it.

"Are you sure you don't want to take off your necklace?" Tristan said, trying to get a hold of himself. He cleared his throat and zipped up her suit. He stopped at the base of her neck and touched the clasp of the necklace with his left handed finger. Setting aside his own agenda, he knew the necklace would be uncomfortable under the suit. He saw the little hairs rising on the back of her neck as his fingers traced the necklace. He could also feel the confusion racing through her mind, and felt a little relieved she was feeling tormented as well.

Instinctively, Serena placed a hand on her necklace, it was such a part of her that she always forgot it was there until someone else noticed. Like so many things in her life, she couldn't explain why she never took it off. It was simply there. It was like she would completely forget it's existence, and every time she tried to take it off, she just couldn't bring herself to do it. It was strange, like a force pulling her hands away from it, and then she would forget all about it. She always assumed it was just a part of her now as she wore it for as long as she could remember.

"I suppose it would be uncomfortable under this suit." She said hesitantly after a moment to regain her composure.

"Here." Tristan said as he pulled gently, grabbing the clasp in his hands he felt a strong jolt of electricity bursting from the clasp. He used all the strength he could, but it was as he feared. Whoever had enchanted this necklace took all the precautions necessary for the necklace to stay there.

"Strange." Tristan voiced his surprise out loud.

"Is it stuck?" Serena asked curiously.

"Seems to be." Tristan said still playing with the clasp as the jolt got stronger with every attempt he made to open it.

"I actually have never been able to take it off, and I can't seem to bring myself to cut it. Family heirloom and all." Serena said, feeling the need to explain herself. As soon as he finished zipping up the suit, she moved away, uncomfortable with the warm feeling his touch left running through her body. She never really had a long term relationship; she just couldn't seem to commit to anything serious. They didn't understand her and always said she was distant, quirky and weird. Brian, her last boyfriend, a nurse at the last hospital she worked at, had even gone as far as to say she should seek professional help for a sexual desire disorder for her lack of sex drive. He continued to use that as ammunition to justify his affairs. It's not that it wasn't somewhat enjoyable, but she just didn't get what the big fuss was about. Besides, she had never had any desire for it before, so why now? And why with someone she had literally just met?

"Ready to go." Serena said with a trembling voice hoping he would think it was just the excitement of finally getting her diving certification. It was then she noticed Tristan's left arm. Yesterday, it had a horrible gash, and it was covered by a significantly sized bandage. Now there wasn't even any trace of injury left. A gash like that would have required stitches at the very least and weeks of healing.

"Oh, it looked worse than it actually was." Tristan said nonchalantly as he noticed she was staring at his arm. Serena's brows furrowed suspiciously at him. But how else would you explain it? A nasty cut like that couldn't just disappear.

"Alright, let's get to it then." Tristan smiled reassuringly as he motioned to the golf cart.

Serena jumped on but remained pensive and quiet. When Tristan glanced at her quickly, pretending he was keeping an eye on his surroundings, he noticed she looked distant. The look on her face definitely reflected the thoughts clouding her mind.

"Excited about starting your diving journey?" Tristan asked, trying to pry open the can of worms. He knew for a fact she was looking forward to it, but something was really bothering her. He could feel a twinge nagging at the back of his mind. She threw a quick glance his way, surprised by the sincerity in his simple question. She could sense he was asking for an honest answer, not just to make conversation.

"Yes, I am." Serena answered with a smile that brightened her whole face.

"But...?" Tristan insisted further.

"But what?" Serena asked coyly feigning ignorance and avoiding his damn piercing almost irresistible gaze.

"There is something obviously bothering you." Tristan answered honestly.

Serena took a deep breath and let it out slowly. It seemed like she had become an open book the second she landed in Hawaii, or at the very least with Tristan. She wondered why he cared so much, after all, he didn't know her anymore than she knew him.

Tristan pulled the cart to a full stop as they reached the training pool. His left hand still resting on the steering wheel, his fingers tapping it. At this point, he knew her better than she knew herself. But he couldn't tell her that.

"Serena," He said gently. " I am responsible for your safety. I need to make sure your head is in the right place and that you're ready before I slap a tank on your back." He explained carefully, hoping to not raise her suspicion.

"I am, I just..." Serena answered weakly, unable to form the rest of her sentence. Opening up to people was not her forte. She was the girl everyone opened up to and dumped all their problems unto. She always took everything with a kind smile and was expected to be the strong one who supported everyone around her. The roles had *never* been reversed. The fact that he was pushing her there felt uncomfortable to say the least. She cleared her throat, feeling like something was stuck there.

"I'm ready. I just have a slight headache." Serena answered hesitantly. It was a simple answer, but it was honest. Although Tristan knew *slight* was an understatement. He was silent for a few moments, deciding how far he should push her. He knew too well the headaches would only disappear completely once the amulet stopped blocking her powers.

"That's not a major issue, the pool isn't deep enough but if it bothers you even in the slightest..."Tristan said then turned to look at her, their eyes locked. "You need to tell me. Your safety is my concern and diving is not just about you, it's also about your partner and keeping each other safe." He explained in his deep voice.

Serena could see the concern in his eyes and she wondered how she had gotten so lucky to meet such an impressive man. He seemed so caring and gentle behind his tough, strong exterior. She understood he took responsibility for his interns seriously, in fact, she could sense he seemed to carry it as a heavy burden on his shoulders. All the employees couldn't stop raving about the awesome work environment and how Tristan was like a caring father figure. But, it seemed to go further than that with her. Was it just with her? Was she imagining the look in his eyes? The tightness in his jaw every time he looked into her eyes?

"I understand." Serena answered with a nod. This was all new and strange to her. Why did he make her feel so vulnerable? His brown eyes were so magnetic, making it ever so hard to look away. There was something commanding about them, yet kind. Tristan nodded in reply and climbed out of the cart. Serena took a deep breath as she looked at the pool, excitement filling her once more as she followed Tristan. Together they took the diving supplies to the edge of the pool. Once everything was in its place, Tristan took a few minutes to run through the tank and regulator setup. She had watched all the training videos, but it was always good to review it and see it live. He handed her a weight belt with what looked like twelve pounds of weight hanging on each side.

"We will start with this and adjust as we go."Tristan said.

Serena nodded as she grabbed it with both hands and slipped it on. Once everything was ready, they jumped in the pool and slipped on their fins and their buoyancy compensator vest which held their tanks securely. Tristan handed her a mask. He grabbed his, spit in it then spread it around with his fingers.

"Trick of the trade, helps with the fogginess." Tristan said with a smirk as he noticed Serena's questioning stare.

"If you say so." Serena responded with a shrug.

"Didn't we just have a discussion about trust?" Tristan asked, raising his scarred eyebrow at her.

"You talked about trusting *me*. I still haven't decided if I can trust *you*." Serena said, the corner of her mouth curling into a teasing smile even with her efforts to remain serious.

"Hmm. Perhaps I should sign us up for some team building workshops before we go shark diving then." Tristan said thoughtfully. Her eyes widened in shock and horror. It seemed he struck a chord.

"I'm not sure which terrifies me more, the shark diving or the workshops." Serena said with shock. Of course, she was more worried about being shark bait, but something about being in proximity with Tristan also made her strangely uncomfortable.

Tristan chuckled. Serena was surprisingly witty, and it was sexy as hell.

"Spitting in your mask is a brownie point to avoid the workshops." He said, pulling the mask on his head.

"Well then, I better get to it, don't want to miss out on THAT brownie point." Serena said feigning great annoyance. With that, she spit in the mask, whooshed it around, rinsed it out and put it on.

Tristan couldn't help but grin. She looked ridiculously cute with all that equipment on, making him wonder just how good she would look swimming without it. He fought the urge to continue that thought. He tilted his head, taking another look at her.

"What?" Serena asked. Tristan stepped closer, his body a few inches away from hers. She hated the way she caught her breath when he stood close to her.

Gently, Tristan pulled out the hairs that had snuck under the seal of her mask, leaving a trail of heat everywhere his fingers touched. She looked up, loving that she could finally stretch out her neck to look up at someone. She had always disliked how difficult it was to find a man who was taller than she was, and by taller, she didn't mean an inch, but a full head taller. It made her wonder what rock he had crawled out of.

He pulled away, grabbing his regulator and pushed the purge button to let out some air.

"Ready?" Tristan said as he pulled his mask down.

"As I'll ever be." Serena answered with a sigh of relief as she grabbed her regulator to let out some air through the purge button. She didn't want her first breath out of a regulator to be full of surprises.

"We go down slowly and sit at the bottom here. We will take our time and make our way to the deep end slowly." Tristan instructed carefully. Serena gave a thumbs up as she placed the strange and uncomfortable mouthpiece of the regulator in her mouth. Slowly, Serena lowered under water into a sitting position at the bottom of the pool, instinctively holding her breath as her head became submerged under water. She closed her eyes and took another deep, slow breath as she remembered she was actually supposed to breath. It wasn't as easy as she had thought it would be. After all, human brains were not programmed to breathe underwater. But, with a little bit of coaxing and focus, she was soon breathing regular breaths. She jumped slightly as Tristan surprised her by touching her hand. He gave her a thumbs up and waited until she did the same before he signaled towards the deep end.

They spent about two hours swimming back and forth around the whole pool before Serena felt completely at ease. As they reached the shallow end for the last time, she couldn't help the gigantic smile crossing her face. Suddenly her mask started to flood as her smile cracked the seals leaving her in a panic as it filled with water. She erupted out of the water pulling her mask off.

Tristan followed quickly enough to see her rip her mask off in a panic. He was grinning from ear to ear at the detriment of Serena who glared at him in frustration.

"It disturbs me how you find my torture *funny*." Serena said as she yanked off a fin, losing her balance toppling right into Tristan's arms. His warm hands caught her lower back to steady her as she put her hands on his muscular chest. He had an attractive salty musky smell to him that reminded her of the ocean air early in the morning as the sun rose on the horizon. That fresh ocean smell before the heat descended and settled in the air.

"What is it about you?" Serena asked softly, her voice trembling ever slightly at his touch. She was avoiding his mesmerizing gaze, but he raised her chin up, forcing her to look at him.

Cursed Fates! Tristan cursed silently as he couldn't believe he was struggling to stay away from her lips, pulling him in like the world's strongest magnet. But he knew he was fighting something more than just his strong Atlantean primal instincts and desires, he was fighting a power created by the Olympian gods themselves. His breath became ragged and so did hers as he gently traced the line of her perfectly set jaw. The defiance in her eyes melted into a desire that called to him, demanding him to take her physically and seal the bond. There was *nothing* he hated more than being manipulated by the Olympians and their greedy hunger for power. No, he would not put his agenda ahead of Serena's wellbeing even if it killed him. But damn it, he realized he was in way over his head. He broke away suddenly, clearing his throat and leaving Serena gasping for air like he had stolen her last breath.

"Whenever you get water in your mask, just press against the top of it with your palm looking up towards the surface and blow through your nose. That'll clear the water." Tristan explained as he made the motion on his own face then turning away to unbuckle his vest, letting it fall into the water. Truth was, he had to look away from Serena, fearing what he would see there.

What the hell was that? Serena thought to herself, her hands still trembling from the shock from that moment. It was almost as if she had an out of body experience, watching someone else in Tristan's arms being overwhelmed with an inexplicable desire to...no. The realization that she could lose control shook her to her core. Because if he had taken her right then, she wouldn't have stopped him. What was wrong with her? She never believed in magic, but this was as close to being under a spell as she could imagine. She turned away to take her equipment off, finding herself wanting to get away as much as she wanted to run back right into his arms. She could have never expected how this day would turn out.

CHAPTER 11
TRITON

Another day came and went. Unfortunately, it was impossible to stay away from Serena completely. She was his intern, his responsibility. But, between her shifts at the cafe and her few shifts at the Marina, he was able to keep her busy enough to keep her from her open water diving. He had decided to continue doing his best at controlling the pull of the bond until he spoke to the culprits. Perhaps his mother had been right and there was something they could do? Wishful thinking at its best, but it was worth a try. Serena was more than ready for open water, but she simply wasn't prepared for what would follow. They managed to keep her busy for a few weeks by learning to care for the animals and sliding a few pool diving exercises to delay the open water certification. Triton felt they could manage to drag it out for a little longer if necessary. This woman's world is about to collapse, not to mention the other godly dangers that would follow. The longer he waited to make her face this reality, the longer she would be safe. Wouldn't she? There was no denying she was excited to get her open water and he knew they wouldn't be able to keep her away from it much longer.

Triton pushed the door to the gates and followed the path leading to the backyard of the villa. Coming around the corner, he spotted them in a warm embrace, Laka, Hawaiian goddess of beauty, love, and fertility. She was a tall, beautiful woman who always wore a Hawaiian flower in her long dark brown hair. She waved him over with a friendly gesture, but soon realized by the look on his face and the trident he held in his

85

other hand that he wasn't here for a friendly visit. He walked defiantly, angry and she knew beyond the shadow of a doubt that he was aware of his predicament. Lono, Hawaiian god of peace, music learning and cultivated foods. He was a shorter, stouter handsome fellow who loved to cook. He bore shoulder length, thick curly black hair hanging from his head and he held a cocky smile as he turned to face Triton.

"Pu'ole," Laka said, dropping her husband's hands to give Triton the good Hawaiian embrace by leaning her forehead against his. Triton pulled away almost abruptly, finding it difficult to remain cross with someone he had called a friend and ally in this realm for so long.

"What's the matter?" Laka instantly asked incredulously with great concern.

"Mind explaining this?" Triton asked, showing the blue glowing mark of the bond that ran from his fourth finger up his left arm.

"Well, it clearly looks like a bond mark." Lono answered innocently, the smirk still on his face. Lono was a gentle soul, and it had surprised Triton that he would have gone this far. He didn't think Lono could have come up with this scheme on his own. Perhaps he had underestimated the lengths he would go to with Laka to restore the peace of their realm.

"Enough with the games, you need to undo what you've done!" Triton barked, his eyes glistening with frustration. Laka was taken aback by his tone of voice. She had never seen this side of him before.

"It cannot be undone. I had no choice! She had to be protected at all cost!" Laka said defensively as she studied Triton intently. Triton closed his eyes tightly to calm himself as he turned away, feeling Serena's confusion in response to his outburst coming through the bond.

"How little you must think of me! We all have choices Laka, you chose the wrong one. I would have protected her either way." Triton sneered. Refusing to look at them and trying to keep his emotions under control. The magic in her pendant kept the powers of the bond mostly at bay, but it didn't take long before Triton realized that strong emotions still slipped through. He had to be careful.

"It is not you we do not trust hale aikã." Lono said affectionately patting his friend on the shoulder.

"You know better than anyone the Olympians do not always have the earth realm's best interest at heart. Look around you! It is clear their interests come first at the detriment of this world." Lono said in frustration, not towards his dear friend but towards forces who were supposed to protect this place. The truth was, Laka and Lono were tired

86

of watching the earth realm being destroyed over the centuries. Ever since the prophecy was foretold, forces were growing against the Olympians causing havoc in the earth realm. Greed, consumerism, the destruction of nature causing earthquakes, tsunamis and more. This was unacceptable and has to be stopped. Triton knew this. The time he spent in this realm made him see exactly what the damage was. Everyone knew Triton was loyal to his father to a fault, and the choice would be too difficult for him to bear. So, Laka and Lono made the choice for him.

"This will ensure her safety, it is the only way, and I think you know this." Laka said, placing a hand on his chest while looking deep into Triton's eyes with her irresistibly calming gaze.

"And in return you've put my life at risk." Triton answered glumly.

"Your life was never at risk." Laka said, obviously surprised by Triton's statement. Triton realized by the honest shock on her face that she honestly believed it.

"You're naive Laka. Some will stop at nothing to halt this prophecy." Triton replied, his gaze distant as he focused on feeling Serena. She was at the cafe serving a customer and she froze for a moment as she felt something poking at her mind. She couldn't understand what it was, but she sensed it.

"Pu'ole," Laka said pleadingly, taking his hands in hers. "It is too late to stop it now. Lono and I have always known that she was part of your destiny, we have seen it. If you look deep down," Laka placed a hand on his chest, her hand growing hot, making the blue thread of the bond glimmer and shine ever so bright all the way to his heart. "You were miserable by your father's side, and the bond would not have worked if the fates did not intend to bind you to her...I am not Aphrodite, who follows Zeus' order to bind only for political matters. The bond is there because it was meant to be." She explained softly. He remained quiet for some time, letting the words sink in. There was something so genuine about Laka and Lono that made him feel things he had not felt in a long time. Perhaps the gods were spending too much time away from humanity that they forgot why they needed to protect it. Most of them would rather deny the humanity within them instead of accepting the great part it played in their very existence. They had fought for humans' existence as much as their own thousands of years before when Cronus wanted its destruction.

"The necklace she wears cannot be broken. It is heavily protected; I have tried without success." Triton explained in resignation. There was no arguing with Laka's logic.

"Pu'ole," Laka said gently. "To break it, you must first complete the bond that binds you." Laka explained, but not clearly enough. Triton didn't understand the logistics of the bond. After all, they hadn't seen one done in ages, thanks to Zeus. But he was curious about what she meant. He turned to face her again, the look on his face clearly indicating his confusion.

"Why do you think Zeus refuses to bond Atlanteans?" Laka asked, trying to lead him to his own conclusion.

"Because the implications of the power they can wield could be a threat." Triton said knitting his brows. Obviously, there was something he was missing by the look on her face.

"Only if the bond is complete." Laka said with a look that clearly waited for him to magically know where she was going with this.

"It's easy to bind the mind, tether two together, make one impossible to hurt or kill without hurting or killing the other, which was the reason for its creation. To make a match political, calculated even...but what they did not account for is what happened once that bond became sacred, with mind, body, and soul. In fact, this is how the humans began the tradition of consummating unions. Binding two people that the fates have destined to be together..." Laka trailed off, still waiting for him to understand.

Triton wasn't surprised by this fact. Aphrodite was the one who had formed the bonds of marriage to be a sacred vow between two people. Reinforcing with consummation seemed logical if she was attempting to make it sacred especially amongst the humans. It was all starting to make sense.

"Wait," Triton said, deeply frowning, the weight of what Laka was saying finally sinking in. "Are you saying Zeus and Aphrodite only intended the bond to be for political use and protection?" Triton asked. She nodded, confirming what he was saying.

"Do you think Zeus would have ever let this come to be if there was a chance for two Atlanteans to bind their powers together?" Laka asked Triton gravely, aware he knew too well what the answer was. It made perfect sense. Zeus couldn't allow anyone to hold this much power. It could be devastating to the balance. Triton finally understood the reason why Zeus forbade Aphrodite to bind without his consent. His jaw tightened with the sudden realization. Laka was trying to say that when she created this bond between him and Serena, she believed they were destined to be together and would be an unstoppable force.

"You understand?" Laka asked, even though his expression had not changed much.

"You're telling me I have to have sex with her to break the spell of the amulet without her understanding the ramifications of it all? I cannot, will NOT stoop to that level!" Triton said defiantly, disgusted by Laka's insinuation. He understood loud and clear, but he bluntly refused.

"How long will you be able to resist the pull my friend?" Laka asked curiously knowing just how powerful the pull would be.

"As long as I can." Triton snapped angrily as he put distance between them. He understood their motives, but he wasn't sure he would be able to forgive them for putting him in this precarious situation.

"And what about Serena?" Lono asked. Triton glared at him at the mention of her name.

"What about Serena?" Triton asked defensively.

"You have your powers to help you resist this bond, she does not. She will unknowingly make it more difficult for you. The longer you wait, the less you will be able to fight it. The bond is much more powerful than your resolve." Laka warned. She loved and respected that her friend wanted to give Serena time, but it was time that neither of them had.

"And whose fault is that?" Triton asked, glaring at Laka and Lono. "A bond is meant to be consensual. Or, at the very least between two who are aware of its existence!" Triton exclaimed, closing his eyes to focus on controlling his anger.

"You've seen Serena Triton," Laka said sadly, realizing the impact of the situation. "Without you, she is in grave danger. We did this to protect her." Laka added persistently using his name to get his attention. Perhaps her and Lono had underestimated his integrity and how much this would tear him apart.

"No Laka, you did what Atlanteans always do. You did what you wanted at someone else's expense." Triton stated sourly before he turned and walked away.

Laka wanted to go after him, to explain herself so he would understand their true motives. They had seen what could happen to Serena if they didn't intervene, they wanted to protect her. But Loko held her back.

"No Ku`uipo, let him go." The god of peace said gently as he pulled her into his arms. He knew full well they had to give him space and time, even if that was the most difficult thing to do.

CHAPTER 12
SERENA

Serena sat at her kitchen island, holding her mug in both hands, elbows resting on the counter revisiting her diving certification experience and wondering why she felt her progress had stalled. Since that amazing first day in the pool when she finally felt in her own element, it felt like Tristan has been avoiding her. Was it that moment they shared? Did she make Tristan feel uncomfortable? Was it something she did? Ailani, god bless her sweet soul, took her under her wing and has been great at filling Tristan's mentor shoes. She completed all the mandatory pool sessions with her, showed her the ropes for running the Marina and even showed her Tristan's secret stash of snacks. Serena felt like she was more than ready for her open water exam, but she just couldn't pin Tristan down long enough to set a date. She has waited for this moment for as long as she could remember and it all hindered on Tristan. Why was he avoiding her? She had approached Ailani about the subject and Ailani had sweetly replied he was busy preparing for the upcoming graduation ceremony for his students and interns. Hawaiians loved to celebrate rites of passage and this was no exception. The Marina had a work program for high school students to earn their required volunteer hours with the hope to inspire future biologists and prepare them for College. The end of the semester was fast approaching and Tristan took the graduation ceremony very seriously. It was a reasonable explanation, but Serena still couldn't help but feel like Ailani was not telling her the whole truth. Maybe she was overthinking it ? She couldn't shake this inexplicable desire to be near Tristan. She felt like she was being pulled towards him but couldn't get near him. She felt like she was going crazy, like she had an itch she just couldn't scratch, however for some reason she didn't feel like she was suffering alone. It was difficult to explain, she felt her thoughts but they were not always spoken in her voice. Was she experiencing emotional dissociation? Was she losing her sanity? Did she take too big of a risk coming here and her subconscious was trying to sabotage her? She placed her fingers on the amulet out of habit and fiddled with the stone to calm herself. It always grounded her when she was anxious, confused or disturbed. Panic gripped her briefly at the thought of Tristan trying to remove it. She couldn't imagine not having it around her neck. It was her lifeboat. Was it simply because Tristan was afraid it could get damaged or caught in something? She followed the cord around her neck to the clasp and tried to open it but couldn't. She slid the clasp under her chin and fiddled with it some more, but it just wouldn't budge. Biting her lip, she thought it was strange how she never tried to take it off. Her cat jumped up on the counter and meowed getting her attention, pulling her back to the present moment. She pet her head gently and the cat started purring, bringing her some sense of ease and comfort. She had never seen a cat be so intuitive before. This cat seemed to know what she needed. Her phone dinged in her backpack alerting Serena to a text message. She pulled it out of the front pocket and saw it was from an unknown number. She looked at her phone, curious to see who it was. *Hi Serena, Tristan here, there is a luau for the staff of the Marina at Kaiona Beach Park starting at six tonight. Forgot to mention it earlier. You are very welcome to join us.* She stared at the phone, not sure of what to make of it. Of course, she had given him her personal information. He had her number in his file. She wasn't used to being included in social events, especially not this type. She had chosen to come to Hawaii for this very reason, this was her opportunity to take part in the culture. *Thanks, will be there.* She texted back. Kaiona Beach was not far at all, and she still had a few hours to relax a little. The condo she purchased came with a few toys, amongst them was a kayak she has been dying to try. The locals kept telling her she should try kayaking to Mokulua Islands. They were two beautiful islands visible from her condo. They are beautiful, within paddle distance and abundant with sea life. It would be easy to do and conveniently close to Kaiona Beach that she could paddle from there. She studied the guides and was confident she could make the trip. There were three different currents meeting up around the island making it slightly challenging if you didn't know any better. She went to her little storage shed outside, grabbed her life vest, pulled out the paddle and orange kayak. Pushing her sunglasses down from her head, she made her way to the beach. As she reached the water, she quickly noticed the water was rougher than she expected. The northern side of the island usually didn't get higher waves this time of the year due to the reefs protecting the beaches a little farther out. She had taken a few indoor kayaking lessons before she moved, but it was nothing compared with where she stood now. She put on her life vest and dragged the kayak knee deep into the sea. She took a deep breath and tried to get into the kayak, but the waves wouldn't let up. It took her three tries before she managed to secure herself into the kayak. The water was rough, but she was too stubborn to give up the fight, lined herself up with the waves and aggressively paddled forward. The ocean was not going to win this one. She started paddling further out to get away from the shore, feeling triumphant, but realizing her goal of reaching the island might have been a little overzealous. She took her time adjusting to the rhythm of the waves and matched her paddle strokes to keep herself in the proper position. Reading the currents felt surprisingly natural and she could tell she would not be able to get to the Mokulua Islands and headed directly to Kaiona beach instead.

Approaching the beach, she could see small figures popping up as she got closer. She still had about an hour before the event, but she could see them setting up the luau, maybe she could help if they needed it. She let the waves push her towards the beach and prayed the ocean wouldn't humiliate her as she made landfall. But alas! As she pulled a leg out the kayak to get out, a strong wave hit her kayak on the beam, and she was over. When she broke the surface, she nearly died of a heart attack when she came face to face to Tristan.

"Shouldn't let the waves catch you on the beam like that." He said with his unmistakable grin. Startled, she put her hand on her chest as she lost her footing and fell backwards towards her kayak. Tristan caught her arm in time to keep her from crashing into it. Another wave pushed her right against his bare chest. He held her tight at the elbows, to allow her to get her footing. His face was a mere inch away from hers as their eyes locked.

"Thanks for the advice, I would have never thought of that captain obvious." Serena retorted sarcastically, maybe a little too sourly. Why was he always around to witness her humiliation? But the bigger question was why did her heart want to leap right out of her chest?

"Hey, I was just trying to be helpful." Tristan explained defensively as he let go of her arms just as another wave hit, making her lose her footing again. This time, she struggled but did not lose her balance. She grabbed her paddle with aggressive determination. She wasn't mad at him, he was only trying to help, but the smirk on his face, and the way he made her feel just made her blood boil. She couldn't explain why she felt uneasy around him. Every time she saw him now, the strange tingling sensation running through her entire body only grew stronger and she just couldn't understand what was happening. She never believed in love, especially at first sight. She always thought people were just foolish to believe in such a futile concept. In her mind, there had always been a scientific physical and chemical reaction that attracted two people together. Nothing more. Serena couldn't understand this "spiritual" connection for lack of a better word. Nothing could explain this, and it disturbed her like nothing else ever had.

"I can do it." Serena protested as Tristan kindly grabbed her kayak to pull it up on the beach ignoring her plea and dragged it high enough that it wouldn't get sucked back into the sea. Serena followed closely behind him. He could almost feel her footsteps stomping behind him. She threw the paddle inside the kayak and followed him as he joined a group of people setting up the luau. She was drenched, but still had about an hour before the sun set to dry out. She shook out her messy bun to allow the soft Hawaiian breeze in a sad attempt to put herself together.

Serena found the event captivating. They had a firepit setup with wooden benches encircling it. She couldn't believe how much food there was. She had heard about the festive side of the Hawaiian culture, and this was no exception. The food was laid out perfectly over four picnic tables. They had everything you needed to make poke bowls to salads, sushi and to even make your own pizza. On another table were beautifully decorated fruit platters with mangos, pineapple, grapes, and cheese. Drinks for all tastes displayed on another. A sixth table hosted dozens of lei's, some made of white, purple and yellow plumerias to celebrate newcomers and another pile made of strung deep green leaves, some kind of berry and spaced with small white seashells. She let her fingers trail over the pretty, strange leaves and wondered what the differences were between them. She was sure they had to hold different meanings. The Hawaiians were a ceremonial people, and every detail had a purpose.

"Those are kukui leis," A soft familiar voice commented from behind her. "They are sewn with polished kukui nuts and green mock orange leaves. They represent an important rite of passage, mostly ceremonies of graduation, or a passage to adulthood." She explained, her gaze studying Serena intently. Serena turned to see Ellie standing there, but hardly recognized her. The way she presented herself at the cafe made her appear stout, but now Serena realized she was athletically built. She wore a floor length white one shoulder bandeau dress with green Hawaiian flower designs making her green protruding eyes sparkle. She had glistening thick blond hair tied in a gorgeous braid snaking to one side of the body down to her waist and a gold metal leaf headband on her head. Around her neck, she wore a golden necklace with a sparkling moonstone dangling inside a crescent moon pendant. Her skin was lightly tanned highlighting her red plump lips. Serena sensed there was something different about Ellie today. Ellie had a deep stare that made her uncomfortable. She had always considered her having such a friendly demeanor, but she was quite different tonight. Her eyes held something deep, almost ancient, and wise, maybe even calculated. Next to her standing obediently was an unusually large grey husky with piercingly blue eyes. It seemed strange and completely out of place that someone would have a husky in the warm Hawaiian climate. He had no leash and did not budge from his master's side.

"They are so beautiful!" Serena exclaimed in amazement, as she turned to face Ellie. Serena jumped in surprise as she felt something lick her hand. Looking down, she giggled at the tingling sensation from the lick of Ellie's dog. The husky stretched his neck to sniff her.

"Prometheus" Ellie said firmly. The dog whined but with one look into his owner's eyes lowered its head and laid at her feet.

"Sorry about that." Ellie said apologetically.

"It's okay." Serena responded as she reached down to pet the animal who responded gleefully by wagging its tail. Normally, Serena wouldn't dare pet a stranger's dog, but Ellie didn't seem to mind, and she had sensed the animal was keen on her.

Ellie watched her carefully. Prometheus wasn't shy or aggressive with strangers, simply careful and obedient. Ellie looked curiously at the necklace adorning Serena's neck as it flickered slightly when she touched the animal.

"Fancy meeting you here." Liam's familiar voice said slyly. With his hands in his pockets, Liam took his place beside Ellie and the dog laid between them. He looked quite radiant with the sun shining on his bright blond hair making it look golden. He had taken his shirt off and slipped it casually over his left shoulder. Serena only smiled, trying to avoid looking at the well-cut muscles of his upper body. He wore a pair of aviator sunglasses which he lifted onto his head.

"Sure is." Serena responded flirtatiously. Did they know anyone at the marina? Or was this some strange coincidence? "Are you guys here for the luau?" Serena asked curiously, unable to help herself.

"No, we live close by. We just finished a shift at the cafe and wanted to chill out with a nice little walk." Liam answered as he petted the dog's head gently. He frowned as he noticed Serena was drenched from head to toe, her wavy wet hair drying in the wind, she still looked stunning. Liam wondered if Serena even knew how divine she looked.

"I was trying to make it to the island before heading out to the marina luau." Serena started to explain motioning to the kayak on the bank as she noticed the stare down she got from Liam.

"I see the waves won." Liam said with a chuckle. Serena's cheeks flushed as she scowled at Liam.

"I just need a bit of practice." Serena said defensively with a shrug.

"I can take you to the island tomorrow if you'd like?" Liam offered, biting the inside of his left cheek. Albeit, she looked adorable when she was humiliated, he was trying to make her feel at ease. He knew the waves in the winter could be treacherous especially with the three currents merging causing havoc making getting to the island impossible unless you knew the secret route.

"That won't be necessary." Tristan said as he shouldered his way in between Liam and Serena. Serena threw him a questioning look. "We are already heading out there for some sea turtle tagging." He explained taking a sip of his beer. Serena wondered if she imagined it. Did his voice sound a little possessive? And did she just catch Liam glowering at Tristan? She glanced at the three of them as they looked at each other in an awkward silence.

"Uh… Tristan, this is Liam and Ellie." Serena introduced trying to break the obvious tension in the air.

"Liam," Tristan growled, with a slight bow of his head. Serena could definitely detect something strange between the two just by the way they pronounced each other's name. Like the sound off their lips was somewhat painful.

"Tristan." Liam greeted back but Serena thought it lacked the friendliness and kindness she had been subjected to and loved.

"Ellie." Tristan greeted more respectfully this time to the young lady almost bowing completely. Serena wanted to ask if they knew each other, which seemed obvious to her, but Ellie moved before she could.

"Let's get some punch." Ellie said as she grabbed Serena's arm moving her along. Serena's eyes glanced up at Tristan in confusion. Ellie nodded slightly at Tristan as she passed by him. Prometheus followed her closely.

CHAPTER 13
TRISTAN

Tristan and Liam watched Ellie and Serena leave and waited for them to be completely out of earshot before speaking. Liam was shorter and less bulky than Tristan, but he stood as if he towered over him. Liam's face darkened as he leaned in just inches from Tristan's face.

"Need I remind you who you were talking to, *Tristan?*" Liam asked quietly with cold authority, trying not to catch too much attention as he stared at Tristan. Tristan's jaw clenched tightly as he bit back everything he felt like saying, knowing it wouldn't be good for him. With the bond pulsating through his entire body, his instincts were on fire to defend and protect Serena. He knew the likes of Liam, and he wanted him far from Serena. Nevertheless, he knew his place

"No." Tristan bit back forcing himself with every ounce of his being to sound apologetic. He lowered his head in respect even if it's the last thing he wanted to do. He knew his place. Liam's face softened immediately, as if the reverence was enough for him to back down.

"Just where do your loyalties lie, *Tristan?*" Liam demanded; his eyes narrowed as if they were looking into Tristan's soul. Tristan never dealt with Liam personally, but there was no denying he knew just how to remind you of his higher rank. Tristan's eyes instinctively fell on Serena.

"From the kingdom of the deep blue sea, the son of its king shall set her free." Liam mumbled with a distant look crossing his face, deep in thought over the words fumbling out of his mouth. A smile crossed Liam's face as the words seemed to suddenly make sense to him. "Good. Keep it that way."

Liam said to Tristan, slapping his arm as he followed Tristan's gaze watching Serena standing at the punch table indulging in the Hawaiian drink with his sister Ellie. Liam's face softened as he backed away and crossed his arms over his chest.

Tristan wanted to question Liam further, but the stern look in his eyes indicated that the subject had to be immediately dropped. How was it possible? There had never been any doubts in Tristan's mind that someone with great power was involved. If Liam and Ellie were in this together, it would explain a lot.

Ellie poured some punch into a cup and handed it to Serena. It was obvious her mind was still on the men as she watched them carefully. Serena took a sip; the alcohol was present but not overwhelmingly so.

"What is the story with those two?" Serena finally asked, unable to stay off the topic, the question eating away at her curiosity. From the looks of it, they were having a very heated discussion and by the glances coming her way, it seemed she was the topic of the conversation. Tristan's deep brown eyes locked with hers, and even though she couldn't explain it, her cheeks burned red and she now *knew* for certain the conversation was about her.

"A very long history." Ellie answered almost coldly, making Serena look back at her. Ellie was obviously avoiding her question, her glance still locked on Liam and Tristan. Serena spent the last few weeks working with them both. She never felt anything so distant and unwelcoming from them before. Ellie nodded to Liam and both men walked up to them.

"Well, we hope you enjoy the festivities." Liam said, his kind smile returning to his beautiful face making it almost impossible to tell it had seemed threatening a few seconds before. Liam nodded to his sister, who took his arm.

"Thank you, see you tomorrow." Serena said waving them goodbye still baffled. She looked at Tristan who seemed to avoid her gaze completely.

"I better go, I need to get ready for the luau." Tristan said, sounding like a dog with its tail stuck between its legs which seem completely out of character to Serena. He saw some men waving him over. Serena wanted to say more, to ask more questions, but he was gone before she could mutter a word. The rest of the evening was pleasant enough. They asked everyone to take a seat around the fire, leaving room for the dancers to take their place. Unlike what she had seen in videos, she was delighted to see male dancers. Instead of the stereotypical female dancers, the men were dressed in hula skirts, leaf leis, matching crowns and wrist bands eagerly waiting to dance. To Serena's great surprise, one of the male dancers was Tristan. He looked dashingly handsome with a neat man bun, placed low enough for the crown to sit on. He had black tribal lines painted on both sides of his face. Serena could not take her eyes off of Tristan. Ailani and him made some welcoming speeches that were followed by the audience shouting "Pai, Pai". She made a mental note to ask the meaning when another girl she recognized as a Marina staff member whispered in her ear.

"Pai Pai means good, good. It is in acknowledgement, in respect of the person speaking. Welina i ka 'ohana means welcome to the family." She explained carefully to Serena. She smiled and joined in. They started by recognizing the young staff leaving for college with the kukui leis, and then went on to acknowledge the new staff. Serena didn't expect to be called up since Ailani had already welcomed her with a lei on her first day, but they called her up anyway. Ailani gave the same speech and everyone shouted "Pai Pai".

"Welina i ka 'ohana Namaka." Ailana said, gracefully placing a flower crown on Serena's head, and placed her forehead on Serena's for a precious moment. Letting go, Ailani motioned to Tristan who walked forward and placed a lei around her neck. They locked eyes again before closing them and when he placed his forehead on hers for the hawaiian greeting, it sent a wave of heat through her body. The embrace seemed to last longer than with Ailani, but Serena knew it was probably just the same. When they pulled away, a sad smile crossed his face leaving her disturbed as she walked back to her seat. Sitting there, she struggled to pay attention to the rest of the ceremony. She barely noticed when Ailani stopped talking but was brought back to the moment when the loud hawaiian drums started beating and the men began to chant and dance. She was completely captivated by it all. The fire burning in the pit, the loud drums, the men shouting and singing while dancing...it was mesmerizing. She wasn't sure when exactly it began, but she started to notice her surroundings becoming blurry, as if they were fading away. Then she started to get dizzy and couldn't concentrate on what was happening around her. Everything seemed so loud. She stared at her empty cup sitting in the sand. She only had the one cup and she doubted it was strong enough to make her feel this way. Before she knew it, the music stopped, and she figured it would probably be best if she went home. It was then she remembered she had the brilliant idea of kayaking to the beach earlier in the day. She was in no condition to jump in that cursed thing anytime soon. If this was caused by the drink she had, then Hawaiians sure knew how to pack their Hawaiian punch. She had never been drunk in her lifetime. She felt like it was a total waste of time and money, and she had never understood the attraction to it.

A strong sense of disorientation filled Tristan and he glanced at Serena. She sat in her chair with a distant look on her face. He was glad when the ceremony was done, and he quickly told Ailani that he was going to bring Serena home. He watched as Serena got up, her face turned white as a ghost and she lost her balance. He rushed to her side in time to steady her.

"I'll take you home." Tristan said a little too abruptly. He was a bit curious as to how she could get this drunk. With the blood of Zeus in her veins, it should have never affected her the way it did. Even with strong powers keeping her essence from surfacing, it could not change that fact.

"I can Uber it thanks." Serena said, yanking her hand away as she glared at him. She didn't appreciate his tone.

"I've got your kayak loaded up on my jeep, let me take you home." Tristan insisted but with kindness. He knew Serena was overwhelmed by emotions that didn't belong to her and he needed to get her home.

Serena closed her eyes. There was a strange, loud ringing in her ears making her dizzy and her stomach churned. She took a deep breath. "Fine." She simply said realizing she should get home sooner rather than later.

Tristan took her elbow, gently guided her to his jeep and helped her settle into her seat before driving off. There was something odd going on. The intensity of the wave of confusion he felt coming from Serena was far beyond drunk.

"What does Namaka mean?" Serena asked curiously, breaking the silence. Her head lay back and her eyes were closed trying not to wretch. Ailani called her that when she first met her and used the term again during the ceremony.

Damn Ailani! Tristan cursed to himself. He had hoped Serena hadn't noticed, obviously that wasn't the case.

"It's a term of endearment." Tristan finally answered with unease after pondering how to answer the question. He knew he was threading a fine line, but he was trying to avoid further questions. It wasn't a lie per say but he knew too damn well he was avoiding the answer.

"You didn't answer my question." Serena could feel he was avoiding the question, which only served to make her even more curious.

Tristan's jaw clenched, unsure how to answer the question. It was clear that even though the powers of the bond between them were still controlled by her pendant, she could still unknowingly sense some of his emotions, making lying difficult. He pulled the jeep into her parking lot and stopped the vehicle. Staring at Serena's cozy little two-story villa in front of him.

"Namaka is the Hawaiian goddess of water and the sea." He finally answered after a long pause, he watched as a frown of confusion crossed her face. Before giving her a chance to question him further, he opened his car door and jumped out. Tristan opened the door to his jeep and held out a hand to help Serena.

"That's a strange endearment." She said confused as she took his hand.

"Perhaps you remind her of the goddess." Tristan answered hoping it was enough to stop this line of questioning. It seemed to work as Serena remained quiet, walking in front of him. He followed closely behind her as she stumbled along the stone pathway to her front door fumbling with her bikini top to grab the key she had securely tied there. Serena grumbled in frustration as she could hardly manage to steady her hands enough to get the key. Her face gleamed victoriously as she finally yanked them free and turned to face Tristan. Her eyes widened as she felt the straps of her biking fall into her shirt and the weight of her ample breasts broke free. She didn't miss the way Tristan's eyes dropped to her chest. She bit her lower lip, as her cheeks burned. She was certain she felt his yearning when she saw his jaw tightened and his gaze continue. She noticed him grin as she turned away nervously to tie that bikini top back up. The sudden movement was too quick for her physical state. Her head began to spin violently and she fell back against his body. Tristan held her at the waste, trying to steady her. She closed her eyes tightly, leaning her head back against his thick solid chest. She let go into the safety of the warmth of his strong hands on her hips and his hot breath tickling her right ear. Instinctively, she tipped her head to the left making his lips dangerously close to trailing down her neck. A shiver ran through her entire body as she imagined just that. *What is wrong with me !* She thought trying to shake off this intense lust washing over her.

As they stood still, he took a deep breath, inhaling the intoxicating sweet scent of vanilla and coconut coming from her soft wavy hair. Why did those damn breasts of hers have to be so fucking perfect? He was aware of the effects he had on her as the goosebumps appeared on her body. He couldn't move, entranced by the flood of desire he felt coming from her. *Cursed Atlas father of all Atlanteans!* He swore silently at himself. He foolishly thought keeping his distance from Serena would somehow help, but it only made things worse. Laka and Lono had been right all along. The more time passed, the more the want, the more the need, and the more the lust grew stronger. It didn't matter what he was told about this bond, he saw it as nothing more than a curse that had been forced upon them both. He could feel his body growing stiff and pulled himself back before she could feel it on that nicely shaped ass of hers. He resisted the urge to praise the gods out loud when Serena dropped her keys.

He picked them up for her, and Serena held her breath as she couldn't resist looking at his ass as he bent over. He kept a hand on her elbow as she still swayed. He unlocked the door and pushed it open to let Serena stagger in, following behind her. He closed the door behind them and saw a hall stand across a small closet. He dropped the keys on the stand. Serena tried to take her sandal off but failed miserably. She lost her balance, grabbed at Tristan in a moment of panic and they both fell back against the wall. Tristan braced himself on the wall by placing a hand above her head and found himself inches from her face. His lips were so close to hers she could almost taste them. Her breath was ragged and her heart was pounding loudly in her chest. She looked up at him and saw the intense look on his face inviting her mouth to join his.

He stared into those vibrant green eyes and felt entranced. He could feel the heat filling her body. He knew he should pull away. For the first time in his life, he was afraid all the powers he held would not be enough to stop himself from going too far if he gave into the temptation of those luscious lips of hers. He balled his hand into a fist in frustration as he used his inner powers to fight the bond, making him tremble.

"Why are you doing this to me?" She whispered with a confused frown as she touched the side of his face, tracing his jaw line. She had wanted to enjoy the simplicity of life here on this beautiful island. Everything was going according to plan until she met Tristan and felt this irresistible attraction to him.

"I'm not doing anything, Serena." He said in a gentle whisper, his eyes never leaving hers. He tucked a strand of hair behind her ear, using all the self-control he had to not kiss that beautiful neckline of hers. He wasn't lying. He had nothing to do with what was pulling them together.

"This is not nothing." Serena said as she took his hand and placed it on her chest, her hand resting on top of his. He felt the pounding of her heart, although he didn't need to. He felt exactly what she meant.

"How much Hawaiian punch did you have?" He asked huskily, cocking his scarred eyebrow. And there it was. He might as well have thrown a glass of cold water in her face.

Serena gathered all the strength she could muster and tried to push him back but it only made her dizzier. She closed her eyes tightly as tears threatened to surface. "Only the one glass, apparently Hawaiian's know how to spike a punch." She answered, greatly confused by the circumstances. She supposed she couldn't blame Tristan for assuming she had too much to drink, after all, she was acting quite strange. She opened her eyes again, wanting to look away but couldn't.

Suddenly Tristan saw a golden sparkle in Serena's eyes. He has seen only this once before, in the King of the God's eyes Zeus. Her face began to change, showing longer lashes, clearer skin, redder lips and her hair's waves becoming beautifully defined curls. The changes were unmistakable. He realized then the necklace she wore was not only a prison to her essence, but a glamour hiding her truly divine goddess form. It was then he remembered Ellie had taken Serena to the punch table. He suddenly felt concerned and asked, "Serena, who gave you that drink?"

"Ellie." Serena answered softly, opening her eyes, perplexed with Tristan's tone. His face remained passive, but she could see something there. But how could he possibly think Ellie had anything to do with this? "So the Hawaiians don't make their drinks more potent?" She asked, confused and unknowingly seductive.

Somehow, Serena's answer didn't faze him much. He glanced at the pendant hanging around her neck and he noticed for the first time that it sparkled erratically. Whatever Ellie had done had weakened the power to the point the glamour spell was failing. Serena's essence was fighting it's way out, making the pull of the bond stronger. It would be so easy at this point to see his plan through to the end.

"Tristan," She whispered inquisitively as he had not answered her question.

"What did it taste like?" Tristan asked. Serena frowned, not understanding where he was going with this.

"Uh...hawaiian punch and something else...like honey or nectar." Serena answered, trying to find the right words.

Anger flashed in Tristan's eyes as she said the word *nectar*. Sweet nectar of the gods. If he had any doubts of Ellie and Liam's involvement, they were gone now. It couldn't be a coincidence.

"Perhaps Ailani put too much rum in the punch." Tristan finally answered as he cleared his throat and used all the control he could muster to pull away from her.

Serena felt frustrated, almost angry at his retreat. She leaned her head back, feeling another wave of nausea as he pulled away. Tristan saw her face pale suddenly, the glamour seeming to return with the distance he put between them. He looked around, noticing the stairs close by that probably led to her bedroom.

"Let me help you upstairs." He said moving in closer and grabbed her arm. As he moved closer he watched the glamour fade revealing those golden eyes once more. He knew then Laka and Lono had been right about his involvement in breaking the amulet's hold. *From the kingdom of the deep blue sea, the son of its king shall set her free.* Liam's words echoing in his mind as he guided her up the stairs and helped her to her bed.

Serena wanted to change into her pajamas, but her head was spinning too much to change. She laid back and closed her eyes and everything instantly went dark.

Tristan watched as she drifted off to sleep as soon as her head hit the pillow. He let out a sigh of relief and turned away to leave. As he reached the front door, he heard the hissing of a cat. As he turned to see the furball a few feet away, he noticed the cat collar had a dangling medallion with a symbol he clearly recognized.

"You have nothing to fear, Queen of the Nereids, I will not harm your daughter." Tristan said simply as he turned away and left.

CHAPTER 14
THETIS

She sprung out of the water and landed on the rock platform of the cavern. It was dimly lit by two torches holding Atlantean flames. Flames that had been burning in this dark place for centuries. Atlantean flames were straight from the hearth of Olympus and were renowned to never burn out. They were safely guarded by Hestia, goddess of the home and hearth. It had been long since she had set foot in this very place, an old dark forgotten portal to the far corner of Atlantis' ocean kingdoms. A kingdom belonging to Poseidon himself. He had eyes everywhere and being in this place meant every precaution would have to take place and she could not wander off too far without being sensed. Only very few secret meetings have taken place over the past few centuries, however they have increased over the last twenty-nine years. More careful planning had been crucial for the success of their plan. It wasn't a small feat to meet a daughter of Zeus without anyone's knowledge. Especially since she was the one who had helped her hide the offspring in hope to finally bring down the Olympian Queen. Thetis had never forgiven Zeus for forcing her to defy the fates, but she was mostly angry at Hera. Hera had been jealous ever since she caught her with her husband in a loving embrace. When Apollo had foretold the prophecy, it seemed the queen had done everything to get rid of her. Sure, she bore great children with

Peleus but over the centuries, the bloodline has weakened. The status of her children has grown less significant by the day. She felt the rage boiling like a volcano building pressure, waiting to explode. The corner of her mouth tipped into a smirk as she thought of the pleasure she would have in seeing Hera's face when she found out about Serena. The love she had with Zeus was one of a kind and she knew Zeus could only adore Serena. How could he not? She would be the most powerful Atlantean to ever exist. Zeus had always been a far better king than Cronus, that fact was undeniable. He had even made sure to have women in power on Mount Olympus as a show of good faith. But women were his weakness, and Hera was a major defect. Hera was a conniving little bitch and she did everything to get rid of anyone that went against her and her husband, especially his illegitimate children. The number of illegitimate children Zeus had fathered was far beyond any other Atlantean or Olympian. Hera managed to make most of them disappear. Leaving a trail of bitter and disgruntled Atlanteans willing to help get revenge against the queen. Even some Hera was completely unaware of. Some of which were sitting right in front of them at Olympus.

Hera had managed to plant the seeds of bitterness even with other Olympians like Hephaestus. Hera had made Zeus cast him down from Mount Olympus with the hopes he would die, simply for not having the "good looks" of the other Olympians. Thetis herself had rescued Hephaestus. She took care of him, mended his wounds and welcomed him into her home, becoming his foster mother, which only fed Hera's hate. The Olympians were beautiful people, and Hera could not endure Hephaestus' presence amongst them until his reputation for forging the most formidable weapons, armor and jewelry spread across the universe. Then and only then, he would be welcomed back with open arms. Hephaestus had decided to remain in his forges on earth and simply visit Atlantis when needed. He wisely chose the volcanos as powerful tools to forge his work. He could not deny his foster mother's request to build a pendant capable of holding great power.

There was also Demeter, who could not forgive Hera for having Zeus allow Hades to kidnap their daughter Persephone and take her to the underworld. Hera convinced Zeus not to do anything about it.

Even Apollo, whose oracle had predicted the offspring, had reason to be angry with Hera for encouraging Zeus to attempt to outrun the fates. And the list went on and on. No one dared to challenge Zeus or Hera. For twenty-nine years Thetis kept the offspring hidden away for protection. *The sun shall shine on the divine. On her thirtieth flower moon she shall fully bloom.* The last words of the oracle echoed through Thetis' mind as she reached a smaller cavern with another pool and waited. Above her, the moonlight shined through a small hole in the cavern ceiling, casting its glowing shadow in the moonpool. Her eyes rested on the cavern wall across the moonpool. A Greek symbol hid on a protruding rock, a symbol hidden by the gods and only visible to Atlantean eyes. It was shaped like an A, but the horizontal bar was an arrow pointing to a bow shaped like a thin crescent moon. It had been created by the moon goddess herself, Artemis. Just like the moonpool, a doorway to Atlantis. Unlike many other doorways to Atlantis, this one was hidden from the rest, and sadly, only accessible on a full moon. Although inconvenient to say the least, she had no other way to meet with them without risking her life. Even meeting this way could prove to be fatal if Poseidon came to realize what was happening. If she touched the moonpool, Poseidon would instantly feel her presence and it would be all over. The hidden delta Greek symbol above the secret doorway glimmered in a bright blue iridescent light catching her eye and sending a wave of relief through her. The meetings were risky and always a race against the moonlight. They didn't have much time, and it was quickly running out. She watched as the rocks became translucent as a figure appeared through the portal. A young, cloaked woman appeared with a large husky dog at her side. Her face was hidden in the shadows of her cloak, but Thetis need not see who it was.

"Lady Artemis." Thetis bowed gracefully in respect of the Olympian goddess.

"Thetis." Lady Artemis acknowledged. Her tone expressionless as it always was. Artemis was nothing but a true lady of high court, being a daughter of Zeus herself and on the council of the Olympian gods. She spoke with respect, but Thetis knew her place, and it was not equal to the goddess herself.

"Time is short." Artemis stated as she noticed the reflection of the moon in the moonpool.

"Yes, my lady," Thetis said, straightening her shoulders in an effort not to stutter in the presence of the goddess. She knew her place and how quickly a goddess such as Artemis could squash her with a snap of her fingers if she felt so inclined. She had to remain respectful if she wanted to retain the goddesses' favor. The more distance Serena put between her and her mother, the less Thetis remained a necessity. Her time of usefulness was nearing the end and Thetis knew she had to tread very carefully. Thetis pulled off her pendant from around her neck and handed it to the goddess who glimpsed at it but did not reach for it. "Its power is fading quickly, I am not sure-" Thetis explained but without a chance to finish.

"Are you questioning the fates, Queen of the Nereids?" Artemis snapped gracefully.

"Of course not my lady," Thetis responded, bowing her head in reverence. "The offspring is surrounded by too many things weakening its power, including the son of Poseidon himself." Thetis pleaded. She had been able to keep her far from anything that could weaken the pendant until she moved away. But now, it was difficult to know how long it would hold with Poseidon's son Triton frolicking with her daughter.

"Is she now?" Lady Artemis asked bemused, raising an eyebrow. "You should know, Queen of the Nereids, that the oracle has spoken once more." Lady Artemis added gleefully.

Thetis bit the inside of her cheek in an attempt to hide her surprise, but not much could be hidden from Lady Artemis' scrutiny. It used to be that Thetis could hear the oracle's predictions, but Apollo took her power away when Zeus banished her to the earth realm. The Olympians obviously enjoyed rubbing her nose in her loss.

"Has she?" Thetis asked, swallowing hard.

"*From the kingdom of the deep blue sea, the son of its king shall set her free.*" Lady

Artemis quoted the words her brother had shared with her.

Thetis sighed heavily and slowly, closing her eyes. She knew too well what all this meant for her. Lady Artemis and her brother Apollo, both protectors of the young until they come of age. They had given their favors to Thetis in order to protect her daughter, knowing full well that if the other Olympians were to find out, she would be killed.

"Lady Artemis, please, she is not prepared-" Thetis started to say pleadingly.

"There is no one else to blame but you for choosing to hide her heritage from her." Lady Artemis cut her off, holding up a hand to silence her. "You were well aware your daughter would only be protected by our favors until she came of age, and the day is soon coming. Be assured she is in great hands with the son of Poseidon." She said firmly.

Thetis sneered at the thought of her daughter's fate in the hands of any offspring of Poseidon, who was by far, equally promiscuous as Zeus. Last she'd seen, Triton seemed more interested in frolicking with Serena than anything else. But, she knew there was nothing she could do or say to change the goddess' mind. Her luck had run out, but she couldn't help the anger coursing through her veins at her helplessness. She had come so far and used every favor possible to protect her daughter. If Lady Artemis and Apollo had decided the favor had run its course, there was nothing she could do about it. As much as Thetis tried to suppress her anger, her powers responded. Suddenly the wind picked up, her long hair began flowing furiously around her as the water in the moonpool began to bubble and rise. Sensing the rise in power, Artemis called her quiver and crescent moon shaped bow in response. In a swift motion, Artemis pulled an arrow out of her quiver, notched it into her bow and shot it at Thetis. The arrow hit her in the right shoulder, throwing her back, pinning her against the cavern wall. A normal arrow would never stick to such a surface, but Artemis' Atlantean arrows could go through anything. As quickly as her bow and arrow appeared, they disappeared. Lady Artemis walked up to Thetis, looked her dead in the eyes and commanded:

"I will forgive your insubordination this time, but make no mistake,

Queen of the Nereids, I will not suffer any further mingling from you regarding anything connected to the great prophecy." She turned away, glancing at the reflection of the moon in the pool, noticing the doorway was about to disappear. Without one more word to Thetis, she vanished through the doorway to Atlantis.

Thetis took a deep breath, afraid to move as horrible pain shot through her shoulder and the rest of her body. She was an immortal in this world, but not to an Olympian's weapon. It could send her right to Tartarus. She attempted to change forms, but the Olympian's arrow drained too much of her powers. With both hands she grabbed the arrow. She took a deep breath and used all the power she could muster to pull the arrow out of her shoulder. She let out a terrible scream of pain that echoed through the cavern as the arrow slid from her shoulder. She collapsed on the floor of the cavern, overtaken by pain.

CHAPTER 15
ARTEMIS

Stepping out of the portal, Lady Artemis no longer felt the need to hide herself and slipped the hood of the cloak off her head. She followed the path out of the cavern, Prometheus following closely as he always did. As she stepped out into the moon lit sky, she stopped noticing a figure sitting on a rock nearby. Her brother Apollo sat gazing up at the full moon with one leg up and his arms wrapped around it as he sat waiting patiently for Artemis.

"Apollo." Artemis called out to get his attention.

"Already back little sister?" Apollo asked teasingly, his eyes never wavering from the moon. Artemis was, by a few hours only, the eldest of the two. He knew it made her jaw clench in annoyance every time he called her that. He refused, even after thousands of years, to let go of the childish mockery as it never failed to have the desired outcome.

"The Queen of the Nereids has been dealt with." Artemis said refusing to give into his childish games. But it was too late, her tone was annoyed to say the least and Apollo always relied on that fact alone to be satisfied.

"And you believe she will actually stay out of the way?" Apollo asked in disbelief. Old habits die hard; of that he knew for certain. Thetis had become extremely predictable, and he knew too well her mother's instincts wouldn't allow her to stay away.

"Our work is done in this realm, my dear brother." Artemis said with confidence that Apollo did not share.

"And what makes you so sure?" He questioned doubtfully.

"We must trust in the fates Apollo." She said reassuringly as she joined him and set a sisterly hand on his shoulder.

"Forgive me if I don't share your optimism dear sister, but too many have tried to fuck with the fates and challenge the prophecies!" Apollo exclaimed with disgust. When Apollo exposed the prophecy long ago, most of the Olympians helped Zeus to suppress it. Artemis' brows furrowed deeply at the curse words and tone of voice her brother used. Spending time in the human realm in this age apparently had bad influences on his choice of language. It was quite offensive to her ears. She slapped him hard behind the head.

"Watch your language brother!" Artemis scolded. "Talking in this manner will only create suspicion in Mount Olympus."

"Those gods need to lighten up a little." Apollo mocked as he rubbed the back of his head. His sister was not someone to mess with on a good day. She was more than a match in strength and if looks could kill right about now, he would be dead.

"Careful planning and the betrayal of many have led them to put all their faith in our hands *brother*. The least you could do is show some respect!" Artemis scowled. Apollo finally turned to look at his sister. What she saw was not disrespect but an all-knowing fear of what Zeus was capable of. It was the influence and power Zeus demonstrated over the centuries that Apollo feared. Apollo respected the oracles and couldn't stand their belligerent attempt at silencing them and cheating the fates. Artemis' eyes softened as her understanding grew.

"We've done everything we could to protect Serena and set her on the path the fates have weaved for her. There is nothing else for us to do." Artemis said gently now. Apollo stood, staring into his sister's eyes as their height was equal.

"I will finish what we've started here sister, and then I will come back to Olympus." He said firmly with a playful tone that made her frown once more.

"Apollo," She said firmly. "Leave the goddess alone." She warned, knowing her brother too well. She regretted the words as soon as she said them, for she knew he would see this as a challenge now. He had never been one to resist the temptation of taking a woman and she knew this one, being a goddess, would definitely not be an exception. The corners of his mouth curled into a defiant smile.

"Apollo." Artemis said his name again firmly, hoping it would somehow lessen his resolve. But she knew he would persevere. He always loved the challenge of soiling the virgin maidens that had pledged their allegiances to her.

"Ah dear little sister, we can't just disappear without making sure everything is in order. Besides, I would like to indulge in a few more frugalities of this realm before going back to the dullness of Olympus." Apollo said with a grin that betrayed his intentions.

"She's not a virgin maiden you know. This realm holds nothing sacred anymore." Artemis said in disgust in her last attempt to change his mind, but by the comical frown that just crossed his face, she knew it only fueled him further.

"Ah, but she's never indulged in the Atlantean frugalities my dear sister." Apollo responded with enjoyment. Atlanteans could have sex with humans, as they often did, but they were built for pleasure between their own and could only be truly satisfied therein.

"Don't be long." Artemis said with a sigh of disappointment, surrendering her useless plea as she walked away from her brother's challenged and amused disposition.

CHAPTER 16
SERENA

Serena sighed heavily as she tucked her sunglasses into her purse. She looked through the door of the cafe, relieved to see only Tracey working today. She had fallen in love with the place from the first day, but somehow, today she just wasn't feeling it. After the night she had, her mind was in a fog. She unfortunately remembered what happened with such harrowing detail, she wished she had the excuse of a drunkard who never remembered anything. She was disturbed by the fact that Tristan seemed certain that Ellie had something to do with what ailed her, even though he attempted to change the subject. She couldn't understand what Ellie's motives would have been. Serena had never heard of a drug that had the effects she experienced, unless it was some sort of hallucinogen she had never heard of in her ten years in nursing. She pushed the door open and was glad to see the cafe filled with customers who would gladly keep her distracted. In fact, she managed to put away her purse, put on her apron and get to work without so much as having to say hello to Tracey. It remained this way for almost three hours. Tracey threw a few smiles her way and she smiled back politely. But she remained pretty quiet herself. Serena had too much on her mind. She could not escape the image of Tristan's lips barely an inch away from hers. But what got her was the physical response that followed instinctively, heat rising through her body and her heart pounding out of her chest. She just met Tristan a few weeks ago and barely knew him. How is it possible that all she wanted to do was tear his clothes off and allow him to do whatever he wanted to her?

"Serena?" Tracey called out, snapping her out of her reverie. Serena had been wiping down a table and staring outside blankly.

"Someone's got you wound up." Tracey said with amusement as she picked up the last of the dirty plates and coffee mug off a table.

"What?" Serena asked dazily.

"You've been wiping that table so clean I think you'll take the lacquer right off." Tracey explained with a giggle as she untied her apron.

"Oh." Serena replied simply, forcing a smile. She looked at the clock and realized it was only two hours until close. She wondered why Tracey was putting her apron away and getting ready to leave.

"Liam called about half hours ago and told me I could leave early if it was quiet. Ray has to go into work earlier and I need to get home to the kids." Tracey explained throwing her purse on her shoulder. Serena was surprised at this. She had never closed up the cafe and had no clue what needed to be done.

"Don't worry, Liam said he would be here to close with you." Tracey explained after seeing a look of dread cross Serena's face.

"Alright, thank goodness!" Serena said with a sigh of relief.

"Enjoy working with the boss!" Tracey winked as she stepped out. Serena only smiled, feeling slightly lighter now. The door rang as someone walked in and Serena stood from behind the counter and smiled as she saw Arianna standing there looking around as if she was in a strange place.

"Hey Arianna!" Serena called out happily surprised to see her. She was a strange young girl but there was something endearing about her.

"Hello Serena." Arianna said with a warm smile.

"Would you like a piece of dessert with a coffee or something?" Serena offered.

"Coffee?" Arianna asked as if she had never heard of such a thing.

"Lemonade then?" Serena offered knowing she had seemed to really enjoy that. Arianna nodded. "Just take a seat and I'll bring it out." Serena said pointing at a table facing the front windows. She went to her counter and picked out two slices of chocolate mousse cake then got the lemonades, set them on a tray with dessert forks and joined her. Arianna eyed the dessert curiously as Serena placed it in front of her. She took the fork hesitantly and stared at it. She watched Serena dig into her cake and did the same, her eyes widening as it melted in her mouth.

"This is divine!" Arianna said with a mouthful.

"It sure is!" Serena agreed, still finding it strange Arianna had never had a simple chocolate mousse cake before.

"Did you run today?" Arianna asked as she took another big bite then took a sip of lemonade.

"No, I didn't get a chance." Serena answered with a shrug. She hadn't felt like it after the night she had. She barely managed to get out of bed in time for her shift, never mind getting herself out there to run.

"So, which beach is your favorite so far?" Serena asked, trying to carry out the conversation again.

"Lanikai beach is wonderful, and the water is less turbulent than the south shores." Arianna answered.

"I haven't had the chance to hit the south side of the island yet. Hopefully I get a chance to do that before my classes start." Serena said feeling disappointed she hadn't taken the time to tour the entire island like she had wanted to do.

"I've been meaning to take a day trip driving around the whole island, would you like to join me sometime?" Serena asked. A beam of joy flashed in Arianna's eyes.

"What a lovely idea!" Arianna exclaimed.

"Awesome, I'll have to check my schedule at the Marina to see when I can swing it and I'll let you know." Serena said, finishing the last bite of her cake then taking a sip of her lemonade as she saw Liam pull into the parking lot in his black Charger.

"Speaking of which, you never told me your father's name." Serena asked Arianna curiously. A frown crossed Arianna's face.

"Oh…" Arianna trailed off obviously uncomfortable with the simple question. She caught a glimpse of Liam coming out of his car, her eyes widened in what looked like shock.

"I have to go!" Arianna said in a rush of words as she stood quickly. "I forgot I have something to do."

"Thank you for this lovely experience." Arianna took the time to say as she touched Serena's arm in a friendly gesture.

"Oh! Ok, you're welcome. I'll catch you later then." Serena smiled as she watched her almost sprint out of the cafe, crossing paths with Liam and strangely bowed her head with a curstie as she passed by him, exchanging words. Serena stood, piling their dishes on the tray then made her way to the back counter. Four girls walked in so she left the dishes on the counter to go take their orders.

She was busy cutting up pieces of dessert for the customers and preparing their coffees when Liam finally walked in looking charmingly handsome sporting aviator sunglasses.

She smiled and shook her head as all four girls watched Liam take off his glasses and stick them in his t-shirt front pocket. He turned towards them as they giggled, pointing fingers in his direction.

"Hello ladies." He greeted, with a charming smile that made the girls blush. Liam joined her behind the counter, watching Serena put the whip cream on one of the specialty coffees. There was a shadow of sadness on her face he hadn't seen before. She was always happy and at peace, but not today. She placed everything on a platter and went to give the girls their order. She remained courteous and professional but wasn't herself.

"Did someone shit in your cornflakes this morning?" Liam asked as she still hadn't even said a peep yet.

"I'm sorry, I didn't sleep well last night." Serena answered distantly as she wiped the few drops of coffee and crumbs from the counter. Liam took her hand gently to make her face him. As Serena finally looked up at him, she just couldn't unsee the threatening look he had in his eyes the night before. The man standing in front of her right now seemed so gentle and kind, which confused her. His blue eyes were so calming, charming, and kind. Maybe there was a reasonable explanation.

"Did anything happen at the luau?" Liam asked with concern as he stepped forward, closing the distance between them. Instinctively, Serena pulled back and crossed her arms on her chest.

"I'm not too sure *what* happened last night." She said uncomfortably with a deep frown.

"Have you eaten anything today?" Liam asked with great concern. His voice was calming and gentle making her tense shoulders finally relax as she sighed.

"No." She responded leaning her left hip on the counter for support.

"Let me take you out for a bite to eat, we will close early today." Liam said almost pleadingly. Serena bit that lower lip of hers, as she did when she was perplexed about something. Liam wondered if she had any idea how seductive she was when she did that.

"I guess." Serena answered. She caught the customers waving at her in the corner of her eye and she hurried to their table.

"Can I get you girls anything else?" Serena asked nicely, putting on her 'server' smile. The girls moved closer to her.

"His phone number?" One of them said in a whisper. The other girls giggled.

"I'll get him to bring you your bills and you can ask him yourself." Serena replied with a smile. She walked back to the counter with a grin from ear to ear. She punched into the tablet and printed out four bills.

"It's not my pretty face they want." Serena said arching her brow and batting her eyebrows as she handed him the bills. Liam chuckled as he took them.

"I'll keep that one for me." He winked as he grabbed the bills and went to see the girls. Serena busied herself cleaning everything off as Liam flirted with the four college tourists who did everything from leaning forward to show off their breasts, to untying their ponytails to let their hair fall onto their shoulders to try to get his attention, to twirling a loose strand of hair around a finger. Liam always had that effect on women, that was obvious from the first day she met him. He sure could turn those heads anywhere he went. She couldn't blame them. His chiseled body, the blond hair, the blue eyes, and that charming smile was simply irresistible.

119

Liam finished closing the café for the day quickly and soon he was locking it up behind them. He motioned to his black Charger parked in the driveway as he unlocked it, pressing the unlock -button on his keychain. Serena settled into the soft black leather seats and realized Liam had a more lavish lifestyle then she thought. She wondered if he had earned this lifestyle or if he inherited it from his parents. She thought it strange that in all the weeks she worked at the café, she had not once seen their parents. She had only dealt with Liam or Ellie.

"I haven't even had the chance to meet your parents yet." Serena exclaimed with a frown.

"Oh. They are spending the next few months visiting some relatives in England." Liam lied. But Serena had no reason to believe otherwise. They soon pulled into a nice restaurant nesting across the beautiful Lanikai beach called Buzz's Original Steakhouse. She heard a lot of great things about this place but hadn't had the chance to go yet. Buzz's had a gorgeous wrap around porch for outside dining, built around a huge two-trunk banyan tree. Even the roof of the porch was built around the tree trunks, giving it great charm. They took a seat near the back railing, with a great view of the ocean and the two Mokulua Islands in the distance. The birds chirped in the distance and Serena closed her eyes instinctively to enjoy what felt like standing in the middle of a tropical jungle. She couldn't help but take a slow deep breath and smile peacefully. Liam watched her intently, leaning his elbows up on the table. He relaxed as Serena's peaceful demeanor returned.

"Can I get you guys something to drink?" The server asked, waking her out of her reverie. She wore a black skort with a white bolero with red hibiscus flowers wrapped around her waist, a black t-shirt with the restaurant logo and her name tag reading "Nai'a." Her long thick black hair was braided behind her back and a red hibiscus flower pinned neatly at the top of it. Serena peaked at the drink menu but hadn't had the time to look at it.

"Is there anything you recommend?" Serena asked as her eyes skimmed the menu.

"Sure, the '58 years on the beach' is really great. It has Naked turtle rum, shaken with lilikoi syrup, pineapple juice, amaretto, house made sweet n sour, creole bitters and nicely finished with a float of Myer's." Nai'a explained making Serena's mouth water.

"Sounds great, I'll get that." Serena said, rubbing her hands together in excitement. Nai'a turned to Liam and a flirty smile crossed her face, the one every girl had when they saw him. This guy was like a giant walking flirt magnet.

"Anything for you sir?" Nai'a asked, batting her eyelashes, and biting the end of her pencil with her perfectly white teeth.

"Just a Honolulu beer please." Liam said through his charming smile.

"Coming right up." Nai'a answered before turning away. Serena couldn't help but let out a chuckle.

"What?" Liam asked innocently. Glad to see Serena back in her usual mood.

"Nothing." She answered by pressing her lips together to stop herself.

"No please, enlightened me." Liam begged.

"You just have an effect on women." She answered looking at the Islands in the distance trying to avoid his gaze.

"I don't know what you're talking about." Liam responded, faking innocence. "Besides, I don't care about other women." He pointed out to get her attention. Serena looked at him in surprise. There was no denying Liam oozed charm and delight with his handsome dimples when he smiled. His perfect complexion was to die for.

"Except you seem unfazed by my irresistible charms." Liam said after forcing a sigh and faking a pout on his perfect lips. Although he was being playful, the smile on Serena's face vanished.

"Liam, I-" She struggled with the right words to say. Liam placed a soft hand on hers, his fingers tracing hers gently.

"Serena, I'm not asking you to marry me," Liam explained. "I'm simply trying to tell you I like you." He added reassuringly. Serena didn't feel reassured. She pursed her lower lip again. She wasn't looking for anything serious right now, maybe not even ever. So why couldn't she just let go and have fun for a change? Life had always been about goals and seriousness and coming to Hawaii was supposed to be about change and fun.

"God!" Liam exclaimed with a low grunt.

"What?" Serena asked with concern.

"Do you realize how incredibly sexy you are when you do that?" Liam said, raising a brow as he leaned back in his chair in time for Nai'a to bring them their drinks. Serena felt her cheeks flush and she was grateful for her interruption.

"Ready to order?" Nai'a asked, pulling out her notepad and pen.

"I'll have your 'Ground Sirloin Steak Special', rare, with an order of hot artichokes." Liam said, seeming to know the menu quite well. Nai'a turned to face Serena, the charming look on her face vanished to a mere polite smile.

"Actually, that sounds delicious. I'll have the same but medium rare please." Serena asked. Nai'a nodded and offered nothing more to Serena. She turned to Liam.

"Coming right up." She said with a flirty smile again. They waited until she was out of ear shot, looked at each other and chuckled.

"I think you underestimate the effects you have on the male populace." Liam said deflecting, taking a sip of his beer. Watching Serena with amusement as she choked on her drink. Now that was something she hadn't heard before.

"I'm sure if you asked about my last disaster of a boyfriend, he would disagree with you." Serena finally managed to say as she took a gulp of water. Her heart felt heavy at the words, she hadn't allowed herself to think much of him until now.

"Obviously, he was a complete idiot." Liam said, starting to feel sorry that someone like Serena had clearly been living unhappily up until she moved to Hawaii.

"I have to agree with you on that one." Serena answered without even thinking. She was never really sure why she wasted her time with him. Maybe deep down she felt the need to fill the empty, lonely, and dissatisfied part of herself. Truth was, she never felt like she belonged. Like she was living someone else's life, until she came here.

They finished their meal quietly; Serena's mood had changed again, and Liam could tell she had gone back to the state of mind he had been trying to get her out of. But the evening was still young. He paid the bill, and he took her home. Liam was a perfect gentleman, coming around to open the door for her. She wasn't fooled by his charms though; she knew too well he was trying to have some 'fun' with her. He walked her to her front door, and she took her keys out, biting her lower lip again. Liam let out a grunt in the back of his throat as he lifted his hand and traced her lips, pulling her lip from her teeth. He moved closer, placing his other hand in the small of her back, his lips close to hers as he pulled her body against his.

"Want to come in?" Serena barely managed to say after swallowing hard. Liam only smirked before kissing her, softly at first, then deepening the kiss as he moved her back against her front door. His body pressed against hers, she felt his warmth and his body stiffen with desire. She smiled as he kissed her neck and his hands slid under her shirt to touch her skin, sending goosebumps all over her body. She couldn't deny the tingle she felt from his touch, igniting a fierce lust she never knew existed. It was nothing compared to what she felt when Tristan touched her. His touch was caring, warm and almost magical. It dug up something deeply profound and quite irresistible. Maybe this is what she felt she needed to release with Liam? After all, Tristan had belligerently pushed her away when she had shamefully thrown herself at him. Perhaps it was that sexual frustration and tension that needed to be let out.

"I guess that means yes." Serena barely managed to say as her hands wrapped around his neck.

"Open the door." Liam said in her ear as he bit her earlobe. She fumbled around, trying to concentrate on opening the door as Liam continued to make it difficult to do so. She managed to get it open then Liam slammed it shut as he followed behind her.

Chapter 17
Tristan

Tristan was laying under the golf cart trying to fix the wiring issue he suspected was causing the occasional shorts leaving staff stranded with supplies regularly. They had other carts available, but really, he needed something to distract him. So, he pulled the cart into his hangar bay and got to work. He was trying to get around the frame of the cart when his mind became flooded with intense emotions. Serena. Whatever she was doing, she was confused and... aroused. He cursed at his hands for being too big to fit in any holes he could use to access the problem. He rolled out from under the cart and stood. He would have to take some of the pieces apart to get the access he needed. He grabbed a wrench from the table. He wanted to push Serena's thoughts aside, but the intensity of her arousal was hard to ignore. He sensed a strong presence mixed into those emotions: Apollo. His blood started to boil, his anger rising and his grip tightened around the instrument. Even if Serena was unaware of their fates being bonded together, the last person he wanted to have their hands on her was the god of the sun and music. He couldn't help his rising rage as he closed his eyes. He wanted to reach out to Serena's mind to stop her somehow. Tristan had refrained from doing so to not confuse her, but he couldn't stand by and let Apollo put his hands on her. Angry and frustrated he focused on them to push his mind a little further, just enough to touch hers. He roared as he sent the wrench flying across the room smashing against a wall, making a loud satisfying 'clunk' as it landed.

"Woah, what did the wrench ever do to you, Pu'ole?" Ailani said as she stepped out of the trajectory of the flying wrench. Tristan's face softened and drained of color as Ailani could have been a victim of his foul mood.

"I'm...sorry." Tristan apologized as he turned away shamefully. Ailani picked up the wrench and brought it to Tristan.

"Something is obviously bothering you." Ailani said, dropping the wrench on the table next to Tristan.

"What possibly gave you that idea?" Tristan answered sourly as he wiped his greasy hands on a rag.

"I think you need to take a deep breath and calm yourself." Ailani said, motioning with her hands. She has never seen him this frustrated or angry before.

"How am I supposed to *calm* myself while I'm fighting this gods damn curse!" Tristan snapped and threw the rag on the table then rested his hands on his hips. He fought the urge to close his eyes as he would only sense her turmoil and feel worse than he already did.

"Ah, so this has to do with Serena." She said studying him. His jaw twitched slightly, enough to give her the answer. "It is only a curse because you're fighting it Pu'ole." Ailani answered. She knew too well the longer Tristan waited, the worst it was going to be for him and Serena. She wanted to reach out and reassure him with a friendly touch, but things were still frigid since their last altercation.

"It is a curse because it's been forced upon two unwilling parties and one which has no idea about anything." Tristan answered through his breath as he turned away from her. Ailani left then, knowing it was best to leave him be.

CHAPTER 18
SERENA

They had barely made it to the stairs before they both started to rip each other's clothes off. Their shirts were off, and Liam swiftly unhooked her bra freeing her ample breasts and throwing it behind him while the other hand cupped one and teased her nipple. It felt amazing, yet there was a part of her who still seemed disconnected somehow. She shoved it aside and decided she deserved to have some fun. Liam's hand went to her shorts, undoing the button, he slid his hands to grab both butt cheeks and lifted her up. She wrapped her long legs around his waist, and he moved to the stairs. He placed her down carefully as he pressed his body against hers and moved to suck on her breasts. Serena gripped his hair as one of his hands moved into her pants to the hot wetness between her legs. She couldn't believe the size of him as she felt his erection pressed against her. She wanted, no desperately needed to release this tension that had been building with Tristan, but her mind was telling her otherwise. Tristan had coldly rejected her. Suddenly, a sharp pain exploded in her head. She let go of Liam's hair and she grabbed her head with both hands in pain. It felt as if someone had yelled, no shouted angrily inside her head and it resonated with excruciating pain. She couldn't explain it, but it felt like Tristan's rage. Liam froze, looking up he saw the pained expression on her face.

"Serena?" Liam called out her name, panting from the moment of passion, trying to figure out what happened.

"My head!" She screamed. She closed her eyes tightly, panting heavily, trying to frantically calm herself. Liam placed a hand on her head gently and let out a breath. Serena looked at Liam in confusion. Was she imagining the golden glow of his arm, running all the way to her head, his hand suddenly feeling warm and soothing? She took a deep breath and closed her eyes. Her breathing slowed as the pain subsided, leaving behind a numbing sensation. A strange feeling of dread and regret followed that didn't come from her. Liam took her left hand, noticing the strange blue glow running from her fourth finger going up all the way to her heart. Serena watched as he traced it with his fingers.

"Triton." Liam cursed the name under his breath. But it all made sense, the way he had jumped in at the beach instinctively staking his claim. Liam had not seen anyone bonded in centuries and nothing could have prepared him for this. It explained everything. He pulled away; a strange smirk crossed his face. Serena felt confused. She looked at her hand and watched the glowing blue light slowly disappear. She wondered if there were any lingering effects of the hallucinogenic drug Ellie dosed her with the night before. She sat frozen on her staircase half naked and trembling. She looked up at Liam, her eyes in a haze, filled with questions.

"Liam?" Serena asked in a trembling voice. But he did not answer. When he finally looked at her, he was calm and collected.

"Your world is about to change Serena. Be grateful you have *Tristan* there to help you." He answered pointing where the strange glowing had been on her left-hand moments ago, and then turned around to leave.

"Liam!" Serena called out in frustration. What was it with men leaving her hanging? "Did Ellie drug me last night?" She asked defiantly. Feeling like an idiot for her moment of pure weakness.

"Drug you?" Liam repeated with a chuckle without turning to face her.

"I know she put something in my drink." Serena said accusingly, beginning to dislike his amused tone. A loud bang of thunder made her jump, it sounded like it had exploded right above her house, rumbling everything around her. It was followed by a heavy downpour. Serena thought it was strange. There had been no clouds in the sky nor any indications of bad weather in the forecast, but the way the evening was going sent a chill down her spine and made her more confused than she had been in her life. Liam glanced up then over his shoulder.

"Seemed like it worked." He replied with a cocky smile as he walked out, Serena following behind him.

"What worked?" Serena persisted with her questions.

"You'll find out soon enough." Liam mumbled with a grin on his face as he walked away into the pouring rain.

CHAPTER 19
TRITON

Watching the calming motion of waves crashing in the distance of Lanikai beach, Triton waved his hand, making his Atlantean conch shell appear. He took a breath, closing his eyes as he focused on who he was trying to summon, then blew. Almost instantly, Hermes appeared next to him, his caduceus in hand, staring out at the sunrise alongside Triton. Hermes was one of the few who could travel and transport between realms and would be the only one who would be able to help him. But dealing with the god of trickery was not simple.

"Ah my dear Triton, I can understand now why you've left the comfort of your father's kingdom for this." Hermes said leaning against his caduceus finding the scenery of the sun rising above the water bursting in beautiful colors simply to die for. Hermes was dressed in a Hawaiian shirt and matching shorts which suited the young athletic human figure he chose. He stood a little under six feet tall and had long slicked back golden blond hair and wore a pair of Dolce & Gabbana sunglasses.

"What can I do for you?" Hermes asked, slapping Triton on the shoulder in a friendly gesture. Triton glowered at him and Hermes backed away giving him some space.

"I need to see the god of the forge." Triton barked; he wasn't in the mood for Hermes' chipperly attitude.

"You want me to take you to Hephaestus?" Hermes asked, rising a brow in surprise. Triton had not traveled far out of Atlantis in centuries and had never required much of his assistance, nor had he ever heard of Triton speaking to the Olympian. It had been a question more of a curious nature than anything else. Triton glared at him. "Alright, alright no need to be aggressive about it." Hermes said in his defense. He took Triton's right arm and hit the sandy ground at his feet with his caduceus sending them through a dark portal instantly and reappearing inside Mount Etna in Italy. Triton had not traveled this way very often; in fact, he couldn't remember the last time he did. One thing for sure, he didn't enjoy it. It felt like being blinded by a thousand stars and shot down a roller coaster track. Triton's stomach flipped with the g-force. He didn't have much of a choice, this was the fastest method by far, and he knew it. Hephaestus had chosen to remain in the earth realm where he worked tirelessly using the great volcanoes around the world as forges making weapons, jewelry, armor etc. He didn't care much about the Olympian lifestyle since he was blatantly thrown out when he was a mere young child. Even though he had been invited back, and offered Aphrodite as a wife by Zeus, he wasn't foolish enough to believe it was out of the kindness of their hearts but rather for their own gain and purpose. They wanted to keep him a satisfied ally as he was simply the best forger to ever exist. Triton stood silently at the edge of the volcano. He sighed and started down the long hot staircase that led to a peninsula sitting in the middle of the lava where his workshop was located. Triton could see the tables covered with forging instruments and forging stoves. Triton spotted the strange looking automatons lined up along the path to protect Hephaestus. He had never visited Hephaestus, nor really spoken with him personally and felt a little intimidated as he often did when having to deal with Olympians. As he should be, they were powerful and fearless, and had been so for an exceptionally long time.

"No need to fear the guy. Sure, he doesn't get many visitors and might be slightly anti-social, but he won't hurt ya." Hermes said, trying to sound reassuring. Triton glared at him again, wondering if he could trust the god of trickery. Hermes followed closely behind, as sweat poured out of every pore of his body. He slipped his t-shirt off to help cool himself, but it was pointless. When he reached the peninsula, he turned down the pathway leading to the smithy workshop. As he reached the end of the path, two automaton guards he thought to be merely statues came to life and stopped him abruptly, Hermes crashing into his back.

"Must you follow so closely?" Triton growled at Hermes over his shoulder.

"My bad," Hermes said with a chuckle. "I'll wait for you right here." He said crossing his arms on his chest.

"Thou shall not pass." Both automatons spoke loudly and simultaneously to catch the attention of their master who stood bent over a working table, hammering at something he was working on. When he stood to look, hammer in hand, Triton understood the rumors he heard of the fearless looking god. He had to stand higher than seven feet tall, a chiseled muscular body decorated with battle scars. He wore only knee length pants which showed his golden robotic left leg from the knee down, sweat dripping from his forehead. Smelling the scent of salt and seaweed, he knew it was someone protected by Poseidon's favor.

"A son of Poseidon in my forge." Hephaestus said, spitting on the ground before returning to his work.

"We need to discuss the offspring of Thetis." Triton called out to Hephaestus, knowing using the Queen of the Nereids name would get his attention. Hephaestus stopped hammering at the mention of the name and the corner of his mouth twisted into a smile. He closed his eyes and whispered some inaudible words in Greek, making the automatons back down and return to their statue like guarding positions. Triton joined the god of fire, and he stood in silence for some time simply watching him work. It was obvious he wasn't going to be the conversation starter.

"The necklace that was made for the offspring," Triton said as he watched him intently. A small muscle in the god's jaw twitched slightly, which was the only indication of a reaction. "She needs something similar made." That caught his attention with a tilt of the god's head as he studied Triton quietly, awaiting the rest of the request.

131

"You wish to silence her powers once more?" Hephaestus asked curiously.

"No, that would be pointless. The fates have spoken." Triton answered. He had no intentions of fucking with the fates as the others had. His life depended on Serena's life and vice versa now, it wasn't simply about him. Besides, it was obvious her powers could not be contained much longer, which proved the immense power coursing through her veins.

"Then what is it that you seek?" Hephaestus questioned, raising his voice, and sounding slightly annoyed.

"Something that will help her control it better. She has been living under the spell of the current necklace. Once the amulet's power fades, there is no telling what it will do to her." Triton said knowing he wasn't sounding very clear, but in truth, he had no idea what he was really asking for. There was no one way to know what would happen if, and when the power of the necklace would fail. But if Serena was going to be the most powerful Atlantean to ever exist and since all her essence had to be kept chained and withheld, who knew what was going to happen once it was released. Triton thought it would be wiser to be prepared.

"Hmm." Hephaestus scoffed. "You have no idea what it is you are asking, and what would you, son of Poseidon, have to offer in return?" He asked, hammering once again.

"You have bestowed your favor upon Serena have you not? You are an Olympian; you would know what she would need." Triton asked slightly irritated, his tone making Hephaestus look up with a frown, fighting not to display a smile on his face. When an Olympian bestowed a favor upon someone, whether it be a mortal or a demi-god, they became protected and the said Olympian could sense their presence, distress and they would have to protect them. Hephaestus found it intriguing that Triton had spoken the name with meaning and a little more emotion than someone who was not personally and emotionally invested.

"The bargain is between us, son of Poseidon, and I will require a favor from you when the time comes." Hephaestus commanded as he continued to hammer. Triton clenched his jaw. He had hoped his plan would work and had expected this would happen. The Olympians were notorious for their bargains and favors, but the last thing Triton wanted was to owe any of them anything. He couldn't be certain if the favor had been bestowed to Serena or perhaps to Thetis.

"Fine." Triton agreed begrudgingly. Hephaestus stopped what he was doing and wiped the sweat from his forehead before reaching out his left hand. Triton looked at his hand suspiciously. First of all, Atlanteans didn't use a handshake to seal a deal, the words spoken were enough to be binding. Second, he was using his left hand. Triton took the hand hesitantly, to which Hephaestus grabbed firmly, forcefully twisting his wrist to flip Triton's hand. He lifted a brow curiously as the blue line of the bond glowed from Triton's fourth finger up his arm.

"I see my *wife* has been busy." Hephaestus said with surprise. He caught a glimpse of the glow, even if Triton had attempted to keep it out of sight. He was surprised that his wife, of all people, went against Zeus and involved herself with this plot to reinstate the prophecy. He narrowed his eyes, studying the bond mark closer. Triton tried to pull his hand away, not wanting the culprits to be found. It was better if it was believed Aphrodite was responsible then some demi-gods living in the earth realm. Hephaestus was curious, it looked like Aphrodite's work, but there was smell to the power that didn't quite belong to his wife.

"The oracle spoke of her thirtieth flower moon." Triton pressed on attempting to change the subject with the looming deadline. Hephaestus dropped Triton's hand and glared at him with intent.

"I will find you when it is ready." Hephaestus barked, not liking being given a deadline and the fact Triton was deliberately trying to change the subject.

"Now, be gone." Hephaestus ordered waving Triton and Hermes away.

"Of course." Hermes said with a gracious bow. He touched Triton's arm, slammed his caduceus on the ground and they disappeared into the dark portal.

*****

Tristan walked up Serena's front doorsteps and stood hesitantly at the door. She hadn't shown up for her shift and was not answering her phone which was out of character for her. She was always so eager to work, showing up early, and Tristan knew something was wrong. He could sense she was still somewhat asleep, but had a sleepless night, shaken by the events that took place the night before. Her world was starting to unravel, and he wasn't sure how she was going to handle it. He silently cursed Thetis for being so reckless and selfish in doing this before he knocked on the door. No answer. He knocked louder, still no answer. He closed his eyes, hating to use their connection again since he had lost his temper.

"Serena. Open the door." Tristan spoke at the door knowing she would hear. He felt her move around and he waited patiently.

CHAPTER 20
SERENA

Serena laid in her bed with her eyes closed as her head pounded. She was used to the headaches, but this was far beyond what she has ever experienced. It took her hours to fall asleep, unable to calm her trembling hands and her state of mind after the incident with Liam. Nothing made sense to her, and she was questioning her sanity.

"Serena. Open the door." Tristan's voice echoed not only outside but as if he was standing beside her somehow. She opened her eyes tentatively and felt as if someone hit her over the head with a hammer. She closed them tightly again rubbing her head. Moving was difficult, so she rolled herself out of bed onto her bedroom floor, thankful for the cozy carpet. She opened her eyes again, expecting to see Tristan standing nearby, but no one was there.

"Serena?" Tristan called out firmly again. Serena frowned and looked around again, trying to focus on her surroundings. How was it possible that his voice sounded like he was standing right there? She struggled to get on her feet, peaking at the mirror in front of her. She looked like a mess and she was still naked. She painfully pulled open a drawer, quickly picking a tank top and a pair of shorts. Passing through the doorway of her bedroom she saw a hair elastic on her dresser which she grabbed on her way out. She paused in the stairs, feeling lightheaded, hoping Tristan had given up and left, but as her eyes closed, she knew he was still there. As she made it to the front door, she could see his shadow through the frosted class confirming her unfortunate thought. She leaned on the door, finding the coolness of the glass comforting. She waited there, not really wanting to see anyone, especially not Tristan. After all, he was the source of her state of mind wasn't he? But, he stood there waiting for her to open the damn door. She stepped back and with a heavy sigh she grabbed her hair twisting it into a messy bun then opened the door a crack.

"Tristan." She mumbled softly unable to look him in the eye.

"Serena, are you alright?" Tristan asked gently.

"Do I look okay to you?" Serena snapped as she glared at him, instantly feeling guilty.

"Serena-" He started to say but she wouldn't let him finish.

"I won't be in today." Serena cut him off, trying to sound less irritated but failing miserably. She tried to close the door but to her surprise Tristan stuck his foot in to stop it. Tristan wasn't clueless, he could feel the turmoil going through her head accompanied by intense pain, but he knew what would fix it: the one thing she was probably staying away from. He pushed the door open, not wanting to force his entry but she wasn't going to let him in and he had to do *something*. Serena backed away to let him in, having no other choice as Tristan was simply bigger and stronger. She honestly had not expected him to simply come in without being welcomed.

"Please come in." She said sarcastically, still avoiding his gaze. Tristan realized then she was avoiding looking at him because there was fear in her eyes, and after what he had done the night before, could he really blame her?

"We have work to do today." He said after clearing his throat. He wasn't really helping his case by having forced his entry.

"Tristan I just can't be out in the sun today." Serena said, rubbing her head as the headache still hammered strongly.

"There's an easy solution for that." Tristan said as-a-matter-of-factly.

"Really? I'm sure glad you have all the answers." Serena snapped again.

He frowned, obviously she wasn't going to make this easy. He took her arm and started dragging her towards the back-sliding doors.

"What are you doing?" She pulled back as he slid the doors open, not understanding what he was trying to do.

"You need to go for a swim." Tristan said simply as if it was the most logical thing in the world. Serena shook her head in protest realizing where they were going.

"Swimming is the last thing on my mind right now!" She protested as she backed away from him, but Tristan followed with determination, closing the distance between them quicker then she could move away.

"Serena, trust me, it will help you." Tristan said firmly. A slash of anger crossed Serena's face, if he thought she glared at him before, he hadn't seen anything yet.

"Trust you?" Serena almost shouted angrily. "How can I trust you after-" She stopped herself, afraid of sounding completely out of her mind. She closed her eyes tightly as a wave of pain shot through her head, giving Tristan the opportunity to catch her, sweeping her up in his arms forcefully.

"Tristan!" She yelled, kicking and thrashing. She tried to fight back but it was pointless, he was much stronger than she was and pretty soon he was stepping into the water. He waited until the water reached his chest and let himself sink, holding on tight with his arms around Serena's waist who was fighting frantically for him to let her go.

"Serena, close your eyes and relax." Tristan said calmly, sounding as clear as if they were sitting on dry land. Serena always liked the sound of his voice, it was deep and scruffy. It soothed her ears and calmed her in a way she couldn't explain. Serena knew there was no point in fighting him, she obeyed. She closed her eyes trying to ease the reflex to swim to the surface for air. As she relaxed, she felt a strange sense of calmness over her like a tingling crawling up her body slowly from her toes. It was the strangest thing, and the most soothing feeling she had ever felt in her life. The feeling reached her head and instantly calmed every corner of her mind, chasing away all her anxiety, soothing all the pain hammering behind her eyes. It was sensational. She wondered if this is what it felt like to get high on drugs. It was then she realized Tristan's hold had relaxed and she could have broken free of his grip but chose to stay there, finding his presence grounding. It seemed like quite some time had passed until her lungs started to burn, begging her to break the surface to catch that sweet breath of air. Then that strange intense burning sensation returned behind her ears. She touched them as the pain became almost unbearable again. She opened her eyes, expecting the burn of the salt water, but nothing. She felt the sand in her toes and pushed herself up, surfacing with Tristan. As she took a gasp of fresh air, the burning sensation immediately disappeared. Looking up at Tristan, she wanted to be angry with him but how could she? Her questions were not answered, in fact, this only added to her confusion, but at least the pain was gone.

"Ready to go to Mokulua Islands?" Tristan asked, lifting his scared brow in a questioning frown. He was relieved to see her smile again. That smile on her lips lighted up her whole being and everything around her. A divine smile that made her so stunning to watch. If only she was aware of the true power she held in that beautiful smile. Serena started laughing almost uncontrollably, feeling all the tension leave her body.

"You just don't give up do you? Seems to me you went to quite the length to get me to say yes." Serena said with sparkling eyes.

"You don't know the half of it." Tristan said with a wink. Serena splashed him with a hand before swimming away towards the shore. He followed behind her deciding to give her this little moment of victory. As she reached the patio doors of her home, she squeezed the water out of her hair and sighed as she saw how much of a mess she actually looked like.

"I'll get the kayak." Tristan said with a smirk as he looked at her from head to toe.

"I have one." Serena said motioning to her shed as her cheeks burned a nice crimson color.

"I brought a tandem. Thought it would be easier if I guided you to the route for your first time." He said, trying not to laugh at the thought of her last kayaking attempt. Serena twisted her shirt to get as much water out as she could before she stepped inside.

"Fine. I'll freshen up while you get it then." Serena opened the door and ran up the stairs quickly, putting on her bikini, and a fresh pair of shorts. She took her hair mess down and knew she didn't have time to detangle it, so she split it in two and braided each half quickly on each side of her head. She plucked her sunglasses off her dresser with her bottle of sun lotion and splatted some on quickly on her arms, shoulders, neck and face as she ran back down the stairs. She saw her water shoes sitting near her front door and slipped them on her feet. It was then she realized she hadn't seen her cat for a few days. She felt a pang of sadness at the thought that perhaps it had finally found her way home and wouldn't return. She slipped her sunglasses on, locked her doors and ran out the back door again. Tristan had not waited long for her, in fact, he thought she had managed her 'freshen up' moment quite quickly for a woman. She literally simply changed and tied her hair into those cute braids snaking each side of her body and chose to wear a cute red bikini top with red shorts. He watched her obviously looking around the back of her house for something, then joined him.

"Looking for something?" Tristan asked curiously.

"Oh, I haven't seen my cat in a few days. Well, she's not really my cat, she just showed up out of nowhere, so I figured she just found her home." Serena answered sadly. She hadn't thought she could get attached to an animal, but strangely enough, she found its presence comforting when she found herself home alone.

"Maybe." Tristan said quickly, sounding strangely uncomfortable. He threw a life vest at her doing his best to avoid the subject, but he could sense that it meant a lot to Serena. He could understand being far from home and feeling alone. He himself had taken time to find friendships that were now the world to him. But other than Liam, Ellie and himself, she had no one but her cat.

"Don't worry, she'll be back." Tristan said confidently in an attempt to cheer her up as he handed her a paddle. She smiled as she slipped on the vest, appreciating that he obviously cared enough to help her.

"I'll take the back, you take the front." Tristan instructed as he took a backpack and slid it at his feet in the kayak. They both managed to climb on without a hitch, but the perfectly calm water helped greatly. As they made their way out to the open, finding their synchronisation, it became quite enjoyable for both of them. When they finally arrived near the island, Tristan stopped paddling.

"Serena, look." Tristan said pointing overboard. He couldn't help but smile as he watched Serena peak over, her eyes widening in amazement as she gasped at the dozens of sea turtles swimming gracefully right under their kayak. It was obviously her first experience seeing the Hawaiian sea turtle.

"The hawaiians call them the "honu"or 'ea. They play a very important role in the hawaiian cultural traditions in mo'oelo. They even have them in their Kumulipo." Tristan explained feeling like he was playing the tour guide, which really, he knew he was.

"Mo'oelo? Kumulipo?" Serena asked curiously. She loved the hawaiian language and wanted to learn but she hadn't gotten that far yet.

"Mo'oelo is their stories, legends or myths. Kumulipo is their sacred creation chant telling their mo'oelo of the creation." Tristan answered passionately. He loved indigenous people, especially hawaiians, for their faith in the creator and their deeply ingrained love and respect for nature and its inhabitants. Serena could hear how much the Hawaiian culture meant to Tristan by the tone of his voice. It was clear he loved them dearly. She had never asked him how long he had been here, or if he was born here, but either way, he still considered this his paradise like she did, perhaps more. They reached the route where all three currents of the ocean met, and Tristan had to steer them in a specific pattern to be able to guide them to where they could coast their kayak. Serena was glad she had Tristan with her, she realized she would never have made this on her own, at least not without getting wet. They reached the bank and Tristan hoped out, holding the kayak securely for Serena to get out. Once she was out safely, and dryly, he grabbed the backpack, opened it and pulled out two masks with snorkels, then reached inside the kayak for two sets of fins.

"Put this on." Tristan instructed Serena as he handed her a pink mask with matching pink and black pool fins. Serena adjusted the strap of her mask while Tristan pulled the kayak high enough for it not to float away. He then pulled his mask on and as he reached for Serena a smirk crossed his face. She looked adorable with the flashy pink mask on her face.

"What?" She asked incredulously, a line appearing on her forehead as she frowned.

"Nothing." Tristan answered with a chuckle.

"Well, I'm sure I look as exceptionally hot as you do." Serena retorted the words slipping out before she realized what she was saying. Tristan's smile grew.

"You sure do." Tristan answered with a chuckle, Serena's cheeks burning red and hot. She turned towards the water trying to escape the embarrassing moment, Tristan following behind her with a dive bag in hand. Once in the water, Tristan guided them towards another flank of sea turtles. They didn't tend to be in much of a hurry to leave around these parts. Once they were right on top of them, he motioned to Serena where they were heading. Tristan dug in his backpack and pulled out a square tracking box they needed to stick to the carapace of one of the turtles. He dove in, Serena following behind, watching his every move. He got behind one of the turtles, with one hand, he hung onto the turtle's carapace and with the other, he pressed a button on the tracker and stuck it gently against the top of the turtle's shell. He gave Serena a thumbs up and signaled her to go to the surface, knowing she would soon feel the need to get some air. Once on the surface again, he handed Serena a tracker which she took hesitantly and gave her a thumbs up with a smile. She nodded and followed him as he dove back under. She was nervous, not because she was afraid of the gentle creatures, but more that she was afraid to hurt them somehow. She stopped herself and looked around, it was like they could read her mind. Three sea turtles turned and swam towards her. One got so close it even nudged her hand gently like a cat wanting to be petted. She smiled, letting water through her mask while stroking the turtle gently on its head. She grabbed the edge of its carapace, activated the tracker then placed it on the turtle. The button activated a soft seal that seemed to click onto the animal and activate the signal. She put pressure on the top part of her mask above her nose, then

141

blew out some air to let the water out of her mask. She stood still as another turtle nudged her hand to grab its edge of its carapace. She grabbed it with both hands and the sea turtle began to swim faster and faster like an underwater ride. It was all she could do not to giggle and let more water inside her mask.

Tristan watched intently, thinking she was beyond graceful and divinely beautiful. Her braids floated behind her trailing along her slender body, her nice ass and great legs. She was unknowingly in her own element here. About five other turtles joined them, encircling her as she was pulled along. She finally let go as the pain behind her ears returned. That strange burning sensation that seemed to appear every time her lungs began to beg for a gasp of air. She kicked with her legs and surfaced, taking a big breath of air through her snorkel after blowing out the water. Tristan swam to her, taking the tube out of his mouth.

"Want to continue?" Tristan asked knowing by the smile on her face that she was enjoying herself too much to protest. Serena gave a thumbs up grinning from ear to ear. They dove back under, deeper this time to reach the reefs. Serena stopped abruptly as she heard a strange sound resonate. It sounded like a loud foghorn of some sort. She was puzzled knowing it was virtually impossible to hear such a noise underwater, especially since it didn't sound close. She turned to look at Tristan who swam towards her. Serena backed away slightly as his eyes flashed a blue luminescent color. It was gone so quickly she wondered if she had imagined it. Perhaps it had been a ray of sunshine reflecting in his eyes? But his eyes were brown, and the reflection of water and sunlight couldn't have made that color. A line formed between Tristan's eyebrows and if Serena didn't know any better, she would think he was worried about something. He grabbed her hand firmly pulling her to the surface and back towards the beach. The touch of his hand sent goosebumps all over her body. Tristan used his free hand to grab his fins which he managed to slip off using his feet, not letting go of Serena's hand who struggled ungraciously to do the same. Obviously, he had done this much more than she had. Tristan helped her, and when he went to turn away, she pulled him back. They faced each other, their bodies nearly touching.

With her free hand, Serena touched the side of his face tentatively. There was uncertainty in his eyes as she searched for what could possibly explain what she had seen flash in those beautiful brown eyes. Her hand lowered to rest on his chiseled chest muscles.

"What was that noise?" Serena asked, still holding his gaze. It wasn't the question she wanted to ask, she wanted to know about him, who he was, why she was pulled to him in a way she couldn't explain and couldn't resist. Tristan barely flinched, holding her gaze firmly, hardly showing any emotions.

Tristan was perplexed and it took everything he had to keep calm and composed.

"Sounded like some sort of horn." Tristan managed to answer, knowing too well it was a full-blown alarm. If she only knew how intoxicating her scent of vanilla and coconut mixed with sea salt did to him. It was then he saw it again. Serena's eyes changed to a sparkling golden color and the features of her face softened. He glanced at her necklace; it was flickering again. He backed away, putting distance between them and watched the glamour fall back into place as her eyes and features changed back. Serena didn't miss the flicker in his eyes and the muscle in his jaw tightened ever so slightly. He wasn't lying, but he wasn't telling her everything.

"I've never heard any horns sound like that." Serena thought out loud, knitting her eyebrows in a deep frown.

"It's a 'Pu'ole horn. The Hawaiians use it for important ceremonies, and there must be one close by." Tristan explained stretching the truth.

"Pu'ole?" Serena asked curiously.

"Pu'ole is a large conch shell named after the Greek god Triton, as it was what he used." Tristan answered in his best historian voice. The corner of Serena's mouth lifted into a smile, finding his explanation amusing. She didn't miss how he had spoken, as if any of that Greek mythology was written history.

"What is so amusing?" Tristan asked.

"I've just never heard anyone talk about Greek gods in past tense, like they existed." Serena answered, her smile widening, making her whole face shine. Her smile quickly vanished as Tristan cocked his scarred

143

eyebrow. *You don't even know half of it.* He thought. As she stepped back and looked at him, she supposed if anyone could be a god, Tristan would definitely match the description.

"You do?" Serena asked tentatively, cursing how difficult it was to read him.

"What do you believe?" Tristan asked curiously, crossing his arms over his chest.

"I…" Serena trailed off biting her lower lip. There was something in his tone that made her hesitate to answer, not wanting to insult him somehow, but couldn't help to remain honest. "Just can't believe there's a bunch of neurotic selfish gods floating around up there not giving a damn about us down here. And you didn't answer my question." Serena finally answered by motioning to the heavens then glaring at Tristan with her sparking green eyes.

Tristan clenched his jaw wishing he didn't find her so damn hot when she bit that lip. He chuckled at her response. If Zeus heard those words coming out of her mouth, he'd have smoke coming out of his ears, and Serena may not have any of that pretty hair left on her head.

"Believe in immortal beings *floating* in the clouds? No." Tristan finally answered as-a-matter-of-factly. Serena fixed her gaze on him, her eyes narrowing. He was so unbelievably hard to read, it was frustrating to no end. He seemed to have no issues reading her.

"What do you believe in then?" Serena asked, rephrasing her question. She couldn't help but feel like there was something there.

"Greek mythology has been around for a long time; don't you think something so detailed and intricate could have some truth to it?" Tristan questioned her in a challenging tone.

Serena could feel he was pushing her to something, but she wasn't sure what he wanted to hear. The truth? "I don't know Tristan." She answered truthfully with a sigh. That was the whole truth. She had never really stopped to think about any of it. Just like everyone else, she had simply passed it all off to crazy wild imagination from a long time ago. There was too much in her life that just didn't make sense. She looked up at Tristan who just stared at her with those brown eyes of his, arms still crossed over his chest. Their eyes locked in a moment. Tristan cleared his throat and turned away towards the landing where they had left the kayak. What was it about him that made her feel like he was keeping something from her, it was driving her nuts?

CHAPTER 21
SERENA

Tristan stopped dead in his tracks, Serena bumping into him from behind. This guy was solid, it was like running into a wall. They had reached the spot where he had left the kayak, except it wasn't there.

"Sorry," Serena mumbled before she saw what he was staring at. "Did someone steal our kayak?" She asked in outrage, hands on her hips.

"It seems like it." He simply answered, his blood boiling. *Cursed Atlas!* He silently cursed with no doubt in his mind regular mortals were not responsible for this.

"How rude!" Serena said angrily as she swirled around as if to find the culprit, but there was no one else in sight. "What are we supposed to do now?" She said, sounding exasperated. Tristan chuckled silently; she was adorable when her temper flared. Tristan turned, looking at Kailua beach in the distance.

"We have two options; we can wait for someone to come along." Tristan said nonchalantly. Serena winced. She could see small figures on Kailua beach in the distance, but no one would be able to tell they were in distress.

"Or?" She urged Tristan, waiting for him to give a better option.

"Swim across." He finally answered, motioning the shores of Kailua beach.

"Sure, with my super fin powers I can handle that no problem." Serena exclaimed sarcastically.

"It's not as bad as it looks." Tristan replied, detecting her lack of enthusiasm at the idea.

"I'd rather not be shark bait." Serena pointed out. She had watched shark week on the national geographic channel and knew there were plenty of shark attacks in Hawaii.

"I've been tracking the sharks that could potentially enjoy gnawing on your pretty flesh, they haven't been in these parts for some time." Tristan said comically. Serena's cheek turned a nice shade of red and she wondered how he could be so eager to swim this far out in the ocean.

"What about Deep Blue?" She argued. Deep blue was one of the largest female white sharks that had been spotted by divers in Oahu feasting on a sperm whale carcass a few days ago. Tristan was surprised Serena knew this information.

"It wasn't anywhere near here, and besides, as pretty as you look, you're not as attractive to her as a sperm whale carcass." Tristan teased trying to sound reassuring. His confidence didn't waver, making it easier to even consider the ridiculous idea.

"What about tiger sharks? Weren't there almost a dozen attacks in the last year? I thought I read an article on two snorkelers who actually swam from here to Kailua beach and didn't get so lucky." Serena said, rubbing her upper arms nervously as her eyes gazed at the open water.

"Then we wait." Tristan said as he watched her body relax relieved to hear him say the words.

"How long do you think it'll be before anyone shows up here?" Serena asked, trying to avoid committing to the idea of swimming the long distance into open water. Maybe she had watched too many movies.

"Could be hours, or days." Tristan answered.

"I can't believe I'm even considering this." Serena said with a heavy sigh.

"Most predators feed at night, so it would be 'safer' if we went now then wait until dark." Tristan said, watching her intently. Not that he even feared it, but he was trying to convince her to do this. After all, it seemed like the fates had it planned. Or perhaps simply a meddling

147

Olympian trying to speed things along. He understood her hesitation, but if she only knew who she was, she wouldn't even hesitate.

"Thanks for the vote of confidence." Serena said as she stared out into the distance, her eyes watching the waves. As she stood there pensively, she could swear the waves became smaller with every churn. How strange, she thought. She peaked towards the west, it was late afternoon by now and there was no way they could make it before dark. She bit the corner of her lower lip, there was something eerily creepy about swimming in open water, but even more so in the dark not being able to see what was coming to get you.

"I... can't." She said with uncertainty. She turned away from the water hoping someone would come along. She sat comfortably in the sand and folded her legs up, hugging them. She was drenched from the snorkeling and she had a feeling that although it was warm outside, it could get chilly when the sun goes down. Tristan joined, sitting next to her.

"Did something bad happen last night?" Tristan asked, breaking the uncomfortable silence that had settled between them. In true honesty, he knew something did and the look on her face when she had opened the door was enough to confirm his suspicion. He watched her face intently, her smile vanished, her face paled as her eyes stared out into the distance.

"What makes you think something bad happened." Serena finally asked, avoiding the answer.

"The look on your face this morning." Tristan said solemnly. "You...were afraid of me." He trailed off with uncertainty.

"Should I be?" Serena asked, avoiding his gaze.

"No." Tristan answered. She turned to look at him then, hearing a touch of remorse in his voice. As their eyes met, she thought she could see it there too.

"How well do you know Liam?" Serena asked pleadingly. Tristan looked away, but not before she saw the flash of anger in his eyes.

"Enough to know I don't want him anywhere near you." Tristan answered. *Because you belong to me.* He thought. Serena's eyes widened in shock.

"I don't belong to anyone!" Serena exclaimed angrily as she stood to

148

walk away. Tristan grabbed her wrist, jumping up on his feet, pulling her up a little too fast so she fell into him, their faces a few inches apart. She was so close Tristan could feel her heart pounding in sync with his, her breath was ragged, her eyes angry. *Cursed Atlas father of all Atlanteans!* He cursed silently. He had never in his life had to fight so hard for control. Control over a powerful string pulling them together. Her body so close to his, her glamour fading once more, her eyes sparkling like gold, her perfect features, her luscious lips. He was afraid that if he kissed her he wouldn't be able to stop himself, and that scared the hell out him. He had sworn from a young age he would not be like his father, or like most of the Olympians, hot tempered, possessive, and taking any woman he wanted regardless of whether they wanted to or not. He never thought himself to be that way, controlled by his cursed Atlantean desire, except for this wretched bond that made it damn near impossible to resist.

Serena put her free hand up on his chest, relieved she could feel the heat, his heart pounding as hard as hers, his breath ragged like hers. She closed her eyes tightly, wanting to control the undeniable pull she felt towards a man she barely knew. She was angry with him damn it, why couldn't she pull away? She wanted to pull away, but she did the very opposite and kissed him. He didn't respond at first, letting her sweet lips tease him into doing what he had fought so hard *not* to do. But she was insistent as she bit his lower lip, making him lose all control. He grabbed the nape of her neck, his fingers gripping the back of her hair and he finally returned the kiss, gently at first. Relinquishing all the control he had, the kiss became passionate and relentless. The heat of passion grew intensely between them. Serena's whole body lost all inhibition like she never had before and she wrapped her hands around his neck, pulling him in closer and deepening the kiss. She felt Tristan's arousal and he groaned in frustration as he used supernatural strength to pull her head away, his forehead resting on hers as he fought to steady his breath and regain some control.

"Serena," Tristan rasped in protest, his body trembling with the need to take her. But Serena wasn't giving up so easily, she lowered her hands and tugged at the button of his shorts. He gently pushed her further away from him, needing that distance before he lost himself completely.

Tears of anger and confusion burned her eyes and threatened to fall. She bit her lower lip, shaking now as she struggled to fight something she didn't understand. When she opened them again, she wanted to look away, but couldn't.

Tristan looked into her eyes again, seeing the tears threatening to come out. His eyes softened as he knew this had to be so confusing for her. She had no idea what was going on. How long was he going to drag this torture out for her, for both of them?

"Someday soon you will understand." He said unable to resist the urge to tuck a now perfectly curled ringlet that had escaped her braid behind her ear. His touch sent a shiver up her spine like an electrical current.

"Understand what?" Serena asked in a soft whisper, her eyes pleading.

"This, yourself, who you are." Tristan answered by releasing the back of her hair.

"Help me make some sense of *this*." Serena pleaded as she traced the intricate pattern of the tribal tattoo on his left shoulder. Tristan shuddered under her touch and grunted in the back of his throat.

"I can't." Tristan managed to say, but only in a whisper.

"I don't understand! You know what *this* is! You know what's happening to me and you *can't* tell me?" Serena said, frustration flashing in her golden eyes as she backed away, but his grip held her close. In the distance, the sound of thunder rumbled, appearing out of nowhere.

"You're not ready." Tristan said solemnly, finally letting go, watching her glamour return and hide her divine features. Already her mood was clearly starting to affect the weather and Tristan was startled to realize her powers slipping through the cracks of her amulet's protection.

Serena looked up at the clouds forming in the distance seemingly out of nowhere. She was frustrated at Tristan yes, because she saw now, he was hiding something important, something she needed to know. But if she was truly honest with herself, she was sexually frustrated and it made her angry, because she didn't understand why he was resisting. Where was this sexual tension coming from? She yanked her fins and snorkel from the ground and begrudgingly put them on her feet.

150

"What are you doing?" Tristan asked, unable to control the smirk crawling at the corner of his mouth.

"I'm not sleeping on this island in the pouring rain." Serena answered sharply, spitting in her mask, and backing into the water. *And clearly, I need to get away from you.* She thought.

"Alright." Tristan said grabbing his dive tote, sliding it around his broad muscular shoulders. He grabbed his mask and fins, following Serena into the water, which was also obviously affected by her sudden frustration as the waves began to churn. He hoped they wouldn't encounter any trouble, but he had the feeling they might. Someone had gone the extra mile to make sure they ended back in those waters.

"I'll stay behind you and keep watch, don't stop no matter what happens." Tristan instructed. He wasn't worried about what could lurk in the waters, but he wasn't ready to show himself to Serena yet.

Serena nodded as she stuck the snorkel in her mouth and let herself fall back in the water. She couldn't help the feeling of unease crawling up her spine, only getting stronger as they reached deeper and darker waters. She didn't waste any time, yet she didn't want to burn out her muscles too quickly. She tried to keep a steady pace, her eyes dotting around her for anything suspicious or threatening. They managed to swim for about thirty minutes or so before anything mildly suspicious took place. It started with dark shadows appearing in the corner of her eyes. When she looked though, she didn't see anything, nor would she stop to investigate. *Don't stop no matter what happens.* Tristan's words resonated in her mind.

CHAPTER 22
TRISTAN

Tristan felt prickling along his spine alerting him to unworldly creatures nearby. He wasn't sure how this was possible as what he was sensing *shouldn't* be in this realm. But could he really be surprised? No. He saw the shadows creeping closer, and they were not the ones of sharks. Tristan was curious how Serena was going to react. He saw the figures of wretched sirens emerge from the shadows. He took a deep breath and narrowed his eyes in warning to whoever, or whatever was out there not to dare come any closer. He clenched his jaw, feeling like they might need some help moving Serena away from the wretched sirens. He started clicking his tongue on the top of his mouth, a noise he knew Serena probably wouldn't hear, or anyone else other than who he was calling for. A few moments later, a smile crossed his face as he watched them arrive. He waited until she was safely out of sight and transformed into his merman form. Waving his hand, he made his trident appear. In a swift motion he sent a bolt of power towards the wretched sirens swimming in the distance. The bolt shot out like a thick rope, and once it found its target, he yanked, pulling the wretched siren directly in front of him. He wrapped his hand around its neck, using his powers to restrain the siren's ability to breath. Both knew that with a quick and easy gesture, Tristan could snap its neck and end its life. But the siren thrashed, fighting uselessly to get out of his grasp.

"What are you doing here?" Tristan demanded, his voice rumbling loud enough for the other wretched creatures to hear.

"We were sent to spy on you." The siren struggled to say, her lungs barely able to draw breath.

"Who sent you?" Tristan hissed.

"Lor-Lor-Lord Poseidon." The wretched siren mumbled. Tristan paused only for a moment then clenched his jaw and tightened his face in anger.

"You forget who you are speaking too, siren! Poseidon would never be this reckless!" Tristan exclaimed, his blood boiling. He could accept his father would send spies, he somewhat expected it, but it was clear to him the wretched siren was lying. There was nothing he hated more than being lied to or manipulated. He narrowed his eyes, using his power to press against the mind of the siren, like a thousand pounds of pressure against its brain. The siren screamed in response, the pain unbearable. Tristan released his hold on his powers.

"This is your last chance, siren, who sent you?" Tristan demanded again.

"Lord Poseidon." The siren mumbled again hesitantly. Enraged, Tristan slammed his trident into the wretched siren. The divine weapon pierced the creature's torso, leaving it staring wide eyed in horror. Dark crimson blood oozed from the wretched thing's mouth as its eyes slowly moved back to stare at Tristan's emotionless face. The wretched siren wavered for a mere moment and before it collapsed, Tristan used the trident to throw the siren right into the path of the sharks which had been looming around Serena unknowingly moments before. The four sharks attacked the bleeding siren, in a feeding frenzy, tearing it apart by its limbs. Tristan watched the other sirens watching the scene in horror.

"Send the message to your masters that I will not tolerate anyone who breaks Zeus' law to come to this realm." Tristan commanded, his voice resonating through the water like loud thunder. The sirens gasped at the horrible scene and vanished quickly, not wanting to be next.

CHAPTER 23
SERENA

Serena felt a strange tingle at the back of her neck. Not like the creepy sensation she had been feeling, more like millipedes crawling at the base of her neck, or a light electrical current, slowly climbing up the back of her head, making its way to her eyes. She thought she heard a strange clicking sound, but knew she was probably imagining it. She turned her head again, and suddenly shadows began to take form. At first, she thought she had seen human-like shapes, at least arms, a body, and a head. She shook her head, slowed down her pace without stopping completely, blinked, and looked again. Now she saw dozens of sea rays swimming together, at first towards them, then suddenly veering off into a different direction. Then, out of nowhere, a pod of bottlenose dolphins encircled her, two to her left and two to her right, three in front, and three below. She smiled uncontrollably, of all the things she was afraid would eat her, this was not it. They jumped through the waves simultaneously in playful harmony. She was certain she saw the dark figures of sharks looming nearby. Long slim, shorter back fin, and shiny silver skin with black marks: tiger sharks. Then, taking her attention away from the looming sharks, two dolphins nudged her hands, and she swore she could hear them say: *Hurry, they are coming.* Serena took both hands and carefully hung on to the dolphin's dorsal fin. The dolphins launched forward pulling her along faster then she could have pushed herself. Instead of taking them hours, it took them less than thirty minutes or so before reaching the shallow waters edging the beach near her home. Serena let go of the fins and stopped. She slid her mask on top of her head, the two dolphins faced her in the water. She laughed as each moved forward and touched her cheek in a kissing motion, then as quickly as they had appeared, they disappeared into the wakes of the waves. With the images of the sharks still flashing in her mind, Serena backed away slowly until she was knee deep in the water, able to see if anything were to sneak up on her, then let out a heavy sigh of relief. She took off her fins and a smile plastered on her face.

"That was fun!" Serena said, unable to hold in her excitement. "Even if we could have been shark food." She said, staring into the distance, the two islands seeming so far. She couldn't believe how fast those dolphins had been.

"Nah. Tiger sharks are highly misjudged." Tristan said as he took off his own fins and mask, joining Serena.

"I'm sure it's a huge misunderstanding and we can just go back in there and ride them like we did the dolphins." Serena said sarcastically.

"Of course, if that is what you want, but they ride better with saddles." Tristan answered, with the serious and unreadable look on his face he always carried.

"As excited as I am about the idea, I'm going to let someone else enjoy the experience, sacrifice and all. Besides, I'm getting kind of hungry." Serena responded, her eyes scowling at Tristan as she rubbed her growling belly. She hadn't eaten since her supper the night before, with Liam. The thought of his name made her smile vanish.

"Serena?" Tristan called out, noticing the saddened distant look on her face.

"I'll get us some towels." Serena answered glumly avoiding Tristan's gaze and question. He wanted to grab her wrist again, push her to share what caused her beautiful, serene face to vanish. But he didn't. Instead, he watched her leave. He knew the events of the previous night weighed heavily on her mind and as their bond grew, he needed to keep her away from him before he did anything he would regret. Something Liam had said deeply affected her and he wished he could see through the mist and the memories. Serena's strength, and biggest part of her personality were deeply affected by the pain she experienced from the power imprisoning her very essence. It lay heavy on her mind, even though she had no idea of its existence and it took a lot of her focus and energy to continue functioning normally. He realized it only proved how strong she really was. The pain she was feeling and the inner strength she used to control it was impressive to say the least. He was pretty certain even his mother would not be powerful enough to withstand the side effects he could feel Serena battle every second that passed by. He watched her run down the stairs of her abode, truly impressed by this woman. She lived her life with this pain that could obviously alter her mood, and rightfully so, but chose instead to have this calming beautiful smile even when no one else was watching. Like this very moment as she walked back outside, she tossed the towels on her shoulders and began unraveling the braids on the side of her head.

She threw him a towel as she stepped through the doorway. She frowned as she noticed he was barely wet. How was that even possible?

"Here." She said handing him a towel anyway, watching him pull out his man bun to dry his hair.

Tristan dried himself off, even though water did what he needed it to do, and you could barely tell he had spent the last hour swimming. He stopped as he saw Serena bite that lower lip again and he couldn't help but chuckle. Serena cleared her throat and looked away, her cheeks burning red.

"Thank you for today. It was…" Serena trailed off looking away at the water where the amazing dolphins had jumped away in unison like right out of a dream. "Amazing." She finished off in almost a whisper. She wondered just then what it was about Hawaii that made it seem so extraordinary.

"This place is amazing isn't it?" Tristan asked in response, making Serena look at him. Did he read her mind again or did she not realize she said that out loud?

"It sure is." Serena simply answered, deciding she had probably thought out loud. "Want to get something to eat?" She asked instead as she threw her towel up on the clothesline attached to the back wall of her townhouse.

"Sure." Tristan answered, realizing his stomach was growling at the mention of food. Serena reached out her hand for Tristan's towel, but he simply smirked and threw his own over the clothesline.

Serena locked the door back up and they walked down the alley towards the street. Neither of them spoke. Serena's mind was in its happy place as she relived the wonderful moments, tagging the sea turtles and swimming with them, swimming back from the island, and that kiss. Her whole body flushed with heat as she thought about *that* kiss.

Tristan frowned as he felt the heat rise in his lower gut. He glanced at Serena, her cheeks a nice shade of red and he couldn't help but smile. She probably didn't realize it. It took about ten minutes of silent walking before they reached a nice little building on the beach. Serena stopped and looked stunned as her eyes looked at the empty space in front of her.

The cute little quaint cafe *Chez Lilly* was completely empty. No tables or parasols outside. The inside was a big empty space. There wasn't even a sign. It was like the cafe never even existed. There was overgrowth of weeds through the cracks of the patio stones like no one had been there in a long time. The windows were bare, except for a big "For Sale or For Lease" sign. Serena stood there baffled, unable to comprehend what had happened. How was it possible that a place she had worked the day before had completely vanished?

"How is this possible?" Serena asked herself out loud, her voice slightly trembling. She wasn't sure she could handle anymore weirdness right now.

"Is this the restaurant you were working at?" Tristan asked. A pang of guilt settling in the depth of his gut.

"Yes, just last night I closed the store with Liam." Serena answered, her voice fading. The headache that had plagued her returned ferociously making her suddenly dizzy, her body swayed as everything around began to spin and everything went dark.

CHAPTER 24
TRISTAN

Tristan wrapped an arm around her waist for support and caught her in his arms as she collapsed. Perhaps he had pushed things a little too far today. Physically, she was exhausted, hungry and had pushed her body to the limit. Mixed in with her emotional state and her confusion made it a cocktail for major physical strain. He picked her up in his arms and walked back to her place. As he reached the back door, he waved his hand to use his powers to unlock and open the patio doors. He chose the back door to avoid unwanted attention. He walked in and placed Serena on her living room sofa gently, using a throw blanket he found resting on a chair to cover her. He walked to the kitchen and opened the fridge, there were two chicken breasts and a few veggies sitting on the shelves. Not much, but he could whip up something. He opened the cabinet doors, searching for everything he needed then started cutting up the veggies and the chicken. Throwing some oil and butter in the pan, he threw the meat in. He reached for the fridge door and froze. He was certain he heard the violent meow of a cat. He opened the fridge door to grab some sauce and he heard it again. He placed the sauce on the counter and walked to the back patio door. There sat the black cat staring at him intently. It scratched the door earnestly, desperate to be let in. Tristan reached for the handle; his eyes still locked with the cat. He wasn't sure if he should, but decided she deserved to be here more than he did, so he opened the door. The cat ran inside straight to Serena's side on the sofa, sniffing the air as if looking for something. Tristan went back to his cooking, grabbing a wooden spoon to make sure nothing stuck in his pan.

"You're cooking for her now." Thetis said none too impressed as she leaned her elbows on the kitchen island opposite of Tristan who continued his task without flinching.

"Your daughter is in need of sustenance." Tristan plainly replied, turning on the sink tap as a precaution. He was a god of the sea, in total control of all forms of water.

Thetis looked at her daughter again and watched her intently. Serena had a frown on her face and her features clearly showed she was distressed. Her face was pale and the lines on her forehead deep.

"What did you do to my daughter?" Thetis questioned, her eyes narrowing to examine her daughter further.

"Perhaps you should have considered the dangers and pain you were putting your daughter through when you decided to hide the truth from her before you start pointing fingers at me, queen of the Nereids." Tristan answered calmly as he poured the meal onto a plate.

"How dare you!" Thetis hissed as she launched herself at Tristan, flying through the air with her powers, but she was no match for him. He simply lifted his free left hand calmly, using the running water to put shackles around her feet to stop her in her tracks. Thetis strained against the bind, testing its strength, and glared at Tristan.

"I am not the enemy." Tristan said, his voice deep and commanding.

It was then Thetis saw the blue glow running up the arm he used to bind her. Her eyes widened. No, this couldn't be. She thought.

"I cannot harm her." He responded simply as he caught her eyeing the glowing bond on his arm. Tristan was just like his father, tall, handsome, and exceedingly difficult to read. She saw the same hidden tenderness behind those brown eyes and noticed they were filled with apprehension, possibly towards a situation he had no control over. Her shoulders slumped in resignation as she took a deep breath, the realization sinking in.

Feeling Thetis relax through the shackles he had created, he released her, then she made her way to her daughter. She sat on the edge of the sofa, studying her daughter's beautiful features as she moved a strand of hair from Serena's forehead. She took her left arm and studied it, the blue glow barely showing but brightening as she touched it. She sighed as she closed her eyes. It suddenly made sense to her now why Lady Artemis and Lord Apollo had withdrawn.

"You have no idea what I've had to do to protect my daughter." Thetis said solemnly with great regret. "The prophecy foretold of a child, and everyone assumed it would be a son. When I finally got pregnant, I thought for certain it would be so. Oh, how I was wrong." She continued with great sadness.

"Prophecies are always cryptic. They are meant to guide us, not control us." Tristan replied as he platted the food. He had no idea what had transpired or how she came to get pregnant, not that he wanted to know.

"When she was born, I knew being a daughter of Zeus would ensure she would be powerful. But I couldn't be sure she would be the child of the prophecy. I sought out some help, and we decided to keep her hidden until she became of age." Thetis explained with remorse as she fingered the pendant.

"Hephaestus made the pendant, Artemis and Apollo helped you with the rest." Tristan voiced his suspicions out loud. Thetis arched a brow and turned her head, the corner of her mouth curling in a half smile. Seemed like someone had been busy meddling in her affairs. She didn't acknowledge anything; she didn't need to explain herself to anyone especially not to the son of Poseidon.

"Did you ever stop to consider the pain she would suffer?" Tristan asked a little too sourly for her taste.

"Pain?" Thetis asked, obviously perplexed by his question.

"How could you not foresee that this power she held was too strong to contain? She lives with an incredible amount of pain." Tristan explained accusingly. It wasn't difficult for Thetis to hear the concern in his tone. He couldn't understand even if she spelled it out for him.

160

"I... didn't know." Thetis said hesitantly, remorse eating at her conscience.

"If you would have paid some attention to her-"

"Do not speak of something you cannot understand son of Poseidon!" Thetis snapped coldly, obviously disgusted he would dare judge her when he had no idea. She stood slowly, her eyes flashing with anger.

Tristan knew she was right; he had no idea what she had been through. Who was he to judge? All he knew is too many had put this damned prophecy ahead of Serena's wellbeing. What was going on with him? If the fate of the universe was hanging in the balance wasn't it all worth it? The truth hit him like a dozen blades in his gut. Instinctively, the bond demanded that Serena's safety was a priority, and it was, but to what end? He was so lost in his thought he didn't see Thetis walk over to him.

"It is up to you now." Thetis said, forcing a smile on her beautiful face as she touched his arm in a motherly gesture.

"I have done all I could..." Thetis trailed off swallowing back a sob of despair. She had fought against everything she had to keep her daughter safe. She had kept her distance, ensuring Serena could be a strong independent Atlantean who needed no one to stand on her own two feet and it had killed her. No, no one could understand the sacrifices she had made to mold her into the woman she was today. Strong, independent, defiant, everything she needed for what was to come. Although she made sure Serena didn't depend on anyone, it had made her long for companionship. She had been unable to build meaningful relationships, but it was better this way. Fate obviously had a better idea when they wove Serena and the son of Poseidon's fate together.

"I will take care of her." Tristan said firmly.

"If you truly care for Serena, you will do what *needs* to be done." Thetis pleaded with urgency as she touched the matching necklace around her neck.

Tristan looked away as Serena started to stir, when he looked back at Thetis, she had morphed back into her cat form.

CHAPTER 25
SERENA

Serena was climbing up a set of stairs carved out of stone inside what looked like caverns. It was dimly lit, and she looked around for the light sources. Every few feet there were torches lit with a strange blue flame. She reached the top of the stairs and the landing pooled out into the mouth of a humongous cavern lit by the same torches strategically placed all around to create just enough lighting. The torches created a majestic effect against huge stalagmites hanging from the cavern ceiling, making the shadows dance across the space.

"Hello?" Serena called out, her voice echoing and bouncing off the walls. Ahead was a pool of some sort, and from the steam rising from its surface, she guessed it was a hot spring. She walked to the edge of the spring, and noticed the same carved stairs going into the pool. She dipped her right toe in curiously and pulled back instantly. It was hot. Not only that, but the sensation sent a burst through her body like nothing she had felt before. It felt like an enveloping warmth crawling up from her right leg all the way up to the tips of her hair. She shivered with pleasure. Serena bit her lower lip in anticipation as she stepped down into the steaming waters of the hot spring. She closed her eyes tightly as pleasure swarmed every inch of her body, like thousands of ants crawling up towards her head. She let out an uncontrollable moan as she plunged her whole body under water, unable to resist the urge to fill her entire being with this divine feeling. She stayed submerged under water with her eyes closed, wanting to enjoy every second. It was like having warm hands caressing her entire body. Her lungs began to burn, begging her to break the surface to take a breath, but she couldn't let go of this. The intense burning behind her ears returned with a vengeance. She snapped her eyes open to understand this familiar sensation that plagued her every time her lungs were deprived of air under water. She pushed herself off the rocky bottom and broke the surface. As she gasped for that sweet breath of air, the pain vanished once more. She frowned, deeply perplexed by these occurrences. Was the water pressure affecting her ears somehow? Was this what it was supposed to feel like when your ears refused to equalize with the weight of the water? It didn't make any sense. The pool simply wasn't deep enough to explain that phenomenon. She felt a prickle on her skin, like a thousand needles lightly touching the pores of her entire body followed by a wave of what she could only explain as pressure coming towards her. The water rippled behind her. Before she had a chance to turn around, strong and gentle arms wrapped around her waist and pulled her against his familiar form. She smiled as she recognized his salty, musky scent. Tristan. She closed her eyes, leaning her head against him, letting herself sink back into the water with him. His head leaned against hers, his soft breath in her ear, slowly making her whole body heat up with desire and wetness growing between her legs.

"Serena." Tristan whispered in her ears. His hands caressed her stomach, then split. One hand struck one breast and the other plunged between her legs. Her body arched against him with pleasure as his fingers teased her entrance, her moans echoing in the cavern. The air suddenly changed around them feeling colder and crispier. She opened her eyes to watch a strange fog appear and she could see her breath in the air. She felt a different, subtle change in the hands touching her and the hairs on her body stood up. Something was wrong.

"I will enjoy taking your innocence from our existence." The voice sneered in her ear. It was no longer the deep rough voice of Tristan. She

163

struggled to move away, but his grip tightened around her. She looked up and saw his face. He had short, light brown hair, his face bore light brown stubble and cold icy blue eyes. His left ear adorned by a large hanging brass cross earring.

Serena sat up suddenly, panting heavily as she awoke from her dream turned into a nightmare. Beads of sweat trickled down her spine as she gripped the throw blanket tightly against her chest for comfort. Her cat jumped her on her lap, purring and rubbing against her hands as if to coax her into petting her to relax. She took a deep breath and let it out as slowly as she could, then released the blanket and reached to pet her cat.

"There you are. How did you get in here?" She asked rhetorically as she pet her cat's head gently. She jumped in surprise as her phone buzzed announcing a text message. She picked up her phone from the coffee table, not remembering putting it there. In fact, what was the last thing she remembered? She peaked outside and realized it was dark. *Serena, I'm sorry I couldn't stay, I got called in at the Marina, Duncan apparently had an issue with Miss Pettigrew. Left you something to eat. I'll check on you later. Okay?* She chuckled. Miss Pettigrew was a Humboldt penguin who sometimes would give you attitude if you didn't watch yourself around her. Miss Pettigrew had Serena running after her a few days before as she ran off with the golf cart keys that had slipped out of her pocket. She bit her lower lip, not sure how to respond. It was then she saw the platter on the coffee table. He had laid it out perfectly, a chicken and vegetable stir fry neatly decorated with a flower made with fresh basil as the petals and a cherry tomato as its center. A tall glass of orange juice with a straw holding a white and yellow plumeria flower. It looked and smelled delicious. She smiled, her heart melting over the sweet gesture. She was surprised, somehow not pegging Tristan as a cook. But what did she really know about him? She picked up the fork and took a bite, it was delicious. *It's okay, I understand. Thanks for the food, it's delicious! And for the amazing day!* She wrote as she swung her legs down on the floor and took another bite of food. She realized then she was famished as she stuffed another mouthful. She hadn't eaten since the night before, and the day had taken its toll on her as she devoured the rest of the food in no time. She looked up in surprise as her doorbell rang. Maybe it was Tristan? She had a peephole on her door, but this was Hawaii, the crime rate was low and she never felt any kind of danger before so she didn't use it. As she swung the door open, her smile vanished as her blood ran cold. A strange man stood at her entrance with a frigid smile and icy cold blue eyes. He was a few inches taller than her, light brown hair, and a short stubble beard. Around his neck was a leather cord with a large brass arrowhead, his left ear adorned by a large hanging brass cross earring. Her eyes widened as she realized he looked just like the man from the nightmare she had woken from. She moved to slam the door shut, but not quickly enough. In a fast motion, he shoved her back against the wall. She opened her mouth to scream for help, but the man motioned with his hand and she felt an invisible force holding her mouth shut leaving her frantically touching her face. He flicked his hand and the door slammed shut behind him, the dead bolt locking. She backed away in a panic, tripped on a sandal and she tumbled on her ass.

The man advanced, his grin widening with every step as Serena crawled backwards to move away from him. Out of nowhere, her cat sprung in between them hissing threateningly.

"Quite the feisty guard dog you have there." He said with a chuckle, his eyes falling on the medallion hanging from the cat's neck. "Well, if it isn't the cunning woman of the hour herself." The man said, crossing his arms over his chest. Serena watched in amazement as the cat transformed into none other than her own mother.

Serena mumbled in confusion, trying to speak without success. The man glanced from Serena to her mother and a look of amusement crossed his face. He applauded slowly.

"Thetis," He tisked. "You raised your daughter as a human?" He laughed sadistically.

"What do you want, Ares?" Thetis finally spoke with clear disdain.

"Now now, who could resist coming to see what the big fuss was all about?" Ares asked, cocking an eyebrow.

165

"You've seen she's no threat to anyone, now leave." Thetis commanded.

"Out of my way queen of the Nereids." Ares said with annoyance flicking his hand again. Serena watched in horror as the motion sent her mother flying through the air crashing right into the kitchen island. The sheer force leaving her motionless on the cold floor. Serena shrieked as she saw the pool of blood forming around her mother's head, tears filled her eyes in terror. She quickly got on her feet and sprinted towards the back door.

"Not so fast." Ares said flicking a finger. An invisible rope wrapped around her feet and she tumbled forward hitting her face on the ceramic floor. Before she knew it, Ares grabbed her by the hair and yanked her to her feet. He turned her around to face him. Serena put her hands on her head, his grip so tight she could feel her scalp burning with pain as a trickle of blood ran down her nose. Ares wiped it off with his thumb, then pushed her back against the wall.

"What do we have here?" Ares said as he looked her over, his eyes studying her nicely shaped legs, hips, her ample breast and then focused on the amulet glowing on her skin. He traced it with a finger and let it slide along her shirt collar sneaking a look down into her shirt. Serena attempted to fight back, punching him in the head, but although her Greek mythology knowledge was flaky at best, she knew he was the god of war.

"Feisty like your mother I see." Ares said as he flicked a finger again, sending invisible shackles to tie those hands behind her back to subdue her. "There, much better." He said as he touched the amulet, watching it flicker under his touch. Curiously, he pulled on it and smiled as it released its electrical current. He yanked it with all his might, nothing.

"Clever little wench." He said impressed. As he studied it, he thought he recognized the craftsmanship: Hephaestus. "So, you truly are powerless." His voice filled with disappointment. He wasn't sure what he had expected but this wasn't it. He had expected at least somewhat of a fight. His eyes lowered to her breasts again, the heat rising in his body as his eyes filled with lust.

"Aphrodite is definitely going to have a fit when she finds out she will be losing her title as the most beautiful woman." He fingered her nipples pinching them under his fingers, finding her scent difficult to resist as he sniffed her hair. Atlanteans had a strong attraction to other Atlanteans, the pheromones oozing out of their pores was simply irresistible to their own kind. Especially one as exquisite as this one. She smelled of sweet vanilla and coconut. Serena struggled against the strange invisible bonds. Everything was bonded except for her head, she waited, watching as he smelled her hair. With all the might she could muster, she head butted him right in his nose. He stepped back as he groaned in pain, then simply chuckled, finding her feistiness simply sexy as hell. He moved closer, pushing his body against hers, pressing his erection against her crotch as he placed a strong hand around her neck to prevent her from trying anything else.

"You are simply divine." He said as he grabbed a strand of her hair, letting it slide between his fingers. Tucking it behind her ear he grabbed at something behind his back, pulling out a dagger. Serena's eyes widened in surprise as he brought the dagger to her throat. She shrieked again, tears rolling down her cheeks.

"No need to fuss, Zeus' blood runs in your veins, it would take much, much more to kill you." He whispered in her face, his breath smelling sweet yet musty. He lowered the dagger, tracing her neck, collar bone, and down to her shirt. He turned the blade to its sharp side and cut the front of her shirt open. With one hand, he untied her bikini from her neck before using the dagger to cut the front and letting it fall to the ground. He moaned with pleasure as her breasts fell free. He encircled them with the tip of his dagger before tracing her abdomen down to her shorts, he cut the string, then the sides and watched them fall to the ground. He then proceeded to do the same with her bikini bottom. He grabbed her by the hair again and dragged her to the living room. Serena glanced at her mother, still lying motionless on the cold floor. Ares shoved Serena on the couch face first and threw his dagger on the coffee table, shattering the plate she had eaten from moments before. She closed her eyes tightly as he untied his pants. At this moment, she felt completely paralyzed and helpless. Her mind scrambled to hold on to something, anything as Ares explored her body and violently began ravaging her. She envisioned herself in a room devoid of any light. It was the dark room of her empty mind. Even though she couldn't explain it, she knew somewhere in there was someone else. She had felt it, his presence growing stronger every day. A small figure appeared in the distance and she walked towards it. He seemed small and so far away, and no matter how fast she tried to get to him, the farther he seemed. She paused a moment, panting for breath. Using all the strength she could muster, she screamed out for help, her vocal cords tearing like claws clawing through thick walls of paper.

CHAPTER 26
TRISTAN

Tristan finally finished cleaning up Duncan's mess. Turns out, Miss Pettigrew decided she wanted to play and while letting Duncan chase her, she managed to make a mess, spilling buckets of food and water everywhere but in the pools. Once everything was put away and he sent Duncan home, Tristan grabbed another set of clothes from his locker. He wasn't going to go check on Serena smelling like dead fish and penguin shit. He pulled on a fresh white tank top and grabbed a water bottle. He unscrewed the cap and gulped it down. Midway through the bottle, he felt her call him, no, a desperate scream for help. He dropped the bottle, which landed and spilled everywhere. He didn't care, he ran like he never had before. He didn't know what was wrong but the emptiness and despair he felt through her mind scared him. He thought of nothing else but to get to her as quickly as possible. Nothing could stop him, not the bystanders watching him run with superhuman speed, nor the beachers staring in disbelief as he plunged into the ocean transforming into his merman form midair. It took him less than five minutes to reach Serena's beach side home. He called upon the powers of the sea with his hands as he walked towards her back patio door, transforming the water into human sized spears at his sides. As he reached the back patio doors, his heart sank as he saw Ares on top of Serena's naked body with his hand holding the back of her hair.

"ARES!" Tristan yelled as he launched his wave made weapons. The water missiles flew past him, shattering the patio glass door into millions of pieces before dissolving. Ares looked up with an evil grin as he lifted Serena's head high enough for Tristan to stare into her terrorized eyes as he dared to finish then pulled out of Serena.

"Son of Poseidon, joining the part-" Ares said sheepishly but Tristan cut him off by waving his hand to summon his celestial golden trident. He pointed it aggressively at Ares sending him flying across the room. Ares hit the wall and collapsed on the floor. Ares stood, dusting himself off with a chuckle. He buttoned his pants back up then flicked his hand, releasing his power on Serena, his eyes never leaving Tristan. It was then he saw the blue glow crawling up Tristan's left arm. He looked at Serena's left arm disdainfully catching a glimpse of the same glow.

"That explains it." Ares said with annoyance as his smile faded. Ares was no fool, staying to fight Triton near his element was foolish. He did not anticipate being interrupted. He had plans to finish what he came for once he took his moment of godly pleasure. But now, there was a bond involved, there was no way he could kill the offspring without starting a full-blown war against Poseidon.

Triton simply stared at him with rage as he lifted his trident again.

"She's all yours. Exquisite if I do say so myself." Ares said provokingly as he waved his hand and disappeared.

"Cursed Atlas!" Tristan shouted in anger as he sent another pointless beam of power. It collided with the wall with an explosive bang.

Serena sat up, placing her trembling hands on her ears to muffle the noise as she cried out. Tristan dropped his trident, making it disappear before it crashed on the floor. He walked to Serena who stood naked and stumbled backwards to get away from him in fear but only to collide with the battered wall behind her.

Tristan stopped himself, a few feet away from her as he saw her standing there, fear in her eyes, naked and broken. His heart felt like he had been stabbed by the very trident he yielded.

"Serena." He called out gently, stepping forward.

"No," She cried out, raising a trembling hand to stop him in his tracks. "Who are you?" She asked with tears rolling down her face. Next to them, Thetis began to stir, waking from her unconscious state.

"You know-" He started to answer.

"No," She cut him off, shaking her head. "No more lies." She cried out.

"I am Triton, son of Poseidon." Triton finally admitted as he lowered his eyes unable to look at hers. Serena's body began to shake violently as she began to sob. She let her body slump to the floor, hugging her legs tightly. Triton grabbed the throw blanket from the sofa wanting to cover up Serena who flinched as he got near her.

"I'm just going to put this on you." Triton said gently. Serena simply nodded.

Thetis moaned in pain, trying to move without great success. Triton saw the pool of blood and knew she was in rough shape. She was immortal in this world, but that didn't mean she couldn't be in pain and take days to recover. He walked over to her battered body, kneeling next to her as he placed a gentle hand on her head. She had a big gash on her head, and from the damage done to the kitchen island, he could only assume she had collided with it. He stood, waved his right hand to summon his conch shell. He closed his eyes, took a deep breath before blowing it. *Hermes, messenger of the gods.* He waved his hand again, making his conch shell disappear. He walked to the kitchen counter and turned on the tap water, leaving it on then he knelt back down next Thetis. He held out his hand towards the tap water and it began to flow towards his hand. As the water reached him, he guided it to Thetis until it touched her head, using it to heal her.

Hermes appeared in the living room.

"Woa! Holy mother of Zeus!" Hermes said as he stepped back, away from the broken glass of the shattered patio door, stepping on a few pieces which crunched under his feet. "You certainly know how to throw a party." Hermes exclaimed taking in the damage around him, his eyes resting on Serena who starred out into space barely glancing at him. "Who do we have here?" He asked curiously as he studied her. Her forehead had a gash, and she was holding onto a blanket for dear life. Her long dark disheveled brown hair hung loosely around her. Her green eyes glazed, her body shaking. Hermes had been around too long not to recognize the signs of trauma. This poor girl was in shock. He looked over at Triton who used all his focus to heal a body lying flat on her back. She was a tall beautiful dark brown-haired woman he clearly recognized.

"Say, would you look at that. You've found them both." Hermes said with obvious surprise.

"Hermes, I need you to find Laka and bring her here." Triton said, slightly annoyed by his chipper attitude with the severity of the situation.

"Just the gorgeous Hawaiian goddess of love? Because I wouldn't mind bringing along that fine specimen of a husband of hers." Hermes said eagerly as he picked up a dagger from the coffee table. He instantly recognized the etching along the handle to be a weapon of the god of war.

"Just Laka Hermes!" Triton barked impatiently.

"Ok man, I got it. No need to bite my head off about it." Hermes said defensively as he flipped the dagger and caught it. Perfect weight, just like you would expect from a weapon of the god of war. Like most Olympians, Hermes was certainly not fond of Ares. He was a dick on a good day, much less on any other occasion.

"Now!" Triton shouted as he waved the water away, finishing the task of healing the queen of the Nereids.

"I'm on it, I'm on it." Hermes replied with a sigh as he hit the ground with his caduceus and disappeared. Triton waited by Thetis' side, but his eyes were locked on Serena who stared blankly at him. Her eyes were dry now, but her body still shook.

Thetis moaned as she opened her eyes slowly, expecting everything to hurt but pleasantly surprised when nothing did. She turned and saw Triton, taking a mere second to register and remember what had happened.

"Serena!" Thetis cried out in fear as she sat up suddenly. Triton might have done an amazing job with his healing, but her head still spun, and she stumbled as she stood, using the edge of the counter to steady herself.

"Be careful." Triton said, but his warning fell on deaf ears. Thetis stumbled to her daughter, sitting down next to her, leaning on the wall to support herself. Serena stared into space, her face blank and her eyes bright red from the tears. Thetis reached out to stroke her daughter's hair, but she flinched, looking at her mother as if looking at a stranger.

"Serena, sweety?" Thetis said gently in a soothing motherly way.

"What...how...you..." Serena mumbled looking dazed. Triton closed his eyes, and with a deep breath he tried to focus on Serena, but her mind felt like a dark empty room. It was as if she had withdrawn into the depths of her mind, unable to cope with what was happening. Triton stood, walked over to Thetis, and took her by the arm gently, helping her up to her feet away from Serena.

"Queen of the Nereids," Triton spoke to Thetis who did not respond.

"Thetis," he said gently, turning her to face him.

"I know this may sound strange, but Serena is not here right now." Triton explained glumly, trying to hide his growing concern. Hermes appeared at that moment with Laka at his side.

"I don't know what you mean, she's right there." Thetis replied in dismay, tears filling her bright blue ocean eyes as she motioned to her daughter. Laka walked by Triton, nodding at him, her eyes filled with empathy and went straight to Serena. As she knelt by her side, she placed a glowing hand pulsating with her divine power on Serena's head.

"I'm afraid you are right Pu'ole." Laka said as she stroked Serena's hair before standing again. "We must take her to Kahuna Pahia in Maui." She instructed.

"I do not think having a male Greek god around her is going to do her any good." Thetis protested. Triton and Laka glared at her, both understanding that Serena would be in a far better state if it wasn't for her mother.

"You are wrong, Queen of the Nereids. Triton is the *only* one who can bring her back." Laka said as she placed a loving hand on her friend's arm, giving it a warm squeeze to convey his importance in this situation. Triton nodded, not too sure what she meant, but knowing he had to get her out of there. Triton and Laka both looked at Hermes who stood back quietly leaning against the crumbling kitchen island.

"Oh, were you talking to me?" Hermes asked as he stood feeling the eyes on him. Triton glared at him. "Alright man," He said as he walked up to them, his eyes studying Serena's predicament. His brows furrowed, breaking his cheerfulness. He didn't know the girl, but she looked pitiful. He flicked his fingers. Serena went from being naked and covered by a blanket, to wearing a comfortable pair of jean shorts, white bikini top covered by a grey crochet net sweater, a pair of white sneakers and her hair neatly double braided. Everyone stared at him.

"What?" Hermes asked dubiously. "You weren't planning on taking her anywhere looking like she'd been attacked by the souls in the river Styx, were you?" He asked with annoyance.

Triton tightened his jaw, hating that Hermes was right and more thoughtful than he gave him credit for. Of course, he didn't know him at all.

"Thank you for your thoughtfulness." Laka replied with a warm smile.

"See how easy it is to be nice, man?" Hermes asked with a scolding glare at Triton who rolled his eyes.

Triton walked past him, slipped an arm under Serena's knees and picked her up in his arms. He wasn't sure if Serena was going to protest, but she simply buried her head in his chest and closed her eyes.

Hermes took Tristan's arm, slammed his caduceus on the ground and they disappeared leaving Thetis behind.

CHAPTER 27
SERENA

Serena opened her eyes slowly. Her whole body felt light as a feather, as if she were floating on a cloud. A sense of peace filled her and her mind felt quiet and empty making her wonder if perhaps she had died. She wiggled her toes, then her fingers. Her eyes blinked, adjusting to her surroundings. The sky above was a perfect blue with a few white fluffy clouds floating about and the sun shined brightly. She heard some noise bringing her to focus. It buzzed in her ears and she realized they were the sounds of insects. She looked around, moving her head slowly, she was laying a field of tall soft grass and some sort of purple flowers. She inhaled the sweet scent and recognized it as the soothing scent of lavender. She sat up slowly, still unable to see past the flowers. Taking the time to notice how she felt, she wondered where she was. This certainly wasn't Hawaii, neither did it feel like a dream. She stood slowly and her eyes widened in amazement at the beauty of her surroundings. Butterflies fluttered through the fields. In the distance, beautiful snow capped mountains decorated the landscape. Never ending hills laid before her eyes and she spotted a beautiful bubbling stream ahead. She began to walk towards it slowly, enjoying the refreshing peacefulness settling into her being. It was unlike anything she had felt before. A bliss she couldn't put into words. Birds chirped around her and she noticed the green forest beyond the stream. As she reached the clear stream, she knelt down to touch it's welcoming freshness.

"I wouldn't do that if I were you." A soft strong voice said thoughtfully. He studied her as she stood, her long dark brown curly hair flowing with the soft breeze and her white satin dress adorned with a golden girdle. As she looked at him questionably, her green eyes sparkled a strange familiar golden color he had seen before. They were filled with endless curiosity as she studied him through long dark lashes. "Not unless you're planning on making your visit more of a...permanent nature." He explained before she had a chance to ask.

Serena studied the man standing in front of her. He stood tall with a strong muscular body hiding beneath a black, neatly pressed dress shirt with the top buttons undone. He had a square set jaw underlying strong yet kind features outlined by a very short black stubble beard and piercing brown eyes. He had dark brown, almost black slicked back hair. His hands were tucked into the pockets of his high quality black dress pants. She had no idea where or who he was, but there was something comforting about his cheeky smile. There was so much Serena wanted to ask, but she couldn't seem to form any words. Who was this man?

He stepped forward, closing the distance between them as he studied her intently, his eyes resting on the pendant around her beautiful long neck. He recognized the pattern of the wire wrapped amulet. It was the symbol of the Queen of the Nereids. He could clearly see the resemblance and there was no doubt in his mind the woman was no other than Thetis' daughter. He could smell the scent of her powers pulsating around her, mixed in with two other strong life forces he clearly recognized as his nephew Apollo and his niece Artemis.

"Where am I?" Serena finally managed to ask, her eyes scanning her surroundings in amazement.

"Elysium." He answered simply. "I'm curious, it is my job to know all the souls that come through here, but I don't seem to know you?" He asked deeply intrigued, fishing for information. He pushed at the corners of her mind, but the pure raw power she held wouldn't let him in. He could normally see into a person's soul but this one was a mystery. She couldn't be human. No human had that power. Yet the look on her face indicated she had no idea who he was or where Elysium was.

Serena's brows furrowed deeply as she pondered his answer and question. She had never heard of Elysium before, was it a country or city she had never heard of? And what did he mean by souls? His question strangely tugged at her, although she didn't know the answer she felt compelled to come up with one.

"I'm Serena." She answered, unable to resist the pull she felt from him as she glanced at him with a questioning, confused look.

"Welcome Serena, I'm Hades." He introduced himself as he held a friendly hand to greet her. She took his hand tentatively. He grasped it with both hands and held it. His touch was warm, gentle and welcoming but there was something dark behind his eyes and she couldn't decide if she should be afraid.

"Thank you." Serena answered hesitantly. She had so many questions burning in the back of her mind, but they seemed to vanish before she could ask them.

"Feel free to roam about. But, stay away from the waters. You...are not ready to touch it yet." Hades explained kindly as he hesitated on the ready part. Serena frowned, confusion running through her, but she turned away and decided to explore this 'Elysium'.

CHAPTER 28
HADES

Hades narrowed his eyes as he studied Serena and watched her walk away. Then with a snap of his fingers Hermes appeared next to him.

"Explain to me how I have an unknown, alive guest in my midst." Hades demanded firmly his gaze still on the beautiful woman walking in the distance. Hermes followed his gaze, his features softening at the sight of Serena.

"Serena. Daughter of Thetis." Hermes answered after a moment of silence. Hades turned and arched an eyebrow as he stared at Hermes. "And Zeus." Hermes said, answering Hades' questioning glare.

"Hermes, Zeus banished the Queen of the Nereids centuries ago. What am I missing?" Hades asked his tone condescending as frustration crept in.

"I may have *forgotten* to mention that the Queen may have proven more cunning than he expected." Hermes said with unease. Last thing he wanted to do was piss off the ruler of the underworld. Hades tightened his face as his anger began to surface.

"Hermes, did we not have an agreement? You keep me informed on what my brother is up to, and I let you roam around here as you wish?" Hades asked calmly. Hermes hated how Hades remained calm and collected when he was angry. It made it hard to prepare for his outburst. But then again, that was Hades. Unlike Zeus, he rarely lost his temper. But it only made his punishments that much more effective.

"There really wasn't much to tell until now. Everyone was looking for this offspring and someone who shouldn't have found her did." Hermes explained nervously.

"Let me get this straight: there was an offspring on the loose capable of destroying my brother and that wasn't much to tell?" Hades asked his tone a little more aggravated now. A smirk crossed his face as a mental image of queen Hera discovering that her plans to squash any future bastard child of Zeus who would overthrow her went flying out the cosmos. "Can't believe I missed the look on the Olympian's face the day they found out." Hades contemplated out loud. Many thought that Hades had gotten shafted when he was given the underworld to rule, but really, he had his own kingdom with no outside forces to worry about. He enjoyed sitting back and watching the others scramble like a bunch of undead without a master to protect their way of life.

"It was quite entertaining to say the least. I thought Hera was going to blow her own head off her body." Hermes said and they both chuckled.

"Who found her that shouldn't of?" Hades asked curiously. Hermes pulled out a dagger and handed it to Hades who took it to examine it. It took him a mere second to know exactly who it belonged to. It stunk of Ares' power.

"Ares." Hades mumbled disdainfully. No one liked the god of war, and Hades was no different. He was definitely not the smartest one of the bunch, but Hades had to admit he had the guts to get things done when no one else did.

"Let me guess, he wanted to have his fun." Hades said with disgust as his eyes drifted to Serena in the distance. He felt something traumatic in the back of her mind, but he couldn't access it. He hadn't been able to search her soul because she wasn't a soul.

"The Queen of the Nereids, she raised her daughter without any knowledge of her heritage." Hades said making his own assumptions with what he could deduce from his encounter.

"Hermes, how is my newfound niece not aware of how powerful she is?" Hades asked with great concern and consideration.

"Seems like the Queen of the Nereids had some help, an amulet made to hold her powers until she becomes of age." Hermes explained with the little bit of information he had, and it wasn't much to go on. Hermes studied Serena's figure, she looked different. Serena glanced in his direction, as if sensing she was being watched. Her sparkling golden eyes looked right at him.

"She looks different." Hermes thought out loud.

"You said the amulet imprisoned her powers, perhaps it also serves to hide her true divine form." Hades stated. He felt the amulet's power, it was something to behold. That much power had to affect her somehow even physically. Humans would not know what to make of her in this form. Her beauty was beyond anything he had ever seen, putting Aphrodite's looks to shame.

"Is it possible she unknowingly split her divine form here and left her human one in the earth realm?" Hermes asked pensively.

"Perhaps I should visit the earth realm and see this hypothesis myself." Hades said with amusement. He visited the realm rarely, and only did so during the six months Persephone was visiting with her mother Demeter. He had to get his rocks off somewhere. But Persephone was in the underworld and they had a bargain, he never left when she was there.

"Not sure what the Queen was thinking when she imprisoned her own daughter's powers." Hermes answered with a disturbed frown. He couldn't understand what possessed the Queen to deprive her own daughter of her own essence.

"For protection, no doubt. The Queen will do anything to protect her children." Hades said with admiration. She had come to the underworld, bargained with the fates, and even faced the river Styx and more. Hades knew she would give her own life for them.

"I suppose you of all people would know that." Hermes chuckled knowing Hades had been subjected to the Queen's relentless efforts for her children like Achilles. She had managed to secure his invincibility, granted, someone still managed to find his weak spot and kill him.

180

"She has no idea who she is, yet in an obviously traumatic situation she managed to use her divine powers to split a part of herself here to find refuge for her damaged soul." Hades concluded.

"Well, that would certainly explain the state of the other part of her in the human realm." Hermes agreed with surprise. He didn't know Serena, but he couldn't help but admire the obvious power she held to be able to accomplish such a feat without even realizing what she was doing.

"Zeus will not take Ares' actions lightly. It sounds like I will soon have an Olympian to torture to my liking." Hades said with an evil smile of amusement crossing his features as he handed the dagger back to Hermes.

"If you're planning on telling Zeus that is." He added with a questioning frown before Hermes took the dagger back.

"And miss my chance to give you such a present?" Hermes said with a chuckle. They both caught a glimpse of Serena in the distance and Hades' face darkened. Contrary to popular beliefs, Hades took his role as ruler of the underworld extremely seriously. He was a kind ruler, not the grim reaper the myths portrayed him to be, even though he never fought to change the rumors. He needed people to believe it, to fear him. It was part of keeping the balance of things. Although justice changed over the centuries, it still needed to be dealt with. Hades was very honorable, and the truth was Hermes enjoyed his rule better than Zeus, which is why he had eventually decided to be a part of Hades' kingdom rather than reside under Zeus' rule in Atlantis. Hades was fair, taking great care of the souls coming through the underworld. It was that concern for the souls he saw in his eyes as he watched Serena.

Hades was the only god who respected the fates, knowing too well defying them would bring some dire consequences. He lived by a better code than the rest of Atlanteans, never forgetting what brought the downfall of their father Cronus to begin with and that they had been created as guardians of life in the universe. He never agreed with the decision his brother took to banish the Queen of the Nereids which is the real reason why he stepped out of the Olympian council. He wanted to make sure the fates knew he wanted no part of their decision nor the consequences that would follow.

"If she has no idea of her powers, then being split is going to be a problem." Hades stated with concern.

"I heard a daughter of Aphrodite speak of a bond that was created between your niece and Triton." Hermes said.

"A bond with a son of Poseidon?" Hades asked with gleeful surprise, a smirk crossing his face.

"A bond woven by the fates." Hermes explained. He loved seeing the amusement in Hades' eyes. Hades chuckled then. Ah the fates! They could be ruthless to punish those who defied them. Bonding a daughter of Zeus with a son of Poseidon was the ultimate punishment considering Zeus was the King and Poseidon his right hand. Binding a powerful son of Poseidon with the most powerful offspring of Zeus, what sweet justice indeed.

CHAPTER 29
TRITON

They arrived at the upcountry slopes of Maui's pristine Mount Haleakala, where the beautiful and serene grounds of the Lehua cottages nested comfortably surrounded by the Makawao Forest reserves. The tropical style cottages were set amidst two acres of aromatherapy herbal gardens, tropical fruit trees such as guava, papaya, bananas, avocados, and native tropical flora. They had appeared on the lanai leading to what looked like the main cottage. The door opened before they even had the chance to reach it. In the doorway stood a tall woman with long black hair adorned with a hawaiian tropical crown. She wore a green strapless wrap around dress with a white plumeria flower lei around her neck. She reminded Triton of Laka in the kindness resonating through her smile. Kahuna Pahia was a priestess of Laka in some form or another, a devoted native hawaiian to her people and her way of life. She was a healer of souls and a demi-god, daughter of Lono. Laka gave him a smile as she put a hand on his arm, signaling him to stay back. Triton nodded in understanding and waited patiently. Laka went to greet Kahuna Pahia, embracing her with the Hawaiian greeting, forehead to forehead. Laka placed a gentle kiss on Kahuna Pahia's forehead. They spoke quietly as they threw a few glances their way. Laka was probably explaining the circumstances as a frown of empathy crossed Kahuna Pahia's face before she waved them over.

Triton joined them and the Kahuna touched Serena's sleeping head gently, her eyes narrowingly studying her.

"Come." The Kahuna said with a motion for them to follow. She took them down a path crossing beautiful blooming gardens, the sweet scent of jasmine and plumerias filling their noses. They finally reached a smaller cottage tucked behind the heavenly gardens with a distant view of the ocean. She opened the door and motioned for Triton to enter. He followed behind her as she guided him to a separate bedroom with a cozy queen size bed. The Kahuna flipped the blankets and moved back. Triton laid Serena down gently, carefully covering her. He tucked a loose strand of hair behind her ear, she looked serene again and he wished he could wipe the sheer look of horror he had seen on her face that had burned into his mind. He expected the reality would be difficult to understand, but he did not account for Ares fucking things up more.

"Come Pu'ole," The Kahuna said as she took his arm. "We must prepare a cleansing ceremony." She persisted as she could clearly see Triton's reluctance to leave Serena's side, but he followed. They went through the gardens again but this time Laka set herself to work picking some fresh herbs while the Kahuna grabbed some drying herbs on a line she had hung nearby. Triton knew nothing about herbal medicine and such. Growing up underwater left him attune to water healing and using mostly seaweeds and underwater plants, but he followed her. He admired herbal healing, after all, the gods had put everything the humans needed at their disposal. Albeit they were destroying those very tools. He picked and sniffed some herbs, some smelled delicious while others were very pungent. Laka picked up some lemongrass and sweet basil, her eyes never leaving her concerned friend.

"What are you afraid of Pu'ole?" Laka asked, studying his tense features. She knew Triton too well. He remained quietly pensive as he continued eyeing and touching the plants as a distraction to the question. Laka grabbed his arm and turned him to face her.

"You are afraid of what you feel here," She said as she touched his chest. "Is a product of the bond. It is the opposite Pu'ole." She said gently, turning his face to look him straight in the eyes. Things had been distant between them since he had confronted her and Lono, but she cared for Triton like a brother. "Your love for Serena is real."

Triton closed his eyes. *Damn goddess of love!* He cursed silently. She knew how to read people, it was part of her gift, especially reading love. He had in fact begrudged this cursed bond because of how he felt, terrified it was only a byproduct of the bond.

"Laka-" Triton tried to say.

"You do not understand that my bond was only going to work if love was involved. I could not do otherwise." Laka explained, her eyes pleading for him to understand. He nodded simply, unable to bring himself to say anything.

"How did you know?" Triton asked curiously. Laka and Lono did not have the gift of prophecy and did not have access to the oracles. The only way they would have known is if someone told them.

"*In the depth of the deep blue sea,*" Laka began to recite the words of the prophecy.

"*The son of its king shall set her free.* I am well aware of this prophecy Laka." Triton said pensively. Those words had been thrown at him more than once.

"But you have not heard it in its entirety Pu'ole." Laka said with a smile.

"Oh?" Triton replied with a curious frown.

"*The sun shall shine on the divine. On her thirtieth flower moon she shall fully bloom. From the depth of the deep blue sea, the son of its king shall set her free. Ye the daughter of the mighty king of the sky, with the son of Poseidon her fate shall we tie. A love stronger than a bond of power, will remain unbreakable and shall be even mightier. Together they shall restore the gods to their humanity, for in her we have woven pure serenity.*" Laka recited with her eyes closed. She inhaled slowly as if letting the words sink in for the hundredth time. And so, she should. Prophecies were often difficult to decipher, but this one was clear enough once heard in its entirety.

"We were wrong, Triton." Laka said apologetically.

"Wrong about what exactly?" Triton asked, uncertain what she was referring to.

"Lono and I believed that you would set her powers free and push you to do something you were not willing to do." Laka answered as she opened her eyes slowly to lock with her dear friend. It was hard not to see and hear the sincerity of her words. Triton frowned deeply, thinking about each word she had recited. It was not like Atlanteans to apologize, and it was as good as he would get.

"You think the prophecy refers to her now and the state she is in?" Triton asked rhetorically. Laka simply nodded. "The flower moon..." He said trailing off.

"Is in a few days." Laka finished for him. "We have work to do." She said as she slapped his arm in a friendly gesture. She finished collecting some herbs and Triton followed quietly as they made their way to a clearing. There was a fire pit there, and Kahuna Pahia stood looking at the skies darkening signaling the rainfall approaching.

"We will have to do the ceremony inside; the rain will be here for some time." The Kahuna said as she turned to face them, then was on her way. She guided them back to the main cottage and opened the sliding doors revealing a big enough space. Zafu meditation cushions placed neatly in a circle around a metal bucket in the center of the room. Triton watched as the women busied themselves setting up candles around the room and placing methodically some herbs in the bucket. Kahuna Pahia was in and out, bringing in food and water bottles, placing them near the circle.

"This ceremony is going to be lengthy; you will need all your godly strength." Kahuna Pahia said with a gentle smile as she noticed Triton's quizzical frown. Laka pulled out a golden flask with a Greek symbol and she handed it to Triton.

"Ambrosia." Laka said. "Better be prepared." She smiled. Triton wondered where she would get the sweet nectar of the gods from, but one thing he knew for sure; Laka was very resourceful. Triton's face changed; his eyes unfocused as if traveling to a distant place.

"Serena?" Laka asked solemnly. Triton closed his eyes, the lack of emotions and feelings he couldn't sense from Serena was overwhelming. It took all his self-control to not run to her and take her in his arms. He tried to focus on her to feel what she needed, but the bond was still clouded with the amulet still at work.

"Bring this to the goddess." Kahuna Pahia said as she handed Triton a tray of fruits, cheeses, and some bread. "Bring her when she's ready." She said with an understanding smile. He nodded as he took the tray and made his way to Serena's cottage.

CHAPTER 30
SERENA

Serena opened her eyes and had to blink a few times before her surroundings became clearer. She lay in a cozy country style decorated room with a huge window with what seemed like a great outside view. Her head pounded with incredible fury and she rubbed her temples as she sat up slowly. She walked to the window, squinting from the light even though it was gloomy and rainy outside. The view was stunning. Gardens filled with tropical fruit trees and flowers and beautiful towering hawaiian mountains in the background. She wondered where she was. Everything was slightly fuzzy. She tried to focus on what she remembered last; Ailani was there with her mother, yes, she had appeared out of nowhere with a hot looking guy. How was this all possible? She spotted Tristan coming down the path with a tray of food. He looked devilishly handsome with his blue denim jeans and white t-shirt. She frowned angrily as she looked at him, not believing she still couldn't help her attraction to him. How was she supposed to remember that he was actually Triton? She shamefully didn't know much about Greek Mythology. Did it explain her irresistible attraction to him? Did he hold some sort of mesmerizing power over her? She knew Poseidon was the king of the oceans or something of the sort. The door of the cottage opened, and Serena sighed heavily before she set out to meet him. Triton seemed surprised when she joined him in the living room.

"I... brought you something to eat." Triton said hesitantly, unable to look her in the eye.

"Seems to me there's enough there for the two of us." Serena said sharply as she sat on a chair looking at the layout of food. Her stomach growled loud enough for Triton to hear as she studied the food when the heavy aroma's hit her nose. Triton didn't move.

"You can sit, you know, I don't typically bite." Serena said dryly. Triton sat across from her but didn't touch the food.

"So, you are Triton." Serena said as she stuffed a piece of deliciously fresh mango into her mouth.

"Yes." Triton answered as he leaned his elbows on his blue denim jeans.

"Triton. Like in the little mermaid movie, with Ariel?" Serena asked curiously. Of course, that was a fictional Disney movie, but her reality had just been shattered and she couldn't tell what was real or not anymore.

"Not quite." Triton said with a chuckle unable to help himself.

Serena studied Triton, his deep brown eyes avoiding hers uncomfortably. There was something irritating about his answer to the reference she made to Disney. It was too vague even though it had been meant as a joke more than anything else.

She felt he was keeping something from her. It was then she realized where she had seen those deep brown familiar eyes of a certain redhead. Arianna had always avoided or changed the subject when she tried to get her to give her the name of her father who she said worked at the Marina.

"She's your daughter." Serena muttered out loud as the realization struck her. Triton looked at her then, a frown crossing his face.

"What?" Triton asked, unsure what she was referring to. Her thoughts were unclear and confusing.

"Arianna is your daughter." Serena said her eyes glaring at Triton who seemed confused by what she was saying.

"I don't have a daughter named Arianna, Serena." Triton answered deflecting and Serena knew it.

"A feisty red head with a great sense of adventure who is extremely curious about humans and apparently about me. She appeared out of nowhere and said she followed her father here." Serena said sharply, annoyed that he was avoiding answering her questions. Triton clenched his jaw, realizing who Serena was talking about.

"Don't tell me her name is actually Ariel?" Serena asked with surprise, the look on his face was enough to give her an answer.

"Unfortunately, it seems Disney profited from my daughter's unfortunate sense of adventure and her name is the only true fact in any of that rubbish." Triton finally said with obvious resentment, not really feeling the need to discuss this topic. It was a sore subject for him. What he had to do to get his daughter out of that Danish author's grasp was not something he liked to reminisce about. He couldn't believe she had bluntly disobeyed again and managed to escape his guards' grasp to follow him here. He should have known she wouldn't be able to stay away especially if he was here. Serena felt her face drain of color and her stomach churned at his words.

"Triton, please tell me you're not actually married?" Serena said as she swallowed hard. Not that it would surprise her to say the least, Triton was thousands of years old, and she couldn't expect him to remain single all that time, but the thought of him being married to someone else simply made her feel sick to her stomach. She almost had sex with him.

"No." Triton answered plainly, avoiding adding any details to Serena's frustration. It was always short and evasive answers that drove her nuts. "But you can't expect me to have lived this long without-"

"No. I don't." Serena cut him off sharply before he had a chance to finish. The fact was she was relieved just to know he wasn't. But she wasn't foolish enough to think that a Greek god of all people did not have sex for thousands of years. There was still something disconcerting about the fact he had been with thousands of women and she didn't want to think about that.

"So, you're a..." Serena trailed off wanting to change the obvious uncomfortable subject. She couldn't seem to remember what they called a male version of a mermaid.

"Merman. I can be if I choose too." Triton answered, holding his hands nervously. This was a strangely uncomfortable conversation. Serena laughed and choked on a piece of pineapple. She took a sip of water.

"It's funny is it?" Triton asked. It was great to see her laugh, but he wished he could get rid of this uneasy feeling in the pit of his stomach like there was something off about Serena.

"Well, it's kind of ironic that a *merman* was teaching me how to scuba dive." Serena said, the term still strange on her tongue.

"I needed something to do in this realm and since I love being underwater, it seemed a logical choice." Triton explained as he grabbed a piece of bread.

Serena frowned and bit her lower lip. Realm? It was going to take her time to digest, and research all this.

"There is alot Serena, which is why I didn't want you to be thrown into this all at once." Triton answered, staring at the piece of bread in his hand. He looked up as he sensed emotions rising, albeit anger, at least he was finally feeling *something* coming from her.

"Maybe you can start by explaining how you do that?" Serena snapped as she grabbed a piece of bread and stood to look out the window.

"That is complicated." Triton said with a sigh as he took a bite of his bread. Serena chuckled sarcastically.

"That is complicated?" Serena repeated sarcastically with a chuckle. "How is any of this not fucked up?" She asked, glaring at him furiously.

"Serena-" Triton said as he stood.

"Don't you dare Serena me!" Serena shouted motioning him to stay where he was. He moved to close the distance but she backed away from him. She hit the wall and he stopped a few inches away from her, leaning one hand above her head.

"Don't you understand I could have taken you any time I wanted? The torment was real for me too, Serena." Triton said sharply, trying to stay calm. He knew her anger was misguided, but none of this was his own doing and she was hitting every chord.

"So, you are no better than Ares then? You just use your merman powers to-"

"Do not compare me to that piece of shit Olympian." Triton sneered now fighting to control his hot temper itching to come out. "And even less to a wretched siren." There was no greater insult than the two things she had just accused him of. Serena flinched from his tone, realizing she had just crossed a line she didn't understand. She looked into his eyes then, his face so close and the heat growing between them.

"Then please," Serena pleaded. "Tell me why after... what happened all I want to do is fuck you." She asked, begging for nothing less than understanding. She had gotten savagely raped, and her mind couldn't comprehend why in the midst of it all, she still wanted Triton. Triton's eyes soften now, forgetting why he was angry with that pitiful look in her eyes. Her words stung as it was out of character for her. But her human way of thinking couldn't grasp the Atlantean desires nor the bond power that was pulling her to do something that just didn't make sense.

"The only way I can explain this," Triton said gently as he touched the side of her face. "Is that fate has bound us together, magically binding our minds and souls. The day we first met, that spark you felt, was the bond." He explained.

"You... felt that?" Serena said with surprise.

"I have, and everything in there," Triton answered, touching her chest. "And here." He touched her head with his fingers. "Ever since then."

Serena frowned, it explained quite a few things. That presence she couldn't explain and what she had felt in the back of her mind. Feelings, emotions, and thoughts sometimes came out of seemingly nowhere. *So, you can read my mind?* Serena thought.

"Yes." Triton answered with a smirk.

"But I can't read yours." Serena stated. She sensed things but not like what Triton had just demonstrated.

"Oh, but you have." Triton replied with a chuckle. "You just didn't realize it."

"So, we are bonded together, mind and soul...?" Serena repeated trying to make sense of it. But like everything else, she couldn't wrap her head around it. Triton nodded.

"The bond is meant to bind mind, body and soul. It will only continue to pull stronger until the bond is complete." Triton watched as Serena's eyes widened with understanding.

"I see." She said, closing her eyes trying to ease her thumping heart back into her chest. She took a deep breath and opened her eyes again. "So, I've been tormenting you as much as you've been tormenting me?"

"You have no fucking idea." Triton said exasperated. He found that word offensive but couldn't find any better word for it. Serena bit her lower lip as her fingers trailed his collar bone. Triton's suspicions were confirmed when his closeness failed to weaken her amulet. Her goddess form seemed to be gone however the pull of the bond has increased to an irresistible level. What else could explain her lust?

"Serena, please..." Triton begged for her to stop, afraid now more than ever he wouldn't be able to stop himself. But she pushed on relentlessly, kissing his ear, his neck and then tasting his lips. Triton grunted in frustration, he felt Serena was using this to distract herself. He feared the bond would take over and he would lose all self-control he possessed. She had just gone through a traumatic event. He wanted to respect her and give her the time she needed to heal. Serena could sense Triton struggling to let go, the conflict in his eyes was obvious. Everything in her body told her she needed to be close to him. Like destiny needed her to be one with Triton to make her whole. She needed to find a way to let him know he would not hurt her with his touch. She touched the side of his face, pulling his head closer to look straight into his eyes, then leaned her forehead to touch his in the Hawaiian embrace.

"Triton, I *need* you to trust me as I have trusted you so far." Serena said softly as she took his hand, locking her fingers with his. She squeezed it reassuringly before she guided his hand to her breast. She felt the heat rise in his hand as he cupped her gently. He closed his eyes and nested his head on her shoulder. Intoxicated by the smell of vanilla and coconut from her hair, he allowed himself to accept her invitation then began kissing her passionately. He cupped the back of her head, pulling her in closer as he knitted his fingers through her hair.

Serena eagerly responded by grabbing the waist of his jeans to unbutton them then she pulled his zipper down to free his impressive hard on. She slid her hands under his jeans grasping his Greek god tight ass then pushed his pants to the floor. She slipped her hands under his white t-shirt, feeling the smoothness of the sculpted muscles of his back as he kissed her neck passionately. A moan escaped her mouth as she pulled his shirt off. Triton stopped kissing her long enough to let her take it off. He kicked his jeans free from his feet. She began to take her own shorts and bikini bottoms off. What was she really doing? It actually didn't matter. Serena let go.

Triton pulled her shirt off and untied her bikini top off, freeing those beautiful breasts of hers. With his hands on her thighs, he lifted her up and pushed her back against the wall ready to take all of her.

Hermes cleared his throat loudly. Triton and Serena froze.

Triton knowingly clenched his jaw and wrapped his arms around Serena. Breathing heavily, Serena leaned her forehead against Triton's as they both fought to catch their breath.

"Hey love." Hermes said winking at Serena with a charming smile avoiding Triton's unimpressed stern expression but still getting a glimpse of his impressive naked body. "Hello to you too." Hermes said, staring down at Triton.

"Knocking would have been nice since you weren't summoned." Triton growled.

"Knocking on a door? Come on, that would take away from the drama my friend." Hermes answered with grand exaggeration, seemingly not affected by Triton's obvious annoyance. Triton's lips thinned as he closed his eyes, taking a deep breath to calm himself then released Serena from his protective grasp. He stood motionless, wanting to shield Serena as she scrambled to grab her clothing to dress herself. She grabbed Triton's jeans and handed them to him with a forceful smile and bright red cheeks. He touched her cheek and kissed her gently before slipping into his jeans and turning to face their uninvited guest, only to find he wasn't alone. Standing quietly next to him, arms crossed and obviously amused by the smirk on his face, was Hephaestus. Serena remained behind the protection of Triton's thick frame. Hephaestus stared at the figure taking shelter behind Triton. The fear in her eyes was unmistakable.

"You have nothing to fear." Hephaestus said, his voice as deep and impressive as the rest of him. Yet, he did his best to smile and look reassuring. There was something familiar in his voice, in his strong presence. He was dressed in khaki shorts and a red t-shirt which seemed to almost burst at the seams trying to support his sheer size. His long dark beard was neatly trimmed but still thick and hanging down to his chest. His warm piercing blue eyes warmed her as he attempted to ease her mind. Serena's whole demeanor relaxed as she stepped around Triton, finally recognizing the visitor.

"Uncle Hephee?" Serena asked in disbelief. Hephaestus grinned, showing a nice white friendly smile.

"Ah! You do remember me my dear!" Hephaestus said with a large grin as he opened his arms for a warm embrace.

"Of course, it's just been more than twenty-years!" Serena said as he crushed her with his warm embrace. She remembered the bear of an uncle visiting often when she was little and was relieved to feel the same safety as he took her in his arms. She had fond memories of the toy robots he always brought her that she treasured. He was very loving and always loved to play with her as a little girl. As much as she fought to keep it together, she buried her head in his chest and cried. There was something so soothing about his familiar embrace that drew out all the emotions she had shoved into a dark place.

"There, there." Hephaestus said gently as he patted her head with his big hand while glaring at Triton threateningly.

"Uncle Hephee?" Hermes mouth silently at Triton who looked even more surprised. This was a Hephaestus that neither of them could have envisioned.

"Are you a... god?" Serena asked hesitantly as Hephaestus wiped the tears with his big thumbs from her face.

"Yes. I am Hephaestus, god of fire." Hephaestus answered with a smile but glaring yet again at Triton. "I know this will be very confusing my dear but believe your mother did everything she could to keep you safe. Olympians are unfortunately relentless when threatened. Trust me, I would know." He said motioning to his golden leg. Serena eyed it then looked at him.

"A threat? I don't understand how I can be a threat to anyone." Serena said as she backed away.

"You are an especially important piece of a puzzle they have tried to burn for centuries. The fates do not appreciate being defied and they will pay for what they've done." Hephaestus said with a weak smile. He opened the flap of his satchel and pulled out something carefully wrapped in cotton. "I brought you something that will help you when the time comes." He said as he handed it to her. Serena studied it, not sure if she should open it. It was heavy enough.

"Now come, let's go for a little walk through those beautiful gardens I see out there." Hephaestus said as he opened the door and motioned Serena to go ahead. Serena followed quietly with Hephaestus shutting the door behind him.

Chapter 31
Triton

Triton and Hermes waited until Hephaestus and Serena were safely out of earshot before Hermes turned to Triton.

"We have to talk, my man." Hermes said to Triton, the look on his face more serious.

"Do we now?" Triton asked curiously as he moved to the window to keep an eye out for Serena.

"I got summoned by Hades." Hermes mustered gravely. Triton turned to look at him. "Imagine his surprise when he found a goddess named Serena walking around in his fields of Elysium." Hermes studied Triton, who barely flinched at his statement. Hermes figured Triton would kill it at poker with his unreadable expression. Perhaps he would ask him for a game sometime.

"How is that even possible?" Triton asked with disbelief. "She doesn't have any of her powers."

"You are in a better position to answer that question, you know more than I do." Hermes replied, rubbing his chin as he thought. "She did look much different though."

"What do you mean she looked *different?*" Triton gritted out.

"Her hair was shinier, beautifully curled, her features and her eyes…" Hermes said distantly as he remembered the divine looking woman walking the Elysium fields.

"Sparkling gold?" Triton barked, waking Hermes from a reverie that made him uncomfortable.

"Uh...behind those divine green eyes, yes!" Hermes exclaimed. "Deserving of Zeus' name, I'd say."

"Her divine form..." Triton said as he rubbed the back of his neck, his eyes falling again on Serena.

"That is what Hades suspected." Hermes confirmed as he joined him and followed his gaze. "Uncle Hephee. Oh, the irony!" He said with a chuckle.

"I just don't understand how." Triton mumbled, trying to come up with a reasonable explanation.

"Yeah, me either. Never thought I'd see the day when the great Hephaestus was reduced to *uncle Hephee*." Hermes said amused. Triton glared at him. "Oh, that." Hermes said after clearing his throat. "Hades said her soul desperately needed healing and it sought out the one place it could heal. Obviously, Zeus will have something to be proud of." He said impressed by the newly discovered goddess. She was the most beautiful creature to ever exist, and she was clearly the most powerful.

"Or to fear." Triton gritted with a deep frown of concern.

"Don't be afraid my man," Hermes reassured, giving him a friendly pat on the shoulder, rewarding him with another glare from Triton. "Zeus is not Cronus. He won't stoop to his father's level."

"I wish I had your vote of confidence, Hermes. And maybe I would have believed you centuries ago, but Zeus has been in power for so long, I'm simply not sure what he will do." Triton said with worry as his brows furrowed deeper.

"Have faith in the fates my friend, that is the only thing you can do." Hermes said in an attempt to reassure Triton.

"What about Hades, can I trust she is safe there?" Triton asked as he realized part of Serena was in the underworld. No one really knew Hades that well. He always chose to remain hidden in his obsidian fortress and far away from the drama of the Olympians.

"He's keeping an eye on her, but she's not a soul, she can't remain there too long." Hermes warned. "As I understand, you have a bond to complete." Hermes said with a wink.

"Not that it's any of your business, but we were rudely interrupted." Triton gritted again even though he wanted to ignore Hermes' curious inquiries.

"It's all in the timing my friend." Hermes said with a chuckle.

CHAPTER 32
SERENA

Serena remained quiet as they strolled down the small, scented path of the gardens. She wasn't sure what to say. It seemed almost everyone in her life had participated in the deception of who she was. Even if her mother had only acted to protect her, deep down she feared her mother had ulterior motives. There had to be a bigger reason she kept something so vital from her.

"You have decided to make this little piece of Elysium your home?" Hephaestus asked. Serena halted at his words; she had heard that name before.

"Elysium?" Serena asked curiously.

"Paradise." Hephaestus answered with a smile.

"Oh, yes. I love it here." Serena replied. If there was something in her life she was sure of, it was she belonged in Hawaii

"I have a forge on these islands. I can visit you more often now that I know where you are." Hephaestus said with anticipation. He had missed his chats with Serena, she was such a smart child and was becoming quite the woman.

"That would be great." Serena said distantly. "How did you and my mother meet?" She asked curiously. She knew Hephaestus was not her mother's brother, maybe he was Zeus'? But she had a feeling uncle Hephee was more than just a distant brother.

"I was thrown out of Olympus, abandoned and left to die. Thetis, your mother, she found me, nursed me back to health and was more of a mother to me than anyone else." Hephaestus explained with sheer reverence and love. Serena could tell by the way he spoke that he had great respect and affection for her mother. It was such a strange concept for her, to hear of mother as the nurturing kind when she had not been so to Serena.

"She gave me a reason to live, a passion for making beautiful things, especially out of things that no one thought could look beautiful." He stopped then, turned to her and touched the amulet resting on Serena's chest.

"You made me this?" Serena asked, her eyes widening in surprise as she touched her necklace. Hephaestus nodded. "Can you take it off?" Serena immediately asked.

"I'm sorry my dear," Hephaestus answered gravely. "I made the necklace and used my powers, but I am not the only one who had to imbue it."

"You mean another god helped?" Serena asked not too sure she understood fully the implications of this statement.

"If you were the child of the prophecy, it needed much more than one strong Atlantean I'm afraid." Hephaestus answered.

"Prophecy?" Serena asked.

"Yes, my dear, a long, long time ago, there was a prophecy that foretold the Queen of the Nereids would bear a child of Zeus who would be more powerful than Zeus himself. A child capable of disrupting the divine order of the Olympians." Hephaestus explained carefully, trying not to overwhelm Serena. She sat on a nearby bench, her head spinning from the overload of information being thrown at her. Hephaestus knelt on one knee in front of her and took her hands on his lap.

"Zeus loved your mother and couldn't bear to send her to Tartarus, so he banished her to this place instead. Serena, how you came to be is a story only your mother can tell. But know this, the fates chose you. You are very precious my child." He said in an attempt to ease some of the pain he could see behind those sad eyes. He wasn't foolish enough to think that there were no challenges ahead for her, but he had faith the fates had chosen the right woman for the job. Serena stared at the wrapped present on her lap, itching to open it and look at it, yet afraid to do so. There was so much she didn't understand, and she had so many questions roaming around in her mind. But she felt numb. The only emotion she felt was anger coursing through her veins and the strange pull of the bond when she was near Triton. She was so lost in her own thoughts that she barely noticed Ailani joined them. Only when Hephaestus stood did she take her eyes off her lap.

"Father?" Ailani said curiously, surprised.

"Ah, my favorite daughter." Hephaestus said sheepishly as he reached to embrace her, touching her forehead with his before kissing it gently. "I knew I recognized the scent of Aphrodite's powers on the son of Poseidon when he came to me."

Serena looked from one to the other dumbfounded. Ailani sat next to Serena and wrapped an arm gently around her shoulders.

"Serena, I am Laka, hawaiian goddess of love. Daughter of Aphrodite and Hephaestus, or as the Hawaiians here like to call him Wahieloa." Laka explained softly. Serena thought it strange how she seemed much keener on how she spoke of her father then her mother. She looked at Hephaestus as if demanding his explanation.

"I did mention I had a forge here did I not?" Hephaestus said embarrassingly. "I made it a home here for some time. Like you and Triton here, falling in love with its people and their way of life." He explained. Serena remained silent. More pieces unfolding in front of her eyes, making her question every person she ever met and if they too were connected to all this shit. Was it all some big joke from what Triton and Hephaestus had referred to as *the fates?*

"What is this?" Laka asked, pointing at the package wrapped on Serena's lap. Serena had been fiddling with the cotton nervously.

"I... don't know." Serena answered hesitantly as she stared at it.

"The son of Poseidon thought it wise to have something forged that could... help her when the time comes." Hephaestus explained to his daughter. Serena stood then, leaving the gift on the bench.

"Do you guys honestly always call people by their parent's name?" Serena asked annoyed to no end as she stood, leaving the gift on the bench, and putting distance between them.

"That is the way of things my dear." Hephaestus replied looking at Laka for some explanation to Serena's outburst.

"It's annoying as hell!" Serena exclaimed, then turned to look at them. "If Elysium is heaven or paradise, what is hell?" She asked curiously.

"Tartarus." Hephaestus and Laka answered at the same time.

"Somehow, it's annoying that a place called Tartarus doesn't have the same effect as a place called hell." Serena said pensively. Hephaestus and

Laka chuckled. Laka stood and joined her.

"We must begin the ceremony shortly." Laka said seriously now.

"Ceremony?" Serena asked, backing away slightly.

"You have gone through some difficult circumstances, and it is good to cleanse you from them before the time comes." Laka explained carefully.

"Ok, can you start by explaining what you all mean when you talk about the *time*?" Serena asked impatiently and honestly frustrated. She was being bombarded at every corner and she didn't know how much more of this she could take.

"The last prophecy about you, it spoke of your coming of age." Laka said with a cheerful smile.

"The what?" Serena asked after a heavy sigh. Could things get any more fucked up?

"The amulet that I created for you cannot be destroyed, but it will cease to work once you come of age." Hephaestus explained, dodging the prophecy question.

"Ok….and?" Serena asked with a motion to keep going.

"I think you understand the immortality that comes with our kind?" Laka asked. Serena nodded. "Humans have an age where a child becomes an adult. We have the same, we all have a *different* time when we reach an age where our powers are at their peaks and we have reached the end of our…physical aging." Laka attempted her best at explaining a complicated subject.

"Ok, so you're saying once I reach a certain age, the amulet will stop working and my powers will…come out?" Serena contemplated.

"*On her thirtieth flower moon, she shall fully bloom.*" Laka quoted the line of the prophecy like she had many times before.

"Thirtieth flower moon…" Serena repeated to herself. She had no idea what the hell the flower moon was, but thirtieth? "My birthday. It's…tomorrow." She said with a heavy frown. She closed her eyes tightly hoping it would help, but as she opened her eyes again, everything around her began to spin. Triton appeared beside her in the blink of an eye to support her.

"What have you done?" Triton barked sternly as he looked at Laka.

"They did nothing." Serena jumped defensively before either of them had a chance to say anything. Hermes joined them as well, looking over at Hephaestus who nodded.

"It is time for us to leave." Hephaestus said gravely. He walked to Serena, squeezing her cheek as he had so many times before when she was little.

"Remember, serenity isn't freedom from the storm," He said, recalling the words he used every single time he parted from her when she was little.

"It is the peace within the storm." Serena finished the quote, closing her eyes as she repeated the familiar words she hadn't recalled in a long time.

"That is why you were named Serena, because you are the peace within the storm the Olympians have created." Hephaestus pressed on fervently wanting to make sure she didn't forget.

"This is for you," Hephaestus said to Serena as he handed the satchel to Triton. "I made you a little something." He said with a smile.

"For when the time comes?" Serena asked, forcing a smile. Hephaestus chuckled, he had such a deep and powerful laugh, it was difficult not to feel its cheerful effects. Even in her current state.

"Yes, when the time comes." Hephaestus agreed.

"Goodbye love," Hermes said as he blew a kiss and winked as he touched Hephaestus' arm, hit the ground with his caduceus and they were gone.

"Now come," Laka said as she turned to Serena. "Kahuna Pahia is waiting." She said as she took Serena's hand who pulled it back hesitantly as a look of concern crossed her face.

"What if I don't want this?" Serena asked with a trembling voice. Could they not understand how overwhelming this all was? How could she not be scared shitless? She was a fucking goddess! Daughter of Zeus whom she had no idea existed until now. Laka and Triton shared a look then Triton turned her to face him. He placed a comforting hand in the small of her back, then the other on one side of her face gently.

"Serena, I know you are afraid of what this all means." Triton said softly. "I've wondered why the fates bonded us together. I thought..." He hesitated, closed his eyes and wished for once Serena could hear his thoughts and feel what he felt so he wouldn't have to speak it. He took a deep breath as he leaned his forehead onto hers, then opened his eyes again. "I thought this bond was a curse, until I fell in love with you. Everything that happens, everything you feel, I feel. You cannot die without it killing me. We are in this together every step of the way, you're not alone."

Serena closed her eyes tightly and Triton kissed her forehead softly. How could her heart not melt with something so raw? She couldn't read his mind, but she sensed through the bond that it was honest. She had never had anyone open themselves up to her in this way and she felt an intense sense of relief wash over her as she knew he was right. For the first time in her life, she wasn't alone. A tear escaped her eyes and Triton wiped it with his thumb.

Laka smiled at the sweet moment, turning away to give them some privacy, then went to pick up the wrapped present on the bench.

"This has to be done now?" Serena asked in a hesitant whisper.

"Yes, I'm afraid we don't have much time." Triton replied solemnly.

"Fine." Serena agreed with frustration as she pulled away from his damn irresistible hotness. Laka started on her way to Kahuna Pahia's cottage ahead of Triton and Serena to give them some privacy. Triton took Serena's hand, intertwining his fingers with hers. Before they knew it, they reached Kahuna Pahia's cozy round brick cottage. It was truly indicative of a native hawaiian shaman. Vines crawling along the walls and flowers growing wildly along its edges giving it the flair of a witch's lair. They walked around to the back where patio doors were left open, probably to allow in the sweet exotic scents of the surrounding gardens and fruit trees. It wasn't raining hard, just a slight drizzle, but Serena shivered as they walked through the doors into what looked like a meditation space. It was an open space with round meditation cushions and a strange cauldron looking bucket in the middle. Handmade beeswax candles had been lit and scattered around the room. One lit candle was placed next to one cushion with a strange looking pile of dried herbs bunched together and neatly wrapped. Serena thought she recognized it as some sort of native American smudge stick she had seen on documentaries. The whistle of a boiling kettle resonated through the room, mixed in with the songs of tropical birds chirping happily in the foliage surrounding them adding to the mystical charm of the place. A woman joined them. She had a charming welcoming smile as she walked to Serena, grabbed her hands then kneeled in front of her and kissed the back of her hands.

"Welina, Nā-maka-o-Kaha'i." The lady said bowing her head in great reverence as she placed the back of Serena's hands on her forehead.

"Please…" Serena said uncomfortably as she pulled her up, bringing her in for a good old hawaiian embrace, touching her forehead with hers. She heard that name a lot around here.

"I am Kahuna Pahia. Our people have been waiting for your arrival for an exceptionally long time, Namaka." The Kahuna said with excitement and pure joy reflecting in her dark brown eyes.

"Nice to meet you." Serena said as she smiled weakly, unsure what to say to what she felt was such an undeserved welcome. The kahuna moved two of the cushions, so they faced each other.

"You two must sit facing each other." She said motioning for Triton and Serena to take their place. Serena sat comfortably; her legs tucked in a cross-sitting position as Triton followed, facing her. He sensed her hesitation and the uncertainty fighting in the back of her mind. She was afraid of the unknown, of what all this meant. Laka made sure there were bottles of water next to them and then sat across from Triton and Serena.

"We will begin. Close your eyes and try to relax and open your mind." The kahuna instructed as she grabbed the herbs and set them on fire then blew them out quickly which released the heavy smoke. Laka grabbed the tea pot in front of her and gave Serena a cup, instructing her to drink from it. As Serena sipped it, it tasted foul yet sweet. She thought she recognized the sweet nectary taste but couldn't remember where she had tasted it before. The kahuna then began chanting in hawaiian. Using the smoke, she encircled them with it but lingered around Serena.

Serena closed her eyes, breathing in slowly to clear her mind and let herself drown in Laka's enchanting voice as she translated the hawaiian words.

"Greatly admired is her Majesty,
The goddess of serenity.

Nā-maka-o-Kaha'i ruler of the sea
The divine ruler to the throne to be.

The arches of rainbows
Beams of colors unequalled.

Creations of fate,
Passing along within the pearly gate.
Look to the brightness of day.
From the vastness of Hawai'i to Kaua'i.
In the heaven's brightness,
The beauty is revealed.

Nā-maka-o-Kahaʻi is her name.
A beautiful flower that never fades.

It blooms on the summit.
On the mountain, Mauna Kea.
Burning bright at Kîlauea
Illuminating Wahinekapu
Upon the heights of Uwêkahuna
Is the sacred cliff of Kaʻauea.
Come forth spirit of the queen of the sea,
To become one with the goddess of serenity.

Greatly admired is Her Majesty.
The goddess of serenity
Nā-maka-o-Kahaʻi ruler of the sea
The divine ruler to the throne to be.

Come forth goddess of serenity.
Adorned with wisdom and beauty.
You will be the beautiful savior of this world.
Nā-maka-o-Kahaʻi is her name.

Kahuna Pahia continued chanting, repeating the hawaiian prayer as Laka stopped translating. There was a strange pull in Triton's gut. It started like a faint dull pain and intensified until it became almost unbearable. He opened his eyes and clutched his abdomen, using all the strength he could muster to remain silent until he could bear it no more. It felt as if someone was trying to rip the internal organs out of his body violently and everything around him began to spin out of control.

"Triton!" Serena called out as her eyes flung open. She stared at him in shock before she collapsed on the floor. Triton watched in horror as the blue glow of the bond turned light gray, which usually only meant Serena's life force was fading and the bond was weakening. Whatever Kahuna Pahia and Laka were doing, it was tearing Serena apart and she lay there unconscious. Triton screamed in pain as he collapsed back on the floor. His body felt pinned as he couldn't move, and he struggled for his breath. He strangely felt as if he was dying as the bond tying him to Serena was being pulled away somehow. Everything went dark.

CHAPTER 33
SERENA

Serena blinked her eyes as they slowly adjusted to her surroundings.

She was not in Hawaii anymore, but found herself leaning against a beautiful weeping willow tree. Her legs were crossed with flowers on her lap that she had obviously been braiding into a crown. She didn't remember doing this and it took some time to realize she was in Elysium. She thought she had dreamed of this place. A distant dream that strangely seemed so real. She had met Hades here; she was certain of it. She was surrounded by an inexplicable peace and tranquility of mind. She felt its healing properties washing away the hurt, pain, shock and horrible dread that had settled in from Ares. It enveloped her like a warm blanket of love and even if she couldn't explain it, it was changing her. She heard whispers that seemed to move with the warm breeze blowing in the fields in front of her and she focused on them. She realized they were whispering a name. *Nā-maka-o-Kaha'i*. She knew her name was Serena, but that notion slowly dissipated and almost sounded estranged to her now. *Nā-maka-o-Kaha'i, it* whispered again, imprinting the name firmly in her mind. She suddenly had the strangest sensation, like she was being watched. She stood and saw a figure take shape and float across the stream of Elysium towards her. She wore a long white flowing dress and had long wavy black curly hair majestically swirling around her body. Warm beautiful green eyes and a kind smile on her perfect face. Triton had been right; the resemblance was uncanny.

"Namaka." Serena whispered, instinctively knowing who was standing in front of her. The ghostly image nodded.

"Nā-maka-o-Kahaʻi was my name. I have been wandering here for centuries waiting for you." The spirit whispered; her lips unmoving but speaking with her mind.

"I don't understand." Serena frowned.

"It is your destiny to take on my spirit so that the goddess of serenity may become one with the queen of the sea." The voice whispered cryptically.

"Are you taking over my body?" Serena questioned, fear rising in the corner of her mind as she was incapable of accepting what the spirit was saying.

"No," The spirit of Namaka spoke gently as she smiled. "Taking on the spirit only, for you will need it for your journey." She explained. Before Serena could respond, the shape turned into a mist and flowed directly into Serena's mouth, ears, eyes, and nose. She gasped and gagged, grabbing at her throat in a panic as she fell on her knees unable to breath, her ears beginning to burn ferociously until it all stopped suddenly. Serena gasped, letting in some sweet air as she laid down and stared at the blue skies in disbelief.

"Hey Siri." Hermes said with a wink as he leaned over her.

"Hermes!" Serena jumped to a sitting position as Hermes surprised her, still trying to catch her breath. If it wouldn't have been for the fact that he scared the shit out of her, she might have laughed at the new pet name he discovered.

"You really like to make a grand entrance, don't you?" Serena asked with a scolding look.

"Wouldn't have it any other way." Hermes teased as he reached out a hand to help her up onto her feet. Serena took his hand and couldn't help the smile forming on her face. Hermes was starting to grow on her.

How could he not? He was hot and with those cute dimples and a smile that brightened his face. You just couldn't help but relax and feel at ease.

"What are you doing in the underworld?" Serena asked curiously, surprising herself with the knowledge of where she was.

"I work for Hades sweet cheeks, but I could ask you the same question." Hermes asked with a feigned serious look on his face and hands on his hips that made him look nothing like the serious look he was trying to portray.

"You work for Hades?" Serena asked, her eyes narrowing. "You're a leader of souls." She said as if thinking about the answer she just spoke. She couldn't explain how she knew this. It felt like someone was whispering the information somehow.

"Look at you, all grown up." Hermes said dramatically as he placed a hand on his heart. Serena chuckled and shook her head. "Where are my manners?" He said as he wiped his hands on his black jeans. "I am Hermes, messenger of the gods." He introduced himself as he reached out a hand.

"And trickery?" Serena added, raising a questioning frown.

"Siri, why get lost in the little details?" Hermes asked, trying to hide slight embarrassment. Serena chuckled.

"Sorry I didn't get that, could you try again?" Serena answered wittingly as she imitated the Siri voice she had often heard on her phone. Hermes chuckled, unable to help himself. He was liking Serena already. He was relieved she wasn't going to be boring like the rest of the Olympians. She was definitely going to spice things up.

"I am Serena, goddess of serenity and sea." She finally said as she took his hand, but instead of shaking it, he knelt on one knee and touched the back of her hand to his forehead. "Hermes-" She started to protest, but noticed Hades standing behind him, hands in his pockets looking amused. He surely had appeared out of nowhere. But then again, he was the ruler of this place was he not? Hermes stood then and stepped back.

"Lord Hades." Serena said reverently as she bowed her head.

"Lady Serena." Hades returned seemingly pleased as he walked to her and knelt on one knee.

"Please Lord Hades," Serena pleaded. "You are in your realm."

"Reverence given where it is due my lady." Hades protested as he took his hand and placed the back of her hand against his forehead as Hermes had done.

"I... apologize for the lack of respect I showed the first time we met...I'm afraid I was...clueless" Serena said apologetically.

"It is understandable under the circumstances. Which brings me to the reason for your visit to Elysium." Hades said as he brushed off her apology as he stood.

"I...had hoped you could enlighten me with the answer to that question." Serena trailed off with uncertainty. There were some questions she didn't seem to know the answer to.

"The fields of Elysium are for those seeking to heal from great tragedy and pain. I believe the goddess in you took you to the only place that could heal your soul." Hades answered charmingly as he smiled reassuringly. Serena frowned pensively, contemplating his explanation. It was all difficult to understand, her knowledge of all this so freshly new.

"Is it this place causing the whispers I hear?" Serena asked curiously.

"Whispers?" Hades asked, raising a brow curiously.

"I hear whispers, like a breeze in my mind. Not all of it coherent, but sometimes I hear answers to things I can't know on my own." Serena answered feeling like she made no sense at all.

"Well, I'll be... seems like you my dear Serena, have access to the same ancient knowledge of the universe only the Olympians have access too." Hades said, obviously amazed and surprised. Serena frowned as she felt overwhelmed again, knowing somehow this wasn't supposed to happen without Zeus' blessing.

"No need to worry about it, my lady. Take the time you need to heal. You are welcome here as long as you need. But I do believe the earth realm needs you." Hades explained kindly.

"Understood. I'm just not sure how...I can go back. I believe I cannot until the amulet has lost its power over my...human form." Serena spoke hesitantly as if searching for the answers.

"I believe you are right." Hades said with a smile. "But no need to worry, the fates will take care of it in due time." Hades said firmly.

"Thank you." Serena curtsied.

"In the meantime, it seems my wife would like to meet you." Hades gritted as he extended an invitation.

"Persephone?" Serena asked. Hades nodded. "It would be an honor to meet the goddess of spring." She said as she took Hades' arm as he offered it.

CHAPTER 34
TRITON

Charon (pronounced Karen) did what he had been doing in the underworld for thousands of years. He steered his boat towards the shores of the living to collect the souls of those waiting to cross the river Styx over to the land of the dead. There were a dozen souls today, each looking grim at his cloaked figure. As always, the human souls were always fear stricken as they had been for the last few centuries when they stopped believing in their existence. It made it even more pleasant to watch the damned souls look upon the void of his features as they became terrorized by something they did not even comprehend. On the other hand, he felt sorry for the good souls destined for Elysium, as few as they were now, lost, and afraid of what was to become of their soul. Dying had become such a dreary thing for humans. He wondered just exactly how they lived their precious lives without believing in anything, without any purpose or thought of what came thereafter. It was the fault of centuries of false education or resentment towards higher beings that had led them to this point. But the humans were not all to blame for their predicament. The Olympians had been created to watch over them, guide them and protect their existence. Instead, they had used them as pawns in their absurd games and for their own enjoyment. For the ones that still cared for them, they felt that guiding them without their knowledge was easier than dealing with their lack of belief or their self-entitlement and blunt refusal of a hierarchy. Indeed, humans refused to be governed by them but, it was the Olympians that chose to act as gods to humans instead of being their guardians. As the souls embarked upon his boat and he tirelessly dealt with souls pleading to be returned to the upper worlds, a soul dropped out of nowhere and onto his boat. Everyone stepped back and some shrieked in surprise. Charon studied the body, usually souls that appeared in the underworld were not unconscious but appeared at the edge of the river Styx waiting for him. He poked the thick body with his staff but to no avail. He sighed in annoyance as he took the hood off his head, causing some of the souls to shriek in terror and jump off the boat. Charon didn't even bother stopping them anymore. It was their own stupidity that led them to this point, and those destined for Tartarus were not even worth breaking a sweat for. The horrid shrieks of the souls who had jumped echoed around them as they got attacked by the damned famished souls of the river Styx. The others stood back too frightened to even breath. Charon bent down and touched the side of the man's face. He smelled of seaweed and musky saltwater. He smelled of Poseidon's protective power. Charon took a deep breath, wondering for a second what he should do with his unwelcome guest. He looked up as three figures appeared at the shores of the underworld. The three fates: Clotho, Lachesis, and Atropos. When they spoke, their voices were like three breezes on a cold winter's night: sharp and chilling.

"*This one must not be harmed.*" Clotho, the spinner of fate commanded.

"*His destiny has been woven into the fate of the universe.*" Lachesis, the allotter followed.

"*Indeed, many great things for him we have planned.*" Atropos, known as the inflexible of the three as she was the one who despised those who defied them and dared to upset the balance of the universe the most. Charon did not speak, only nodded as they disappeared, and he placed the hood of his cloak on his head and continued steering his boat towards the shores of the underworld. With a flick of his fingers, he called upon the leader of souls.

"Yes Charon." Hermes said as he appeared next to him biting into a piece of hawaiian pizza. Hermes had always found it amusing that he had started the humans on a new trend and got them using the *don't be such a*

Karen expression as a dare. Charon had told Hermes the Olympians had as much pull on the humans then he did on his boat. Little did the humans know they were actually referring to the one who would bring their souls into the underworld. Boring and glum in Hermes' opinion.

"It seems the fates do not agree with my wish to throw this body into the river Styx." Charon replied with great disappointment. Hermes stopped chewing as he instantly recognized the hot body of the son of Poseidon laying strangely unconscious in the boat.

"I have to agree with them. Besides, it would be a shame to lose my hot as Tartarus poker buddy before I even get a chance to play one game with him." Hermes exclaimed as he knelt to place a hand on the man's shoulder.

"Just take care of it." Charon replied sourly. Charon did not appreciate losing his bet to Hermes, nor the humans using his name in vain. Hermes studied the body lying there, knowing he was much too tall and too strong to move it himself. He hit the floor of the boat with his caduceus and they both reappeared on the shores of the underworld.

"Trite?" Hermes called out as he tugged at Triton's shoulder. He had sensed the son of Poseidon had appeared. Unlike Serena, he had not split himself physically. His soul was actually here in the underworld. Hermes could sense that Triton had not passed on, he was simply in a deep state of unconsciousness, hanging between life and death. The fates had obviously chosen to bring him here and it probably had to do with Serena. Triton opened his eyes slowly. He was staring up at a darkened sky that felt nothing like the earth realm and smelled like death. The scent burned his nose as he realized someone was kneeling next to him. He turned his head, surprised he could actually do so, and it was Hermes who looked at him with concern.

"Hermes?" Triton rasped in a barely audible whisper. His throat felt horribly dry. It felt as if he had wandered the desert for days deprived of water. He licked his lips and they felt cracked. He sat up slowly studying his surroundings. He noticed a rocky cavernous mountain to his left and then miles and miles of a rocky deserted space separated by a dark river. He caught a glimpse of a long boat floating away from them. Steering the boat was a tall figure dressed in a dark robe, his face covered by the hood of his cloak. It was then he realized it was none other than the psychopomp Charon, the ferryman of Hades who carries souls of the newly deceased across the river Styx that divided the world of the living from the world of the dead.

214

"I am... dead?" Triton grumbled a frown of confusion on his face.

"Nah, Charon wanted to dump your pretty ass in the river Styx when he realized you weren't dead and summoned me to take care of you. Leader of the souls and all." Hermes answered comically trying to ease Triton's mind the only way he knew how. "Such a dramatic arse he is." Hermes said, shaking his head. The myths had always depicted Charon as a scary looking shady character typically looking like a scary skeleton from Tartarus, drawn up to scare the humans. But beneath the dark cloak, the psychopomp's appearance varied upon the soul who looked upon him. If it were a soul destined for Tartarus, they would see nothing but a dark, soul devouring creature. But, if it were a good soul on its way to Elysium or its fields, it would see the gentle, caring soul much like the one of his master Hades. Triton noticed he had indeed somehow crossed the river Styx. He didn't know much about Charon but wondered why he would bother protecting him from the river Styx to begin with.

"Seems like the fates showed up and told them your time had not come yet. Apparently, they like the look of your ass as much as I do." Hermes stated, remembering the scene he had fallen upon when he appeared in Maui.

"Serena?" Triton gritted, a deep line of concern forming between his brows as he thought of her.

"You mean you are not here to play a hand of poker with me?" Hermes asked sarcastically, making an insulated face. Triton closed his eyes and sighed heavily.

"No need to be so dramatic my man, I'll take you to Siri if you promise me at least one game in exchange." Hermes said with dismay. Triton opened his eyes and glared at him. And there it was. Triton knew the god of trickery liked to have his fun just like most of the Olympians and wondered when he would ask for his favor.

"Fine. Just take me to Serena." Triton snapped impatiently.

"Ah!" Hermes shouted as he rubbed his hands together unable to contain his excitement.

Hermes and Triton reappeared inside what was obviously a throne room. Everything was made of glistening black obsidian adorned by an ebony throne as impressive as any Olympian throne could be. Narcissus flowers were etched along its fine cut edges. The tall back of the throne was carved with intricately shaped cypress tree branches and a skull on each peak. Each armrest had the head of Hades' three headed dog Cerberus.

Next to it, was a smaller throne made with tree vines and even though it was simple, the patterns were simply stunning. Triton assumed it had to belong to his wife, Persephone.

"No one's here." Triton said, stating the obvious. Before Hermes had a chance to comment, they turned towards the big marble double doors of the throne room as it opened and watched as a lowly servant walked through.

"My lords," The servant said with a curtsy. "Lord Hades will see you in his salon." Triton and Hermes followed the servant down the dark halls lit by only small torches of Greek fire. Of course, this was the underworld, it would have an endless supply of it. Triton thought. As much as it was dark, there was no sense of oppression with the lack of lighting and Triton wondered if it was only meant to scourge the damned souls. Or maybe he himself had misconceptions of the Lord of the underworld like almost everyone outside of its walls. They walked silently; the only noise was the clanking of their feet on the shiny obsidian floors. They reached another set of black marble doors and the servant opened it. When they walked in, Hades, Persephone and Serena were hovering over a small table with a strange looking bowl with a drink in hand. When Serena turned to look at him, a smile beamed across her divine features making him clench his jaw tighter than he ever had before so that it wouldn't drop to the floor. The woman, no, the goddess that stood there was simply jaw dropping and unrecognizable. She wore a golden satin empire waist dress with a floor length golden laced overlay. Her hair was loosely tied up on her head with golden pins, letting a few perfectly curled brown strands cascade down framing her beautiful face. Her green eyes magnificently sparkled gold against her accoutrement.

"Ah, and the son of Poseidon joins us." Hades said as he sipped from his drink in hand, his other hand tucked in his pocket.

"Lord Hades." Triton said with respect as he bowed his head. Serena looked from Triton to Hades curiously, then that perfect smile vanished with the cheerful color of her cheeks. The drink in her hand slipped out and crashed onto the floor as the realization set in of the only reason Triton could possibly be standing there. Hades said Hermes was going to get *a lost soul.*

"Triton." Serena's voice trembled as she muttered the name.

"No need to worry, sweet cheeks." Hermes said with a charming smile of reassurance. Serena turned to Hades, her eyes pleading.

"Hermes is right, the fates have made it perfectly clear I cannot keep him here." Hades finally answered after a brief moment of uncomfortable silence and a long sip of his drink. Hades could communicate instantly with anyone in his realm and had obviously done so in the time it took him to answer. It became noticeably clear to both Serena and Triton that Hades had brought him here for a specific reason.

"Only," Hades trailed off, demanding their attention as his eyes looked intently between Triton and Serena. His lips thinned from a thought roaming in his head. "I need to make something *very* clear." Hades took another sip of the dark liquor in his glass and he set it down a little harder than he needed to. His face remained calm and composed, his tone chillingly assertive. "As much as I do not like the drama of Mount Olympus and the *wrong* choices my brother has obviously made to defy the fates, he is my brother. I have to sit back and enjoy watching them getting their punishment for such insolence, but *I will not allow him to be threatened.*" He finished emphasizing the last words, sending a chill down Serena's spine and a noticeable clench in Triton's jaw.

"The last prophecy spoke by the oracles has no mention of Serena being a threat." Triton replied plainly. A spark of curiosity gleamed in Hades' eyes at the mention of a new prophecy.

"Serena is not a concern however," Hades turned to the shelf behind him grabbing a bottle of dark liquor. He filled his glass then took his time putting the bottle away. "The goddess of serenity bound by the fates to a powerful son of Poseidon," He said, his eyes taking pleasure in looking over Serena's beautiful features. "It's a different story altogether now isn't it?" Hades asked rhetorically. Persephone, obviously jealous of the wandering eye of her husband, walked around the table and took her husband's arm protectively.

"Pray tell, what is this new prophecy?" Persephone asked curiously. She was herself an incredibly attractive and beautiful goddess. Adorning her mother's beautiful blond hair and perfect complexion, she had nothing to be jealous of. Even if Serena was indeed more beautiful than any of the other goddesses put together.

"The sun shall shine on the divine. On her thirtieth flower moon she shall fully bloom. From the depth of the deep blue sea, the son of its king shall set her free. Ye the daughter of the mighty king of the sky, with the son of Poseidon her fate shall we tie. A love stronger than a bond of power, will remain unbreakable and shall be even mightier. Together they shall restore the gods to their humanity, for in her we have woven pure serenity." Triton recited the words of the prophecy Laka had spoken to him. Serena's eyes flashed from their natural green back to gold as the words resounded in her head. She had not been aware of this prophecy and yet again was reminded by the duplicity involved with the words the fates had spoken through the oracles.

"Lord Hades, I have no ill intentions towards any of the Olympians. And I hope…" Serena trailed off avoiding Triton's glare. "That they are words of a *concerned* brethren and not of a *threatening* nature." Serena said calmly, a playful smile crossing her lips as the glass she just dropped put itself back together, filling itself back up then made its way back to her hand. She took a long sip as a thickness grew in the room pressing against everyone's power. Hades' eyes widened before he had time to keep his composure as he realized just how powerful Serena really was. She sent the weight of her powers towards Hades, pressing on him like a heavy bolder waiting to squash him like a bug. He chuckled and raised an eyebrow as an impressed smile crossed his features. He had obviously been messing with the wrong goddess, thinking her newly found powers were weak. How he was wrong. As much as he wanted to keep his composure, the corner of Triton's mouth twisted in a smile of pure satisfaction. Serena might not have known this, but he had never doubted that without the amulet holding her back, she was truly a force to be reckoned with and this just confirmed it. Serena let go of her powers, never intending to go any further than showing what exactly she was capable of. She knew Hades was not really a threat. This had simply been a dick measuring contest and she wasn't afraid to let them know she could win.

"Of course, my lady." Hades replied, hardly able to hide his amusement. In truth, he was looking forward to watching his brother scramble against the results of his own actions. He had merely been tempted to test just how powerful his niece was and boy she did not disappoint. He was not responsible for bringing the son of Poseidon to his realm, even if he may have hinted otherwise. He used the situation to his advantage to understand Serena's intentions and to spice things up even just a little. The fates were clearly responsible in delivering Triton to his realm.

"Persephone dear, perhaps we should let these two... get better acquainted." Hades insisted. She simply nodded and followed him out the salon, passing Hermes who stood at the entrance with his arms crossed enjoying the events perhaps a little too much.

"I'm sure there are some souls requiring your assistance, Hermes." Hades commanded suggestively.

"No rest for the wicked." Hermes said with a sigh of great disappointment as he disappeared. The servant waited for his masters to exit the room then shut the door behind them, leaving Triton standing there speechless. He had no idea what to say or why he was even brought here.

CHAPTER 35
SERENA

Serena sipped her drink slowly enjoying the scotch as she let it sit on her tongue before she swallowed it. She avoided Triton, overwhelmed by the events yet again. She had just taken on the Lord of the underworld. What in the fires of Tartarus was that?

"You were formidable." Triton answered as he read her thoughts. He wanted to get close to her, to close the distance between them, but he wasn't sure it was the right thing to do.

"Why not, I don't bite...much." Serena said wittingly, reading his mind as she took another sip of her drink, curving an eyebrow.

"Serena, I..." Triton trailed off as if suddenly unsure how to act around the woman he had gotten to know, and to love over the last six months. But the woman he was looking at eerily reminded him of someone he once knew long ago.

"Serena is not here right now, *son of Poseidon*." Namaka teased as she turned and bit her lower lip, knowing it would make his heart race and the heat in his gut rise. Those words sounded so cold, disconnected and even impersonal towards a man she was now almost completely intimately bonded too. She turned to him, closing the distance Triton seemed afraid to do. But could she blame him? The woman standing in front of him was by far not the same frail, broken woman he had left behind in the upper world. Instead, he had come to find a goddess. Her fingers trailed the v neck collar of his white t-shirt as her eyes locked with his. The heat between them rose to a stifling level.

"Lady Namaka." Triton finally said, breaking the uncomfortable silence as he kneeled in front of his goddess, grabbing her hand, and touching his forehead in reverence with the back of it. He looked up from his position on the floor with great admiration filling his eyes. Namaka moved a strand of hair from his eyes, her touch sending tingles where her fingers touched the skin of his face. She pulled him up on his feet and drew him closer as she planted her luscious lips upon his. Triton fought with every screaming fiber of his body to pull away, wanting nothing but the feeling of her on him, but this was not the right moment.

"If not now, then when will it ever be?" Namaka pleaded and for a second, Triton saw Serena's green eyes flicker through the goddess's eyes.

"I am but a soul in this realm, Namaka." Triton's voice deep with certainty and almost a slight touch of pain from denying his body the need to take her. For the first time, they were together mind and soul since her amulet obviously had no power over her in the underworld and couldn't block their connection as it had in the upper world.

"You said to me once the bond was meant to be mind, body and soul. But it has only been able to bind our mind and soul. You were wrong." Namaka said softly into his ear, sending a shiver of pleasure through his body again. Triton pulled back, curving his scarred eyebrow curiously at the goddess.

"What do you mean?" Triton asked.

"I think the fates brought you here so that our souls could finally bond together." Namaka answered with a smile. She almost believed Hades had been the culprit responsible for Triton's presence in the underworld. But the whispers in her mind confirmed otherwise. Triton stood silently pondering the statement. She was right. He had believed they were bonded mind and soul the day they met and shook hands, but he was the only one to feel its effects. Could she be right about this? Why else would the fates allow him to come here? Namaka obviously didn't need his assistance here, that much was clear to him.

"The powers of the amulet are too strong, Triton. Serena was not lying when she told you I needed you to complete her. The power of the bond needs your soul bond to be completed for her to move forward and allow my true goddess to exist peacefully in that human form." Namaka repeated the information as she was beginning to understand it. She tugged at Triton's jeans, pulling him closer as her eyes locked with his. Triton kissed her as he began to understand what Namaka was inferring. He kissed her softly at first but the desire was too strong to hold him back any longer. She teased him with her tongue. She tasted sweet like the spiced liquor she was drinking. He ravished her mouth, pulling her head back with his hand, tangling it deep in her soft flowing hair. The bond was almost too difficult to resist, but with all his might, every inch of power he still had, he pulled away.

"Namaka..." Triton, his voice trembling from the effort it took. Namaka chuckled and with a snap of her fingers they both were completely naked.

"I know you want this, Triton." Namaka said seductively as she toyed with him, trailing the lines of his sculpted abdominal muscles as her eyes locked with his. He closed his eyes, took a deep breath and he grabbed Namaka's wrist as she reached for his now hardened member.

"I am not sure how this is possible." Triton said as he opened his eyes, the tenderness and moment of weakness were gone. Namaka had been dead and gone for centuries. Yes, the resemblance to Serena was uncanny, but to say they were identical was wrong. The woman in front of him clearly looked like Serena. Her mind felt like her, but now she also felt like Namaka. Namaka let out a sigh of disappointment as she pulled her wrist out of Triton's grasp, snapped her fingers to dress them back up.

"Serena is the offspring of the prophecy Triton, but the fates gave her my spirit to help her." Namaka said with obvious disappointment. Triton narrowed his eyes as he studied Namaka intently, trying to understand what she was telling him.

"That does not explain why you are here, in Serena's body." Triton said with slight aggravation.

"The fates gave Serena my spirit, in exchange for my sacrifice, I bargained one last moment with you." Namaka said, her eyes filling with tears as she closed the distance between them, touching the side of his face gently, she kissed him softly, but he didn't kiss her back. He leaned his forehead on hers. Triton had wondered when the fates would reveal their punishment of his involvement, of his compliance with the rest of the Atlanteans' defiance. He thought perhaps they would rip Serena out of his grasp. But instead, they chose a much more effective torture. They brought back the spirit of the only other woman he ever loved. To top it off, in the body of the other love of his life. Fucking fates.

"I don't have much longer, Triton." Namaka said with a sob, realizing that Triton was making the choice, and that he would choose *her*.

"Namaka…" Triton whispered, but didn't move. After a moment of silence, he opened his eyes and stared right into Serena's.

"Triton?" Serena whispered back with uncertainty.

"Serena." Triton smiled and he kissed her deeply, relieved to see her back as herself. There was no doubt in his mind that the fates had bestowed Namaka's spirit to Serena to help her on her quest.

"Am I still Serena, or am I Namaka?" Serena asked confused. He felt her confusion. She had been present all this time, but he was certain Namaka had wiped the memory of her takeover. The problem now was knowing exactly when Namaka took over.

"You are Serena, goddess of the sea and serenity." Triton whispered as he placed his hands on each side of her face. She bit her lip and he felt the thousands of questions roaming around in her head. She opened her eyes and Triton was gone.

"Serena?" Triton called out, touching the side of her face. Serena opened her eyes slowly, her head spinning something awful. She stared at the ceiling, taking a moment to realize she was lying flat on her back on Kahuna Pahia's floor. She felt completely drained, like every negative emotion was sucked right out of her. Even with the exhaustion, she felt strangely liberated. Like the traumatized part of her was gone. Sure, she

223

was furious about what happened to her, but there was a calm within her she couldn't explain. A whisper telling her everything was going to be alright. She still felt somewhat disconnected though, like her mind was divided. Almost like she was in a dream like state. Was she dreaming?

"How long…?" Serena tried asking as she struggled to sit up. Triton took her elbow, helping her up gently.

"You've been unconscious for almost thirteen hours." Triton said with a look of concern plastered all over his face. It had been the strangest, scariest feeling he had ever experienced. Kahuna Pahia was chanting, Laka was translating and suddenly, Triton felt weak, like someone was trying to rip all his internal organs out of his body. Then, Serena collapsed. She looked as white as a ghost, almost lifeless. In fact, Triton felt the tether of the bond was so weak he lost consciousness. Laka had given him some ambrosia and it took him a few moments to collect himself, but he managed to pull himself out of it.

"Here, drink this." Triton said, offering Serena a golden flask. As she drank it, she tasted the sweet familiar taste of nectar.

"What is this?" Serena asked curiously as she wiped her mouth. She wanted to know what this was, after all she had been drugged with it.

"Ambrosia, sweet nectar of the gods." Triton replied. "It heals us, sustains us."

"But that is what Ellie drugged me with?" Serena was confused that Ellie could drug her with such a liquid, if it sustained them or healed them.

"Ellie didn't drug you Serena." Triton said. "My guess is that she gave you the nectar knowing it would weaken your amulet's power over you." He explained as he fiddled with his fingers. Serena knew Triton had to be right as she realized almost everything strange started happening after she saw Ellie and Liam at the Luau.

"Are you going to tell me who Liam and Ellie really are?" Serena asked knowing that everyone in her life was not who they seemed to be, and she was sure it included those two.

"Ellie is Lady Artemis, and Liam is Lord Apollo." Triton answered with honesty but without giving her too much detail.

"The names sound familiar, I know they are part of the Greek mythology, but I don't know much more." Serena said, trying to find something she may have read or heard about the two.

"The important thing to know is that there are twelve Olympians. Zeus ruler of the earth and sky and his wife Hera are the rulers, the king and queen. Then you have his right hand, my father Poseidon who rules the oceans. The rest are all Zeus' children: Artemis, Apollo, Hephaestus, Hermes, Athena, Aphrodite, Demeter, Dionysus and... Ares." Triton explained hesitating on the last one.

"What about Hades?" Serena asked curiously, ignoring the last name he mentioned.

"Hades rules the underworld. He refused to be part of the Olympians, although no one really knows why." Triton said, wondering why she felt so curious about Hades, did it have anything to do with her goddess form being in the underworld? Triton had met the god of the underworld but still knew truly little of him. He only knew what the stories told, and gods only knew they could be vague or blatant exaggerations.

"You should go back to your cottage and get some sleep." Laka said gently as she joined them. Serena had almost forgotten about her. She glanced outside, it was completely dark, and it had to be late as the moon hung high and bright in the sky: a full moon.

"Goodnight." Laka waved and she was off to bed. Triton stood, now feeling back to his normal self. He reached out to Serena, whom he was glad had also regained all her color and vigor. She stood, closing the distance between them.

"Would you like to join me for a midnight swim?" Triton asked curving his scarred eyebrow curiously.

"It's late and complete darkness!" Serena exclaimed with a giggle.

"I can see perfectly fine in the dark." Triton said, the corner of his mouth lifting into a smirk.

"What about sharks?" Serena said with honest fear in her eyes.

"Serena," Triton said with a wide grin. "I am the son of Poseidon, ruler of all oceans. We command all creatures."

"Oh." Serena said as the realization set in. Even in Mokulua islands, they were never in any form of danger?

"No." Triton answered as he kissed her neck softly.

"We are not going to make it there if you keep doing that." Serena said with a giggle as she struggled to pull away, feeling amused that she was the one pulling away for a change. But she felt this irresistible draw towards the water and wanted that swim. Triton chuckled and pulled back, grabbed her hands and they made their way to the ocean. The beach was much closer then she had anticipated, but it still took them a good fifteen minutes to get there. When they finally reached the beach, Serena was amazed at the sight. The moon, almost full, was shining brightly above the ocean casting a beautiful light on the water. He watched her intently as she closed her eyes and took a deep breath. The soft breeze blowing her wavy brown hair loosely behind her back and even if she was not in her goddess form, she surely looked like one.

"Do you know how beautiful you are?" Triton asked as he cupped the side of her face with one hand, the other on the small of her back pulling her closer.

"Trit-" Serena began to protest but Triton wouldn't give her the chance. He kissed her softly, loving the taste of her sweet lips.

"Do you trust me?" Triton asked as he pulled away, Serena trying to catch her breath. She paused for a moment. It wasn't that she didn't, but she could sense he was up to something and it was that she didn't trust. She finally nodded.

Triton began undressing himself, standing completely naked within seconds. He smiled as he noticed Serena's eyes wandered below his waist. Realizing she was caught staring, she turned her gaze away, her cheeks burning a dark crimson color. He watched as she took her turn undressing herself, and realizing his pleasure would be more obvious at this point, he turned away and walked into the water. When the water was up to his knees, he dove in, letting the salt water run through his body and do its thing. It cleared his mind and gave him focus on what he wanted to do, what he needed to do. But in truth, he was nervous. He didn't want to overwhelm Serena more than she already was. He breached the surface in time to watch Serena's perfect figure plunge into the water behind him. He swam closer, until his toes anchored in the sand. Serena popped up a foot away from him with a smile beaming across her face. Her perfect features glowing in the moonlight and her long wet hair clinging to her slim figure. She was built like an Atlantean: the body shape of a tall athlete. Seeing Triton was standing, she let herself sink, thinking she would reach the sandy bottom. Forgetting Triton was taller than she was, she inhaled a gulp of water as she sank underwater. Triton pulled her by the hips, holding her close to give her time to catch her breath. He saw the color of her cheeks return and although he fought the chuckle, he couldn't help the corner of his mouth from curling up and his scarred eyebrow from rising with amusement.

"I fail to see how drowning is funny!" Serena scolded as she pushed herself away from him, splashing him in the face.

"Considering that you are a goddess of water..." Triton trailed off as he grabbed her ankle and pulled her to him as she tried to swim away.

Trying to remain serious, Serena tried splashing him again, but he grabbed her wrist and wrapped his other arm around her waist pulling her close.

"And you want me to trust you. Maybe we need that team building workshop after all." Serena said sarcastically. Triton's smile vanished and his brows furrowed.

"Serena, I would never intentionally hurt you." Triton said his eyes darkened with intention.

"I know." Serena answered as she touched the side of his face gently, sending a wave of pleasure through his body. She kissed him then and wrapped her legs around his waist. Heat flooded between them and he grunted as he stopped. If he didn't, he wouldn't accomplish what he had brought her here to do.

"Ready?" Triton asked, after clearing his throat.

"For what?" Serena asked curiously.

"We are going under." Triton simply answered, giving her a second to hold her breath before he sunk them underwater. He pulled them deep enough so that they were a few feet from the surface, with water above them. They stood still, not needing any weights to hold them steady. Their bodies naturally adjusted to gravity.

"Close your eyes and relax." Triton's voice echoed underwater. His voice was already deep and scruffy, but it almost sounded like a rumble underwater. Serena closed her eyes, still unsure what Triton was trying to do. Soon, her lungs began to ask for air and the burning sensation behind her ears returned. She touched them, her legs still wrapped around Triton's waist. But not for long. As her lungs began to scream and demand she return to the surface for air, the pain behind her ears became intolerable. She pushed herself away from Triton, but he caught her, holding her firmly, his arms wrapped around her waist, her back against his chest. *Let me go, Triton!* She shouted through her mind.

"No." Triton replied firmly. Serena's survival instinct kicked in and she began to thrash violently to break free, but he didn't budge. He simply moved his head away when her elbows or head came too close to his face. As the pain behind her ears was unbearable, she screamed uncontrollably in a panic and her brain told her she was going to drown. It felt as if someone was ripping her ears right out of her head and she started seeing stars. She knew she was going to pass out. *Triton!* She called out, pleading and begging for him to let her go.

"Relax Serena." Triton said as he used the power of his voice to soothe and calm her. Just before Serena felt like she was about to pass out, a burst of oxygen exploded through her and her entire body relaxed. She stayed still, unable to move but focused on taking deep breaths. But from where? She touched her behind her ears, there were three ridges there. *Gills!* She thought.

"Of course." Triton said with a chuckle. Serena turned to face him, the look on her face could have murdered him.

"You've always had them, you just needed a little...push." Triton explained. *You think maybe you could have told me that before you freaked me out?* She thought as she frowned, the lines deep across her forehead.

"You still would have had the same reaction Serena, your human reasoning and conditioning is too strong." Triton answered, crossing his arms on his chest.

"A warning still would have been nice." Serena snapped. Realizing she had just spoken underwater, she touched her lips. Triton smiled as he uncrossed his arms. He backed away from her slightly, wanting to change the mood, he decided now was the time to show her more.

Serena's eyes widened as she watched a swirl appear around Triton's legs and form a beautiful sea green fish tail glimmering like polished sea glass. The scales sparkled with a light glow like the gentle moonlight in the darkest night. He was hugely intimidating and seemed to have grown to almost seven feet tall. His eyes sparkled, the glimmering magnified by the clear glassy ocean water.

"You..."Serena started to say but couldn't find the words. He was stunningly beautiful and it simply took her breath away. She moved forward, realizing that she was actually walking. Albeit, it felt like she was moonwalking in space. She reached out her hand, touching his tail curiously. Even though it was covered in scales, his tail was surprisingly silky smooth to the touch, like the feel of cool, calm, ocean water underneath your fingertips. Her eyes glued to his tail, she pressed her teeth on her lower lip, cocking an eyebrow curiously.

"What?" Triton asked playfully.

"Where's your...How do you...I mean do you have a..." Serena mumbled, unable to let the word out. What was wrong with her? She felt like a giggly ten year old afraid to suddenly combust if she said the evil penis word. Triton burst into laughter, unable to resist from the look on Serena's face.

"Its a valid question!" Serena exclaimed trying to remain serious, but Triton's laughter was contagious.

"Those of us that can transform do." Triton said as he struggled to place his words and get himself together. A shimmer appeared, swirling around Triton's body again as he transformed back into his human form. Serena couldn't help but simply be amazed. Then, she bit her lower lip again, her eyes settling on the said body part resting exactly where it should be. And boy was it ever impressive. Now, the little she remembered about Greek mythology was enough to remind her that the Greek gods were all well endowed. It wasn't just a myth after all.

"And those who can't?" Serena asked, turning away to hide the embarrassment she felt as her cheeks burned when she realized she was staring again and Triton's brow rose in amusement.

"Oh it's there." Triton muttered as he watched her swim away. He wanted to stop her, but knew they should probably get back to the cottage, so he followed behind her. She picked up her shorts and shirt, refusing to look back as Triton slipped on his jeans. He was completely dry, the water only made him wet if he allowed it.

CHAPTER 36
SERENA

Serena remained quiet as they walked back, her mind trying to process everything. It was a lot and sometimes she felt overwhelmed by it all. Besides, she felt she had to focus, her mind wandering to Triton. The need she felt to have him was intense and she had to try to ease her pounding heart and her ragged breath. She felt ridiculous having such a hard time with it. Triton eased up next to her, grabbing her hand, interlocking his fingers with hers giving her this time to process everything. He knew by now that Serena had to overthink everything. It probably came from the human reasoning she had been subjected too all this time. She wanted, no needed to be able to explain everything. Except most of this, she couldn't. They reached the cottage and Triton opened the door for her.

"Chivalry isn't dead after all." Serena said with a cocky smile.

"Only in this realm." Triton said with clear disgust. That was something Triton quickly noticed when he had first begun his search for her. Serena walked to the bedroom, throwing her sandals in a corner. Triton followed behind her, stopping in the doorway, leaning against the frame with his hands in his pockets. He watched her throw her shorts and shirt on a chair then turned to sit on the bed, playing with her hands nervously as she bit that damn lower lip again.

"What?" Serena asked cluelessly as Triton chuckled.

"Sometimes I think you do it just to torture me." Triton answered as he walked to her, using his thumb to pull her luscious lip out from her teeth. His other hand, tucking a lovely wavy brown lock of her hair behind her ear. She closed her eyes, his touch sending a shiver down her spine. She loved the feel of his big masculine hands on her skin. The way her skin prickled and the hairs on the back of her neck stood up. She felt like he was melting her from the inside out. Triton tilted her chin up and planted a soft kiss on her lips as he pulled her onto her feet. He slid his hand up the nape of her neck, loving how her head fit perfectly in it, how soft her hair felt as her hair tangled between his fingers. His other hand caressed the small of her back and slipped under her bikini bottom grabbing her nicely shaped ass. The kiss deepened as he lost himself in the sweet scent of vanilla and coconut of her hair and the tickle of her soft fingers as she trailed the outline of his abdominal muscles down to the waist of his jeans. The jeans that now felt excruciatingly tight as the desire grew with the teasing of her tongue in his mouth. He let go of her head and pulled on the ties of her bikini top, throwing it across the room. He trailed her neck with his mouth as he took a breast in one of his hands, loving that like everything else, it fit in his hand perfectly. Serena arched her back, moaning as he teased her now hardened nipple and when she opened her eyes, he smiled with his damn irresistible curved scarred eyebrow. She bit his lower lip and he chuckled, knowing she was making him pay for toying with her. She unhooked his jeans and tore the zipper open as his hardened member sprung out. She couldn't help but smile at the thought of her inability to talk about this very part of him. Triton untied her bikini bottom and let it drop to the floor, grasping her ass with both hands. Serena tried to remove Triton's jeans, but he was making it difficult to focus, so she moved them down as much as she could and he did the rest with his own legs, pushing them off to the floor. He lifted her and she wrapped her legs around his waist. He moved to the bed, laying her down carefully as he leaned his forehead on hers and one hand caressed her thigh.

"Serena…" Triton whispered her name in a rasp. He craved this moment with every fiber of his being, every part of his body begging him to continue. She had given him the permission before, but she sensed that deep within him was the need for her to allow him to continue, to push further and finally complete their bond.

"I'm all yours, Tristan." Serena whispered softly, using the human name as it felt more personal to her, being who she first fell in love with. She tangled her fingers in the brown curls of his hair, as he had done to her moments before and kissed him. Then with her legs and a quick move of her hips, she pulled him inside her. He groaned, and it made Serena shiver with pleasure, a moan escaping her mouth at the feel of him inside her. Resting on one elbow, he interlocked the fingers of his free hand with hers as their bodies began to rock together.

"Serena!" Triton called out as he lost himself completely in the sway of her hips against him, the heat and tightness of her around him. There was a strange thickness of power building around them like a thick heavy fog and it became harder to breath.

"Tristan!" Serena called back as they reached full climax and she gasped for air. She felt the heaviness and weight of Triton's power pressing against her. They came together, Triton spilling himself into her warmth. A loud noise exploded around them, like thick glass shattering into millions of pieces. Then, bright beams of light exploded out of Serena's body, throwing Triton in a wave of power, through the air and crashing against the wall across the room. She was a human no more. Everything around Serena started to spin out of control as she stood calling out for Triton in a moment of panic, but everything spun too fast, and bile rose from her stomach. She darted for the bathroom on her wobbly legs and threw herself at the toilet and began to wretch uncontrollably as everything became too much to bear. She gagged as the retching spasmed her entire body making her shake violently. A buzzing sound echoed in her mind and slowly grew into thousands of loud whispers screaming to be heard. She grabbed her head.

"Make it stop! Make it stop!" Serena screamed, unable to control it.

Triton opened his eyes, awoken by Serena's screams of pain resonating through his body. Everything hurt, like he had been blasted by Greek fire.

"Serena!" Triton called out as he struggled to his feet. He made his way to the living room frantically searching for the gift Hephaestus had given Serena. *Cursed Atlas!* He cursed as his vision was too blurry and made it difficult to see anything. He finally fumbled around with his hands where he thought he had left the satchel and praised the gods as his hands felt the cotton it was wrapped in. He stumbled back into the room and made his way to Serena where he sat on the floor next to her and leaned against the back wall. He reached over, grabbing her hair gently out of the way of her vomiting.

"Too...much..." Serena tried to talk but wretched again, feeling like she had nothing left but her internal organs to vomit.

Triton blinked a few times, trying to force his vision back. It was slowly starting to improve. He unraveled Hephaestus' present, having no idea

232

what the god of the forge had created for her. A circlet with leather ties. If Hephaestus had made this, it had to be a beautiful piece of art. But with his damn vision, he wouldn't be able to appreciate it. As carefully as he could, he placed it around Serena's head and did the best he could to tie it in the back.

Serena sighed with relief as the whispers disappeared suddenly with the excruciating pressure she had felt in her head. She felt the cold circlet Triton had placed on her head and ran her fingers across her forehead, enjoying the coolness it provided to her burning body. Relieved that she seemed to be done retching, she leaned back against the comfort of Triton's muscular chest as he wrapped an arm around her shoulders to hold her close.

"Holy Fuck!" Triton exclaimed. Serena chuckled weakly as the words sounded so out of character for Triton who seemed too proper for that language.

"Literally. Now I know what holy fucking feels like." Serena mumbled; her voice raspy from the bile that burned her throat. She looked up, searching Triton's face. He looked down and smiled as he was greeted by her sparkling gold eyes and divine features. She truly was the most beautiful woman he had ever laid eyes on, a divine goddess.

"Welcome back my lady." He whispered as he stroked her curly brown hair.

"Thank you, son of Poseidon." Serena said, trying to remain serious but failing miserably as she rested her chin on his chest. The corner of Triton's mouth curled into a smile and his eyes sparkled with amusement at his name off her lips.

"You are so beautiful." Triton said his voice deep with the heartfelt sentiment that melted Serena's soul.

"I just puked like what felt like my entire insides, I think your vision is still defective." Serena said doubtfully.

"I see just fine." Triton replied, his eyes still locked on hers. He was glad she was back to her normal self, and more. He could feel her power, their power pulse together like a separate heartbeat. It was impressive. It was nothing compared to the weight of Zeus' power, it was much, much more.

"Let me show you." Triton said feeling slightly better as he stood, pulling Serena up with him. He wrapped his arms around her waist as he made her face the bathroom mirror. He smiled as Serena gasped in amazement as she touched her hair. Perfect golden-brown ringlets hung down her body, her face almost looked unrecognizable as it was softer, clearer, and her eyes sparkled gold. It was the strangest thing. They were still bright green, but they sparkled gold, how was that even possible? Her hands touched the circlet again, it was a beautiful band with celestial gold and silver, engraved with Irish symbols and encrusted with four sets of two carnelian jasper flame quartz stones which somehow Serena knew all represented serenity. It was stunningly beautiful. Her eyes wandered down to her neckline and noticed her necklace was gone. She instinctively touched her neckline. Amid the chaos, she didn't even feel the necklace fall off.

"Serena, your necklace was also hiding your true divine goddess form." Triton explained as he felt the questions burning in her mind.

"Not anymore." Serena said as she shook her head hesitantly. "I am Serena, goddess of serenity and the sea." She said with a beautiful beaming smile.

"Lady Serena." Triton said as he bowed his head.

"Triton." Serena said in protest as she tried to stop him from bowing again but Triton wouldn't stop. He knelt on one knee, taking her hand, he touched his forehead to the back of it, then pressed his lips on it as he gently kissed it.

"You better get used to it Serena, everyone will bow to you." Triton said with amusement as he stood slowly with a cocky grin on his face. He kissed her then and the heat that grew was different than before. It wasn't an irresistible or uncontrollable pull. It was soft and gentle even when it grew more passionately. Triton loved the feel of her, to grab the back of her head, his fingers tangling in her hair as he kissed her deeply. The look on his face changed as he studied her face, his brows arching into a frown.

"What?" Serena asked.

"You were...not yourself for a few days." Triton said hesitantly as he played with a curl of her hair.

"Triton, I had to find a way to heal from what happened. Although what you call a few days felt a lot longer to me." Serena answered as she bit her lower lip. This was so confusing for her.

"Time in the underworld and Atlantis passes differently than it does here." Triton explained as he pulled that lip out with his thumb and kissed it.

"So, I could have actually been there for a while then." Serena agreed with a nod. It would explain why to a human it would seem rather foolish that she healed rather quickly when in reality, she had been healing for some time.

"My knowledge of the underworld is limited at best, but I do believe it does not follow the same rules of time as this realm does, especially in the fields of Elysium." Triton said. Serena leaned her head against Triton, feeling a little lightheaded even though she had never felt so alive.

"I think the fields of Elysium have a mind of their own. It gives you the time your soul needs to heal." Serena said as she closed her eyes, feeling a little tired. Triton picked her up in his arms. "What are you doing?" Serena asked with a giggle.

"Even we need to rest Serena." Triton said firmly as he laid her down and tucked her in.

"Where are you going?" Serena asked with disbelief, not understanding where he was going since he was also obviously exhausted.

"I…" Triton started to say but stopped himself. Although he had lived in the earth realm for some time now, it was difficult to erase centuries of customs and habits.

"Nonsense, your place is with me." Serena ordered as she patted the spot next to hers.

"You need your sleep." Triton replied, shaking his head in protest.

"You're exhausted too, Triton; we can at least do that together." Serena said, confused.

"Serena," Triton said, raising his scarred eyebrow. "You don't understand yet that Atlanteans have a very strong... drive." Serena's eyes widened in understanding and then laughed at the realization.

"This is not funny." Triton crossed his arms across his chest in protest.

"You're telling me you can't ever sleep with me because what? You can't control yourself?" Serena asked, barely able to contain her laughter at the thought.

"You need your rest, and you look ravishingly beautiful in that nakedness. I won't be able to let you sleep." Triton retorted, not able to withhold his smirk any longer. Serena had a lot to learn when it came to what ran through her veins. The high libido of the gods in Greek mythology was never a secret and was a well-known fact. On top of fighting his own gods' damned genes, he had to fight the bond as well. He pictured having to shackle himself to the bed posts to keep from touching her, but that would be a drastic measure. He wondered how he was going to adjust to this continuous need and desire burning in his gut for her. She stood then, grabbed a bathrobe hanging on a hook against the wall, put it on and wrapped it tightly to hide any skin that could potentially give him any ideas.

"How's this?" Serena asked, cocking an eyebrow, trying to contain her amusement.

"You could be wearing a sack of potatoes and it would do nothing. You would still be the hottest fuckable goddess in the universe." Triton said with a sigh, feeling disheartened. Serena snapped her fingers and her bathrobe changed into a sack of potatoes.

"Still want me?" Serena asked, biting her lower lip as she realized what she had just done, as if she had done this all her life. Triton chuckled.

"Still the best-looking sack of potatoes." Triton said as he pulled her close and kissed her passionately as the heat rose to an uncontrollable level. Serena managed to flick her fingers again and they both suddenly appeared fully dressed in comfortable pajamas.

"You will just have to control yourself Mr. Triton." Serena said attempting to be serious but failing miserably. She pulled him onto the bed, Triton snuggled in spooning next to her. It took a few seconds before she was completely asleep, and he smiled. How was it that he was lucky enough to be the one bonded to such a goddess? Why had he been chosen to be bonded with her? It could have been anyone else more powerful and deserving then he was. Apollo was a powerful Olympian who still had not married, although they had probably avoided the ones responsible for defying them in the first place. It's not that he wasn't grateful, he just found it hard to believe he had been chosen for this. Still, there was something in the back of his mind that told him there was a bigger reason for all of this.

CHAPTER 37
SERENA

She walked up the stairs of a humongous pantheon. The entrance was an archway supported by two marble pillars engraved with intricate patterns she knew she had seen before. As she stepped inside, she remembered she had been there before in another dream. It was a grand room with high cathedral ceilings covered in stained glass brilliantly displaying constellations. Around the room, there were five thrones on each side of her facing each other and two at the very end sitting up above a platform led by stairs. She walked straight down, stopping to admire the craftsmanship and the incredible details of the thrones, each different from the other. She stopped in front of an extremely polished golden throne covered with intricate magical inscriptions. Hung above it, was a sun disk with twenty-one rays shaped like arrows. It was obvious to her that this was the god of the sun's throne but she couldn't seem to find who exactly that was. She was surprised by a high pitched whistling and saw an eagle fly in circles around her head and lower itself until it landed on the back of the highest throne. She walked towards it curiously. The throne, made of black marble with gold lightning bolts etched all over, was so large that seven steps had been built to reach it, each step coloured with a different color of the rainbow. A large blue canopy was laid above it, looking strangely like a blue sky. She studied the eagle, it was beautiful. Instinctively, she lifted her hand towards it.

"This is a sacred place." A deep commanding voice said from behind her. She pulled her hand back and froze. Feeling as if she shouldn't be here and even more, close to this throne. She turned slowly and there stood a tall man. He wore a golden chest plate, framing his chiseled muscles. His shoulders are adorned by golden spaulders shaped like eagle wings. Draping behind him was a white cape embellished by golden lightning bolts embroidered along its edges. His glistening bald head intensified his neatly trimmed salt and peppered beard and stern clear blue eyes that demanded respect. He was strong and imposing yet there was kindness behind those eyes that softened as he studied her intently. He closed the distance between them. He reached up to touch the side of her face, his hand felt warm and gentle yet she still flinched. The last Olympian that touched her left a wound that wasn't completely healed.

"You are beautiful, just like your mother." He said with a warm smile as he backed away slightly to a comfortable distance, as if sensing her discomfort. Serena felt the fondness in the tone of his voice.

"Zeus!" Serena exclaimed, taking a step back at the sudden realization, then kneeled knowing she had to show some respect. He placed a soft gentle hand on her head then lifted her chin to stare directly into her eyes.

"No need to fear me, my child." Zeus said as he pulled her up, his eyes still feeling like they were scrutinizing her intently. A deep frown crossed her face, filled with a mix of concern and confusion. She knew this was a dream, but this felt so real. His touch had felt so real.

"I...am I dreaming?" Serena asked, finally finding her voice yet still unable to look Zeus directly in the eyes. But how could she not be intimidated by the presence of freakin Zeus? He raised her chin again.

"Dreams are the only safe way to communicate, without the unwanted ears of others I'm afraid." Zeus answered with a concern in his eyes, yet they never wavered from hers.

"My mother was banished to the earth realm, forced to live the life of a mere human away from her people, her kingdom, everything and everyone she loved... I had to be kept a secret, to be hidden away and lied to and all this because she feared you were going to send me to Tartarus...how am I supposed to not fear you?" Serena asked her eyes moist as she pleaded to understand why everything had been kept a national secret. In the back of her mind, the whispers told her that her mother was Thetis, daughter of Nereus, queen of the fifty Nereids, who are beautiful water nymph maidens living peacefully and guarding the waters. They lived in the kingdom of Aegean far beyond Poseidon's kingdom's oceans of Atlantis. Serena watched as a look of sorrow crossed Zeus' eyes.

"It is not me your mother feared the most, my child." Zeus said, his tone was melancholic and had a touch of regret.

"You are the king of Atlantis, the ruler of the Olympians and yet you let someone else threaten your children?" Serena asked in disbelief, her tone a little more bitter than she wanted it to be. But how could she not be? Anger flashed like golden lightning bolts in her father's eyes and thunder rolled above them. Zeus chuckled, surprising Serena who stepped back from him.

"I...didn't realize I was being funny." Serena said, her temper flaring even more.

"You truly are my daughter, strong willed and tempered as I see you're already affecting the weather." Zeus said. Serena frowned as she looked up at the sky where the thunder had clapped a moment before.

"Yes, that was all you *daughter*." Zeus said again as he walked up the steps and sat on his throne.

"You cannot come here and pretend you understand thousands of years of existence and make a judgement *daughter*." Zeus said his tone firm and cold, sending a chill down Serena's spine.

"I didn't *come here*." Serena said resentfully, biting back the anger coursing through her veins as she remembered who she was talking to. Standing up to Hades had been one thing, but Zeus' power was much, much greater. It pressed against hers, heavy and thick in the air almost making every breath she took difficult to take.

"No, you certainly did not." Zeus agreed. He liked his daughter's feistiness already. It was clear she had spent too much time with humans without learning the proper Atlantean etiquette and he couldn't blame her for that. Perhaps it would help her bring some humanity back into Atlanteans after all.

"I cannot say who will be against you when you come to face the council." Zeus said gravely as he rubbed his chin with concern.

"Face the council?" Serena asked, taken aback. It was the first time she heard anything about facing the council.

"Ah, I see the son of Poseidon has not told you of the task he was entrusted with?" Zeus asked, cocking an eyebrow with obvious amusement. Serena bit her lower lip, almost making herself bleed with frustration. "Let me enlighten you *daughter*. Poseidon and his son Triton were the ones who discovered your existence. The son of Poseidon, being his father's most loyal and faithful servant was given the task of finding you and he was supposed to kill you." Zeus explained to her enjoying the dismay showing clearly on her face.

"You're lying!" Serena said with a trembling voice as she turned her back on Zeus, tears threatening to spill from her eyes as she felt betrayed by the only one she thought she could trust. The bond on her arm pulsated and glowed brightly and Zeus could not miss it. He closed the distance between them then grabbed her left wrist to make her face him. She flinched and yanked her hand back, but his grip was too strong.

"By the fires of Tartarus!" Zeus' exclaimed, his voice filled with disbelief rumbling through the pantheon.

"Who dared to defy me with...this...?" Zeus mumbled, unable to finish his sentence. His eyes filled with fury, flashing gold as he glared at her and the grip on her wrist tightened shooting pain up her arm.

Serena woke suddenly with a sob escaping from her throat. A bead of sweat rolled off her forehead as she fought to keep the tears from falling. She healed in the underworld, that was true, but she still was not immune to hurt, pain and betrayal. She flipped the blanket as slowly as she could and walked to the window. It was dawn outside, but the dark clouds above threatened the clap of thunder as lightning flashed in the distance. She turned to study the man that was laying next to her, the man she was bound to for the rest of her immortal life. He looked so peaceful, resting on his side with his brown hair hanging loosely around his face. He was completely silent. She could barely see him breathe. In fact, she was almost certain he was breathing through his gills instead of his mouth or nose as she couldn't even see the rise and fall of his chest. She bit her lower lip wondering how long she would wait knowing she wanted to leave. She took a slow deep breath as silently as she could, closed her eyes and snapped her fingers to transport herself back to her home in Oahu. She reappeared in the living room, almost surprised that everything was back the way it was, before it all changed. She stood in the living room, there were no shards of glass anywhere from the patio door Triton had shattered when he had come to save her. No indents on the wall where Ares had landed from Triton's attack. The kitchen island sat untouched as if nothing had happened. She wasn't sure what to think as she had expected to come back and deal with the reality of what had happened, but nothing. As if someone had just wiped out everything that led to her transformation. She jumped in surprise at a knock on her patio door. She turned to see the red head Arianna standing there waving at her. Serena sighed, not sure she was ready to face a child of the man who had betrayed her. She slid the door open.

"I...wasn't sure you would be awake at this early hour. I was walking on the beach when I saw you." Arianna said as if nothing had changed.

"Why don't you come in, Ariel." Serena said solemnly as she opened the door and moved aside for her. Ariel hesitated for a second then walked in, waiting for Serena to slide the door shut before saying anything.

"You know who I am?" Ariel said, confused.

"Yes, Ariel, daughter of Triton." Serena said as she walked to her couch and let herself sink in the cushions. "Your father was not too happy to find out you were here." She said as she clasped her hands together staring in the distance.

"My father knows I am here?" Ariel asked in a panic, but quickly noticed Serena was distant when she simply nodded.

"I...needed to see who was keeping my father in the realm he despised the most." Ariel said shamefully knowing she had been caught. Serena looked at her solemnly.

"Despised this place?" Serena asked with a sarcastic chuckle.

"My father has avoided this realm like the plague. The last time I was here, I thought he was going to destroy it." Ariel said as she sat in the chair across from Serena studying her.

"It seems you caused quite the stir the last time you came here." Serena said, tucking the new found curls behind her ears.

"I fell for a human who turned out to only want to use me for his own fame." Ariel said sadly.

"Men!" Serena scuffed, her emotions flaring causing the blue glow of the bond to shine brightly along her arm. Ariel's eyes widened in disbelief.

"Mother of Zeus!" Ariel exclaimed as she rushed to Serena's side and grabbed her arm. "Is it you he is bonded to?" Ariel asked her fingers trailing the mark on her arm, her excitement clearly visible.

"You know about that?" Serena asked, surprised at how many knew of her predicament before she did.

"I have ears across the walls of our kingdom." Ariel explained her cheeks burning red as the corner of her mouth turned into a cheeky smile.

"I see." Serena said with a deep frown. "Yes, Triton...your father and I are..bonded." Serena confirmed. Shit could not take that beaming smile off of Ariel's face.

"How delightful!" Ariel almost shouted as she stood but she froze as she saw the look on Serena's face. "What is wrong?" She asked with concern.

"It's...complicated Ariel." Serena simply answered, avoiding her gaze. Ariel frowned, her lips pressed together as she considered what to say.

"I cannot pretend to understand, but I believe I can make my own assumptions." Ariel said as she sat next to Serena again. Most assumed she was flighty and superficiel, but that's what she wanted them to think. She knew for a fact Zeus did not ordain this bond, he wouldn't be foolish enough to bond his mighty daughter with her father, it would be disastrous. So, she knew it had to be a bond that was done without their consent. She had watched her father from a distance since he had been in this realm and had never seen him seem so relaxed, at ease and even happy.

"My father has been living miserably in the shadow of Lord Poseidon for a very long time, unable to find peace...and love, until now." Ariel explained touching Serena's shoulder. "Serena, you have freed him and for that I will remain forever grateful." She said with sincere honesty gleaming in her eyes. She loved her father dearly, her mother had left her in his care never to be seen or heard of again. He had done and given her everything to the extent Poseidon would allow. He had even risked everything when she had ventured to the earth realm long ago and she had been forever grateful, vowing to never put him in that position again, until he came here. She couldn't stay away. She had to see what he was up to.

"My father is the best Atlantean there is. He has a kind heart and he loves and serves his father to a fault. He needed this, deserved this." Ariel said again, her voice almost pleading for her fathers cause. It was obvious by her tone that she loved her father very much.

"Ariel-" Serena started to say but she froze. It had started with a slight prickle of her skin and had slowly intensified as Ariel had been talking. Now, it felt like all the hairs of her body were standing up and carrying a strange electrical current.

"Serena?" Ariel asked as Serena's eyes became blank and she became still as a statue. She didn't move, her mind distantly focusing on the sensation. She started to hear a whisper, *Serena, goddess of the sea and serenity I summon thee.* The whispers grew louder as if they were getting closer somehow.

"Can you hear it?" Serena asked in a whisper.

"Hear what?" Ariel asked with a concerned frown. Serena stood, then walked to the back patio door, opened it and began walking towards the water.

"Serena?" Ariel called out, following behind her.

"I am being summoned..." Serena said so softly Ariel almost missed it. Serena knew she could resist the summoning, but she hadn't learned how to yet and it was such an irresistible pull, it was like her limbs moved forward without her command. Of all the powers that she could be lacking, the fates chose this one? She had faced Hades in the freaking underworld and she couldn't find the power to resist a summon? There was trepidation in her gut telling her whoever was summoning her was not quite on friendly terms. As her feet touched the ocean, Serena watched a figure rise out of the water. She had dark jet black hair with random white streaks. It flowed wildly about, although it should have been wet and sticking to her. Her dark brown eyes looked almost black. She was naked, her breasts hidden by her flowing hair. The corner of her mouth was twisted up in an evil grin that sent a shiver down Serena's spine. She glided along the water like she was floating and as she got closer, Serena realized the bottom part of her body was that of a creature resembling an octopus with twelve muscled and menacing tentacles.

"Lady Serena." Scylla hissed as she bowed her head.

"Scylla." Serena muttered under her breath as the name popped in her mind even though she had never seen her.

"It is good to see the spirit of Namaka return as the rightful ruler of these oceans." Scylla spoke with high flattery.

"And you best remember that, Scylla." Serena responded, emphasizing her name. It didn't sound threatening, but the implications of it were clear.

"This is simply a social call, my lady." Scylla said with the smirk on her face still untouched.

"Do you make a habit of breaking Zeus' law by making social calls?" Serena asked, her voice was calm and firm, doing everything she could to portray the demand of respect. Scylla was not here on friendly terms, that much was certain no matter what Scylla's flattery was attempting to do.

"Zeus' law?" Scylla chuckled with a tone of vehemence. Serena took a silent breath, the clouds above them suddenly turning dark and the water around Scylla began to churn wildly. A bolt of lightning shot out of the skies and landed next to Scylla. She clearly clenched her jaw in an attempt to hide her surprise from the slight pain shooting through her body from the electrical currents the lightning conducted. But she didn't move as thunder clapped above them and Serena tried to use the same power she had used in the underworld with Hades, but to no avail. Here, reunited with her human form and wearing the circlet she needed to help control her powers, she realized it also blocked them just enough to keep her from doing what she wanted. Was it possible she had been more powerful in the underworld? Could it be her wavered confidence? She had felt so strong in the underworld, so invincible, like she could do just about anything. Now, she felt the flicker of her powers but it was as if some were just out of her grasp. *Be careful with Scylla.* Triton's voice whispered in her mind like a soft distant thought. She could feel his growing concern with the sense of urgency he felt to be near her.

"What do you want?" Serena demanded, raising her voice to be heard above the now growing storm around them.

"Zeus has done *nothing* to protect this world. Do you honestly think that making it law for us to stay away was really for the good of the *humans*? Join our plight, help us against him!" Scylla asked, her eyes flashing with anger as the waters continued to grow turbulent. Serena narrowed her eyes, her lips thinned from pressing them hard together.

"Do not pretend you have the best interest of humans at heart. I may be young and unfamiliar with my roots *Scylla*, but the waters tell me your intentions are far less admirable." Serena said as calm as the eye of a storm. Scylla's face turned from a devilish grin to fury in the blink of an eye.

"We will see who will pay!" Scylla shouted furiously, her words barely audible through the storm that had formed around her. She dove back into the sea and was gone. Serena closed her eyes, taking slow deep breaths to calm the loud thump of her heartbeat. The truth was, the storm wasn't caused by her lack of temper, it was because she had been...afraid. Something about Scylla had just unnerved her, and the fact that she couldn't tap into her powers as she had with Hades filled her with doubt. She turned away, walking back to her condo as the clouds behind her faded to give way to the bright sunshine and the almost perfectly still ocean waters. Ariel stood speechless, watching the scenery change drastically around them, then flipping her eyes between where Scylla stood moments before to Serena walking quietly back into her home. She frowned, unsure of what to think about what just happened. She knew so little of the situation, but what she did know was that Serena is supposed to be the most powerful Atlantean to ever exist. Why would she let Scylla get away? She should have stopped her.

CHAPTER 38
TRITON

Triton awoke suddenly as his heart began thumping louder than usual.

He sat up, quickly realizing that Serena was gone. He tried to reach out to her, using the power of his mind but she refused to acknowledge him. Something was amiss. She was far, in fact he could sense she had gone back to her home and there was someone else there with her. *Ariel!* He flung the blankets off him and stood in anger as he had hoped Ariel had gone home when she saw Serena had not been there. He changed back into his blue jeans and white tshirt, wishing he had a better change of clothes, but knowing where he was heading would require him to take them off anyways. He flung the door of the cottage open and came face to face with his mother.

"Triton, my son!" Amphitrite exclaimed conspicuously.

"Mother." Triton muttered after a moment of surprise passed, she was the last person he expected to see here. As if remembering who was standing in front of him, he knelt and grabbed the back of her hand and placed it on his forehead before standing again. She returned the gesture by touching his forehead with hers.

"What brings you here?" Triton asked curiously, a deep frown forming on his face as he knew she just didn't pop over to the earth realm for fun. She was dressed in a dark brown leather warrior outfit, looking ready for battle, not for a mere everyday conversation.

"Can I not simply miss my favorite son and want to see him?" Amphitrite asked, raising the same eyebrow her son always did.

"That is highly doubtful." Triton retorted knowing her too well.

"You think you know me so well?" Amphitrite scoffed as she walked past him. Triton sighed in annoyance as he shut the door behind her. He had no time for this.

"I know the facts, and you haven't been in this realm in centuries." Triton replied impatiently, winning him a scolded look from his mother.

"Not only is the tension growing with the new found goddess, but your *daughter* is missing." Amphitrite finally explained. There was a deep concern in her tone that Triton could not ignore. He clenched his jaw, frustrated, enraged that his daughter had managed once again to add to the tension. She was defiant and this time, he wasn't sure he would be able to soften the blow of her punishment. He had jumped through hoops the last time with his own father, convincing him to let Triton deal with her consequences and that it did not require Zeus' attention. But this time, Poseidon would not be so considerate. Triton sighed as he pinched the bridge of his nose and closed his eyes.

"Women!" Triton muttered in frustration, his blood boiling at the two in his life who seemed to persistently test his patience.

"The last time my daughter decided to explore her sense of adventure you didn't even budge, in fact," Triton said as he rubbed the back of his neck, his eyes drifting to the gardens outside the window. "I believe you found it amusing. So spare the excuse that my daughter's adventurous and rebellious tendencies are the reason for your visit." Triton retorted sourly, making Amphitrite frown.

"Something has you tighter than a bladder monster's grip." Amphitrite muttered as she joined him by the window, admiring the beauty of the gardens. She couldn't deny the beauty of flowering gardens and its scents were difficult to beat. Coral reefs had their own appeal, but it just didn't measure up.

"I came to warn you that-" Amphitrite began to explain. Triton snapped out of his distant stare suddenly as he felt Serena's mind fill with trepidation, she was being dangerously summoned. He felt the panic rise and he sensed she realized she couldn't tap into her powers as she had in the underworld. *Be careful with Scylla!* He warned her. He wasn't sure what Scylla wanted. Scylla wasn't foolish enough to think she could take on Serena?

"Curse Atlas! Scylla?" Triton barked, finally looking at his mother who pressed her lips together and frowned.

"Her and Charybdis have breached a guarded portal and managed to travel to the earth realm." Amphitrite answered with a sigh.

"When?" Triton gritted angrily.

"A day or so ago." Amphitrite answered glumly.

"And I was just told about this now?" Triton asked as he waved his conch shell into appearance.

"We sent Iris," Amphitrite answered, glaring at her son, not appreciating his tone. "But she couldn't find you. Apparently you were in a place she couldn't reach you!"Amphitrite responded with concern. The only place Iris could not go was the underworld. Triton's frown dissipated as it dawned on him why his mother had ventured into this realm. She thought he was dead.

"I...am sorry mother." Triton said apologetically as he ran a hand in his hair.

"I feared the worst when I found out Ariel was gone." Amphitrite said, closing her eyes as she recalled the dread she had felt when Iris had said he was unreachable. Her heart had almost stopped, especially following the news of Scylla and Charybdis. Ariel could be reckless when she was desperate. Her last venture out into the earth realm had proven that. When the news came that the alarm from a distant hidden tunnel portal had been breached, she could only assume the worst. That tunnel was for emergencies and only their direct families were aware of it. Someone from the inside had led the enemy right to it.

"Which portal was taken?" Triton asked, fearing the answer.

"Aegea." Amphitrite answered almost in a whisper. Triton closed his eyes. Ariel would have known about this portal. After the last incident, Triton had taken her shapeshifting abilities away so she could not transform into human form. The only person powerful enough outside the walls of their kingdom was Scylla.

"Cursed Atlas!" Triton exploded in fury as he punched the wall. He closed his eyes, breathing heavily to calm himself as he blew his shell to summon Hermes, again.

"Ready for that game of poker?" Hermes said rubbing his hands with excitement as he appeared. He glanced over from Amphitrite to Triton sensing the obvious tension and with a sigh of relief said, "I guess that'll wait." He gritted with disappointment. Amphitrite slowly walked right to Hermes' face, staring at him intently.

"Tell me Hermes, why is it you rejected my summon but yet you answered my son's?" Amphitrite asked curving an eyebrow curiously, unable to hide the annoyance in her voice.

"Simple your royal fishyness, you see Triton here owes me some fun times and I just can't turn *that* down." Hermes explained plainly as if his excuse made perfect sense, seemingly unperturbed by the queen's icy glare. Hermes was reminded where Triton got his death stare.

"Although if you keep summoning me, you will be one busy card player in the near future." Hermes said with great satisfaction at Triton.

"I need to get to Serena." Triton growled.

"For a chance to take a look at that marvelous piece of as...tonishing goddess," Hermes started but a clench of Triton's jaw followed by his arms crossed and a death stare making him mumble himself out of his chosen words. He cleared his throat and quickly hit the ground with his caduceus before it was too late.

They reappeared instantly in Serena's Oahu home. Ariel sat on Serena's living room sofa, hands fidgeting on her lap as Serena stood speechless in the kitchen drinking a glass of water.

"Father!" As soon as Ariel saw her father, she jumped off the couch and backed away, trying to put distance between her and her father, knowing it wouldn't really do much when it came down to it. She had not lied to

Serena about her father's character, he had a kind heart, but she knew this time, she had gone too far. As he always did, his brown eyes glaring at her and his arms crossed over his chest, his silent firm presence didn't even require him to speak. Triton felt Serena's apprehensiveness of the situation. *What is going on?* Serena asked tentatively. She could feel he was angry, no, furious and that most of it was directed at Ariel. *Ariel crossed a line, Serena.* Triton replied a little too abruptly. *She just wanted to follow you here.* Serena replied her heart sank from Triton's coldness towards her, but could she blame him? *No, there is much more at stake, including the safety of the humans of this realm.* He snapped, refusing to even look at her, because he knew if he did, he would lose his cool and he needed to remain composed and firm for this. He had too. The safety of the humans demanded him too.

"Do you know what you have done, *child?*" Amphitrite said her tone was just as cold and composed as Triton. It was clear where he had gotten it from. His father was too hot tempered and always lashed out furiously at anyone or anything that opposed him. But Amphitrite was more calculated and controlled. He had always feared her more than his own father as a child, because he knew she took the time to consider what wiser punishment she would bestow. Whereas his father just always reacted, albeit harshly most of the time, but he was more predictable.

"I...I...I thought she was supposed to be the most powerful Atlantean to exist and that she would dispose of them before they had a chance to hurt anyone!" Ariel cried out backing herself into the patio door, hot tears of fear in her eyes. Serena slammed her glass down a little too aggressively and moved to make her way to Ariel. *No Serena, do not interfere with this!* Triton snapped as he used a hand to motion her to stay where she was. Triton lifted his left hand and his trident appeared. Tears of panic poured out of Ariel's eyes when she realized her father was not going to be easy on her now.

"Father, please... I didn't intend for the humans to be harmed!" She begged with hot, fresh tears burning her eyes.

"There's nothing I can do this time Ariel. You did not just put your life at risk, you put all the lives of humankind at risk. The ones we were created to protect!" Triton said through his teeth, forcing himself to be calm through the haze of his fury.

"Please..." Ariel begged, her eyes turning to Serena, pleading for her assistance. *Triton.* Serena said. *Stay out of it Serena!.* Triton said firmly.

"There is a way to avoid greater punishment through Lord Poseidon or even Zeus." Triton said as he was deep in thought. He could see the desperation in his daughter's eyes and even if he wanted to be angry with her, she was still his daughter. He needed to do what had to be done to avoid Zeus' wrath.

"I'll do anything." Ariel pleaded in a whisper.

"Since you seem to be unable to stay away from this realm, then you will be banished to it." Triton commanded. A look of shock crossed Ariel's face, but before she had time to contest, Triton pointed his trident at Ariel, sending his powers upon her and stripping her of all her underwater abilities. She couldn't transform, and now she couldn't breath underwater either. Ariel gasped, as if all the air had been sucked out of her lungs, then she let herself slump to the ground. She wrapped her arms around her legs and continued to sob softly as she tried to steady her breathing. Triton closed the distance between them, making his trident disappear as he lifted her up and wrapped his arms around her in a fatherly embrace. He held her for some time and no one spoke. The silence deafening and her sobs the only sound that could be heard.

"I will do my best to keep Lord Poseidon and Zeus from giving further punishments, but I cannot guarantee anything." Triton said softly now as he wiped his daughter's tears with his thumb. Ariel simply nodded, unable to bring herself to say anything.

"I have a small place you can stay at, it is not much, but you will be comfortable there. I will take you there now." He said softly. Ariel pulled away, tucking her red hair behind her ears as she followed her father towards the front door. As he passed the kitchen island, he glanced over at Serena who looked up and locked eyes with him.

"Mother, I will get Ariel settled." Triton spoke to her but didn't look back, his eyes still on Serena. *And then, you and I will talk!* He said to Serena.

CHAPTER 39
SERENA

She felt like a schoolgirl scolded by her teacher with the way Triton had looked at her and the tone of his thought.

Amphitrite watched her son and her granddaughter leave without saying even a word. As the door closed behind Triton and Ariel, Serena sighed, leaning back against the kitchen island and rubbed her eyes.

"I am going to assume that you were the reason why he was in a foul mood to begin with." Amphitrite said firmly. Serena looked up, almost forgetting in the heat of the moment about the woman that had appeared with Triton. She turned to face Serena and bit her lower lip. The woman standing in front of her was nothing short of an impressive, beautiful and assertive woman! She looked no older than Serena herself, but in her deep ocean blue eyes she could see ancient wisdom. She had dozens of thick and long brown tresses that fell to her fit waist. Her strong and muscular body was complemented by skin tight upper body leather armor that resembled golden fish scales. Her forearms had four large golden rivets with mermaid symbols on them. Her back had larger versions of them trailing down her spine. She looked ferocious and indestructible.

"I…" Serena trailed off, her words vanishing at the sheer intimidating look of Amphitrite's scrutinizing gaze. What could she say? She didn't know who this woman was.

"I am Amphitrite, daughter of Nereus, wife of Poseidon." Amphitrite introduced herself. Serena caught a glimpse of a cat running down the stairs.

"Well if it isn't the loveliest of my dear sisters." Thetis said with a warm smile, obviously tickled pink to see her. The firm and assertive woman vanished before Serena's very eyes.

"Thetis! My queen and dear sister!" Amphitrite said with a smile. It was that of a warm sister as they reached for each other, forehead to forehead and held each other close. Serena frowned. It was difficult to believe how much of her reality was a lie, yet everything was connected to the Atlanteans. She sighed slowly, wondering if she would ever come to terms with it all. Thetis pulled back then as she noticed Serena's frown of dismay. Leaving her sister, she wrapped her arms around her daughter, holding her tighter then she had in her entire life. Serena stiffened at the unfamiliar gentleness of the motherly display. It was as if she had lived with an entirely different mother all her life. Thetis pulled back, framed the side of her daughter's face tenderly with her hands.

"If you only knew how difficult all this was for me." Thetis said with honest regret.

"But...why?" Serena asked, fighting back the tears now. She couldn't understand. Why would any mother willingly choose to be cold and distant with their child? Why did she have to grow up fending for herself and feeling as lonely as she had? This scarred her so deeply she swore she would never have children of her own.

"I needed you to grow up to be a strong independent woman and to prepare you for who you needed to be." Thetis explained, her eyes and tone of voice begging for her understanding.

"All the good that did." Amphitrite mumbled under her breath but loud enough for them to hear. Thetis glared at her sister.

"The fates knew and understood she would not be able to do this alone, Thetis. How could you think for one second that putting the fate of the universe on your daughter's shoulders alone would be realistic?" Amphitrite questioned as she curved her left eyebrow, the same eyebrow she had seen Triton do so many times before. Thetis pulled back, glaring at her sister.

"I thought it was the only way to prepare her if she was to be the most powerful Atlantean. I wanted to give her all the strength she needed to bear the burden." Thetis replied as her shoulders slumped.

"If I was the most powerful Atlantean? Are you telling me you did all this on a *possibility*?" Serena gritted with disbelief. Thunder rolled in the distance as it responded to her temper and her eyes flashed from green to gold. Never had she felt her temper this out of control, but she just couldn't seem to help feeling so helpless, so lost. Inside, she felt amazing, like she found the part of herself she had been missing all her life. But she felt torn by the lack of knowledge of her real identity.

"The prophecy spoke of a child, yet everyone assumed it would be a son...so did I." Thetis answered solemnly. Serena sighed heavily. She wanted to understand but she knew she was missing too many pieces of the puzzle for any of it to make sense.

"Ok so basically you don't know for sure that I am this child of the prophecy." Serena said with relief. She didn't even know what this prophecy really meant, but she knew it meant some serious shit. Both Amphitrite and Thetis looked at Serena with frowns on their faces.

"Oh, there is no doubt you are the child of the prophecy." Amphitrite said.

"And what makes you say that?" Serena asked as she closed her eyes tightly. Amphitrite grabbed her arm gently and Serena opened her eyes again.

"The fates would not have gone to all this trouble." Amphitrite said as her fingers traced the blue glow of the bond on Serena's arm. Serena pulled her hand back uncomfortably, she was hoping beyond all things that she wasn't who they were all looking for. Maybe if she had just faced Hades, but with what happened with Scylla, she didn't think she was powerful enough. She turned away then sunk back into the comfort of her living room sofa. Leaning her elbows against her lap, she rubbed her face with her hands trying to ease the awful tension she felt.

"Amphitrite is right, I'm afraid." Thetis said but Serena didn't hear regret in her voice then, more like excitement or pride. Her mother *wanted* it to be her, she could see it.

"I'm not ready for this! Now I have to deal with all this weird shit and I'm still trying to deal with...this!" Serena exclaimed with frustration as she motioned to the bond on her left arm.

"You need to work on your choice of words." Thetis scolded her daughter. Serena glared at her mother.

"My *choice of words* is the only thing I still have a choice on." Serena snapped as she stood, her words pressing on her chest and every breath she took seemed to hurt.

"Everything I've ever known is a lie. Everyone I know is part of that lie. I was never given the choice for any of this including this bond to a man I don't even know." Serena said as she closed her eyes regretting the last words as they escaped her mouth. It wasn't a lie, she barely knew anything about Triton other than he was an Atlantean and the son of Poseidon. She knew him more as Tristan, and even then that wasn't much to go on. She felt like she had just married a man she just met.

"Just so we are clear my dear niece, Triton is in the same predicament you are. He didn't ask for this bond. It only made matters much, much worse for him." Amphitrite said defensively.

"You mean he couldn't complete the task of killing me when he found me." Serena said as she leaned her head on the glass of the patio door, enjoying the coolness it provided. Thetis glared at Amphitrite who only took on a defensive stance.

"My son had no choice. He has always been loyal to his father." Amphitrite said.

"Everyone has a choice." Serena answered but the words choked in her throat as she realized what she was saying.

"Of course," Amphitrite chuckled. "Just as much as you did my dear." She said sarcastically, the words burning in her mind. Serena knew she was right. She had sensed Triton's turmoil, the terrible pull he felt between her and the loyalty he had towards his father, and all the other Olympians in his life. She knew, deep down, that Triton did not choose this either and his feelings were so overwhelmingly sincere it almost hurt.

"Do you not realize how lucky you are Serena? You have the power to restore Atlanteans to their former purpose!" Thetis said and as Serena turned her head to look at her mother, she saw the obvious excitement beaming in her eyes.

"How can I feel lucky mother, I know *nothing* about what I'm supposed to restore thanks to you." Serena answered bitterly. All she knew is right now, she felt helpless and lost, far from the powerful confident Atlantean she had felt like in the underworld. She touched the circlet around her forehead. Thetis reached out to Serena, putting a gentle hand on her shoulder.

"Right now, I would really like some time alone." Serena simply said, her eyes locked on the ocean spilling out in front her. Thetis nodded, feeling resigned knowing she had done this to Serena. She motioned to her sister Amphitrite.

"My sister and I have some catching up to do, I'll come back later." Thetis said but Serena barely heard the words as they left through the front door. Serena closed her eyes and sighed heavily. She never thought she would enjoy the peace and quiet of her home, but she felt overwhelmed and needed a breather. But it wasn't meant to be. She had just sunk into her living room sofa when the doorbell rang. She leaned her elbows on her lap and rubbed her face in frustration.

"Just a minute!" Serena shouted as nicely as she could, but she knew she sounded slightly frustrated. As she got to her front door, she hesitated for a moment, remembering who had been at her door the last time. She bit her lower lip, and felt a peaceful calming presence on the other side of the door. Her circlet wasn't letting her tap too much into her powers, but enough to know whoever was there was someone she would be glad to see. It was confirmed as she opened the door and saw her *father*, Pete, standing there hands in the pockets of his blue jeans. He smiled tentatively, a strand of his light brown hair dangled across his forehead.

"Dad!" Serena exclaimed as she threw herself in his arms.

"Woa!" Pete said as he tumbled back and fought for balance, but he wrapped his arms around Serena and held her close. Pete had been the only being who had ever shown her real love and affection, and Serena wondered if he knew she wasn't really his. The thought sent a wave of sobs, making her feel like a ten year old little girl again instead of a thirty year old adult.

"Shhh... it's okay." Pete said as he stroked the back of her head, his gentle words whispered in her ear making her cry even more. Triton had been there for her, but he was part of everything that was happening to her. Realizing that they were still standing in the doorway with the door wide open, she backed away, wiping the tears as she moved aside to let Pete in.

"I'm sorry...come in." Serena apologized.

"Never apologize for being human." Pete said with a comforting smile as he wiped a tear she had missed off her cheek. *If only I was human.* Serena thought but only bit her lower lip. Pete narrowed his eyes and frowned, knowing this look on Serena's face meant something quite serious. There were two times Serena had that look: when she told him her asshole of a boyfriend cheated on her and when she told him she was moving to Hawaii. Serena shut the door behind them and walked past him, avoiding the concerned look in Pete's eyes.

"What are you doing all the way in Hawaii?" Serena asked to avoid the serious questions roaming in Pete's mind. She felt his eyes studying her with concern as she busied herself pulling out two mugs and poured two cups of coffee, then handed one to Pete knowing he took it black like she did.

"Your mother said she would be here for a while and that you could use your dad." Pete said sipping on his coffee, his eyes never leaving her face.

"Are you going to tell me what happened or am I going to have to pry it out of you?" Pete finally asked after a few silent sips from both of them. Serena watched him, handsome by his own rights he was a little over six feet tall, with large thick shoulders. Light brown hair touching the tip of shoulders that he liked to slick back and clear blue eyes that could pierce right through her soul. She always thought he was the most handsome man in her life, and she still believed it.

"I…don't think you would understand…" Serena trailed off, unable to come up with a reasonable answer, something that would make sense for human ears as tears welled up in her eyes and threatened to spill once more. Pete chuckled as he took another sip then choked. He clapped on his chest as he fought to catch his breath and Serena felt the strange unease that came with it. Her lips thinned as she pressed them together and frowned. *Thetis, queen of the fifty nereids, was banished to the earth realm and forced to marry a human named Peleus.* The voices whispered. The voices that were controlled by the circlet and had been scarce and incoherent for the most part. But this, this was clear. But if her mother had married a mere human, Pete couldn't be that human. He would be long dead wouldn't he?

"Serena, I know there is…a lot that's probably been thrown at you…" Pete said tentatively as he reached for her hand and squeezed it. He had always been a wonderful father figure for Serena and as she took a long look into his eyes the voices continued their whispers: *Peleus, husband of Thetis, hero and king, father of Achilles.* Serena pulled her hand back and stood backing away from Pete as the realization set in of what was being persistently whispered in her mind. *When the prophecy was spoken that Thetis would bear a child more powerful than Zeus, he gave her to a human named Peleus, king of Myrmidons and Thessaly. Thetis, unwilling to wed a mortal, refused. She was subdued by Peleus with the help of Chiron, a Centaur, son of Cronus, holding fast as she changed into fire, serpent and many other shapes. Exhausted, she had no choice but to accept her fate. She married the human, a grand ceremony attended by all the gods.*

"You're part of all this!" Serena muttered, a sob catching her throat and making the words difficult as she closed her eyes and shook her head. She didn't want to believe that the man she revered, loved and had known as her loving father could be involved in this. But was she really surprised ? Everyone else in her life was an accomplice somehow weren't they?

"Serena, sweetie what's wrong?" Pete asked pleadingly as he stood. There was unmistakable sincere distress in his voice.

"Peleus." Serena said in a whisper as she opened her eyes and stared right into his. His eyes widened and he took a step back, obviously surprised by her realization.

"Serena…" Pete said as he closed the distance and placed his hand on Serena's shoulders.

"How's it possible? You're….human." Serena asked her eyes pleading for understanding as she looked into the soft eyes of the man she had called her father for so many years.

"It's a long story." Peleus answered with a sigh as he stepped back, then leaned against the kitchen island behind him.

"Seems like everything implicating the Atlanteans is." Serena gritted with frustration as she rubbed the side of her head trying to ease the tension.

"That's…an understatement." Peleus answered with a chuckle.

"So you forced my mother to marry you…?" Serena asked curiously. She wasn't outraged as she knew things were much different back then, thousands of years ago.

"I was young and stupid Serena. When Zeus offered me immortality, I took it without even knowing what I was getting myself into. Then, I found out all I needed to do was allow the Olympians to create a bond between me and this queen which seemed easy enough. Until I actually met your mother." Peleus explained with disbelief, mostly in himself for being so naive and proud. Like most of the heroes created by the Olympians, he thought he was indestructible and capable of doing anything he was asked to do. And who could refuse immortality? Serena chuckled, knowing exactly what he was talking about. The smile vanished again and a deep frown crossed her face as she realized, wondering if Peleus knew who she was.

"So, you knew about me?" Serena asked tentatively, hoping she wasn't stirring something new. She watched as Peleus took a slow, long sip of the coffee then held the cup with both hands. After a few moments of silence, he simply nodded a sad look crossing his face.

"Your mother and I…have been cursed when it comes to children Serena. Achilles was the only one who lived long enough to fight…and I think even you know how that ended." Peleus went on to explain glumly.

It was clear to see the sadness behind his ancient blue eyes. She could see now the remnants of his herohood. He was built like a soldier and had always kept himself fit with various martial arts training and intense cardio workouts. He was the definition of a Greek hero now that she thought of it.

"What about the twins?" Serena asked curiously. Not that she was close to Romulus and Remus. They had tortured her existence as a child. They had settled down somewhat with age though, even if she couldn't call their relationship *close*, they still managed a hug or two when they got together. Her life strangely started to make sense to her now. She had never felt like she fit in, even if Peleus had always been a great father. A great father to a child that wasn't even his.

"We adopted the twins when they were just a few months old." Peleus simply answered as he took another sip. Serena grabbed her mug behind Peleus, who moved aside watching her as she walked around the kitchen island to the sofa, sinking her weight down, staring at the content of her mug.

"Last time I spoke to your mother, she was frantic on the phone, saying something bad happened to you. She couldn't make a coherent sentence. I told her I'd be on the next plane over." Peleus said his voice filled with concern as he joined her, sitting next to her, his knee touching hers.

"I...knew something terrible had happened. I've only ever seen her like this once before." Peleus said, his thumbs thumping the mug uncomfortably. Serena chuckled, not in any way amused, far from it, but with surprise of a mother she couldn't envision.

"And when was that exactly?" Serena asked. She wondered who her mother really was. It seemed everyone knew her as an entirely different person. The picture everyone seemed to paint of her mother was that of a caring and loving mother who would do *anything* for her child. That was not how she saw her at all. But she *had* been different since Ares...no. She shook her head to push away the thought.

"The day your mother realized that even through all her sacrifices, bargains, a trip to the underworld, the fates were going to take Achilles." Peleus said, his eyes distant as if seeing the memory roll out before him.

Serena realized then that her mother had some excruciatingly painful losses.

"Seems to me there's no point fighting against the fates." Serena said bluntly. They literally had everyone's fate in their hands and could pull the thread of your life in the blink of an eye.

"No. There isn't, no matter how badly you refuse to accept it, it won't change *anything*. The only thing you will accomplish is pissing them off, and *that* is a grave mistake." Peleus replied with a pained expression. She looked at him again, seeing the tremendous pain behind his eyes and Serena realized he too had suffered great losses.

"Did someone hurt you Serena?" Peleus asked firmly, his eyes staring in the distance as he sipped on his coffee again.

"I had a quite *unpleasant* first encounter with Ares." Serena sneered with disgust. She watched Peleus' face darken and his jaw clenched with anger, no fury. Something she had never witnessed in her life. He gulped down the last of his coffee and slammed his mug a little too violently on her coffee table. He didn't look at her, nor did he need any more details. He knew the god of war and he knew by the desperation in his wife's frantic call, Serena's face and desperate sobs what it meant. He stood, pulling an old golden coin out of his blue jeans pocket. Silently, he walked back to the kitchen. Serena stood and followed, watching with concern, wondering what he was doing. She watched him put the sink plug in and turn the tap on. Once the sink had a few inches of water, he flicked the coin into the sink.

"I give this gift to honor Iris, messenger of the gods." Peleus said, his voice strong and grave, as if he had done this many times before. Serena watched in amazement as a mist formed from water droplets rising from the sink into a strange water-like mirror about three feet tall.

"I call upon Chiron, son of Cronus." Peleus said firmly. A few seconds later, Serena's eyes widened in amazement as a figure appeared. His upper body was that of a strong muscular chiseled man wearing a leather vest. He had a square face with a set jaw and deep brown eyes with matching neatly combed brown curls hanging down to his shoulders. His face was the image of strength and classical beauty and Serena could see a gentle kindness there that she hadn't seen on any other Atlanteans before. His torso melted into the powerful body of a white stallion with strong hind legs, yet his front legs were those of a strong athletic human and dressed with neat brown leather full leg greaves decorated with golden buttons along the seams. He held a bow in his hands and a quiver hanging at his back. A centaur.

"Master Chiron." Peleus greeted reverently as he hit his fist to his chest in what seemed like a show of respect.

"Peleus, what a lovely surprise!" Chiron exclaimed joyfully as he returned the gesture.

"I wish it were under better circumstances." Peleus said with concern as his brows knitted together, forming deep lines across his forehead. Serena watched as the centaur's gaze fell on her and he locked eyes with her. There was something so familiar in his eyes and she wondered if, like many others, she had crossed paths with him when she was younger.

"And this must be Serena?" Chiron said with a beaming smile that instantly warmed her and put her at ease. Peleus nodded.

"Well my dear, I must say you have caused quite the stir in Olympus." Chiron said with a chuckle, hands on his hips.

"Master Chiron, I believe it's time for my return. My work here is done." Peleus said gravely and Serena noticed the smile vanish from Chiron's face. Nothing more needed to be said. It seemed Chiron understood simply with Peleus' tone.

"I am looking forward to your arrival my dear Peleus." Chiron said, forcing a smile. The window suddenly disappeared.

"Dad, what did you mean by your work is done?" Serena asked. But he didn't move, he leaned forward with his hands against the counter and closed his eyes.

"I didn't simply stay here because of your mother, Serena. I stayed to protect you. Do you understand what the fates want of you?" Peleus asked.

"No." Serena simply answered, leaning her back against the kitchen counter.

"The Olympians were created to protect the universe. Once they discovered they had so much power over the humans and other races, they gave themselves the god status." Peleus answers softly, his eyes staring at the distant ocean through the window above the sink.

"You're saying they are not gods?" Serena asked with a frown as she crossed her arms across her chest.

"There is but one creator, one true god. But giving one great power, comes great responsibility and great risk." Peleus continued. "Once an Atlantean with great power asserts themselves to take the place of a true god, a shift takes place in the balance. The fates are ordained to make sure the balance remains and is respected. Once they see the shift take place, they weave the fate of one to set things straight again. The first war was bloody, since Cronus was an evil ruler who simply disrespected humans, or any life at all. A prophecy was foretold that one of Cronus' sons would overthrow him, and so the war was terrible and hundreds of thousands died. When Zeus won, and sent Cronus to Tartarus, he realized that other creatures from other universes could not dwell within the earth realm as they held too much power there. Slowly, over the centuries, he began to rid the realm by building gateways and guarding them, making it law that no one outside this realm could cross over without his blessing." Peleus explained.

"So, my father is a good ruler then?" Serena asked confused. Zeus had seemed genuinely kind for a moment, until something shifted. She wasn't sure if it was the fear that she would dethrone him? Fear that she wasn't worthy? She didn't know him at all, but from Peleus' explanation, he didn't sound evil.

"He was." Peleus agreed.

"I sense a but…" Serena sighed.

"It is easy to lose your focus, your purpose over the centuries especially surrounded by others who can influence you and steer you in the wrong direction. Who you surround yourself with Serena will affect who you become." Peleus said as he finally turned, putting a gentle hand on her shoulder.

"The fates chose you to set things right, not with war, destruction or death…but serenity. The eye of the storm." Peleus smiled weakly as he touched the side of her face.

"I don't know how I'm supposed to do that." Serena said, swallowing a sob. She felt like such a mess. If she was this Atlantean hanging in the balance, shouldn't she be strong and confident, the woman she thought she was before?

"When it is time Serena, everything will be revealed." Peleus pulled her into him and she threw her arms around him. They held each other for some time before Peleus pulled back.

"I have to go." Peleus whispered as he tucked a curl behind her ear.

"Take this." Peleus dug in his pocket and handed her the same old gold coin marked with Zeus' head he had used to call Chiron.

"This is a drachma and can be used to contact anyone you wish. You can use it to call me if you need me." He said gently. Serena took the coin reluctantly. She didn't want him to leave, she wanted him to stay and help her as he always did. He was the father who told her stories until she fell asleep in his arms as a little girl, and the father who bought ice cream and watched comedies late into the night when she was older. He did everything to make her smile and forget her troubles. But she nodded, unable to say anything in fear she would beg him to stay. He kissed her forehead then left. Waiting until she felt completely alone, Serena reached to the back of her head searching for the ties of the circlet that were tangled in her hair. Too much was riding on her having her full powers and she yearned to feel like she had in the underworld. She cursed under her breath as she began untangling the leather ties. She fumbled in frustration for some time until she was finally able to undo the tight knot Triton had managed to tie. It was tight enough that she was sure Zeus himself wouldn't have been able to take it apart. She hesitated before taking it off completely, afraid of what she had felt before Triton had slipped it on. *Serena, don't.* Triton's voice echoed in the back of her mind with concern. She bit her lower lip, desperate to feel like she had felt in the underworld. To be the Atlantean everyone expected her to be. Strong, confident and powerful. Not this insecure, weak, emotional disaster of a person. She pulled it off slowly and it all came rushing back like a sudden explosion through her mind and body. She dropped the circlet to the ground and ran to the sink to wretch.

CHAPTER 40
TRITON

It took Triton and Ariel less than fifteen minutes to walk to Triton's place, both remaining quiet as they walked side by side. He had chosen a little house nested between two villas on the edge of Waimanalo beach and as fate would have it, strangely close to Serena's place. He had chosen this place because of the privacy the thick shrubbery offered. Triton had never mentioned anything to Serena, but he had been surprised when he had realized just how close they lived to each other. Although, who knew what the future held now and thinking about that made his head want to explode. Where were they supposed to go from here? He had been so focused by Serena's coming of age that he had not even considered the implications of it all. Was he or could he simply return to serving his father? Was that even a possibility? What did the fates really want or expect Serena to do? This world was completely oblivious to their existence and he wasn't sure how she could reconcile keeping things the way they were. Would they be able to defeat Scylla and Cherybdis without causing some disturbances in this realm? Zeus had made sure that anything not from this world could not be seen by the human eye, unless they had Atlantean blood somehow. And what about Ariel? He made the choice to strip her of her Atlantean essence knowing that if his father or even Zeus had her fate in their hands it would be much worse. But he wasn't oblivious to the dangers she would face in this realm. She was currently unprepared to survive here and he was unsure what the impending threat from Scylla and Cherybdis' minions would be. So he would have to remain here for now, but how would Zeus take to that? And what about Serena in all of this? He hated that he had used a forceful tone with her when he told her to stay out of his business, but she had no idea how to deal with Atlantean issues yet. Until she learned, she would have to trust his way of doing things.

This was going to be difficult for them to adjust to. They were just starting their lives together and they would have to learn to get to know each other. Even if Triton had more time to watch Serena, see how she thought, there was still much to learn. She would need time to digest all of this. Unfortunately he wasn't sure if the fates would give her the time she needed. The front of the house was lined with shrubbery with a gate in the middle leading to the front door. The metal gate was locked with a padlock. Triton punched in the code and the little gate unlocked. He opened it, moving back to let his daughter ahead. She silently followed, like a punished animal with its tail between its legs. He felt the weight of his punishment, yet he knew this was the best way he could protect her. He opened the front door and they walked in his humble abode. It was a single story home with compact modest living. The entrance made way to a small living room with a small couch and television which he rarely had the time to watch. A little hallway led to the two bedrooms. The first one was his own, and the second one he had used as an office space and he knew he would have to convert it back to a bedroom for Ariel. On the right side of the hall was a small bathroom and at the end of the hallway nested a little kitchen.

"Ariel," Triton said as he took her shoulders gently to make her face him. Unable to meet her father's eyes, she stared at the ground solemnly. He lifted her chin up and offered her a comforting smile.

"You understand that I could not protect you from Zeus and Poseidon this time?" He asked. She nodded, moisture building in her eyes as she fought back tears.

"I could not let them serve their harsh punishment no matter how much they thought you deserved it." He explained as he traced the side of her jaw with his thumb. His hand seems so big compared to her small face, he could easily cup the entire side of it with one hand. He tucked a red strand of her hair behind her ear as he kissed her forehead and Ariel smiled meekly. There was no doubt in her mind of his love for her. He had put his neck on the line more times than she could count.

"I will get things settled for you and help you adjust to your new life here. I'll set you up with a job at the marina and I am sure Laka will love having you around." Triton said, attempting to cheer her up. He looked up as he felt Serena's mind fill with frustration. As he focused his mind on hers, he could sense she was trying to take her circlet off. *Cursed Atlas!* He muttered under his breath. *Serena, don't.* He warned but he could feel her desperation fueling her determination to take it off.

"What's wrong?" Ariel asked, seeing the look of dismay on her father's face.

"Serena." Triton answered with a sigh.

"She is so beautiful...and wonderful." Ariel said as she thought back on the few times she had the pleasure of spending time with her. She was the most beautiful person she had ever seen and was so patient and loving even towards perfect strangers. She watched a smile cross her father's face that lit up his handsome features and it was obvious how much he cared about the new goddess. Triton wanted to stay and help his daughter settle in somewhat, but he couldn't leave Serena.

"Go to her." Ariel pleaded as she saw the obvious turmoil written on her father's face. "I cannot go far now that I can't go in the water." She said with a sigh. Without the ability to roam the oceans, she couldn't really go far. Her knowledge of the earth realm was too limited to try anything on her own. Triton nodded as he grabbed the keys to his jeep that were hanging next to the entrance door. Serena's place wasn't far, but he needed to get there quickly.

"There is food in the kitchen, make yourself at home." Triton said before he walked out and closed the door behind him. Feeling terrible for leaving his daughter on her own. But, she would have to learn how to live in this world without servants, maids and him.

Even if Serena was only a few minutes away by car, he found himself speeding. She had managed to take off the circlet and he felt the overwhelming waves of her powers flooding her. The tires of his jeep screeched as he pulled in too quickly into her driveway. He ran to the door, using his power to close it behind him and he made his way to the kitchen where Serena stood leaning against the sink retching her guts out. Noticing a hair elastic on the counter, he pulled her hair back into a ponytail as best as he could.

"Where's the circlet Serena?" Triton asked firmly.

"No! Need. To. Control. It." Serena said, shaking her head in protest before she retched again. Everything spun around her and even though she tried to focus, it was impossible through the thousands of whispers resounding in her mind. If only she could silence them. She hadn't eaten anything since this happened last and in her weak state her legs gave in. Triton wrapped his arms around her waist to support her.

"Serena! You cannot control what should have taken thirty years to control in one day." Triton growled in frustration. He spotted the circlet on the floor from the space between the kitchen cabinet and the counter. He leaned her against the counter and then hurried to get the circlet. When he came back around, he stood behind her to put the circlet back on but she struggled weakly, trying to push him back. Without having control over her powers, she sent a wave that sent Triton flying and crashing against the wall, pinning him up against it.

"Serena!" He gritted through his teeth, struggling against it, the circlet still in his hand. Through the kitchen window, he saw the weather change into a vicious storm. Dark clouds, strong winds and heavy downpours coming out of nowhere. Wind funnels could be seen on the water and he knew something had to be done before anyone got hurt. Triton closed his eyes and took a deep breath, letting Serena's power fill him. He intertwined his power with Serena's like vines wrapping themselves together in an effort to help her control her powers. Unlike Serena, he had centuries of practiced control and it was easier to let her powers meld with his own even though her powers were formidable. He pushed back against hers like pushing against a door blocked by a boulder, but slowly, her power moved back and he landed on his feet. Still fighting to get to Serena, he continued to push against her power.

"Serena!" Triton called out not wanting to hurt her in this process but knowing, feeling she had no control of what was happening. He pressed on, trying to be gentle with the pushback until he finally reached her and she screamed as the pressure building against her felt like she was being pressed between two cement walls. Triton struggled to reach around her head but managed to tie the circlet back on. Serena collapsed against him as he finished tying the knot of the circlet, whispering in his ancient language, using his power to seal the knot so only he could take it off.

"Don't." Serena protested weakly, barely able to move as she felt him, knowing what he was doing.

"It is for your own good Serena." Triton whispered in her ear as she leaned completely back against him, closing her eyes as her consciousness threatened to escape her. She stayed there, her breath ragged as she tried to steady it. The whispers had vanished almost completely, leaving behind only a faint and occasional one. Triton held her close, his arms wrapped around her, his face leaning against hers as she trembled from the exhaustion of fighting for control of her power. He closed his eyes and took slow, deep breaths as if coaxing her to do the same. She closed her eyes and focused on it and slowly, she began to follow his breaths and her heartbeat to the rhythm of his own. Her strength slowly returning, he felt she was almost back to normal but didn't move. He felt a tear from her cheek touch his and he turned her gently so she could face him. Forehead to forehead, he opened his eyes but she kept hers closed.

"Why is everyone trying to control me?" Serena asked, her voice raspy from the bile burning her throat again.

"I am only trying to do what's best for you." Triton answered. Her eyes snapped open and her eyes sparkled from green to gold as anger flashed through them. She pulled back, but Triton wouldn't let her go.

"I am sick and tired of everyone using that excuse." Serena said angrily.

"You should be grateful so many care about you to do so." Triton reflected, his jaw tightened as he felt Serena's anger rise even more. He could see shadows coming through the windows as dark clouds lingered from her temper.

CHAPTER 41
SERENA

Serena pushed herself away from Triton. She still felt somewhat drained, but mostly she felt pissed off. Frankly, she was tired of being told that it was what was best for her. She couldn't argue that right now, she wasn't sure who she was. She felt stuck in between Serena, the normal human thirty-year-old starting an exciting new life and Namaka, badass Lady of the sea and serenity. And then there were the expectations. EVERYONE expected her to be this powerful savior of the universe. Yeah, no pressure there at all. Triton had been so proud, so in love with her goddess side in the underworld that she had found it hot and empowering. She desperately wanted to be that goddess, to make everybody proud. This was the reason why she had wanted a new life. Her mother always pushed her hard all her life, pushing her to be the best she could be to the point of smothering her, making her feel like she was never good enough. Her fresh start in Hawaii had given her the peace of mind she had craved for so long. No one to please but herself. Kharma had a sick sense of humour. She sighed. It wasn't kharma, it was the fates, whoever they were.

"Serena, I'm only trying to help you. I have been around for thousands of years, I think I am in a good position to give you that." Triton said, leaning back against the counter studying her intently.

"What about the fact that you were supposed to find me and kill me?" Serena said bitterly, refusing to look in his eyes. She felt his surprise.

"Kill you? Who told you that?" Triton gritted.

"Zeus. He told me you were given the task of finding me and were supposed to get rid of me." Serena answered sharply.

"Yes, that was what I was asked to do." Triton answered simply. He spoke lightly, and his calmness frustrated her even more. He frowned and raised his scarred eyebrow. "Is that why you left me this morning?" He asked curiously.

"Forgive me if I had to digest the fact that the only reason I'm not dead is because you value your own life!" Serena gritted through her teeth. She turned to walk away but Triton grabbed her wrist and pulled her close, his face a few inches away from hers. She refused to look at him, but she could feel his tension growing and his jaw clenching.

"Look at me." Triton said firmly. When she didn't, refusing to give into his demand, he lifted her chin up, forcing her to lock eyes with him.

"Look at me and tell me again the only reason you are alive is because I don't want to die." Triton said his tone was still firm but gentle. He couldn't help it, when he looked into those beautiful golden green eyes of hers, it melted him. But Serena was angry, not just at Triton, but at everyone who took part in lying to her all this time.

"How can I Triton? I barely know you or what you're capable of. I don't understand any of this, the bond, who I am, my powers… I can feel that you are honest now...but I can also feel the terrifying truth that you are a powerful being capable of killing on command." She answered, closing her eyes as she let out exactly what was on her mind. After she had gotten her powers, she had felt his power, the soldier side of him that had led him to fight many battles and kill many. And then there was what she saw him do to Ariel, taking everything that made her Atlantean away from her. She couldn't pretend to suddenly understand their ways, but she had begun to question what Triton was really capable of. He trailed the side of her face gently with his fingers, his soft touch still sending a wave of uncontrollable pleasure through her body. She opened her eyes as he pulled her closer. Their bodies touched now and she felt the same heat growing in his own body as in hers. She opened her eyes and saw it there too.

"I see. You are right. For thousands of years I have been my father's right hand, doing everything that was asked of me without question. That includes killing enemies for the most part. But Serena," Triton whispered as his hand moved to the nape of her neck and his other under her shirt to touch the small of her back. "I...love you. Not because of a bond, but because I am destined too. I cannot harm you and I have to do everything I can to keep you safe until you can do that for yourself." He explained thoughtfully. She felt the sincerity of what he was saying, his words burning in her mind. The bond demanded that he keep her safe and it would ask the same of her.

"So Zeus really wants to kill me?" Serena asked with concern. She had felt the Olympian god had tried to unsettle her, and it had worked. She knew nothing of him and didn't know what to think.

"Zeus loved your mother Serena, and Hera did everything she could to get rid of her when the prophecy was foretold. Like most Olympians, he is ruled by his cock more than his brain and Hera controls that part of his body." Triton explained roughly. There were no appropriate words to use to describe the reality of it.

"Hera...the queen." Serena said as the whispers were coherent enough to make out what they were saying. Triton nodded.

"You have to bring me to face them?" Serena asked fearfully. It was enough that she had faced Zeus, even if in a dream. She couldn't imagine how it would feel like to face ALL of them.

"I...am afraid so." Triton answered hesitantly. "When you're ready." He whispered as he tugged at a perfectly curled lock of hair.

"And other than Hera, are there any others against me?" Serena asked, almost afraid of the answer.

"Not many Serena, most of them voted to keep you alive and to have you face them instead of killing you." Triton replied.

"Like who?" Serena asked, closing her eyes as she felt his hot breath on her neck.

"Other than Apollo and Artemis, let's just say the only ones that didn't

274

vote for you are Hera, Demeter and Ares." Triton answered as he rubbed the back of his neck, hating to pronounce the name of that bastard. Serena frowned, unsure if she should be relieved or confused by this information. She couldn't even begin to understand how they thought, but if they were anything like earth politicians, it didn't mean anything.

"It is safer to think of them that way Serena, except they are not all conniving." Triton replied to her thoughts as he touched the side of her face gently. "Athena is a very wise and good Atlantean. Artemis and Apollo...I think have proven their loyalties. As long as you remember that they are in fact not gods, but beings with a higher capacity for wisdom than humans...but they are not infallible." Triton explained thoughtfully, inching his face closer to hers as his desires grew.

He began to kiss her and she melted under the soft warm touch of his hand on her back igniting the flame of passion between them. She had wondered if the intensity of their desire would diminish once the bond had been completed.

"No, it hasn't." Triton whispered in her ear as he kissed her neck, his deep voice adding to the flame. "This is part of being Atlantean, we love deeply." He muttered before kissing her again, making her shudder with pleasure as he snuck a hand under her shirt to rub a breast. She moaned and his kisses became relentless.

They both froze as they heard a loud conch shell horn.

"I'm beginning to think the fates don't want us to fuck." Serena muttered.

"Please don't feed the same bullshit line you did on Mokulua Island about this being simply a ceremonial horn." Serena said firmly. Triton's jaw clenched nervously.

"I'm afraid it's an alarm. Something bad is coming." Triton answered, a worried frown crossing his face. Then another alarm sounded, this time it was a human Tsunami alert. Serena recalled being told to pay attention to this one and she couldn't help but feel this strange tingle on her skin, making all the hairs of her body stand up. She shivered.

"Any creature that sets foot in this realm sets off alarms the Olympians have set. What your feeling is coming from something that shouldn't be here." Triton said angrily. He had sensed the creatures and it seemed they did not heed his warning and would have to pay the price. Triton let go of Serena and walked to the living room. He had dropped the satchel Hapheastus had made for Serena there when Hermes had transported them back. He grabbed it and eyed it curiously, knowing whatever was in there would probably come in handy soon. He took it and handed it to Serena who took it hesitantly. She opened it and couldn't believe her eyes. A full set of Greek armor and clothing. She pulled out what she thought looked like a dress body armor style. The top part covering her shoulders was made of a dark brown leather with the matching serenity symbols of her circlet stitched along the front seams. The breastplate was bronze and celestial steel that dipped between her breasts to protect the heart. The shoulder straps were a dark red leather with silver medallions carrying the same serenity symbols. Red leather pauldrons hung off the shoulders. The skirt was made of red leather split pieces studded with the same bronze metal symbols, hanging over a white cotton skirt. She turned the dress and somehow wasn't surprised there was no zipper, but corset style with leather cords.

"Put it on." Triton coaxed wanting to see her sexy body in that armor. Serena had never worn anything remotely close to this kind of clothing but she slipped it on. Triton whistled and Serena's cheeks burned red. He went behind her and started threading the leather cords through the loops.

"Ready?" Triton asked teasingly.

"As I'll ever be I suppose." Serena replied, gasping as Triton tightened the piece. Serena wondered who in their right mind found this comfortable? It took a few minutes before Triton tightened it and knotted it off. He took out two dark brown leather arm bands studded with the bronze symbols and he helped her but them on. Then he handed her a pair of red leather open-fingered gloves which she put on. He slipped the long bronze bracers with buckles to fit them nice and snug on her forearms. Serena smiled and chuckled as she slipped on the red leather greaves before Triton helped her fit the bronze greaves on top. She felt like she was dressing up for comicon. And finally, la piece de resistance was pulled out of the bag and Triton handed her roman style leather sandals. She stood and walked to her powder room. She turned the light on to look at herself in the mirror, her smile vanished as her eyes stared into the eyes of a complete stranger. She looked like a Greek warrior alright. Quietly she braided her hair loosely, completing the outfit perfectly. Triton came up behind her, wrapping his arms around her.

"You look stunning." Triton said reassuringly. She bit her bottom lip, almost making herself bleed as tears threatened to spill. Triton turned her around and used his thumb to pull her lip from her teeth, then kissed her red plump lips.

"Everything will be fine." Triton tried to sound comforting as he leaned his forehead on hers. "We need to get going, stay behind me. I have a feeling whatever we find out there is not going to be pleasant." He said. Serena closed her eyes as she took a deep breath, feeling his power push against hers as if to help ease her mind. Then let it out.

"Let's go then." Serena said, trying to sound brave. She felt helpless right at that moment. Triton nodded and they were on their way. Triton picked up speed and broke into a full powerful run. Serena frowned at first then pushed herself to follow, and surprised herself by being able to easily keep up with him. They reached the beach side in no time and Serena almost stumbled as she stopped herself from her sprint. Her eyes widened at the scene. A tsunami about a hundred and fifty feet tall moved towards them menacingly.

ACKNOWLEDGEMENTS

First and foremost, this story wouldn't even have started without Alison Branchaud. I shared a strange dream I had, thinking it might make a decent plot for a story and she was brave enough to listen to my bable. Once I wrote an introduction, she encouraged me to develop this story.

I want to thank my husband Chad for his undying support through this process. He believed in me, in my abilities to write and encouraged me to get this book finished to the end.

Of course, for my family's patience, especially my mom Clotilde, my dad Carl, my sister Véronique and my brother Sébastien in my endless talks and blabbering of my ideas as I got overly excited at times. I know it got annoying at some point but they kept supporting me either way.

All this would not have gotten started without Lee who coaxed me back into writing and rediscovering my love and passion for it after I had set it aside for so long.

Thank you to the very talented Yashushi Matsuoka for bringing to life Serena and Triton. With a few simple questions and amazing talent, you were able to get me and what I was looking for exactly. You managed to bring tears to my eyes everytime I opened the final work.

And last but definitely NOT least, Amanda Ducross for helping me put the whole thing together. You gave me the inspirational motivation and excitement I needed to see this through. Your reactions to the story as we read and edited together gave me so many ideas that made the story what it is today. I couldn't have finished this without you.

Thank you all from the bottom of my heart.

ABOUT THE AUTHOR

Catherine Gagnon is the author of THE DIVINE ORDER OF OLYMPIANS SAGA. As a graduate of massage therapy, she has traveled the world to add different types of approaches and techniques to her skill set and be immersed in their cultures.

Writing since a very young age, she was always fascinated by Greek mythology and its complexity. It was during her training in Hawaii that she fell madly in love with the culture and the people. When she discovered how intricately Greek mythology and Hawaiian mythology were tied to each other in some way or another, she decided to write about the two things that inspired her the most: Greek Mythology and Hawaii.

Follow her on the web at:
https://www.authorcatherinegagnon.com
Facebook: https://facebook.com/authorcatherinegagnon
Instagram: https://www.instagram.com/authorcatherinegagnon

Made in the USA
Monee, IL
09 July 2021